THE DOUBLE GAME

Dan Fesperman's travels as a writer have taken him to thirty countries and three war zones. *Lie in the Dark* won the Crime Writers' Association of Britain's John Creasey Mamorial Dagger Award for best first crime novel, *The Small Boat of Great Sorrows* won their Ian Fleming Steel Dagger Award for best thriller, and *The Prisoner of Guantánamo* won the Dashiel Hammett Award from the International Association of Crime Writers. He lives in Baltimore.

THE DOUBLE GAME

DAN FESPERMAN

CORVUS

First published in the United States by Alfred A. Knopf, a division of
Random House, Inc., New York.

Published in hardback and trade paperback in Great Britain in 2012 by
Corvus, an imprint of Atlantic Books Ltd.

10 9 8 7 6 5 4 3 2 1

A CIP catalogue record for this book is available from the British Library.

Hardback ISBN: 978 0 83789 337 6
Trade paperback ISBN: 978 0 85789 338 3
E-book ISBN: 978 0 85789 339 0

Printed and bound in Great Britain by the MPG Books Group

Corvus
An imprint of Atlantic Books Ltd
Ormond House
26–27 Boswell Street
London
WC1N 3JZ

www.corvus-books.co.uk

THE
DOUBLE
GAME

A PRECAUTION

I no longer believe what I read in books.

Unless, of course, the text states clearly that every word is made up, a product of the author's imagination. I especially take notice when a novelist deploys that oft-used legal disclaimer, the one that says, "Any resemblance to actual persons, living or dead, events, or locales is entirely coincidental."

Sure it is. That statement makes me perk up like a dog that has heard a distant whistle from a cruel and deceitful master. It means truth is about to appear in some elegant and artful disguise.

As for all those dusty "facts" piled in the vast remaindered bin known as nonfiction, well, I've exhumed quite a few such items in this autumn of foraging and funerals, and so many have proven to be false that I've lost faith in their authenticity. Along the dim corridors of the secret world I've come to know best, only the so-called inventions of fiction have ever shed any light of revelation.

But with light come shadows, and therein lies the rub. Shadows hide danger. They conceal death, even love. They must often be avoided, but never ignored. I arrived at these conclusions only recently, although I now suspect that at some deeper level I've known their truth all along.

Let me tell you why . . .

I

The Great Man himself was waiting for me on the phone. I say that without irony. In those days Edwin Lemaster was my hero, accomplished and unblemished, the very sort of fellow I aspired to be but never became. Even my wife, April, sensed the call's solemn importance, although she'd never liked his books.

"Genre fiction," she always sneered. "Spies and secrets, lies and betrayal, blah blah blah."

"You mean like life?" I'd counter, little knowing we were touching on the dynamics of our coming failure.

Yet on that long-ago sunny morning she smiled in excitement and stretched the phone cord to its limit, as if it were a lifeline that might pull me to safety. I grabbed it.

It was June of 1984, Orwell's year of reckoning. The Cold War, after a brief thaw, had safely returned to subzero, and the Berlin Wall remained rock solid. I was twenty-seven, a Washington journalist on the make, poised at roughly the halfway point of my life up to now. Opening my mouth to speak, I felt like a flustered fan who had finally reached the head of the autograph line.

"Uh, Mr. Lemaster? This is Bill Cage."

"Bill, a pleasure. And call me Ed. My assistant Lenore forwarded your request. As you know, I don't usually give interviews, but your letter was quite convincing."

Of course it was. I'd spent hours on it, agonizing over every word. In my latter-day career as a PR flack, nothing I've written has ever matched its persuasive sincerity. Then again, I am no longer paid to be sincere.

"I'll be coming down from Maine for the university lecture anyway," Lemaster continued, "so why don't we give it a try?"

I could barely draw breath to answer.

Why such excitement over a mere scribbler? I should explain. Not only was Lemaster the world's premier espionage novelist, but he'd also been a spy for sixteen years at the height of the Cold War, back when spying was a glamorous profession. "Our le Carré," the American critics called him, although to my mind le Carré was "Their Lemaster."

But for me the appeal went further, and was deeply personal. Having grown up as a Foreign Service brat, I had come of age in the very capitals where Lemaster set his plots, at the very moment in history when they were unfolding. In those days, to walk the night streets of Berlin, of Prague, of Vienna, of Budapest, was to imagine that mysterious and exciting events were occurring just around the corner. And sometimes they were.

My father, also a fan, first put a Lemaster novel in my hands when I was twelve, as an antidote to a gloomy Saturday in Prague in 1969. Within days I was pillaging his shelves for the equally timely glories of John le Carré, Len Deighton, and Adam Hall. Eventually I turned to earlier classics by Maugham, Buchan, Ambler, and Greene. I even read the 1903 Erskine Childers book that supposedly gave birth to the modern spy novel, *The Riddle of the Sands*, its pages haunted by the knowledge that the author had eventually been hanged as a spy. My father had them all, a painstakingly assembled collection of more than two hundred espionage first editions, most of them signed by the author.

Whenever we moved—and in the diplomatic corps that happened about every three years—the books were my back-door passage to our new home, with the characters as my escorts. At a moment in history when other American boys were memorizing batting averages and home run totals, I was steeping myself in the lore of fictional spies. They were my Mays, Mantle, and Maris, and I aspired to emulate them. To be a spy was to survive by your wits in a dangerous foreign landscape, to seek to know everything about others while revealing nothing of yourself—an arrested adolescence in which you merited your country's highest trust even as you traded in its deepest duplicity.

And the writer I always returned to with the greatest anticipation was Lemaster, who seemed more willing than the rest to take me into his confidence. He declassified the world I lived in, elegantly parting the curtains in all their varying shades of gray. So perhaps now you can understand why his promise of an interview left me momentarily at a loss for words.

"Bill?" he prompted. "Are you there?"

"Great," I finally managed. "That would be . . . *great.*"

"Chancellor Stewart has kindly offered the use of his conference room. Shall we say four o'clock?"

"Perfect." At least I'd moved on from "great."

"In the meantime, Lenore will send you an advance copy of my latest. See you next week."

"Wouldn't miss it for the world."

Wouldn't miss it for the world? Had I actually said something so trite? I blushed as I hung up, and for the next hour I half expected Lenore to call back to cancel. Then, determined to make the most of the opportunity, I began finding out all I could about Lemaster's life and times.

The basics were already known to me: He was divorced, childless, eldest son of a Wall Street lawyer. Groton '51. Yale '55. Then two years as a Rhodes Scholar at Oxford, where he became an incurable Anglophile before joining the CIA in 1957. Served throughout Europe. Began writing novels while still an Agency employee. Left the CIA in '73, a month after his third book became a best seller.

I figured there would be plenty more. But in those days before Google and YouTube it was far easier to maintain a low profile, and that's what Lemaster had done. I checked the clip file at the *Post*, the Lexis-Nexis database of publications from around the world, *Who's Who*, the *Reader's Guide to Periodical Literature*. My search turned up loads of book reviews, but only a few profiles, and those were skeletal. Only *Time* magazine and London's *Guardian* had interviewed him at length, and even their stories were mostly about his books and characters. When *Time* asked about his career in spying, Lemaster was charmingly dismissive.

"Oh, I was quite unimportant. A cog in the machine, easily replaced. Anything I picked up for the novels came mostly from hearing what other fellows were talking about, the ones who were doing the interesting stuff."

Frustrated, I retraced my steps, this time combing the material like an old-fashioned Kremlinologist, alert for significance in the backwash of minor detail.

He hunted, but only for birds, never mammals. Fished, but only with a fly rod and he tied his own lures. Liked Bordeaux reds, Alsatian whites. A Red Sox fan who had never been to Fenway, yet had twice been to

Yankee Stadium (and if that isn't the behavior of a natural-born spy, what is?). His thesis at Oxford was on the theme of courtly love in medieval poetry.

I looked up "courtly love." It was all about a knight's idealized, secretive devotion to a specially selected woman, never his wife, although possibly someone else's. He pledged eternal loyalty even if she never loved him back, and wrote her letters under a code name.

It sounded an awful lot like espionage.

At the appointed hour I appeared at the chancellor's oaken chambers with a fresh notebook and a microcassette recorder. Folded in my pocket was a list of forty questions, winnowed from fifty-seven the night before. I wore a jacket and tie, which in those days occurred about as often as sightings of Halley's Comet.

Chancellor Stewart, who turned out to be a school chum of Lemaster's, handled the introductions. His secretary kindly tried not to smile as I wiped a sweaty palm on my corduroys before shaking hands.

Lemaster was taller than I expected, even a bit imposing. But the craggy nose, the lined face, and the stray forelock, curling toward his brow like a comma, were exactly as advertised on his dust jackets. Both he and the chancellor wore tweeds. Stewart escorted us into the conference room, then departed.

"Where would you like to begin?" I asked nervously, feeling like a sycophantic fool.

"Wherever you'd like." He sounded as though he meant it. "We don't even have to talk about the new book unless you want to, although my publisher would probably send me to the gallows for saying so."

His relaxed manner immediately put me at ease, and for the next two hours I enjoyed that rarest of pleasures—a much-anticipated event that exceeds expectations. His answers were witty and expansive, candid and unrehearsed. And although he continued to downplay his career with the CIA—seeming almost sheepish on the topic—in other areas he revealed details I had never seen elsewhere. He even described the exact moment he had dreamed up his greatest creation, frumpy spymaster Richard Folly, who had come to him out of the blue in 1967 as he rode a heaving tram car in Budapest, where I had actually been living at the time. Folly, a perennial loser in love and in office politics, had been the most sympathetic literary companion of my adolescence, and I'd always felt redeemed when he ultimately triumphed on the strength of his nimble, analytical mind.

But the best thing about the interview was that Lemaster spoke just the way he wrote—in complete and flawless paragraphs, rarely hesitating and never doubling back. I couldn't help but compare the painstaking hours I'd spent on the letter, and I surmised enviously that for Lemaster writing must be almost like taking dictation.

Things went so well that the chancellor, with Lemaster's blessing, invited me to join them afterward for dinner at the University Club, where a round of cocktails followed by two bottles of wine further loosened tongues. In those days I was too vain to consider that anything other than my winning personality had prompted his easy collegiality, but toward the end of the meal I learned otherwise. The chancellor had just excused himself to the men's room, leaving the two of us alone for the first time since our interview. Lemaster leaned across the table.

"So tell me something, Bill."

His tone was conspiratorial, and I edged forward. He paused for a swallow of claret, then sprang his surprise.

"How is your splendid father? We once knew each other well, you know."

"You did?" The words were out before I could stop them.

"Oh, yes. We crossed paths here and there back in the day. He was a useful man for people like me. Very helpful."

I had long known that my father's embassy duties sometimes included assisting men who were, as he liked to say, "in a more delicate line of work." I fancied I'd even met a few, on strange occasions when my dad chivvied me along after dark to some unfamiliar café, where we would share a back table with a fellow I'd never seen before and would never see again. None of those men ever stated his name, and at some point in the proceedings my father always suggested that I make a preemptive visit to the men's room, which is probably when he and the mystery guest transacted the evening's real business. I liked to believe then that my role was to help provide cover—a cozy father-son backdrop for some spook in transit. But in retrospect I may have embellished those memories, because at the time I was always waist-deep in some new find from my father's spy shelves, and would have been highly susceptible to any suggestion that clandestine doings were afoot.

What I did know for certain was that Lemaster had never appeared at any of those trysts. And surely my father would have told me if he'd met the man. Autographed Lemaster novels held pride of place on his shelves, although Dad had led me to believe the signatures had all been obtained by enterprising booksellers.

Yet here was the author saying they were pals. Obviously I had missed something.

"Well," Lemaster continued, "I shouldn't be too surprised he never mentioned it. He was a good soldier that way. A real Joe, your dad, and you certainly couldn't say that about everyone on the diplomatic side. A lot of them acted as if we were radioactive."

Before I could respond he raised the stakes further.

"He always spoke well of you, Bill. His son the top student. His son the track star, beating all those strapping Austrian boys 'round the oval. Four minutes twenty-one seconds, wasn't that your mile time? And that flap you got into with that pretty gal of yours down in Vienna, Litzi something or other? That's why your letter was such a hit. Lenore usually tosses those things in the trash, but she made sure I saw yours right away."

So even his assistant knew all these details? I was feeling hurtfully excluded, the foil of some long-running jest. *You were right, Warfield. That lad of yours had no idea!* My discomfort must have shown. Lemaster's expression softened. Then, perhaps in atonement, he offered a small intimacy, just for me.

"Of course, in those days even your father didn't know what I was *really* up to. No one did. I was keeping an eye out for the Don Tollesons of this world."

Now that was interesting. Tolleson was the traitorous creation at the heart of Lemaster's magnum opus, *The Double Game*, in which Folly unmasks his lifelong friend and colleague Don Tolleson as a Soviet double agent. Was Lemaster admitting that he, too, had been a mole hunter? None of his press clippings had even hinted at that.

"So did you ever find one?" I asked. "Who was your Don Tolleson?"

Lemaster frowned, as if realizing he'd said too much. He swallowed more claret, then launched into a paragraph on the nature of betrayal. This time the answer felt rehearsed, and it skirted my question. I tried again.

"But what about you personally? You wrote *The Double Game* while you were still with the CIA. It must have been a guilty pleasure to contemplate betrayal to such depths. Did you ever play with the idea of crossing the line yourself?"

"What, by defecting?"

"Or just by turning. Working for the other side. If only to find out what it was like."

His eyes crinkled in amusement, and at that moment it was clear to me that Lemaster believed he was still talking solely to the son of his old friend Warfield Cage, and not to an ambitious reporter for the *Washington Post*.

He swirled the wine, and something about the way it eddied in the big glass reminded me of a crystal ball on the verge of revealing all. Maybe that was what stimulated my baser instincts as a newshound. Or perhaps I was still feeling stung by my dad's secrecy, or emboldened by drink. Whatever the case, as Lemaster glanced downward, momentarily lost in thought, I slipped a hand inside the lapel pocket where I had stowed the microrecorder. Then, like one of Folly's zealous young acolytes, I squeezed the red button for "Record," setting the tape in motion without the slightest click. I casually withdrew my hand just before he looked up, and upon seeing he hadn't noticed, I was giddy with a sense of accomplishment. For the only time that night, I was the smartest man in the room.

"As a matter of fact," Lemaster said slowly, "yes. I *did* contemplate it. Not for ideological reasons, of course. And certainly not for the money. But it crossed my mind, and do you know why?"

I shook my head, not daring to speak. The revolving wheels of the recorder vibrated against my chest like a trapped bumblebee.

"For the thrill of it. The challenge. To just walk through the looking glass and find out how they really lived on the other side—well, isn't that the secret dream of every spy?"

The words were barely out of his mouth when the chancellor rounded the corner from the men's room, breaking the spell. Soon afterward the coffee arrived, and with it the first glimmers of the sobriety that would restore our previous distance. That night I slept deeply and dreamed for the first time in years of Cold War Vienna.

The next morning, a bit hung over, I agonized over how to handle

Lemaster's little bombshell. No doubt my family connection had allowed me to maneuver into a position of trust. Alcohol had also played a role. And any man unaccustomed to giving interviews was certainly more prone to a lapse. But weren't such factors part and parcel of effective interviewing? Didn't readers of the *Post* deserve the truth? And hadn't I succeeded where even *Time* magazine had failed?

I was reminded of a Joan Didion line I'd read in college, something about how writing was always a matter of betrayal. That's when I realized I couldn't go through with it, not for something as ephemeral as a newspaper story. I felt immediate relief, albeit with a pang of disappointment, but my decision was made. I was too close to the story. I would keep the revelation to myself.

Or such was my intention when Metro Editor Kent Spencer approached my desk an hour later to ask how the story was coming. I described my approach. His downturned mouth indicated he was less than impressed. So, as a teaser, or maybe just to show him what a diligent little questioner I'd been, I found myself saying, "You know, right toward the end of the evening he mentioned something pretty interesting."

Even as I told him I was calculating how to use the quote, after all, by sprinkling it into the final paragraphs. It would be an anecdote to unite the story's major threads. A kicker, as we said in the business. That way I could provide the proper context—the drinks, the off-the-cuff mood, the devil's advocate thrust of my question.

But Spencer was a step ahead of me.

"He said *what*? Are you telling me the author of *The Double Game* actually considered being a double agent? That's a helluva story, Bill. I mean, it's still kind of featury, but only if you go with a soft lead. Who knows? They might even want it out front."

My stomach rolled over. The dangerous animal I had just released from its cage paused to bare its teeth, then leaped beyond reach. I tried to catch it.

"Really, Kent, it wasn't like he was serious."

"C'mon, a quote like that? You got it on tape, I hope."

"Sure, but . . ." In my rush to chase down the beast I had just ensured its escape. If I'd told Spencer the remark wasn't taped, I might have been able to downplay it, even bury it. Instead, my editor now knew it was not only usable but also lawyerproof.

"Great! Lead with it."

"I was thinking more in terms of a kicker. It would make the perfect ending."

"What, then have some turnip on the desk cut the story from the bottom? It's called *news*, Bill. It goes at the top."

So, with a dark sense of foreboding and, worse, of betrayal, I wrote a story saying that spy-turned-novelist Edwin Lemaster had once considered working for the Soviet Union. By the time Spencer and the copy desk finished with it, the tone was downright accusatory, and even my loudest protests couldn't repair the damage.

It was a brief sensation, of course. The wires picked it up before the ink was dry, and by noon one UPI version had even reported that Lemaster "nearly defected."

Lemaster never called, never wrote. He responded only through a press release in which, as I richly deserved, he condescendingly implied that a callow young hack had used an unguarded moment of tipsy speculation to fashion a mountain out of a molehill.

But the strangest reaction may have been my father's. He phoned our apartment even before April was out of bed. He lived in Paris then, one of his last diplomatic postings. In those pre-Internet days he must have spotted the item in the State Department's daily press summary, and then gotten someone in Washington to read him the text.

"Jesus, Bill, what have you done to our old legend Edwin Lemaster? You get him drunk or something?" His tone was strained, like he was trying to keep it light but not succeeding.

"You're the one with some explaining to do. How come you never told me you were friends?"

There was a sharp intake of breath, followed by a pregnant pause. Then, in halting steps: "Did he . . . *He* told you that?"

"Yes."

Another pause, the line crackling from across the Atlantic.

"What else did he say about, well, all that?"

"Hardly anything. Said you crossed paths a few times, that you were 'a good soldier, a good Joe.' Nothing specific. I would've thought you'd have mentioned it at least once."

"There were security reasons. And you . . ." He sighed, groping his way through the static. "You'd have thought I was name-dropping."

"Is that the best you can do?"

I tried to sound offhand, hoping for a laugh, or for more. Dad is a nimble conversationalist, and this was his opening. But he held his ground, and when we hung up a few seconds later it felt as if a veil of secrecy had been lowered between us. Worse, maybe it had been there all along.

But what I didn't learn until recently was that elsewhere, my story had planted the seed of unintended consequences deep in the fertile soil of chance. Blowback, the wonks call it now. Reaping the whirlwind. Although by the time germination occurred, the matter had assumed the nature of a hybrid, its traits drawn literally from all those spy novels I had once read with such youthful interest.

Page by page, I would be lured back into an era when fact and fiction were virtually indistinguishable, yet with consequences that were anything but dated.

2

The envelope poked like a white tongue from my Georgetown mail slot, making it seem that the front door was taunting me as I approached my empty town house at dusk. I was wondering why the postman hadn't shoved it on through until, plucking it free, I saw it was neither stamped nor addressed. Only the formal version of my name, "William D. Cage," was typed on the outside. It was sealed.

Ignoring the bills and flyers piled on the rug, I took it to the living room chair by the window so I'd have enough light to read. I was about to tear it open when the refined quality of the envelope seemed to demand the use of a letter opener, so I rose to fetch a silver one from my writing desk before returning to the chair, feeling instinctively that this wouldn't be something I'd want to read standing up.

Inserting the blade at the end, I flicked it down the crease with the skill of an assassin, releasing a scent that was strangely nostalgic.

Smells like . . . Europe, I nearly said aloud. But that seemed ludicrous, even impossible. So I raised it to my nose, and there it was again, unmistakable, a hint of all those grand way stations of my youth in the depths of their winter gloom—sulfurous coal smoke, hosed cobbles, the chill damp of a low gray sky—even though in Georgetown it was warm and muggy, a summery day at the end of September. Weird.

A single sheet was folded inside. The paper itself looked and felt oddly familiar, the sort of fine, sturdy bond you find only at better stationers. The contents were brief but remarkable:

```
Message posted for you concerning the whole truth
about your onetime acquaintance, Mr. E.L. of Maine.
```

```
To retrieve, use Folly's tradecraft, page 47. Then use
book code, line 11. The dead drop will be known to you,
just as it was to Ashenden from the very beginning.
Welcome to the real Double Game.
```

Well, now.

E.L., obviously, was Edwin Lemaster, still living and still writing, way up in the north woods of Maine, where he no longer granted interviews. The idea that there might be some sort of "whole truth" yet to discover about him was intriguing, but so were the multiple literary references that jumped from the page. Folly was of course Lemaster's Richard Folly, and the tradecraft prompt seemed to be directing me to page 47 of *The Double Game*, probably the hardback edition. Ashenden was an early hero of the espionage canon from the eponymous 1928 novel by Somerset Maugham, yet another author who had spied for his country. I assumed that the wording "from the very beginning" meant I should scan the book's opening pages for some clue as to the whereabouts of the purported dead drop, which, in the spy trade, was a secret place for stashing messages.

The allusion to a book code was, for the moment, over my head. I knew what a book code was—a way for spies to communicate by using a shared literary passage as a decoding tool. But which book should I use? And on what page? And with what set of numbers for line 11? I turned over the note, but the other side was blank.

That's when I noticed the ghostly watermark—the outline of an elaborate crest and the maker's name, Gohrsmühle. Now I knew why it reeked of the Old World. The paper had been manufactured in Germany decades ago, and there was a box of it upstairs in the drawer of my bedside table. I had bought it after we moved to Berlin when I was seventeen, to write letters to a girlfriend I'd left behind in Vienna. My first love, and my first secret correspondence. Only seven sheets of it remained—six now, presumably—and the envelope had almost certainly come from the same box.

I then noticed irregularities in the typeface. Every *i* was slightly raised, and the upper chamber of each *e* was filled with ink. Meaning the note must have been typed on my old manual Royal, a keepsake I had appropriated long ago from a *Post* scrap pile during newsroom renovations. It, too, was upstairs, in a locked attic office.

I am not generally one for dramatics, but something like a shiver passed through me. Whoever left this message had not only been in my house, but he had also taken his time, digging up the stationery and then breaking into my office to type, raising a clatter you could have heard next door. For all I knew, he was still up there. Or maybe he'd made off with everything, my Royal and the whole box of stationery.

Worry turned to anger, and I ran up the stairs two at a time. A practical joke was one thing, a home invasion quite another.

No one was there. The box of stationery was safe in its drawer, minus a sheet and an envelope. The typewriter still sat on the desk. The door to the office was locked, and showed no signs of tampering.

Surely the front door of the house would tell a different story. My neighborhood was hardly immune to crime, and over the years I had invested in a stout deadbolt and an alarm system. But the status light on the system monitor still glowed a benign green, and the deadbolt was unmolested. So were the doorjamb, the kitchen door, and the slider in the back. Every window was secure.

I felt like one of Ian Fleming's Bond martinis—shaken, not stirred. Returning to the kitchen, I poured three fingers of bourbon and drained half of it in two scalding swallows. Only when it began lighting up my nervous system did the real point of this elaborate intrusion occur to me:

It, too, in both style and substance, had been stolen from the pages of an old spy novel.

I stepped to the bookshelves by the fireplace, where it took me only seconds to locate *A Fragment of Fear*, a 1965 novel by John Bingham. While I was at it, I grabbed my yellowed paperback of Maugham's *Ashenden* and the hardback of *The Double Game*, then took everything to the couch.

Flipping through the Bingham, I found what I was after in chapter three, a scene in which the main character receives a threatening note, then realizes it must have been typed on his own typewriter with his own stationery, even though his home showed no sign of a break-in. Bravo. I toasted the intruder's ingenuity and drained the bourbon.

What made this little stunt even more fascinating was that Bingham was not just any author. A titled Brit also known as Lord Clanmorris, he, too, had spied for his country, and he was a fine writer. But his greatest claim to literary fame was by proxy. He was reputedly a model for fictional spymaster George Smiley, John le Carré's very own Folly, and yet another fabled mole hunter. Not to mention that, to my mind, Bingham's best work was a novel called *The Double Agent.* Someone had moles on the brain.

My earlier inclination had been to phone the police. I now dismissed the idea. Rattled as I was, my curiosity was stronger, and if the police got hold of these items I might never get them back. Plus, with no sign of a break-in, and all the materials coming from upstairs, they might even conclude I'd cooked it up myself. A publicity stunt from a man paid to create them.

One thing I could say with certainty—whoever did this either knew me well or had done plenty of research. I could think of only one person who would've spotted all the references in the note, and that was my father. But break-ins and practical jokes weren't his style, and the topic of Edwin Lemaster remained off-limits.

Dad was retired now and still living abroad, although I'd seen him only a few weeks earlier at the funeral of a family friend, Wils Nethercutt. The service, oddly enough, had produced its own quirky Lemaster moment, which I couldn't help but recall.

The burial was on Block Island. Getting there required a drive to Rhode Island plus a ferry crossing, and I arrived just as the doors of the church were closing. I slid into a pew up front where my father sat alone, two rows behind Nethercutt's widow, Dorothy. The church was only a quarter full, a gathering dominated by stooped, white-haired men, some of whose faces were vaguely familiar. A few doddered up to the pulpit to tell old stories about the deceased—spy tales, it seemed, an impression reinforced when a fellow in the back stood to lock the church doors, then posted himself like a sentry.

"Bunch of old spooks," my father whispered disapprovingly, but I was entertained. The stories were lighthearted, even funny, although the narrators kept names and locations to a minimum, as if still living by their old rules.

Toward the end of the service there was a brief stir when heads turned toward the sound of creaking floorboards in the balcony. No one had switched on the lights up there, so all you could see was a thin figure in gray, seated in the shadows. During the final prayer I saw him duck out a door, and he was gone well before everyone began filing out. There was no sign of him at the reception, but an agitated old fellow in a wheelchair insisted loudly that it must have been Edwin Lemaster.

"That pariah?" one of the few women in attendance answered shrilly. "Surely not."

"Easy, Val," someone cautioned. "Plenty of us are still on good terms."

"Why a pariah?" I asked Dad. I was feeling both relieved and disappointed by having missed a fresh encounter with my onetime idol.

"Lemaster was never a favorite of some of the people here."

"Like that woman Val?"

"Apparently. I'm not familiar with her, but she's probably Agency."

"Who's the one in the wheelchair?"

"Giles Cabot. At one time, he and Nethercutt were practically joined at the hip, so no one was surprised when they both retired here. Good to see him out and about."

"What did he do for the Agency?"

Dad surprised me with a direct answer.

"A top deputy in counterintelligence. For that paranoid old nut, Jim Angleton."

"Is that what Mr. Nethercutt did, too?"

"You aren't supposed to know that, but yes. Angleton's people were always a little prickly and superior for my taste, even when they made the rounds of the embassies. But that was the required persona if you worked for Jim: Us Against the World."

"How'd *we* end up being invited to this?"

"Wils was a year ahead of me at Yale, and our fathers were friends. But I imagine it was more a case of Dorothy trying to fill the pews. Not many old timers left from State *or* the Agency."

"Dorothy looks familiar."

"We used to see a lot of the Nethercutts those two years in Georgetown. You were pretty young then."

I went for a drink. Dad sought refuge with a pair of old colleagues from State. They huddled with their backs to the ex-spooks like shipwreck survivors on a raft.

I wandered awhile, intending to mingle. But these were careful people, and every conversation dropped in volume the moment I moved within range. After a while it became mildly amusing, like making the signal come and go on an old radio by touching the antenna.

I worked my way back toward Dad just as a commotion erupted across the room, over by the bar. Once again Cabot, the fellow in the wheelchair, was in the thick of things, except this time a trim fellow in silver hair was leaning down into his face, gesturing emphatically. The tendons stood out in the man's neck and his hands slashed the air. Someone off to the side in a bright blue suit tried to intervene.

"Honestly, Breece, what's the harm in it!" The gesturing man wheeled on him.

"Goddammit, Stu. Stay out of this!"

Cabot spoke up, but his voice was too low for me to hear the words.

"The guy named Breece looks familiar," I said. "Has he been in the *Post*, or on TV?"

"Not if he can help it. Breece Preston is allergic to publicity. But not to attention, as you can see. Poor old Cabot, Preston will eat him alive. Just look at the way he's—"

Dad halted in midsentence. He looked away from the scene and placed a hand on my arm.

"Why don't we get some air?" he said. "I see that the smokers have begun firing up their weapons of mass destruction."

Something had upset him. Or maybe he'd had his fill of old farts refighting past battles. I followed him onto the porch, but not before watching Preston lean down and poke Cabot in the chest, which drew a swift reaction from a husky young man positioned behind the wheelchair. This in turn prompted a challenge from a stout fellow standing behind Preston, fiftyish but sporting a mullet, which made him stand out in this crowd like a carnival wrestler among retired professors. The last thing I heard as the door shut was raised voices, like on a schoolyard when a fight breaks out.

"Think they'll come to blows?" I asked, out in the sea breeze. "The one in the mullet looked ready to rumble."

Dad shook his head and stared out at the ocean. He looked a little pale, but maybe it was the light from the overcast sky. By the time we returned, order had been restored. Preston, Cabot, and their protectors were in separate corners. Nethercutt's wife was off to the side, talking to the older woman, Val, who'd called Lemaster a pariah.

"So do *you* think that was Lemaster up in the balcony?" I asked.

"No idea." He turned away toward the bar.

Later at dinner, when it was just the two of us down on the waterfront at the Mohegan Cafe, I tried to pry out more details about the various players.

"Was the guy in the electric blue suit Mr. Henson?"

"Stu never did know how to dress for the occasion."

"Wasn't he a CIA station chief in Europe?"

"Here and there."

"What do you think Breece Preston and Giles Cabot were arguing about?"

"Haven't the foggiest." A pause, then a frown. "Breece was always a bully at heart."

"Is he still with the Agency?"

"Goodness, no. But he's still in the business."

"Consulting?"

"You've probably heard of his outfit. Baron Associates. Contracts with the Pentagon, wherever the troops happen to be mired at the moment."

"Intelligence gathering?"

"Of a sort. His type always goes private eventually."

"Good money, probably."

"That's part of it. It's more for the freedom. Once you're outside the velvet rope you no longer have to play by the rules."

"Wouldn't that be breaking the law?"

"Where, in Afghanistan? Iraq? Some narco-state? Breece prefers to operate in places where the law has disappeared. If you ever spot one of his people in your rearview mirror, pull over to let them pass."

"You mean like the guy with the mullet?"

Dad looked away, dabbing a napkin at his mouth as if he'd received a blow.

"Where's our waitress?" he said. "I need a refill. Pass me that steak sauce, will you?"

I knew better than to press the point, especially when the next topic he raised was Redskins football, which he loathed and I loved. The next morning, before I was awake, he took the early ferry to catch his flight back to Vienna. I hadn't seen him since.

I considered telephoning him. He would probably get a kick out of all this, especially the Bingham touch with its George Smiley connection. He might even have some leads on who'd done it. It would be midnight there, but he'd always been a night owl.

Then I recalled his continuing silence about Lemaster. In all the years since '84 he still hadn't explained their friendship to my satisfaction, despite plenty of opportunities. Let it wait, I decided. For the moment this secret would be mine alone.

The funny thing was, I hadn't opened any of the cited books in ages, nor had I read a single spy novel. Dad and I both lost interest almost the moment the Berlin Wall came down in '89. For a while I gamely kept up with Lemaster's output. Maybe I felt obligated after having burned him in the *Post*. But he soon lost his edge, tilting toward rightist political themes and straying into techno-thrillers—beloved by the Pentagon but disdained by his oldest fans. Folly hadn't made an appearance since '91, and the title of that book, *A Final Folly*, says all you need to know about how the damn thing ended.

Friends whose literary judgment I trusted occasionally recommended new practitioners, authors who set their spies amid contemporary intrigue in Latin America, Asia, or in the so-called War on Terror. But something in the actions of those brave young men and women who hammered down the Wall seemed to have forever sealed my portal of fascination with the secret world. Spy novels, like the Cold War, lay entombed in my past.

Or so I told myself. For two hundred dollars an hour I suppose some shrink would have explained that fear was what really prevented me from returning, a fear of confronting everything else I'd left behind—my marriage to April, my newspaper career, my hopes of again living abroad, and my fond dream that perhaps one day I, too, might write something worthwhile, even lasting.

All had vanished without a trace, unless you counted our son, David, who lived with his mother and had just turned eighteen—voting age, big on Obama but not so big on his dad. Not that I'd given him much reason to be. It was shocking how little had been required to erase everything—a false step in Belgrade, a few foolish lapses in Washington, a cascade of misjudgment, and here I was.

Yet now, with this cryptic note staring up from my lap like a summons, I felt connected to that previous era in a way I hadn't been in ages, and my emotions were in an uproar. Even if this turned into a glorified scavenger hunt, maybe it was time to start looking for answers. At the very least, I should try to find the dead drop.

Already I was transformed. Seated there, with full heart and empty glass, I was no longer just a lonely PR man with a big paycheck and a spent imagination. I was Folly, I was Smiley, I was page one of a fresh new first edition. I was the boy I had once been, and the man I had never become.

As I scanned the opening paragraphs of *Ashenden*, a flash of insight told me exactly what I needed to do next. So I stood, ready to turn the page. Ready to turn them all.

3

I was on my way to the dead drop. Was that possible? More to the point, was it advisable? In my PR job at Ealing Wharton I'd warned off many a client from come-ons far more sophisticated than the cryptic letter that had just landed on my doorstep, and I was already wary of the sender's motives. What sort of dirty work did he have in mind, and who would be ruined as a result? Perhaps he meant to do me harm.

Curiosity overcame caution, if only because of all the times as a boy when I'd imagined setting out on just this sort of spy's errand—flashlight in hand, an eye out for surveillance, the moon peeping over my shoulder. In those days I was usually on my way to meet a girl, run an errand for Dad, or share a toke by the Danube.

But this was the real thing, or some prankster's version of it, and as I stepped onto O Street a swell of giddiness caught in my throat like laughter. For the moment, any chance of danger seemed worth the price of admission.

I took precautions nonetheless. To give the streets time to empty and darken, I waited a few hours before leaving the house. I also scrounged up an old canister of pepper spray. To pass the time before zero hour I took down some old books to reacquaint myself with my favorite spies. Their debuts were of particular interest since I was preparing for my own, and I discovered eerie similarities.

In le Carré's *Call for the Dead*, George Smiley is summoned from sleep by a ringing telephone. In *The Miernik Dossier*, Charles McCarry's Paul Christopher is yanked from bed in Geneva by the doorbell. In *Berlin Game*, Len Deighton's Bernard Samson waits in the midnight cold of Checkpoint Charlie for a contact who never shows. And in *Knee Knockers*, Lemaster's Richard Folly is lured into the murk of predawn Prague. Such a lonely procession of nocturnal seekers. Literally and figuratively they were all in the dark. Now, so was I, an unlikely initiate to the midnight brethren.

As mandated by page 47 of *The Double Game*, my tradecraft involved a series of switchbacks to ensure no one was following. It felt childish, especially when I spotted a neighbor walking her dog—an Alsatian, meaning it must be Mrs. Pierce from over on Dumbarton. I called out in greeting, but the woman who turned was slimmer, younger. Possibly taking me for a mugger, she quickened her stride, and to avoid alarming her further I doubled back toward P Street. Fortunately there was only a block to go, and I tempered my sheepishness with the knowledge that, while Georgetown was hardly Berlin, these chockablock town houses had harbored many a spook and spymaster at the height of the Cold War.

CIA chief Allen Dulles had lived right around the corner. So had Frank Wisner, the doomed zealot whose mania for covert action sent hundreds of operatives to their deaths. In the fifties and sixties, dozens of Agency men had lived here, gossiping and drinking with pundits and policy makers at rollicking dinner parties that included plenty of charming guests from abroad—British mole Kim Philby, for one.

Dad and I lived here then, during a two-year home posting from '62 to '64, back when the can-do luster of American spying peaked and began its long, steady decline in the wake of the Kennedy assassination.

I remember Dad pointing out Dulles at a cocktail gathering and admonishing me, "Be nice if he speaks to you. He just lost his job because of the Bay of Pigs"—which sounded to me like some kind of farming disaster.

At the age of seven I spotted Mr. Wisner at a neighbor's garden party one Sunday afternoon. At the time I had a crush on his daughter, who was several years older, so I was paying close attention to all things Wisner. Even a kid could tell that her dad seemed pale and beleaguered, a man at the end of his rope, although I had no way of knowing that years earlier he'd suffered a nervous breakdown in the wake of the Soviet invasion of Hungary.

A year later, after we moved back overseas to, of all places, Budapest, my father heard that Mr. Wisner had blown out his brains with a shotgun. I recall feeling bad for his daughter, and wondering if I could improve my standing with a sympathy card.

But my most vivid Georgetown memory was of an autumn afternoon just before my eighth birthday, when murder was the talk of the town. A woman was shot to death on the towpath of the C&O Canal, a pleasant greenway where everybody walked their dogs. The *Post* identified her as Mary Pinchot Meyer, sister-in-law of Benjamin Bradlee, who identified the body. All I knew of Mr. Bradlee was that he was the dad of a school-mate a grade behind me, although the story said he was the Washington bureau chief for *Newsweek*, which sounded important. It felt strange seeing our neighbors' names in a crime story, and I read over Dad's shoulder as he drank his morning coffee.

"Shouldn't you be getting ready for school, sport?"

"I'm done."

"Teeth brushed?"

I bared them fiercely, and he turned back to his reading. A few seconds later he chuckled under his breath.

"What's so funny?"

"Oh, it describes this poor woman's ex-husband, Cord Meyer, as a 'local author and lecturer.' You remember Mr. Meyer, don't you?"

I did, mostly because he was the only person I'd ever met named "Cord." Still is.

"I thought he worked with Mr. Wisner?"

"He does. The paper is being discreet."

"What's 'discreet' mean?"

"You could look it up. Increase your word power, like in *Reader's Digest*."

Dad hated *Reader's Digest*, so I took it for a joke, although I didn't get it.

"Don't you be wandering over to the towpath. That's police business, not yours. And if you cross Wisconsin Avenue on your bike, for God's sake, *walk* it across."

"Yes, sir."

Naturally I made a beeline for the towpath after school on my red Galaxy Flyer. To my disappointment, there was no sign of the crime, so I set out for the next best destination—the victim's art studio in the Bradlees' garage, on an alley behind N Street. The *Post* had evocatively described a freshly painted canvas, still wet from her final brushstrokes, drying on an easel in front of an electric fan.

I negotiated a dogleg turn up the alley, and to my morbid delight the garage was wide open, revealing a roomful of canvases, including the one in front of the fan. What I hadn't bargained for were the two men who turned abruptly at the sound of my approach.

One was Mr. Bradlee, who relaxed the moment he recognized me. But the other man, taller and thinner, stared with probing eyes from behind thick, horn-rimmed glasses. He acted more like a cop than a neighbor, and when he took a step in my direction I nearly fell off my bike. Fortunately Mr. Bradlee put out a hand to stop him.

"It's all right, Jim. It's Warfield Cage's boy." Then, to me: "It's Bill, right?"

"Yes, sir. I'm sorry if—"

The man named Jim interrupted.

"This isn't your business, son. That's what your father would tell you."

It probably wasn't his, either, but I'd been taught not to talk back to adults.

"Yes, sir."

Then he said the strangest thing, reminding me of one of those folk tales where the troll offers a riddle for safe passage:

"Remember, son. Caution is the eldest child of wisdom. Now run along."

"Yes, sir."

I was shaky in the saddle until I reached the wide open spaces of Thirty-third Street. When I described the encounter to Dad, he chuckled just like he had while reading the *Post*.

"Sounds like Mr. Angleton," he said. "Quoting Victor Hugo, no less."

"Who's he?"

"Victor Hugo?"

"Mr. Angleton."

"Oh, sort of an 'author and lecturer,' like Mr. Meyer."

"Why was he in that lady's room?"

"Looking for secrets, I'd imagine. That's mostly what he writes and lectures about."

"What kind of secrets?"

"They wouldn't be secrets if he went around telling everybody, would they?"

Not until my thirties did I find out from some book what they'd really been up to. By then I was working for Bradlee, who'd become executive editor of the *Post*, and I'd long since learned that Jim Angleton had been the CIA's chief counterspy. They'd been looking for Mary Meyer's diary, which described her affair with the late President Kennedy. Since she was something of a lefty, Angleton may also have wanted to scan it for clues to assist his infamous Great Mole Hunt, a paranoid quest in which he ruined the careers of so many trustworthy CIA men that he, too, was eventually forced out.

They found the diary. Bradlee gave it to Angleton, who promised to destroy it. Instead, telling no one, he stashed it in his files.

So that was my neighborhood, a high-toned ghetto of spies and policy makers. And here I was now, decades later, crossing the shadows of its maples and dogwoods as I zeroed in on yet another cache of secrets.

In case you're wondering how I figured out the location, it was a breeze once I read the opening lines of *Ashenden*. The key sentence was right there on page one:

On the house at which Ashenden had been asked to call there was a board up to announce that it was for sale, the shutters were closed and there was no sign that anyone lived in it.

The passage perfectly described a detached house on P Street that my neighbors and I had long been complaining about. It had been gutted for renovation, then the developer went broke and boarded up the windows. In Georgetown you didn't do that, so we raised a stink. City Hall finally sent a crew to replace the boards with tasteful shutters and post a "For Sale" sign. It had to be the place.

Normally a porch light was burning, but tonight the house was dark. As I crossed the tiny lawn I saw why—someone had removed the bulb. The front door had one of those big padlocks favored by real estate agents. Based on Folly's tradecraft, I was looking for a yellow chalk mark on the bricks, but there was nothing out front. I went around to the left and spotted a yellow slash just below the rearmost window. I glanced back at the neighboring house, a mere fifteen feet away. The last thing I needed was someone reporting me to the cops, but all was quiet. The shutters were unlocked, and the sash opened easily when I pressed up against the glass. I climbed through the opening into an empty room that smelled of sawdust and fresh plaster.

I closed the shutters behind me and turned on the flashlight. Sweeping the walls with the beam, I spotted a buff-colored envelope propped on the mantelpiece like a note left for Santa. I fetched it, every footstep a hollow thud. Then it was time to leave, unless I wanted to become a poster boy for Neighborhood Watch.

In my impatience to get home, I ignored tradecraft and took the most direct route. As if to punish my haste, someone called out from behind me just as I reached my street.

"You're out late tonight, Bill."

It was the woman with the Alsatian, maybe thirty yards behind me at the end of the block. The dog was lit by the streetlamp, but she was in shadow.

"I am. And your name is . . . ?"

"Mail service is so slow these days. But I'm glad you finally got delivery."

She and the dog set off briskly in the opposite direction. I hurried after them, full of questions. But as soon as she rounded the corner a rear door opened on a car at the curb. No dome light, no headlights. I broke into a run as they climbed in. A black Lincoln Town Car, the kind embassies used, but the tags were unlit. The car pulled away. Brake lights glowed briefly as it paused at the next intersection, then it sped off.

Now what kind of tradecraft was that, tipping off a target to surveillance? It felt more like thug behavior than espionage. Or was it a signal that someone would be guarding my flanks? Either way, I'd been put on notice. But why would someone with the resources to hire a burglar, a tail, and a driver with a limo need me? Maybe the envelope would tell me.

I shut the blinds, settled onto the couch, and slit open the envelope. Two pages were inside—generic white paper, although the typing was all too familiar. How many hours had this person spent on my Royal? The words "Use on line 11" were typed on the first page above a long strand of paired numbers, presumably for the book code. But in what book? And on what page?

Those questions were answered on the second sheet, although I gasped at its contents. A yellowed page 93, torn roughly from Lemaster's first novel, *Knee Knockers*, was pasted to the paper. So was a sliced-out square from the book's copyright page, which showed that the book was a first edition from 1969. More typescript was below.

This certainly ruled out my father as a suspect. He would sooner torture a small animal than carve up a cherished first edition. If tearing a page out of an old book sounds like no big deal, consider that a first edition of *Knee Knockers* now fetches up to $5,000, double that if it's signed. A defaced volume is practically worthless. Mercenary considerations aside, to any bibliophile this was an act of malice, and it told me that someone was harboring quite a grudge, against either Lemaster or the owner of the book.

But enough of that. There was a book code to decipher, and the numbers were my guide. In each pair, the first one told me which word to count to on line eleven, and the second told me which letter to use. Soon enough I had the message:

You were halfway there in eighty four. Finish the job. Instructions on line seventeen.

Line seventeen began a passage of dialogue between Folly and operative Karl Breeden:

"How long do you think I'll need?" Breeden asked.
"Maybe two weeks," Folly said. "Three tops."
"Any travel?"
"Vienna for sure. Probably Budapest. We'll communicate through the usual channels. Stay where you always do. Use the code name Dewey."
"And from there?"
"Await my instructions in Vienna. I'll be in touch."

Clearly, these were my marching orders. Just as clearly, my quarry was Edwin Lemaster, or rather, the Lemaster who had once worked for the CIA. The message signed off with a sort of warning, typed at the bottom of the second sheet:

Management not responsible if you end up like Mr. Hambledon's description on p. 78.

Hambledon. The name rang a bell, but I couldn't place it. I checked page 78 of *Knee Knockers* and *The Double Game*, but came up empty. I flipped through *Ashenden* in case a Hambledon played a minor role, but he wasn't there, either. Hambledon. I had read it long ago, but for the moment it was lost in the fog of memory.

The mantel clock struck two. Practical matters began to intervene. Ealing Wharton needed me in top form tomorrow, and I would be lucky to get four hours of sleep. I was due to testify on Capitol Hill on behalf of our newest client, makers of the Lattelicious Superluxe, a milk frother implicated in a dozen house fires. Some congressman, scenting an easy opportunity for publicity, had called for a hearing to examine how our client and its regulators had allowed such shoddy merchandise onto store shelves. My job was to take the heat alongside our client's CEO, who was as clueless about PR as his technical people were about wiring. We were meeting at seven to prepare.

But all I could think about as I climbed into bed was whether I should continue this spy hunt and, if so, how quickly I might arrange time off for a trip to Europe. Vienna, of all places. Home not only to my dad, but to my richest boyhood memories.

I was being used, of course. I had no illusions about that. I had often watched my firm's managing director, Marty Ealing, entice some congressman or other to do his bidding with a similar blend of flattery, intrigue, and misdirection. He always made them believe it was in their own interest, when usually it was in Marty's. And by letting them lead the way, they were the ones who encountered any snares and booby traps.

Who, then, was using me, and toward what end? And how dangerous were the booby traps? Those questions kept me awake for the next hour or so, while the name Hambledon fluttered above me like a moth until I finally drifted off.

After what felt like only minutes, the alarm shrieked. I shut it off and lay in the sudden silence. That's when the moth landed on my forehead and whispered its name:

Tommy Hambledon.

He was a spymaster created by author Manning Coles, the pen name of a British mixed-doubles writing team—Adelaide Frances Oke Manning and Cyril Henry Coles. The latter worked for British Intelligence, the former for the war office. They wrote dozens of Tommy Hambledon books. My dad had fifteen, but I owned only one—*Drink to Yesterday*, the first in the series, published way back in 1940.

I threw on a robe, descended the stairs in slippered feet, and retrieved the volume from the highest shelf. Dust puffed from the jacket as I turned to page 78.

At the bottom of the page, Tommy Hambledon told an excited new recruit exactly what entering the spy trade was about to do to his life:

"Yes, it's got you now, and it will never let you go. When once the job has taken hold you'll find that nothing else in life has any kick in it, and apart from the job you're dead. Neither the fields of home nor the arts of peace nor the love of women will suffice."

Under my present circumstances it sounded more like an enticement than a warning, and even as I began mapping my morning strategy for defending the fallen virtue of the Lattelicious Superluxe, in the back of my mind I already knew one thing for sure.

Used or not, I was going to Vienna.

4

You've probably guessed by now that I was an only child, and that my dad was a single parent. Two males, each playing solitaire, yet pleasantly companionable in our vagabond tour of Cold War Europe.

Only one memory of my mother survives, and even it remains in shadow. It is night, and I am two years old. We are living in Belgrade, forever my city of ill fortune. She stands backlit in my bedroom doorway, face in silhouette, features obscured. I am supposed to be asleep, so I shut my eyes as she steps forward in the dark to kiss me. Her lips are cool against my forehead. Her perfume is heady and Parisian, a scent phantom that has stalked me through life, growing fainter by the year.

She left us just before I turned three, then visited a few days later on the weekend of my birthday. Once the candles were blown out and I'd gone to bed, she and my father discussed how to divvy up custody. Then she went off to Greece, where a week later she died in a bus accident on some lonely hill in the Peloponnese. Probably while traveling with another man, I later surmised, although my father never said.

I like to believe that her absence made me a more careful observer. Children let their mothers do a lot of watching for them—keeping an eye out for cars, or for lurking strangers. My father hired nannies and sitters, of course, but I must have sensed that they never had quite the same stake in matters as a mom, so I developed a keener eye, a heightened awareness.

Her absence was at the heart of an ongoing conspiracy by which my father and I carefully avoided discussing delicate personal issues. Doing so would have risked having the subject of her desertion come up, so we spoke instead of the world around us—sports, school, current events. And books, always books. In Budapest, when I was nine or ten, the subject of American spies was in the news, so one night I asked my dad what it was, exactly, that spies did.

"Oh, things that we never see. With an import we can never be certain of. But rest assured, they make a difference, and they're out there each and every day."

"Where?"

"All around us." He chuckled and shook the ice in his cocktail—a gin and tonic, so it must have been summer. "Like God."

It was a surprising answer, considering he'd never once taken me to church, so I asked the logical follow-up.

"Do you believe in God?"

"Absolutely. Life didn't just spring up out of thin air."

"What do you think he's like?"

"Oh, I doubt it's a he or she, don't you? I've never understood why everyone has to turn God into such a human, and not a very nice one at that. A petty know-it-all who demands to be worshipped, and will damn you to Hell if you don't."

Henceforth, the subjects of spies and God were intertwined in my mind. Both came to represent the unknown and the unknowable, which is probably why I was predisposed to like those novels of Dad's. They were textual glances into the firmament.

Now, here I was about to join the priesthood, so to speak, by heading back to Vienna where all those first editions still lined his shelves—signed, dated, and dusted once a week. As a boy I'd occasionally spotted what I thought were glimmers of real characters hiding in their thickets of prose, especially Lemaster's.

"Dad," I would ask, "is this Mr. So-and-So from the embassy he's writing about?"

"No, son, it's a novel. All the characters are made up."

"But—"

"They're not real people, Bill."

And that would close the subject until I spotted the next one, peeping from the pages like a fugitive. Now, based on the messages I'd received, it didn't seem far-fetched to believe that every answer I sought might be found within those books.

But first things first. The secular business of Ealing Wharton awaited. I also needed a plausible excuse to go snooping around in my old backyard of Europe. Cover, in other words. Building a legend, as Folly would have put it. To do the work of a spy, I would have to start behaving like one, especially if someone was already tracking me.

God and spying. Father and son. A mole's two masters. Tandems were much on my mind after my night of eerie visitations. Let the Double Game proceed.

5

My first independent act of espionage in Operation Lemaster, as it would later come to be known in official channels, was to lie to my boss. Easy. Having spent the morning dissembling under oath on behalf of a milk frother, fibbing to Marty Ealing for my own benefit felt as righteous as a donation to Amnesty International.

"Hate to drop this on you now, Marty, but I need a few weeks off. It's personal."

"Personal?"

We were in Marty's office, and I knew I'd said the magic word. To Marty, "personal" is where everything juicy goes to hide, the stuff of leverage and control.

"It's my dad."

Marty frowned. Clearly he'd hoped for something messier, preferably a woman married to someone other than me. I have zero respect for Marty, which is one reason I still run. It takes at least four hard miles along the C&O towpath to sweat out a day's labors at Ealing Wharton.

"He's seventy-eight and lives alone in Vienna." Sensing I was losing my audience, I picked up the pace. "I'm all he's got, and, well, you know how it goes at that age."

"Say no more, Bill. Hell, after the way you wrapped that committee around your *middle finger* this morning"—Marty always telegraphs his punch lines—"how could I say no? We'll work out any adjustment to your compensation later."

My second act was to phone Arch Bascombe, an old colleague from the *Post* who was now an editor at *Vanity Fair.* Might he be interested, I asked, in a freelance piece on the espionage career of author Edwin Lemaster?

"Isn't he the one you burned in that interview piece way back when?"

"At least you remember."

"So you finally got to the bottom of that?"

"Getting there. Headed to Vienna tomorrow, in fact."

"I'll bite. On spec, of course. And I can't cover expenses."

"Understood. But a letter of introduction would help. You'd be surprised how much weight that still carries in the Old World."

Bascombe was charmed by the idea, and the price was right. He emailed me an official-looking letter on magazine letterhead. My cover was set.

I then telephoned the one person in Washington whose opinion still mattered to me. My son, David.

Like a politician who pays too much attention to approval ratings, I'd been making something of a comeback with David during the past year, and nothing had pleased me more. While it would be nice to think my own efforts were responsible—I'd taken him on some college visits during his senior year of high school, and in the spring I'd attended all his lacrosse games—the real reason was his own maturation. Not only had he become an engaging and interesting young man, he had learned not to hold a grudge.

He was a freshman at Georgetown, right across the neighborhood, and we had dinner once a week. Now that he no longer lived at home, I was at last on equal footing with his mother for shared time. I wanted to let him know I'd be going abroad.

Fortunately he was free for the evening. He picked Martin's Tavern, a hangout at Wisconsin and N within walking distance for both of us. As always, I arrived ten minutes early. Once you've deserted a child, you never again want him to enter a room where you're supposed to be waiting and find it empty.

Martin's is one of those places with English hunting prints on the wall and a brass rail at the bar. I ordered a pint of ale and settled into a booth. David arrived on schedule. Salazar, a waiter familiar with all the regulars, directed him to our table.

I stood to give him a hug, a greeting he'd recently begun reciprocating.

"You look good, David." He was flushed from a workout. He'd be playing college lacrosse in the spring, but they already had him running and lifting weights. I loved watching him play because his motor never quit. It made me believe that somewhere inside him beat the heart of a distance runner, although I knew better than to say so.

"You look good, too, Dad. What'd you do, quit your job?"

He was perceptive in that way, like his grandfather.

"Next best thing. I'm taking some time off. Going to Vienna to see your granddad. After that, who knows? But I'll be gone a few weeks."

Salazar took our standard order—the Delmonico for David, lamb chops for me.

"How are your classes going?"

"Not as hard as I thought they'd be."

"That comes later, when they know you've let your guard down."

Sensing the onset of a fatherly lecture, he nimbly changed the subject.

"So how come you never told me about the history of this place?" He beamed as he said it, in the manner of all college freshmen bursting with new knowledge.

"Martin's has a history? I know Washington never slept here."

"Spies. It was a KGB hangout in the seventies. Some big-shot controller used to meet his boss here. Before that there was Elizabeth Bentley, the Red Spy Queen. She'd come here for drinks during the war, then meet her contact at a pharmacy down the street. Then there was the Russian defector, Oleg Kalugin, who ran out on his CIA contact from a restaurant right across the street, where the Five Guys is now. And about six blocks from here is where crazy Jim Angleton used to have his three-martini lunches, sometimes with Kim Philby. They were buddies, you know."

"Whoa, now." I took a big swallow of ale to hide my unease. The one topic I didn't want to raise, and he'd raised it. "Where'd you learn all that?" Not from a sealed envelope slipped beneath his door, I hoped.

"I'm taking an intro to European history since World War II. For the Cold War he had us read *The Spy Who Came In from the Cold*. Awesome book. It made me want to look up all the spy stuff that happened around here. I kept thinking of all those novels of yours, so I've been checking out some of them from the library."

Like father, like son, like grandson.

"Don't bother with the library. Just ask. Or come and take them; you've got a key."

It then hit me with devastating suddenness that David would have made the perfect accomplice for whoever was orchestrating my adventures, and for a millisecond I was perched on the edge of hurt and disappointment, thinking he would now reveal all with a belly laugh at my expense. A spy book caper, cooked up to spoof me. Just as quickly the moment passed. There were too many details he wouldn't have known, and he certainly didn't have the means to have broken into the house at the dead drop. And this was David, not some client at Ealing Wharton.

"Holy shit," he said quietly. He was looking over my shoulder.

"What is it?"

"She looks just like Elizabeth Bentley. But it can't be."

"The Red Spy Queen?"

"Bentley wore a red carnation and carried a copy of *Life* magazine. And that woman over there . . ."

I turned and saw a slender woman alone at the table by the door. Attractive, late twenties. A red carnation was pinned to her navy business suit, and she was flipping through a magazine. I caught Salazar's eye, figuring I'd ask if he knew her. About then a noisy party of six burst through the door, blocking his way and obscuring our view.

"Yes, Mr. Cage?" Salazar had finally made it through the maelstrom.

I kept my voice low, although the new arrivals were making quite a commotion.

"That woman by the door, the one with the flower on her lapel."

He glanced over his shoulder, then frowned.

"By the door?"

The arrivals eased toward the back, clearing the view. The table was now empty.

"Wow," David said. "That was awesome."

"Never mind," I said. The puzzled Salazar left to attend to the rowdy newcomers. If David hadn't been there I might have wondered if I'd seen her at all, but now I was wondering if she was the woman with the Alsatian.

"Something I should probably tell you about this trip," I said. "I may be doing some work over there that's a little, well, unorthodox."

"For Ealing Wharton?"

"God, no. I'd never stick my neck out for them. Freelance stuff. For *Vanity Fair*."

"Wow. You're writing again?"

I was pleased by his excitement.

"Maybe. In fact, I'm looking into some old stuff from the Cold War." I realized I'd said too much when he connected the dots right away.

"So do you think that woman with the carnation—"

"No. I don't. But keep an eye on the house while I'm gone, if you don't mind. Take all the books you want. If you get a strange text from me now and then, take it in stride, but don't tell anyone else. And, for God's sake, whatever you do—"

"Don't tell Mom?"

"Yes."

"I wouldn't do that." Then, as if something had suddenly occurred to him. "Is that what you think I've been doing all these years? Reporting back to Mom?"

"No, not at all. It's just that—"

"Is that why you never confide in me about, like, anything?"

"That's not true."

Or no more true than it had been for my own father. It then struck me that the children of divorce were the original double agents—faithful to two masters at once, yet almost certainly favoring one over the other in secret.

"David, I hope you realize how much I've always regretted that you grew up with only one parent in the house. I know it was never easy. For you or your mother."

"You grew up that way. You seem to have turned out okay."

"True. But death didn't give my mother much choice." I'd never told him that she ran out on us. "My exile was voluntary, and stupid."

"You wish you'd stayed together?"

"I wish I'd been mature enough at the time to at least give it a try."

"That's pretty much what Mom says."

Which didn't make me feel any better. Even after sixteen years the judgment stung, mostly because it was true.

David forked in a mouthful of steak and followed it with potatoes. At least one of us still had an appetite. He was right. I'd never offered him much in the way of personal revelation, but maybe tonight was a start.

I glanced again toward the table by the door. A busboy was clearing the dishes. She'd left behind her magazine, and when the busboy picked it up I looked at David and he looked at me.

It was an old copy of *Life*, with Joseph Stalin on the cover.

6

This was not the Vienna I'd known as a boy. Riding the S-Bahn into the city I sat among Turks and Arabs, their chatter clouding the air like gnats. When the Turks got off, Bosnians got on. Orange commuter straps swayed overhead like hangman's nooses, and as usual after a transatlantic flight I felt like the walking dead.

Out in the streets, police cameras stared from every corner. A tram line I'd once used no longer existed. When I went in search of coffee to help me recalibrate—*the* signature drink of Viennese living—the first place I saw was a damn Starbucks. Still, it was caffeine, and after a few swallows my outlook improved.

Some things hadn't changed. Pedestrians at crosswalks still waited dutifully for the light, and old women still glared when I crossed anyway, the embassy boy back to his old tricks. In the clipped green expanses of the Stadtpark, grown men still peed behind the sparsest of cover, a habit that now seems reasonable with public toilets charging a euro. This being a Sunday, practically everything was *geschlossen*, just as it would have been thirty-five years ago.

Most reassuring of all was Vienna's enduring beauty—block after block, stacked and frosted like a wedding cake. Yet, to my more experienced (jaded?) eye, the imperial magnificence looked brittle—as if the city's aging face had received an injection of Botox and could no longer crack a smile.

My dad was a late riser on Sundays, so I'd told him my flight was getting in hours later than it really was, meaning I had a few hours to kill before arriving on his doorstep. He'd been oddly thrown by the idea of a visit on such short notice.

"Day after tomorrow? Goodness. Well, I'll have to do some juggling, but yes, of course, Sunday would be perfect! I'll reserve a table at Figlmüller, and to hell with the tourists. A schnitzel and a Gösser will have you feeling right at home."

Juggling? Was I that hard to prepare for?

I set out on a long walk, part of my usual plan for beating jet lag by avoiding naps at all costs. It was cloudy and cool, and I kept an eye out for tails, especially slender women with red flowers or leashed Alsatians. So far, only the cameras were watching.

Shortly after one-thirty I reached my dad's stately old building, a block off the Graben in the Hofburg quarter. I pressed the button by his name, shoved open the door on his answering buzz, then rode the tiny caged elevator to five. He was waiting in the hall dressed in his usual Sunday uniform of tan corduroys and a blue Oxford.

"The prodigal returns!" His stock greeting. "Let me take your bag, you must be exhausted."

He had laid on quite a spread. On the dining room table was a beaded pitcher of orange juice next to a carafe of coffee. Slices of meat and cheese were arrayed like playing cards on a china platter alongside a basket of croissants and bowls of yogurt, muesli, and sliced fruit. A full Vienna *Frühstuck*, even at this hour, and the gesture was touching. It reminded me of how anxious I'd been to please David two days earlier, and I wondered if parents ever stopped feeling as if they needed to launch a charm offensive whenever their grown children came home.

"I hope you're hungry, or would you like a lie-down first?" Using the British term.

"I'll eat. It looks great. Then a shower, maybe. But I need to stay vertical."

"Of course. Your stoical approach to jet lag. Here, let's take your plate to the living room where it's not so damn gloomy. I'll bring the coffee."

He drew open the blinds to a view of old rooftops beneath brooding clouds.

"A cross-country sky," he said. "Isn't that what you used to call days like this?"

"I did. Looks like one of those days when our coach would run us ten miles through the Vienna woods."

I could smell the trail as I said it—black mud and fallen leaves. Dad had come to all my races, screaming with surprising passion for a sport he'd never known. I think he appreciated its perfect meritocracy. No manner of favoritism or fakery could make you finish even a second faster. To a diplomat, that must have seemed miraculous.

"Reading anything good?"

His favorite question, and with the perfect backdrop. Bookshelves lined the two walls that got the least sunlight, so the bindings wouldn't fade. The espionage first editions were on the far left, easy to spot by the shiny plastic covers over the dust jackets, the mark of a collector, although he'd read every copy at least twice. Dad certainly wouldn't have needed hours to remember Tommy Hambledon, and it again occurred to me that he might be playing at least an advisory role for my mysterious controller.

"Funny you should ask," I said. "I've been going through some old Lemasters."

"You make it sound more like business than pleasure."

"In a way, it is."

"How so?"

"Are you sure you don't already know?"

He frowned, puzzled. It seemed genuine.

"I'm here on a freelance assignment. Trying to ease back into a little journalism."

"Wonderful!" He'd hated it when I gave up writing, and he almost never asked about my work at Ealing Wharton. "What's the story?"

"Something you might be able to help me with. *Vanity Fair* wants a piece on the espionage career of Edwin Lemaster. That's why I've been going through the books. Searching for clues to what he was really up to."

Dad wrinkled his nose.

"Who put you on to this?"

The one question I didn't want to answer. Dad was as sharp as ever.

"I got a tip in the mail. Anonymous."

"The most reckless kind, for all concerned. Didn't you take a big enough bite out of him the first time?"

"You act like that was my fault."

He shrugged. I sipped coffee, waiting to see if he'd take sides. Maybe he already had.

"You know, I came across a review a few years ago that dated his entire decline as a novelist to that interview of yours."

"Never saw it."

But I had, of course, and one particular paragraph had lodged in my mind:

Ever since his "confession," Lemaster has lost his edge, seemingly more interested in proving his loyalty than in honing his craft. His latest book, a techno-thriller in which Uncle Sam's minions are portrayed only in the brightest hues of red, white and blue, completes his descent into mediocrity.

"The funny thing," Dad said, "is that Agency people didn't even raise an eyebrow about the whole confessional part."

"Really?"

"It was his other slip that pissed them off."

"There was another slip?"

"Think about it. Think of everything he told you."

I did. I drew a blank until my father filled it in.

" 'I was keeping an eye out for the Don Tollesons of this world.' He was a mole hunter."

"Well, yeah. That was pretty obvious."

"And what does that tell you about who he worked for?"

"The Soviet desk?"

"Oh, come on."

"Jim Angleton?" My father smiled but said nothing. "I didn't think Counterintelligence had its own field men. Not overseas, anyway."

"Nobody else thought so, either, including most of the CIA."

"So it was off the books?"

"Everyone's except Angleton's, which he kept in a safe."

Angleton yet again. Dead for more than twenty years, yet still coming up in my memories, and in my conversations with both David and Dad. And why not? Everything I'd ever read about him made him sound like the bizarre creation of some novelist, which of course made him seem real, eternal. He was the original Cold Warrior, one of the first to play the postwar game against the Soviets and play it well. In his hobbies, as in his work, he was a detail man, a miniaturist—tying flies, breeding orchids, combing files, hunting moles, deconstructing poems. Deeply suspicious, yet blinded by Anglophilia and his friendship with Kim Philby, whose betrayal drove him over the edge. And now I'd learned that Ed Lemaster had secretly worked for him.

"Turns out," Dad continued, "that Angleton had three operatives, all of them ostensibly employed by the Soviet desk but in reality reporting to him. Which meant they were paid twice, of course."

"So even within the Agency there were double agents, sort of."

"That's certainly how the Soviet desk saw it. Angleton called them his 'flying squad.' Apparently only a few of his assistants knew about it."

"Where'd you hear all this, the funeral?" He smiled cagily. "No wonder I couldn't get anything out of you at dinner."

"Of course, by the time Lemaster let the cat out of the bag in that interview, Angleton had been in retirement eleven years. But there was still hell to pay. You saw what those people were like. They still argue about crap that happened in 1948, so you can imagine what kind of a row they'd have over—"

He was interrupted by a ringing telephone, a land line jangling down the hall in his bedroom. It startled us both, but him even more. He looked over at the clock on an end table, then back at me, then again at the clock, which seemed strange, but I said nothing. It was exactly two o'clock.

The phone continued to ring.

"Excuse me," he said, sounding shaken. He headed off toward his bedroom. I took up a position at the end of the hall to listen.

"Cage," he said, answering in the Austrian style. There was a pause. Then, sternly and in German: "No. This is Warfield, but William is here. Are you sure that's who you wish to speak to? Very well."

Then, louder and in English: "Bill, it's for you."

His brow was creased as he handed me the receiver. He hovered in the doorway as I answered, rude by his standards.

"This is William Cage."

I turned my back for privacy, but sensed his lingering presence. I'd been back for half an hour and we were already spying on each other. The answering voice was neither tense nor urgent. It was an older man, Viennese accent. The line was clear, so the call was probably local.

"This is Christoph, at Kurzmann Buchladen." A bookstore. "I have your special order, delivered today in the name of Dewey."

There it was, the promised message, although I hadn't expected it so soon.

"A delivery? Now?"

"We are closed Sunday. We open tomorrow at eight o'clock. On Johannesgasse."

"Where did you—?"

He'd hung up. When I turned around my father was staring from the doorway.

"Was that Kurzmann's?"

"How'd you know?"

"I'm an old customer, although not for years. Did you special-order something?"

"No."

I toyed with trying the name "Dewey" on him, but if I told him that, then I would have to explain more than I was ready to. His reaction to the phone call had already aroused my suspicion, and, judging from what he said next, my reaction had aroused his.

"Do they have something for you?"

"So he said."

"And you're sure you didn't order anything? You're *positive* that that call came from completely out of the blue?"

"Yes."

He eyed me dubiously, probably because of the guilty look on my face. But he was hiding something, too. We moved back to the living room and, like boxers returning to the ring, took up our previous positions. Then, for whatever reason—the strange call, the jet lag, or even the sight of all those spy novels, these words spilled from my mouth:

"This is almost like something out of a Lemaster novel, don't you think?"

He reacted as if I'd slapped him.

"Why do you say that?"

"I don't know. Maybe because it is? Do you remember any scenes like this? Or could I be thinking of another author?"

"All right, Bill. Enough." His tone was stern, as if I was in high school again and he'd just found a roach clip in the bathroom. "Who told you to ask me these questions?"

"Nobody."

"Likely story, but I suppose after that wacky funeral nothing should surprise me. I did wonder what sort of repercussions would come out of that unholy mix of people, but I never imagined you'd be part of them. So, who did you speak to before flying over here? Someone at State? Or maybe even the Agency?"

"The CIA?" I didn't have to fake sounding incredulous because I really was.

"So the Agency, then. Is that the real reason you're here?"

"Dad, no one told me to ask you anything." He gave me a long look, unconvinced. I stared right back. "Have I ever been able to lie to your face and get away with it?"

"No." He seemed to relax. "But *something* made you ask."

"My imagination, probably. Why'd you assume I'd been talking to the Agency?"

"Ask Christoph."

"The bookseller?"

"When you pick up the delivery. Ask him why I'd think this was some sort of job for the Agency. Ask him as well who else has been in touch with him on this matter, and for God's sake do it discreetly. Then tell me what he says."

"You're serious?"

"Absolutely. And, son?"

"Yes?"

"If you're thinking this is some sort of lark, or intellectual exercise, then I urge you to disabuse yourself of that notion straightaway."

"Based on what?"

"That's all I'm going to say until you've talked to Christoph."

At first I thought he was bluffing, but as the silence lengthened, Dad stared out the window into the gray afternoon. I coughed and picked up my coffee cup, but it was empty, so I set it back down, uncertain what to do next. We still had five hours to kill before dinner, eighteen before the bookstore opened. It was going to be a long and awkward afternoon.

7

I arrived five minutes early, only to find that Kurzmann Buchladen was already open for business. There was even a customer ahead of me, a dissipated-looking fellow in a long wool coat and a floppy brown hat that slouched on his head like a dumpling. I took him at first for a wino, then noticed how assiduously he was working the shelves, like an ingenious piece of farm machinery that can simultaneously harrow, weed, and cultivate. Three volumes were tucked beneath his left arm and a fourth bulged from a coat pocket. He looked up as the door shut behind me, jingling a bell. Then he wrote me off as inconsequential and resumed his harvesting.

I looked around. Sellers of rare and antiquarian books are often messy housekeepers, but even by those standards the conditions at Kurzmann's were unforgivable. The framed prints and maps hanging from the walls were dusty and crooked. Several had cracked glass. The watermarked ceiling was beaded with moisture—a death sentence for all that cloth and pulp below—and the musty air smelled faintly of cat urine. Mounted on the wall behind the register was an ancient color engraving of Prince Metternich, Europe's original celebrity power broker, the Kissinger of his day. He glared out at the merchandise in apparent disdain.

Creaking floorboards drew my attention toward the back, where a short balding man in an unbuttoned vest emerged from the gloom. A tape measure was draped around his neck, as if he were a tailor who'd been called away from his sewing.

"Yes?" he asked in English, pegging my nationality. He ignored the other customer, and looked surprised by my presence, which was odd given yesterday's phone call.

"Are you Christoph?" I asked in German. He answered in the same language.

"Do I know you?"

"You telephoned yesterday about a special order. I'm Bill Cage."

A book slapped to the floor in the aisle where the other man was browsing. He snatched up the dropped copy and glanced my way with a gleam in his eye, or maybe I imagined it. The only noise was the muffled sound of rush hour traffic from the Ring, half a block away.

"Ah, yes," Christoph said. He shuffled toward the register. "Your book has arrived."

"For someone named Dewey, you said."

He shot me a sidelong glance but said nothing.

"Well, is it or not?"

Stopping behind the counter, he glanced toward the harvester, who was working at a more deliberate pace than before. Then he glared at me and hissed beneath his breath: "Do you always conduct your business so sloppily?"

He quickly turned away and, with some effort, climbed a stepladder to a long shelf stuffed with books. Yellow labels scribbled with names poked from every copy, although the amount of dust suggested that most of the customers had either died or forgotten their orders. But my parcel looked clean as a whistle when he pulled it free. It was wrapped in brown butcher paper and tied with a crisscross of white string. Something about this presentation stirred a distant memory that I couldn't quite place. The name "Dewey" was written on the butcher paper in black ink. Christoph handed it over, still glaring.

"Fifty euros, Mr. . . . . ?"

"Cage."

"Yes. Mr. Cage."

"Fifty? That's practically seventy dollars."

"The price is marked. You can take it or leave it."

I got out my wallet.

"Will that be all, sir?"

"No. I have a question." He winced and glanced behind me. There was no sound at all from the harvester. Feeling his eyes on my back, and remembering my father's warning to be discreet, I lowered my voice to a whisper.

"My father told me to ask you why he might suspect this was some sort of job for the Agency." I felt like an idiot. "You know, the CIA?"

"Please, Mr. Cage."

He, too, was whispering, and if his tone had been icy before, it was now tremulous with anger. Then he switched to English and spoke loudly.

"If there are other *special orders* you wish to discuss, perhaps it would be easier to do so in my office, where I have full access to the records of my inventory."

"Okay. Fine."

He led the way, footsteps loud and choppy. The harvester returned to his labors, but Christoph still hadn't shown the slightest interest in him, even though the fellow could have walked out with his books at any moment without paying. He certainly looked the type.

We negotiated a switchback hallway, then climbed a winding staircase to an even gloomier corridor lined with more books. Many were leather-bound and ancient, others relatively new, the titles flashing by like signs on the Autobahn. *Portnoy's Complaint* in German, an old *Atlas of the New World* in Spanish, an anthology of Charles Addams cartoons. When we reached the end of the passage he withdrew a set of keys, fiddled with one or two, then unlocked the door to an office as clean and modern as you'd find in any bank, although it, too, was filled with books—his choicest copies, to judge from the bindings and titles.

The décor was Formica and chrome, with everything in perfect order—papers in stacks, pencils in cups. An iMac with a 21-inch screen held pride of place. Christoph sagged into a massive chair upholstered in black leather. He didn't motion for me to sit down, but I did anyway, in a smaller seat of matching leather. There was an electric kettle on a window ledge next to packets of tea and filter coffee, but he made no offer of hospitality. From the rigid set of his jaw it was obvious he was still furious.

"I only brought you up here out of respect for your father," he began, switching back to German. "Otherwise, I would have kicked you out of the store."

I repeated my question.

"All I want to know—and my father told me to ask, so it's not like this was my idea—is what made him think this might be a job for the Agency?"

"*He* told you to ask me this? Warfield Cage?"

I nodded. Christoph shook his head in disbelief.

"How do I even know you're his son? Do you have any identification?"

I felt foolish justifying myself to this old gnome, but I dug out my passport and showed him. He again shook his head.

"Your father was once such a careful man. If this is his idea of a joke, tell him I didn't laugh. Have you perhaps done something to anger him?"

"Not unless we count your phone call. He thought that was *my* idea of a joke."

"Please believe me when I say that I don't normally ask about these transactions, but how did you happen to become the new representative for Dewey?"

"Who is Dewey, anyway?"

"Just answer me."

I wasn't sure what to say. I certainly wasn't going to tell him everything.

"Even if I knew, I wouldn't feel comfortable telling you."

"Well, thank God for that, at least. I was beginning to think you were utterly hopeless. All I will tell you—all that I *can* tell you, Mr. Cage—is that I haven't engaged in this sort of business for thirty-seven years, and frankly I never thought I would again. But when I did do it before, the name was always the same as now. Dewey. No surname, no address, just Dewey. The parcel, wrapped just like yours, would always arrive through the door slot over the weekend. I would be notified at home by telephone on Sunday morning, whereupon I would call your father promptly and exactly at two o'clock to tell him to come and pick it up."

That at least explained my father's startled reaction.

"Is that what happened this time?" Then I remembered the other question Dad wanted me to ask: "Who else has been in touch with you about this?"

"This time there was no phone call, only a note to my home, and then the parcel, delivered to the store. No one else was in touch."

"Who sent the note?"

"There was no name. Please, Mr. Cage." He was wringing his hands now.

"So, was my father the only one who ever came for these books?"

"I am not saying that. I am not even saying they were books, since I never opened the wrapping to check. It is even the same price as before, except in those days of course it was in schillings."

I picked up the parcel and fiddled with the string, causing Christoph to practically spring from his chair.

"Please, Mr. Cage, not here! I don't want to see it, and I don't want to know."

Where was all of this fear coming from? I put down the parcel, which seemed to calm him. Then he gave me a long look, which led to a question.

"Tell me one other thing, Mr. Cage."

"If I can."

"Are you in league with any Russian friends in this affair? Older ones in particular?"

"No. Why do you ask?"

He shook his head.

"It's probably not important."

"Then why did you ask?"

"As I said. Not important. I'm sure I've been imagining things. This entire Dewey resurrection has been very disconcerting." He stood abruptly. "Good-bye, Mr. Cage. I am gratified your family still feels it can trust its business to me. I have always been a man of discretion, and will remain so despite your behavior. But you must go now."

He briskly chivvied me out of the office, but didn't follow me downstairs. When I reached the ground floor the store was empty, but there was a pile of euro notes on the counter by the register next to a handwritten list of titles.

Christoph had unsettled me enough that I decided to seek shelter before making another move. Stuffing the parcel in a coat pocket, I walked into the street, looked around quickly for surveillance, then ducked into the first *Konditorei* I could find, just down the block. I sat in a rear corner, facing the door, and as soon as the waitress took my order I put the parcel in my lap.

My handler had just upped the ante. Obviously he'd meant to rattle both Christoph and my father, and he had succeeded. Christoph, in turn, had rattled me. It was also obvious that my handler had intended me to learn that, long ago, my dad had been part of an established network for relaying information, with Dewey as a code name. But who were the other links in the chain? What did any of this have to do with Lemaster, other than the code name in his novel? And why had Christoph asked me that odd question about Russians? He'd claimed that he hadn't handled a transaction like this in thirty-seven years, so I counted back to 1973—the year my father and I left Vienna for Berlin. It was also the year that Lemaster, basking in the glow of his first best seller, had quit the CIA.

I fingered the string. The temptation to open it now was too great, so I looked around furtively before untying the knot and folding back the paper. The contents were anticlimactic. It was a German softbound edition of Lemaster's *London's Own*, a special book in that it was the volume in which the beleaguered Folly, seemingly past his prime, had finally turned the tables on his Soviet nemesis, Strelnikov. But there was nothing special about this edition, a dog-eared paperback from a fifth printing of a translation. I was about to open it when a man's raspy voice made me jump half out of my skin.

"Fifty? For *that*?"

It was the harvester from Kurzmann's, pulling up a chair as if we were old friends.

"Personally, I wouldn't give you a fiver for it. Two if you were lucky." His right hand darted across the table and snatched the book away. He tutted as he turned to the title page. "No. Not even signed." To my relief, he handed it back.

His fingernails, which I would have expected to be chewed or dirty, were clean and manicured, and his hands looked soft. His face was unshaven, but he smelled freshly showered, and his eyes were a clear, sober blue, if a bit careworn. He spoke German with a lowbrow Berlin accent. The general impression he made was of someone who'd begun cleaning up his act but hadn't quite finished. He carried an elegant cane of varnished oak topped by a wolf's head of carved ivory, which he propped against the table.

"Who are you?" I asked.

"I'm glad you spoke up so clearly back there at Christoph's. I'm not sure I'd have recognized you otherwise."

"You know me?"

"From many years and many places." He rose nimbly to his feet. Books bulged from both pockets of his overcoat. "I trust that your father is well. A wonderful man. And in case you're wondering, I'm not the only one who followed you here, although I'd have thought you'd at least notice the other one. She's far more attractive."

I looked around quickly, half expecting to see the slender young woman from Georgetown. The only other customer was an old man nibbling strudel at a far table.

"Oh, she's long gone. Took off the second you left the store. For now I'd say you're quite safe." Then he crouched at my side and whispered in my ear. "Of course, that's subject to change if you keep announcing yourself as 'Dewey' everywhere you go."

He stood and checked his watch. "I should be going. Work to do." He headed for the exit, thumping the cane against the floor with every step.

"Who are you?" I asked again.

He turned to face me as he opened the door.

"Tell your father that Lothar sends his regards. Farewell."

Then, with a tip of his hat and a flap of his coattails, Lothar was gone, although for a few seconds more I heard his cane, tapping as urgently as an SOS.

Now, who the hell was Lothar? A bit player for hire, or a chance interloper? A goad or a threat? And who was following me? Or was that something Lothar had made up to rattle me, another part of his act?

I returned my attention to the paperback and noticed a bookmark peeping from midway through the text. It had a logo at the top from an antiquarian bookstore in Prague, with an address right around the corner from the apartment where my dad and I had lived when I was fourteen. The store's name, Antikvariát Drebitko, immediately triggered a memory that, in the context of this morning's events, was mildly disturbing. My father had twice sent me there to pick up exactly this kind of parcel—a book wrapped in butcher paper, tied with string. That memory, in turn, unlocked another: I had carried out similar errands in Budapest when I must have been only ten or eleven.

Had my father employed me as some sort of clandestine courier? At one level it was exciting, but now I could also see it from a father's point of view, and I was appalled. Anything might have happened to me.

I opened the book to the marked page. At the top was a single hand-written word in block letters, next to a time:

BRÄUNERHOF. 10:30.

Below, a passage of the novel was marked off:

Folly unfolded his reading glasses, which were smudged and scratched, an old pair that had been bent, dropped, sat upon, and left for dead in a dozen different cafés. He wondered why he didn't just buy a new pair. Something to do with loyalty, he supposed, the comfort of the familiar. They maintained their wobbly perch on the bridge of his nose as he studied the map, the streets of Berlin coming alive to him like old friends after a long absence. Just by tracing his finger along the route he could see the rendezvous point as clearly as if it were right there in front of him— a yellow phone booth in Zehlendorf, next to the bakery on Teltowerdamm. He knew the routine, too. Arrive on time, shut yourself inside, dial a number—any number—and then wait for the contact to appear at the door, checking his watch, acting like some impatient asshole that needed the phone right away. Hang up, open the door, and receive a parcel in passing as the stranger slid past you into the booth. Then keep on walking as if nothing out of the ordinary had just occurred. Anyone could do it. Even a spy past his prime with an old pair of specs and an outdated map.

Well, that seemed clear enough. A brush pass, as they said in the trade, and it was to occur in less than an hour. Obviously my handler was picking up the pace, an urgency that made me wary. But the location made me smile. The Café Bräunerhof was a place of importance in my life, a wellspring of pleasant memories, and unless it had turned into some sort of chic WiFi hotspot, I was quite happy to make it my next stop.

8

A Vienna café is a perfect place for a secret rendezvous, because it doesn't matter if either side shows up on time. The beauty of these establishments, from the grandest to the plainest, is that you can spend hours doing absolutely nothing without arousing the slightest suspicion. Even in our age of twittering impatience, a Vienna café is all about the art of refined indolence, reasonably priced. You go there to unplug, not to connect, and the entire staff is trained to assist you.

The transaction is blessedly simple: Purchase one cup of coffee—pricey, but only if you intend to gulp it down and leave—and in exchange you may linger as long as you like. Your waiter, dressed in a dinner jacket, won't even give you a dirty look, but he will attend to your every need without complaint. Tip him generously and he probably won't even remember you were there to begin with, in case the authorities ask later.

So there I was at the Bräunerhof on a fine Monday morning with thirty-six minutes to spare, surveying the scenery from my former favorite table, along the side wall farthest from the entrance. To my amazement, everything looked exactly as it had in 1973, the last time I'd been there. The big windows up front spilled pale sunlight onto a row of wooden booths beneath twelve-foot ceilings. Beige walls, stained by nicotine, were hung with mirrors shaped like lozenges. There were coat racks between the tables up front, and I remembered that on rainy days they always reeked of wet wool. Plush benches ran down either side of the café to accommodate customers at smaller tables for two. In the middle of the room a pastry cart was backed against a cabinet table piled with newspapers on bamboo rods. Stationed in the back was the key location for my upcoming appointment—a phone booth built of varnished wood, with a small window in the door. In the old days it would have been a risky choice for a rendezvous. Customers occupied it at all hours. Now it was a charming anachronism, seldom used.

My nostalgia for the Bräunerhof was easy to explain. At the age of sixteen I'd been sitting at this very table, playing hooky from school, when Litzi Strauss walked into my life. I'd come here to hide out, and to eat one of the café's sublime omelets along with a warm strudel. To wash it down I ordered coffee *Obers*—with cream—my dad having taught me at an early age to caffeinate in order to cope with those European mornings when the sun didn't rise until nine.

I remember the moment perfectly. My bill was paid, and I was contemplating where to go next, when Litzi strolled in with a toss of blond hair and a flicker of the most expressive brown eyes I'd ever wanted to dive into. She was a little tall for my taste, but judging by her furtive movements, she was a fellow renegade, also gone AWOL. I caught her eye as she paused by the newspaper table. She smiled fleetingly, then chose a copy of the same paper I was reading. I took it as a positive development—call and response, sign and countersign, as if we were already in secret communication.

In those days I was often awkward around girls, and I'd already guessed she was slightly older than I. Yet, for some reason—her welcoming smile? the lingering high from the toke I'd just shared with my friend Brenner in the Stadtpark?—she seemed within reach of my romantic capabilities. This rare burst of confidence made all the difference in my eventual approach. For once I was not like the fumbling Richard Folly or the morose George Smiley. I was instead, however briefly, more like one of those dashing fellows who were forever cuckolding my heroes.

She took a seat along the same wall, at the second table down, a mere six feet to my left. The electric effect of her presence seemed to make the wool stand up on my sweater. The waiter took her order, then she opened her paper with another glance my way. Sensing that the opening might be my last, I spoke up with uncharacteristic nerve.

"Meeting someone?"

"No. You?"

I improvised. "Harry Lime."

"From that silly movie, you mean?"

"*Silly? The Third Man* is only one of the greatest films ever made. Written by an even greater novelist."

"Graham Greene's too Catholic for me. The book's not even a proper novel, you know. He wrote it originally as a screenplay. Did you know that?"

Of course I did, thanks to my father, who had nonetheless indulged me with a paperback of the book Greene eventually published. It wasn't really an espionage tale, but it was rife with spylike duplicity, and prescient in its late-forties depiction of Cold War tensions. So yes, I certainly did know it. But mostly I was thrilled that *she* knew. It wasn't the sort of arcana girls usually came up with. She was preaching to the converted, and we both knew it. In my excitement I blurted a non sequitur.

"He lived around the corner, you know."

"Graham Greene?"

"Harry Lime, the Orson Welles character. In the movie they say his address is Stiftgasse 15, but they shot all his apartment scenes at Josefstadt 5. It's the building with those Venus sculptures out front. Or whatever they are."

"Maybe you can show me, after I've finished my coffee."

"I'd be glad to."

"As long as no one from my school sees me first."

"Same here." We laughed, the kinship of fugitives.

As we went out the door a few minutes later she actually took my arm, a gesture that felt exciting and old-fashioned at the same time, and at that moment I knew I was on to something more profound and special than any previous flirtation. We were together until the day I moved to Berlin, roughly a year later. The relationship changed us both, mostly for the better.

All this reminiscing broke my concentration, and when I checked my watch it was only a few minutes before 10:30. Wondering if my contact had also arrived early, I scanned the room for likely suspects.

To my left, in the corner booth up front, were a middle-aged man and woman, both wearing scarves. A small "Reserviert" placard indicated they were regulars, entitled to a *Stammtisch*, or customary table. They were discussing the German satirist Kurt Tucholsky. To their right sat a quiet elderly woman wearing a double strand of pearls. Along the opposite wall, facing me from across the room, was a young couple too absorbed in each other to notice anyone but themselves. Out in the middle was a table of three women, late forties, very proper in manner. To my right, a young male professional type in suit and tie who had come in on crutches.

Figuring I had better clear the decks by settling the bill, I nodded to the waiter, who arrived promptly and stated the total. He uttered a polite "Danke" as I named an amount that would allow for a hefty tip. While he was making change, the door opened, and I couldn't see around him until the new arrival had passed and was on the way to the back. I was mildly surprised to see it was a woman, but she disappeared down the corridor toward the rest rooms before I could see her face. It had to be my contact. It was time to enter the phone booth.

I did as the script demanded, turning my back to the window as I deposited coins and punched in a number. I mumbled a few words of nonsense into the mouthpiece, and when I'd judged that a minute had passed, I turned to see if my contact was waiting, so that the exchange could take place.

The newly arrived woman stood just outside the door, staring back at me through the glass. We both gasped. Even after more than thirty years, I recognized Litzi Strauss right away, and she clearly recognized me as well. We stood motionless with our mouths open for a few seconds, then I opened the door. Next I was supposed to take whatever she handed me and keep on walking.

No way.

Instead, I fell back on a much older script, one that I had rehearsed only once.

"Meeting someone?"

"No. You?"

"Harry Lime."

She laughed and fell into my arms. Then, remembering what had reunited us, we disengaged somewhat awkwardly, and she withdrew a sealed manila envelope from beneath her coat.

"I believe I'm supposed to give this to you."

"It's called a brush pass."

She rolled her eyes, just as she had years ago when I mentioned *The Third Man*.

"I think now I'm supposed to be on my way, never to see you again."

"Terrible idea. Let's go for a walk."

She smiled and nodded, and as we reached the door she put her arm through mine. I actually blushed. Not in embarrassment, but in a flood of memory. It was so powerful that I had to take a deep breath once we were out in the sunlight.

"Did you know it would be me?" she asked. She was flushed, too.

"No. How 'bout you?"

"Are you kidding?"

We were speaking German, right back to our old ways.

"Then whoever is pulling the strings knows me even better than I thought."

"You're not the one who arranged this?" There was a note of concern in her voice.

"No. So you don't know who's behind this, either?"

"I thought I did. An old friend from university asked me for a favor. I was supposed to be passing material to a corporate headhunter for a friend in Salzburg, things he was too nervous to send by email. What about you?"

"It's a long story," I said. "Got time to hear it?"

She smiled.

"Of course. But aren't you going to open that?" She nodded at the envelope.

"And ruin our reunion? It can wait. How many years has it been?"

"Do we really want to count?"

"Where to, then? Harry Lime's?"

"Certainly, but I'm afraid you won't like it very much." There was a gleam of mischief in her eyes as she towed me toward Josefstadt with her hand warm on my arm. What a strange sensation it was, to leap so suddenly across a chasm of decades only to alight on the same sidewalk you'd left from.

As we rounded the corner I saw what she meant. The marble façade of Harry's grand old building was now covered by scaffolding and a huge sheet of plastic, with a full-color ad for a Burger King Whopper. Marty Ealing would have loved it.

"The death of art," I said.

"Seeing as how there are ten museums within a block of here, I doubt one hamburger will topple the empire. But it is annoying to see it every time I look out my office window."

"Where do you work?"

She pointed back across the square, toward the grandiose expanse of the Austrian National Library.

"You're a librarian?"

"An archivist. Old letters and manuscripts, mostly."

"I suppose now you're going to tell me you're married with eleven children."

"One husband, an ex. No children, I'm sorry to say."

"I have an ex as well. But a son, he's eighteen."

"Lucky you."

"I am lucky, even though he grew up mostly with his mother."

I thought of my parting conversation with David, and wondered what he would think of this little scene, and of Litzi.

"Let's have lunch," she said. "Buy a baguette and eat in the park. It's too nice a day to go back indoors."

I immediately agreed.

I suppose I should have wondered right then how my handler had managed to bring about this reunion, and how he knew so much about my past. But for the moment, on a beautiful morning with Litzi's arm through mine, my mind was on anything but spying.

So off we went to lunch, heedless of anyone but ourselves.

9

Had you asked me to predict how Litzi would look after all this time, I would have erred on the side of frumpy. As a girl she had her mother's fair complexion and blond hair, but her mother was also a standard-issue hausfrau, stout and sturdy, with a face as puffy as bread dough. Her father, from Bohemia, was thinner, with hollow eyes and prominent cheekbones, the face of a refugee. It was clear now that Litzi had borrowed the best from both sides. Fair complexion, but with features winnowed to their essentials. A few worry lines, but not enough to shake her air of earnest calm, although there did seem to be a hint of past disappointment in the depths of her eyes. Her blond hair was touched by gray, but she still had the posture of a dancer, lithe and graceful. It made me wonder how I was measuring up, then I told myself to stop, that we were far beyond that now.

We bought sandwiches at a bakery and walked to a park on the far side of the National Library, where ravens stalked the green and cawed for handouts. We sat at the base of a fountain and talked for a while about our lives and our jobs and what had become of the years while the water gurgled behind us. Then she nodded toward the sealed envelope, which lay at my feet in the grass.

"Well, are you going to tell me what this is all about?"

In all those spy novels, of course, the oldest and best advice was to trust no one. The same was true when I'd been a journalist, and more so at Ealing Wharton, where your level of mistrust was roughly proportionate to your annual bonus. But I had long ago noticed something about people who followed this advice. All of them seemed to wind up alone. I knew because I was one of them.

Today, I decided, I would act sixteen again, if only for the afternoon, if only for Litzi, and if only because for the moment I no longer wanted to be alone. Besides, she and I had lived through a lot together, some of it anything but child's play. If anyone had been battle-tested to protect my secrets, it was Litzi Strauss.

"How much time do you have?"

"As much as we need. While you were buying lunch I texted my office. They believe I'm at an urgent appointment that will keep me away for most of the afternoon."

"Do you remember all those Edwin Lemaster books my father had?"

She rolled her eyes and smiled, a wary but willing audience. I continued talking, and told her everything. She didn't interrupt once, and was silent for a while when I finished.

"Amazing," she finally said. "In my work I sometimes spend hours going through old letters, or some diary from centuries ago, and I'm always struck by how much those people come to life for me. But these are made-up characters you're talking about, yet it's like they've stepped right off the page. It makes me wish I'd been there to meet the fellow who delivered the envelope to me. He looked so strange."

"You *saw* him?"

"I wasn't supposed to. Karl, my friend in Salzburg, told me someone would drop it at the library's reception desk with my name on it."

I turned over the envelope. "Litzi Strauss" was written in the same blocky handwriting that had been on the parcel from Kurzmann's.

"I figured it would probably be delivered by a courier service, but the other arrangements were so strange that I wanted to check, just in case, so I asked our man at the reception desk to note the exact time when the envelope was delivered. Later I checked the day's footage from the security cameras, and there he was."

"You're a natural, Litzi."

She smiled shyly. "Maybe I am. And it was no courier service, let me tell you! You should have seen him. A chilly morning on the first of October and he's wearing an undersized summer-weight suit of that crinkly blue and white material you only seem to see in America."

"Seersucker?"

"Yes! Seersucker."

Something tugged at a hook deep in the pond of memory, but Litzi was off and running.

"The front pocket of his jacket was stuffed with pens, a whole row.

At first I even thought he was wearing some kind of ID badge, but no, it was all pens."

Whatever had been nibbling at my subconscious now struck with full force. I began reeling it to the surface.

"A seersucker, you said."

"Yes."

"With a pocketful of pens?"

"Yes."

"Was he wearing glasses?"

"Sort of an old-fashioned pair."

"And he was fat?"

"Maybe not fat, but a little overweight. Soft-looking. Do you know him?"

"Was he carrying anything else?"

She thought about it.

"A briefcase. A thin one, with a big tag."

"Unbelievable."

"You *do* know him."

"Where's the nearest bookstore?"

"Only a few blocks, you know Vienna. Why? Who was he?"

"I have to show you something."

She impatiently led the way to a *Buchladen* that was far neater than Kurzmann's. All the while she pressed me for answers, but I didn't want to spoil the surprise, and was hoping my memory wasn't playing tricks on me.

I made a beeline for the novels and checked the A's, for Ambler, Eric. Fortunately his books have made a comeback in recent years. You can now find paperback reprints both in the U.S. and abroad. A German version would be fine, as long as they had a copy.

"What are you doing?" Litzi asked for what must have been the third time.

"Looking for your courier."

And there he was, right next to a copy of *A Coffin for Dimitrios*. Or, rather, there was the book, *Judgment on Deltchev*, a fine little novel from early in the Cold War that Ambler had published in 1951. I'd read it cover to cover on the train from Prague to Vienna a week before turning fifteen.

I took it down and flipped through the pages. If I was correct, the reference came fairly early. Yes, there it was on the first page of the second chapter. I handed it to Litzi.

"Last paragraph. Read it."

The passage describes the novel's hero, Foster, as he arrives in an unnamed Eastern European capital, where he is met by Georghi Pashik, a shifty man of mixed loyalties. Pashik played a pivotal role in the plot, and his mysterious presence had stuck with me long after I finished the book. Here is the English version of what Litzi read:

I saw him standing on the platform as the train drew in: a short, dark, flabby man in rimless glasses and a tight seersucker suit with an array of fountain pens in his handkerchief pocket. Under his arm he carried a thin, black dispatch case with a silver medallion hanging from the zipper tag. He stood by a pillar gazing about him with the imperious anxiety of a wealthy traveler who sees no porter and knows that he cannot carry his own baggage. I think it was the fountain pens that identified him for me. He wore them like a badge.

Litzi's eyes widened. Then she put a hand to her mouth and laughed. "Oh, my God! So now I'm living in a novel, too?"

"As a librarian, you should be honored."

"Archivist. Dealing with facts. When I was a girl I read *Emil and the Detectives*, just like everyone else. Then I grew up. But this *is* quite a coincidence."

"It's intentional. It's my handler's way of telling me how well he knows me. He's been yanking my chain, and now he's yanking yours."

"But what if I'd never checked the video?"

"You did, though. That's what matters, and he was ready for it. He had his man dress for the occasion, just like he was playing a role." I took the book from her hands, hefting it like Exhibit A for the prosecution, although I wasn't yet sure of the charges, much less of the suspect. "Obviously someone is taking this very seriously."

"May I ask a question?"

"Of course."

"Why are you doing this? If it's serious, like you say, then why take the risk just to go chasing after your past? Isn't the present enough for you?"

"Do you think that's all this is?"

"Certainly it's part of it. Your interview with Lemaster. Your father's little missions to the bookstore. Me. It's almost like an analyst was taking you back through a series of repressed memories."

"I never repressed any memories about you."

"Didn't you?"

"What's that supposed to mean?"

"You've always hidden things from both of us. So have I."

"We have?"

She shook her head, like she couldn't quite believe I didn't agree. Or maybe she was just being Litzi, provocative for its own sake, the way she'd always been.

"You Austrians. A nation of Freuds."

"You Americans. So innocent about the world, except when you're trying to run it."

That sort of broke the mood. We left the bookstore and wandered aimlessly up the block. She briefly took my hand, squeezing it as if to make peace, but neither of us said much for a minute or two. I think we realized we'd reached a crossing point. It was time to either say good-bye or find some pretext to keep the day going.

I knew which option I preferred, although the sealed envelope tucked beneath my left arm was making demands of its own. Litzi checked her watch.

"My office must be wondering if my appointment is ever going to end."

"You could always text them again."

"Saying what?"

"That you're meeting an old friend for a drink."

She stopped in the middle of the block. Pedestrians eased around us. I watched her face as she considered what to say next.

"And after we have this drink, what then? Dinner? Probably with another drink, or a bottle of wine? Then we go back to my apartment to talk about how wonderful things used to be. And maybe then, because we are both lonely and unattached, we decide to make love for old times' sake, or for new times' sake, or for however we decide to justify it. Is that what you have in mind?"

I knew better than to answer. This was the Litzi I remembered, frank and analytical, offering the good with the bad in equal doses, whether you were ready or not. She picked up the thread on her own, as I'd known she would.

"No matter what may have brought us together, Bill, we are not living in one of your old books, and I am not some sort of second chance. I have loved many times since we knew each other, and some of those men meant far more to me than you ever did. My husband's name was Klaus, and if my womb had not fallen to pieces then we would have raised sons and daughters, more than you could count. So I suppose what I am saying is that, while this is very nice, I don't wish for either of us to be burdened by expectations."

I smiled, which seemed to surprise her.

"I'm glad you still get straight to the point, Litzi. Although you've thought things through a little further along than I have. Not that I object to where you ended up, with the two of us in bed. But in the life I've been leading, sometimes a drink is just a drink. So would you like to have one, or should we call it a day and leave the rest to our memories, repressed or not?"

She smiled back.

"I'd forgotten how easily you could always disarm me. Me and my Austrian earnestness." She took my arm. We resumed walking. "Let's have that drink, and then dinner. Then you can take me home, but I won't invite you upstairs. If you're still around tomorrow? Well, maybe. But for tonight, how about Restaurant Sperl?"

"God, no. My dad stuffed me full of schnitzel last night at Figlmüller. And if we go to Sperl we really *will* talk about old times. I'd rather hear about all these men who were so much better than me. Pick someplace new."

We still talked plenty about the past, of course. All the while the envelope remained with us, unopened, like an unstamped passport for entry to the rest of the week. Neither of us mentioned it until around nine o'clock, after our waiter had poured the last of the wine Litzi had so accurately predicted we would drink.

"I think it's time," she said, nodding toward it. I'd placed it on the table. The waiter had put the bill on top of it, but I knew she wasn't referring to paying.

"I think so, too. Drum roll, please."

"No drum roll. It would sound too much like a firing squad."

"Oh, I doubt it will be that grim."

But when I slipped the paper free I saw right away that the tone of this message was more somber and urgent than that of the ones before it. My handler was raising the stakes.

"TAKE HEED!" was handwritten in block letters atop a book page that had been sliced neatly from a copy of le Carré's *Smiley's People*. Not another first edition, I hoped. There were two pages from the book, and a third from another novel. On the Smiley pages, three brief passages were marked in black ink. Taken as one item, they read like this:

"Moscow Rules. I insist Moscow Rules."

"And what were the contact procedures exactly?" Smiley asked.

"The safety signal was one new drawing-pin shoved high in the first wood support on the left as you entered."
"And the counter-signal?" Smiley asked.
But he knew the answer already.
"A yellow chalk line," said Mostyn.

Handwritten afterward, again in block letters, was a street name, "Köllnerhofgasse," but no number, and no date or time.

"Does this mean you're supposed to meet someone?" Litzi asked.

"Looks like it. And by Moscow Rules. I guess they want me to make sure I'm not being followed."

The third page came from a copy of the novel *Spy Wednesday*, by William Hood, an ex-spy who began his CIA career in Vienna, where he helped run a Soviet double agent in the 1950s. He had ended it as one of James Angleton's top deputies—so there was Angleton's ghost yet again. After retiring, Hood had helped former CIA director Richard Helms write his memoirs. When he wrote about spy tradecraft, you could bank on its authenticity, and a tidy example of that was staring up at me from the excised page, in two marked passages:

Earlier that week, Roger Kyle had seen the numerals 3-4-7 jotted boldly across the top of page 222 of volume two of the phone books arranged alongside the bank of pay telephones in the Vienna Central Post Office.

Kyle fished a pen from his pocket and drew a line through the numerals. The emergency meeting would be on the third day of the week, Wednesday. At four, the next digit, in the afternoon. The safe house was at Frankgasse 7, the third number.

"So now you're supposed to go look at some phone book at the Post Office?" Litzi asked.

"Does the Central Post Office even have pay phones anymore?"

"I don't know. But the doors are unlocked till ten. If we leave now we'll just make it."

I'd once known the old post office well, and remembered it fondly. Christmas packages had arrived there every December from my grandparents. Dad always took me on the twenty-third to pick everything up, then we'd stop for a wurst and fries on the way home, dripping grease and sweet mustard onto the packages.

Litzi and I got there eight minutes before closing time. Only three other people were inside—a woman mailing a letter, a sweeper half in the bag, and a security man preparing to lock up. Lo and behold, there were still pay phones, with a handy supply of Vienna directories. When I flipped to page 222 of the second volume, three numbers were scrawled across the top in the same block handwriting that had been used in the message.

2-4-11

"Well, there you go," I said, feeling the same satisfaction I did whenever I completed the *New York Times* Saturday crossword. "Two, the second day of the week, means Tuesday, tomorrow. The four means four p.m., at number eleven, presumably on Köllnerhofgasse. Once I get there, all I have to do is look for the safety signal to make sure the coast is clear."

"That's the same time as the rendezvous in *Spy Wednesday*," Litzi pointed out. "How did that one go?"

"The agent never showed. He'd been kidnapped to Moscow to be executed."

"Well, that's promising. What about the contact in *Smiley's People*?"

"An Estonian named Vladimir. The KGB shot him in the face."

Litzi shook her head but couldn't help laughing.

"Moscow Rules don't sound very reliable."

"I'm sure the third time's the charm."

"Maybe someone should come with you."

She said it with a smile, but also an unmistakable note of caution. That, plus Lothar's earlier warning, reminded me that to some people this sort of information never lost its potency.

"I'll be all right," I said. "Vladimir was old and arthritic and walked with a cane." Fleetingly, unavoidably, I thought again of Lothar, who also walked with a cane. "I can still outrun most people as long as they're over forty."

"Don't joke about it." Her smile was gone. "Those other messages sounded kind of fun. Not this one."

True enough. Yet I found myself almost enjoying the aura of incipient danger, especially if it provided a handy pretext for seeing Litzi again.

"You're as curious about this as I am, aren't you?"

A shrug, an enigmatic smile.

"I suppose I wouldn't mind getting to the bottom of things."

I suppressed a laugh.

"What?" she asked.

"'Getting to the bottom of things.' Those are the words Holly Martins said to Major Callaway in *The Third Man*. Do you remember what Major Callaway said?"

I quoted it to her in English, trying for my best impersonation of Trevor Howard in the role of Callaway.

"Death's at the bottom of this, Martins. Leave death to the professionals."

This time she didn't smile. With good reason, as it turned out. Major Callaway was right.

10

I'd texted my father to tell him I'd be late, but I hadn't told him why. I felt guilty about that because I knew he was eager to find out what had happened at Kurzmann's, and by the time I kissed Litzi goodnight it was nearly eleven. True to her word, she didn't invite me upstairs, but we were meeting again tomorrow.

Dad and I had muddled through the balance of the previous evening with the help of food and lager. Figlmüller lived up to its end of the bargain by serving schnitzels the size of catcher's mitts, but even that old comfort hadn't eased things between us. I still had lots of questions, and I'm sure he had a few.

As I approached his apartment I saw that the lights were on. I was counting on the news of Litzi to serve as an icebreaker. He had always been fond of her, although I couldn't help but remember his strange reaction the first time I'd mentioned her.

"What's that name again, son?"

"Litzi Strauss."

"Litzi. How unusual. Is she a Jew?"

"*What?* Does that matter?"

"Certainly not. It's just that Kim Philby's first wife was a Litzi from Vienna. Litzi Friedmann, a Jew. That's why I asked. But your Litzi's a Strauss. Doesn't sound Jewish."

"She's not *my* Litzi."

"Well, not yet, anyway."

My blush told him all he needed to know about my ambitions on that front, and he nodded in approval.

"I'm happy for you, son. Love keeps us on our toes."

"I never said I was in love." Redder still.

Another knowing nod, then he said smugly, "No, I suppose you didn't."

Stung, I struck back below the belt.

"Being in love with Mom didn't seem to keep you on your toes."

The light went out in his eyes, and his subsequent surrender made me miserable.

"You're right about that, son. Good luck with her all the same."

He never asked about her in any meaningful way again. Small talk only where Litzi was concerned, and I was the poorer for it.

I found him waiting up for me in the living room with only Johnnie Walker Black for company. Judging by the level in the bottle, they'd gotten comfortable. I was tipsy from the wine, putting us on an equal footing.

"Long day?" he asked from his easy chair, a hint of concern in his tone. "Hope it wasn't Christoph keeping you out so late, filling your head full of nonsense?"

"Christoph couldn't get me out of Kurzmann's fast enough. I ran into an old friend. Litzi Strauss."

He brightened instantly.

"Wonderful! How is she?"

"Currently unmarried, looking well, and I'm seeing her again tomorrow. Those are the three things you really wanted to know, right?"

"I suppose so." He smiled at my peace offering. "But tell me about Kurzmann's. I've been wondering all day."

"It was pretty strange. He hardly told me anything, except that he hadn't taken a special order like that since the year we moved to Berlin. He did mention the whole routine you used to have. The Sunday phone calls at two on the dot. The plain brown wrappers tied in string."

"Your delivery was wrapped that way?"

"Same price, too, except in euros. Or so he claimed." Dad shook his head in amazement. "But he wouldn't say what the transactions meant, or who they were for."

"Probably because he didn't know, and he never would've jeopardized the arrangement by asking. That price looked even higher back in the seventies. Christoph made a pretty penny off those little visits, but I suppose they were his fee as middleman."

"Middleman for what? And what was your role?"

"I was a courier, plain and simple. It was my job to make the pickup, then drop off the item later in the day at another address, which was also relayed by phone, some voice telling me that my shirts were ready. There was a code. The name of the cleaner's was always the street, and the stated price was the address."

"Not very sophisticated."

"Not if the line was bugged. But the embassy checked pretty regularly in those days."

"Who was the 'they' in all this?"

"You can probably guess."

"The Agency?"

"That was always my assumption."

"Then tell me one thing. A truthful answer, straight up yes or no."

"If I can."

"Were you CIA?"

"No."

He said it immediately and without wavering, his eyes looking straight into mine. His face and hands were calm, no gestures to betray either nerves or uncertainty. Then why did I still not believe him? He must have sensed my doubt, because he then opened up in a way he never had before.

"Look. When I say no, I mean absolutely, unequivocally no. But at various postings I was State's liaison to the Agency. It's unofficial. You'll damn well never find it in Foreign Service job listings, but every embassy has one, and when you and I were living in Europe, I was usually the guy. So I did a few chores for them. It came with the job."

"Like those meetings we used to go to, with those men who never gave their names?"

"What?"

"C'mon. You don't remember dragging me to all those bars and cafés?"

He seemed annoyed.

"I met lots of old friend in cafés and bars. No doubt I sometimes took you along. But I wasn't meeting spies for the Agency. Other than those few courier assignments, I never knowingly did *anything* for the Agency beyond a little consular paperwork—cleaning up a few passports, doling out visas for some of their émigrés, that sort of thing."

Well, that was one youthful illusion shattered, provided he was telling the truth. Then he had a question for me.

"This package Christoph gave you—did you open it? Because that's certainly something I never did."

"Never?"

"Why risk finding out something that could get me in trouble? What if I'd been hauled in for questioning by some foreign government? I might've lost my job, or worse. Was I curious? Sure, but never tempted. And I believe I asked you a question."

"Yes, I opened it. I took it down the street to a little *Konditorei* and sat in the back. It was nothing special. A German translation of *London's Own*. Fourth printing of the paperback edition, unsigned."

I withheld the part about "Dewey" and the enclosed message. If he offered more maybe I'd reciprocate.

"Right after I opened it I was accosted by this strange old troll who must have followed me from Kurzmann's. His name was Lothar, and he sent you his regards."

Dad surprised me by smiling broadly.

"The one and only? German fellow, looked like he might have just pulled an all-nighter with Mick and the Stones?"

"With a cane that he taps like a telegraph."

"Complete affectation, but he's entitled. Lothar Heinemann is a legend. Book scout extraordinaire."

"Book scout?"

"How do you think I tracked down half my collection?" He waved an arm toward his shelves. "Some of the choicest finds were his. Ask Lothar to find a needle in a haystack and he'll be back inside a week with five to choose from, plus a sewing box. He's a genius. The problem is finding him. And, frankly, keeping him sober."

"Booze?"

"Worse. Although I hear he's been clean for years. Used to be very popular with Agency people. Ran off the rails for a while in the early seventies, but by then he was out of my price range. Too many other people wanted the same kind of stuff."

"Agency people collect spy novels?"

"God, yes. At least half a dozen, to hear Lothar tell it, but I could never get him to spill names. Lothar was always pretty cagey about who he was scouting for. But I do know one collector who never hired him. Edwin Lemaster."

"*He* was a collector?"

Dad gave me a smug look that suggested I should've known all along.

"That's how we became friends, since you've always wanted to know. Talking about books. I was a little surprised he didn't bring it up back in eighty-four."

Finally.

"So where did you meet? And what year?"

"Oh, it must have been the late fifties. But I didn't get to know him all that well until later, around sixty-seven. He'd just started writing *Knee Knockers* when we ran into each other at a bookstore in Budapest. He wasn't comfortable telling the Agency about his little writing project, understandably, so I became a sounding board for his ideas—the plot, the characters. He loved the genre as much as I did, and wanted to be a part of it. I remember the day well. It was at Ferenc Szondi's old store on Corvin Square."

"Didn't you send me there once to pick up a package? Wrapped in butcher paper, even?"

"I'm sure it was more than once."

So I was right.

"Those were Agency errands?"

"Lord, no. Do you really think I'd have dispatched my ten-year-old on a mission for the CIA?"

A second illusion now lay in ruins, albeit one I'd concocted only that morning. Obviously my childhood hadn't been as exciting as I thought, and I could only smile at my overactive imagination. It was the fault of those books on his shelves. Gazing up at them now, I easily recalled the way they'd once fired my youthful fantasies.

I knew the vital statistics of his collection by heart: 222 novels by 48 authors. Eighteen had worked for intelligence agencies, six more for a foreign ministry or a war office, so you knew the pages were spiked with disguised secrets.

By now you may have concluded it was mostly a Cold War library. While that aptly describes the ones I read as a teen, his holdings were far broader and deeper. More than a quarter of his first editions were published before 1950, and even *The Riddle of the Sands*, from 1903, wasn't nearly the oldest.

There was Rudyard Kipling's *Kim* from 1901, with its Great Game intrigues of British India, and William Le Queux's *Strange Tales of a Nihilist* from 1892. The oldest was James Fenimore Cooper's *The Spy* from 1821, a tale of a double agent for George Washington. Dad's two-volume copy was so fragile that he'd placed it off-limits, which made me curious enough at the age of fifteen to track down a reprint in an embassy library. I realized by the second sentence, which ran to a breathtaking eighty-five words, that I'd never finish. Yet it was Cooper's first best seller, and he showed surprising prescience about the future of spying by having Washington tell the hero, "You must descend into the grave with the reputation of a foe to your native land. Remember that the veil which conceals your true character cannot be raised in years—perhaps never."

You've probably never heard of most of the earliest authors, but some were hugely popular. Le Queux, for one, although to me he was a hack. Manning Coles, of the Tommy Hambledon books, took the quality up a notch, as did John Buchan, and then Ambler. And of course there was Joseph Conrad, who not only produced *The Secret Agent* in 1907, but a 1911 sequel, *Under Western Eyes*.

It was only in the mid-fifties that Cold War tales came into vogue, and even those were dominated for years by a pair of rakish Brits—Ian Fleming's James Bond and Desmond Cory's Johnny Fedora. Fedora is largely forgotten now, but he was in print two years before Bond. JFK made all the difference for Fleming when the dashing young president revealed he was a Bond fan. Sales took off, and Hollywood took notice. Fleming also had the better pedigree, having worked in British intelligence with everyone from Kim Philby to Graham Greene.

Dad harrumphed that Fedora and Bond were "cartoons for the drunk and oversexed," yet he collected all sixteen Fedoras, and all fourteen Bonds with their beautiful jacket illustrations by Richard Chopping. He also grabbed up the first five books in Donald Hamilton's Matt Helm series—another man of action, and far worthier than the spoofy film portrayal by Dean Martin—and all four books in Adam Diment's series featuring Philip McAlpine, a groovy Austin Powers prototype.

The more cerebral spies whom we now think of as the genre's exemplars didn't start showing up until '61, with le Carré's Smiley, and at first even he was more concerned with solving murders than digging out moles. Then, in '62, Len Deighton gave us something darker and more genuine to chew on with *The Ipcress File*, with its anonymous hero (a spy who didn't acquire the Harry Palmer name until the books went to Hollywood). The following year le Carré published *The Spy Who Came In from the Cold*, which made even Graham Greene gush, and afterward things were never the same.

Lemaster's arrival at the end of the sixties led an American charge joined by Charles McCarry, Robert Littell, and even the political pundit William F. Buckley Jr. (I refused to read his Blackford Oakes spy novels after coming across two pedantic groaners in the first three paragraphs: "Johnny got orotund when he was tight" and "At Yale, mere registrars don't summon students thus peremptorily.")

The early seventies ushered in a golden age of Lemaster and le Carré, plus Deighton and Adam Hall with his knotty string of Quiller novels. By the eighties, even some of the genre's older hands had returned—Graham Greene, Ted Allbeury, Helen MacInnes, and E. Howard Hunt, the ex-CIA man notorious for his role in the Watergate scandal. Dad has seven Hunt novels dating back to 1942, and they're not bad. Richard Helms used to give copies to friends back when he ran the Agency.

At the height of the Cold War, publishers were churning out so many spy novels that it was hard for collectors to keep pace. There was a spin-off from a comic strip (*Modesty Blaise*, by Peter O'Donnell), a quasi-spoof by an established literary author (*Tremor of Intent*, by Anthony Burgess, of *A Clockwork Orange* fame), and even a few Russian titles with KGB heroes by the Soviet writer Yulian Semyonov. Finally, William Hood, the aforementioned Angleton deputy, joined the fray with the novel that Litzi and I had just seen a page of, *Spy Wednesday*. His second novel, *Cry Spy*, published a few months after the collapse of the Berlin Wall, was the last non-Lemaster title my dad collected. The following year I gave him a signed copy of le Carré's *The Secret Pilgrim*, but he handed it right back and told me he was off the stuff for good. Soon afterward I did the same.

"Bill?" My dad called out through the haze. "Are you drifting away from me?"

"Sorry. Must be the wine. And the jet lag, of course." But now I had a question for him. "Why did Lemaster never use Lothar?"

"For him half the fun was hunting down the titles. Of course that only piqued Lothar's curiosity. Whenever I'd bump into him in some far-flung bookstall he'd always ask if I knew what Ed was up to."

I noted the use of Lemaster's nickname, the first time Dad had showed such familiarity.

"How well did you know Lemaster?"

"Mostly as a fellow book hound. And not as well as I thought, apparently."

"What do you mean?"

"He's the kind of person you warm up to right away. Witty, engaging. Seems to open up in a hurry. Makes you feel like part of his inner circle. But after a while, you realize that's as close as you're going to get. Sort of like those old book clubs that used to lure you in with those great offers—any four for a dollar!—then, boom, no more freebies. Full price only."

"Was it for professional reasons?"

"Not completely. But I've never known for sure. He was an enigma that way, and I've never heard differently from anyone else."

"Why didn't you tell me this before?"

"He was doing secret work, son. His movements, his whereabouts, his contacts. All that, even the little things, had to be kept under wraps, even after he'd quit. He made that very clear to me."

"But *you* knew. Why do you think he trusted you? You weren't even in the Agency. Whatever happened to 'Trust No One'?"

"Life. Life is what always happens to 'Trust No One.'"

A curious comment, and there was probably more behind it than Dad wanted to tell me. I could live with that. He had already been far more generous than I'd expected.

Now it was my turn to give. Not everything, of course. If he could hold some items in reserve, so could I, especially since what I had to say wasn't going to be easy for either of us. I poured a shot of Johnnie Walker, swallowed, and waited for the little explosion of heat to reach the bottom of my throat.

Then I delivered the news.

"There was a name on the parcel I picked up today," I said. "Dewey."

For a moment I thought Dad was going to choke. His knuckles whitened on the glass.

"Why are you ambushing me with this so late in the day, and when I'm half in the bag? What's your game, son?"

"Easy, Dad. Christoph said it was the name on your parcels, too. So I'm curious."

"Christoph never should have told you that. I suppose I deserve it for telling you to ask that damn fool question about the Agency."

"So who was he?"

"Dewey was a name without a face, presumably a code name for the next link in the chain. As soon as I dropped off the parcel I'd go to a phone booth—a different one every time—and dial a number that was on the sales receipt. Someone would pick up but would never say a word. I'd announce that Dewey's package had arrived, and hang up. Were those your instructions?"

"No." I hedged my answer, or maybe "lied" would be the better word. "I'm awaiting further instructions, which I'll receive tomorrow."

Dad frowned skeptically. He swallowed more whisky.

"You need to give up this ridiculous assignment, son. The sooner the better. Obviously someone means to do Ed harm, and by picking you as the agent of destruction they're using you against me as well, and probably putting us both in harm's way."

"Against you? How so? Toward what end?"

"Whoever is behind this knows things that it would be in your best interest not to find out."

"Meaning there's still something you're not telling me."

"It's for your protection. Always has been. Here you go stirring up old coals, trying to start a fire when you have no idea who'd get burned, just like you stirred things up back in eighty-four with that story on Ed, and look where that led. Do you think he was the only one whose career was damaged?"

"Did something happen to you?"

"I'm talking about *you*! Do you really believe you'd be slaving for those bootlicks at Ealing Wharton if you hadn't set certain forces in motion?"

Never before had he spoken so harshly about my job. It stung, even though I shared his opinion. I must have reacted as if I'd taken a punch, because he quickly moved to make amends.

"I'm sorry. That was uncalled for. I know you're not there by choice. Alimony, child support, it couldn't have been easy." He looked at his glass, as if the whisky might be to blame. "These are things I shouldn't be saying."

"What *are* you saying? You know why my career ran off the rails. It had nothing to do with the Lemaster story."

Belgrade, that was why. The city where I lost my mom in '59 became the city where I lost my profession in '92. It was the year I finally landed a posting as a foreign correspondent, only to be denied a work visa by the Yugoslav government, which prompted the *Post* to recall me. Temporarily, they said, but things never worked out, and for me it was the beginning of the end. There was more to it than that, of course—newsroom politics, declining budgets, a marriage already strained by conflicting agendas. But in the "for want of a nail" category of small events leading to major consequences, Belgrade '92 was the most apt summation for why I wound up divorced and working in PR. Beware the thwarted man. He will almost always make an unbearable ass of himself.

"You're absolutely right," Dad said. "I had no business going there. I apologize."

"Well, you're not going to stop me."

"Of course I'm not. Because you still seem to think this is some sort of crossword puzzle you can solve at your leisure and then toddle on home to write about it."

"And why can't I?"

"Well, the Russians, for one thing."

"The Russians?" First Christoph had mentioned them, and now my dad. "Why the Russians?"

"Don't you read the papers anymore? Look at who's in charge. An ex-KGB man who generates half his power by telling outdated ghost stories about NATO and the United States. Those freewheeling days when Gorbachev and that drunk Yeltsin were opening all the old files are gone. No more fresh start."

"So you're saying the Cold War is back in vogue?" I was joking, but Dad didn't crack a smile.

"I'm saying that for this crowd and all its henchmen, it never ended. And considering the ultrasensitive nature of the work Lemaster once did—"

"Mole hunting, you mean."

"Yes. That sort of material retains its shelf life for as long as the principles survive."

"Dad, you're talking about things that happened thirty, forty years ago. And some of it probably wasn't even that important then."

"I once felt that way, too, just after the Wall came down. All those little chores I'd done suddenly seemed quaint and harmless, fun stories to tell my grandchildren."

"Well, there you go."

He shook his head.

"Somebody set me straight."

"Who? When?"

"It was early ninety-one, during my final overseas posting. A rather pushy fellow with a crew cut visited me at the embassy office in Berlin. Bit of a knuckle dragger, but he had top clearance, and he took me back into a part of the building that was normally off-limits, even to the liaison chaps like me. He sat me down, and with no preamble whatsoever told me that in no way, shape, or form, was I ever to breathe a word about my 'Dewey' errands."

"Why?"

"People like that don't give you a reason. I told him I had no intention of telling anyone, and that I'd always been very good at keeping secrets. Then he lectured me. 'When I say you're not to discuss these matters,' he said, 'I mean with anyone, up to and including congressional investigators, Agency security officers, and the president of the United States.'"

"Interesting choices."

"I thought so. Of course, I couldn't let that go without telling him that his brand of reticence might not conform to my sworn oath as a Foreign Service officer."

"What did he say to that?"

"'Honor is a wonderful thing, Mr. Cage. But do you really think an oath is worth destroying an entire career?'"

"Jesus."

"Yes. Although later I wondered if I'd been unduly impressed. Apparently some of my colleagues concluded he was a bit of a joke."

"There were others?"

"At least one that I know of. Ted Barr, a liaison like me, with lots of European postings. Turned out he'd done a few Dewey errands as well, same general time period. Of course, I didn't know this until years later. It was the mid-nineties when I ran into Ted at some Foreign Service gathering for old Iron Curtain hands. Ted had figured out I was involved because he'd eventually gotten curious enough to look into it further. He'd even managed to dig up the guy's name, Ron Curtin, plus a code name for his boss, Thresher. Said he was preparing to file an official complaint, up through channels, and asked if I wanted to sign on."

"Did you?"

Dad shook his head.

"Chickened out. Ted Barr was still in the field, practically a free agent. But I was working for the assistant secretary. He wouldn't have appreciated his deputy getting into a scrap with the Agency. I politely declined but asked him to keep me posted."

"And?"

"Two weeks later Ted Barr was dead. Car accident in Tuscany, one of those narrow roads with hairpin turns. He drove a little roadster. The police said his brakes failed."

I swallowed hard and sipped more bourbon.

"Had someone cut the line?"

"No one ever said that. The report only said 'failed.' I checked. Quietly, of course."

"So you don't *know* it was related."

"How can you ever know with something like that? But I've always wondered."

I couldn't help but notice the similarity to how my mother had died, although in her case there was never any mention of brake failure, and she was riding a bus in Greece, not a sports car in Italy.

"If you stay with this," Dad said, "that's what you'll be up against. At some point, anyway."

"But that was, what, fifteen years ago? This Ron Curtin guy probably isn't even working anymore."

"That's what I thought until Nethercutt's funeral. His hair is longer now—a mullet, isn't that what you called it?—but I recognized his face right away. Same build, too."

"Breece Preston's bodyguard?"

He nodded.

"No wonder you suddenly needed some fresh air. So is Breece Preston 'Thresher'?"

"I don't know. Nineteen years ago Ron Curtin could've been working for anyone. For obvious reasons I haven't felt inclined to check."

"Why would Preston care about any of this?"

"Good question. From all I ever heard, he and Lemaster were only fleetingly connected, but apparently that contact goes way back, to Ed's first years as a field man."

"Sounds tenuous."

"Maybe. But Preston always did have a mania for protecting 'sources and methods,' as the Agency calls them. And whoever Thresher is, or was, he seems hell-bent on keeping past matters under wraps. So you see?"

"Point taken. I'll be extra careful."

"Careful isn't good enough, son."

"I'm working for a magazine, Dad. Even if it is Breece Preston, he and Curtin aren't with the Agency anymore. They won't know what I'm up to until the story's out."

Dad shook his head, seemingly exasperated.

"You don't understand how it works with these people. They stay connected forever. It's the nature of their business. If you keep stirring things up, he'll get wind of it. And when he does, he'll set something in motion, God knows what. And by then it will be too late to get out. For all you know, it already is."

"Then I might as well follow it to the end."

"And I thought *I* was drunk. At the very least, give it some thought.

Maybe in the morning you'll feel differently. You'll do that much, won't you?"

"Sure, Dad. I can do that."

He nodded, but looked spent, at least ten years older than when I'd come through the door. He scanned the bookshelves, and in following his gaze my eyes alighted on the long line of Lemasters. At the far left was *Knee Knockers*, the author's debut, and I remembered Lemaster telling me how he'd first sketched out Richard Folly while riding a tram across the Danube. It must have happened around the time he and Dad became friends, which made me want to read it again, if only to search for traces of my father.

I stepped across the room and pulled down the copy in a rustle of plastic.

"Do you mind if—?"

"Not at all," he said wearily. "Take it to bed if you want."

I turned to the title page and saw the author's signature. Considering what I knew now, I wondered why Lemaster hadn't personalized it with a short note. But like most collectors, Dad was a purist about these things. I flipped through the opening chapter, and my mouth fell open. Page eleven was gone. When I went back to the front I saw that a square had been neatly sliced from the copyright page. This was the volume my handler had defaced for the message in Georgetown. Whoever had been in my house had been here as well, prowling among these shelves.

"What is it?" Dad asked. "What's wrong, son?"

I laid the book open on the end table next to him and showed him the damage. He withdrew a pair of reading glasses, then gasped and coughed. He put a hand to his chest.

"Just what in the hell is happening?" Then, turning toward me: "Did *you* do this?"

"Dad, no. Jesus. But I've seen the pages, the torn parts anyway. They were part of a message someone sent me in Georgetown, but I had no idea they'd come from your copy. None. It was part of the anonymous tip. It's the whole reason I'm here."

He shook his head, dumbstruck. I'm sure he saw this as a deeply personal attack. I did, too. He shut the book and gently set it down.

"You should go to bed, son. We both should. We've done quite enough damage for one day. Just keep your options open, will you? If that's even still possible."

"Yes, sir."

"To bed, then."

But he stayed up. Even as I tried to fall asleep, I heard Dad prowling the shelves down the hall, methodically ransacking his collection as he looked for further victims—the whisper of riffled pages, the thunks of books being stacked, the slide and shuffle of more volumes being pulled for inspection. At first it was nerve-racking. Eventually it lulled me to sleep.

I awoke around four, fully alert, which always happens on my first nights abroad. The apartment was silent, but somewhere a light was on. I grabbed the old bathrobe I'd worn as a boy and padded down the hall.

Dad was asleep in his easy chair in a solitary pool of light, head back, mouth open. A novel was splayed against his chest, and piles of other books covered every level space. Some forty volumes in all were out, and there was no telling how many he had already returned to the shelves. Lines of dust marked the empty spaces, which shocked me a little with its evidence of decline. The air was musty from the disturbed pages.

Apparently what had finally halted his labors was the same thing that always stopped us whenever we went foraging—one book had beckoned more than the others, and he'd been drawn to revisit a favorite scene. When I saw the title, *The Spy Who Came In from the Cold*, I knew it would be open to the final page, where Alec Leamas and his lover are shot dead at the Berlin Wall. Dad had always cited it as a sublime encapsulation of the Cold War—small people crushed by the machinery of competing empires.

It was the UK first edition from Gollancz, with an orange cover illustrated by a boxed quote of praise from J. B. Priestley. Dad would hate to see the binding treated this way, so I carefully picked it up from his chest. It was indeed open to the last page.

I placed it on the end table, where another volume was splayed facedown. This one was nonfiction, a collection of interviews with Graham Greene. When I checked to see what had caught Dad's eye, a comment about Kim Philby leaped from the page:

"I can understand a man's temptation to turn double agent," Greene said, "for the game becomes more interesting."

It was an eerie echo of Lemaster's remarks in our interview. For the professionals, I suppose, the game was everything. Isn't that what was driving me as well? The excitement of discovery, the pursuit of the unknown. I knew then that I would keep going, no matter what Dad wanted, but I no longer had any illusions that it would be a romp, a mere puzzle, and Litzi needed to know that as well.

Shutting the Greene book, I pulled my robe tighter and took a blanket from the couch to cover Dad. I switched off the lamp and returned to bed.

Hours later I awakened to the smell of bacon and coffee, an American breakfast. Dad wore a suit and tie, a signal that urgent matters were afoot.

"Where are you going this morning?" I asked.

"Oh, here and there." His mood was grim, businesslike. "Unless you're about to tell me you're quitting this fool's errand and heading home."

"Did Holly Martins quit when Major Callaway ordered him home?"

Dad was not amused.

"In real life, Holly Martins would have wound up facedown in the Danube. Here are the morning papers. Give Litzi my regards, but please keep her out of this."

"Don't worry. That's the first item on my agenda."

"Good."

He said nothing further about his plans, and I said nothing about my upcoming appointment. Yesterday the precautions of Moscow Rules had seemed frivolous. This morning they felt like smart planning. Dad grabbed his overcoat and paused by the door.

"Son," he said, "at some point you're going to have to level with me about everything that's going on, and about what you're really looking for. I'll leave it up to you to decide the best moment for that."

"Yes, sir."

It made me feel about thirteen, like I'd been grounded. After he left I listened to the clank and whine of the descending elevator. Then I poured more coffee and took it to the living room, where I found none of the chaos that had greeted me at four a.m.

Dad had opened the blinds to a full wash of autumn sunlight, and he had reshelved every book. Even the lines of dust I'd noticed the night before had been wiped clean, like fingerprints from the scene of a crime.

12

Litzi and I met at the Bräunerhof, of course. A strudel for her, an omelet for me. But my appetite was off, especially once it became clear that Litzi still regarded our appointment as a lark. It was my duty to set her straight, and to talk her out of coming with me, even though the last thing I wanted was to cut short our time together.

Her kiss the night before had been warm but unfamiliar. We had changed in so many ways, and aging was only part of it. The long slouch into disillusionment had marked us both, and I think each of us recognized it in the other. Yet I was certain that the boy and girl we'd once been were still within us, aching to come out and play. But would that ever happen if I sent her away now?

"Tell me again about this business of Moscow Rules," she asked. "Why is it so important?"

"It means you're supposed to be extra careful, because you're on enemy turf. So you use an elevated level of tradecraft."

"Bill, we're in Vienna."

"In *Smiley's People* the old Estonian, Vladimir, was in a nice park in London. The KGB shot him anyway."

"In a novel. At night. During the Cold War. I looked it up online when I got home."

I took her hand. She smiled, but I didn't.

"Litzi, I know this may seem like harmless fun. I felt that way for a while. But it isn't. To some people, anyway. Which is why I'd feel a whole lot better if you sat this out. Then, when I'm done, if you still want to see me—"

She frowned and let go of my hand.

"You've been talking to your father, haven't you?"

"How'd you know that?"

"Has he warned you off me?"

"He's warned me off everything *but* you. And he'd be furious if something happened to you because of me."

I told her his story about the beefy guy at the wedding, and the warning about old secrets that had anything to do with code name Dewey. She watched me closely, reappraising. Then she took back my hand.

"So this is supposed to make me less likely to come along?"

"Litzi, it's not a game."

"Of course it isn't. It also isn't an old letter from an archive, where everyone has been dead for five hundred years. From what you're saying, this is still alive and breathing. For me that's a plus, not a minus."

"Alive, breathing, and possibly lethal."

"I can take care of myself, Bill. Or have you forgotten our last great adventure?"

"As if that would be possible."

Indeed, while my imagination had embellished all those café trysts with my dad, and my youthful errands, the weekend Litzi was referring to had been truly audacious, and might easily have ended in disaster. And, just like now, the whole thing had been my idea.

It went like this:

Just after my seventeenth birthday, and only three weeks before Dad and I were due to depart for his posting in Berlin, Litzi and I disappeared together on a farewell excursion. Three nights and four days, all on our own, without telling a soul.

If the itinerary had been solely up to me, we probably would have hopped a train to Switzerland—Bern, Geneva, or some alpine lodge. My main goal was to establish the means, motive, and opportunity for sexual congress, because at that point we were still virgins. We'd had several notable near misses—frantic, half-naked encounters when we'd narrowly dodged discovery by her parents, by my dad, and, memorably, by a Vienna policeman on foot patrol in the Stadtpark, well after midnight.

Litzi had bolder ambitions. She proposed a whirlwind tour behind the Iron Curtain—hop across the Czech border to Prague, then onward to darkest East Germany for stops in Dresden and Berlin before returning to Vienna by overnight train. We would thrill to the cloak-and-dagger doings of the beleaguered locals while enjoying the freewheeling sexual atmosphere reputedly engendered by three decades of godless Communism.

It took weeks of planning to secure the visas and tickets, a chore in which I secretly (or so I thought) availed myself of Dad's consular connections. Each of us left behind a note saying we were sleeping over with friends for a few nights. By the time everyone figured out what was really up, we were well across the border. To our way of thinking, it was our launch into adulthood.

The first day went well enough, once we got over the initial awkwardness of traveling as a couple. Czech border authorities hardly glanced at our passports, which I found a little disappointing, and the atmosphere that we at first regarded as mysteriously oppressive soon began to seem merely drab and gloomy. If anyone was keeping tabs on us, we were too wrapped up in each other to notice, especially once we reached the faded glories of Prague, which in those days was coated liberally with soot and decrepitude. We shared sausages and tall mugs of pilsner—ID? Who needs an ID? This was Bohemia!—and I happily showed her all the places where I'd hung out as a fourteen-year-old, and the square where Soviet tanks had rolled in just before I turned twelve.

The only real disappointment was our innkeeper, who, far from being a Marxist libertine, assigned us to rooms three floors apart, then watched our comings and goings like a strict old aunt. We slept together anyway, dodging her on the creaking back stairway. It was bliss, I have to say, although I've often wondered if Litzi felt the same, since seventeen-year-old boys aren't exactly the world's most solicitous lovers.

It was while waiting for departure to East Germany at the Prague train station that we first noticed someone shadowing us. A man in a brown wool coat seemed to take a special interest as we moved from a baker's kiosk to the newspaper stand. Then he conspicuously followed us onto the platform.

We had window seats in one of those cramped compartments with facing benches, three passengers per side, and a sliding glass door with curtains. The compartment was full, and rank with sweat. Our watcher flitted past the door at least four times during the three-hour ride to the border, and on each occasion he made a point of looking at us through the glass. Finally Litzi stood up and brusquely closed the curtains, an action almost immediately countermanded by an old matron seated by the door who scolded Litzi in a surly burst of Czech. Litzi, who knew a little of the language, told me later she'd said, "The rest of us have nothing to hide."

We remained on edge as we arrived at the border, but even though the document checks took forever—the East Germans were thorough, as Germans usually are—within an hour we were back under way, and the man in brown was nowhere to be seen. We relaxed as the train crawled along the banks of the winding Elbe, enjoying a dusky view of fairy-tale beeches and rolling hills.

I switched on a light and took out my book, a novel by ex-spy E. Howard Hunt, who at the time was awaiting sentencing for his Watergate crimes. I'd chosen it mostly for its title, *The Berlin Ending*, since that was to be the final city on our tour, and my next home.

The train wasn't due to stop until Dresden, so when the brakes shrieked and the cars groaned to a halt at a small mountain village a few miles east of Bad Schandau, everyone looked up in annoyance. By then it was nearly dark, and no passengers were waiting on the platform. Then I saw a dozen or so *Volkspolizei*, or Vopos, come pouring out of the tiny station house, flashlights swiveling, whistles blowing.

Litzi looked at me, and the crabby woman by the door watched us both as if her worst suspicions had been confirmed. There were heavy footsteps in the corridor, followed by muffled shouting. Several Vopos ran past our window. Another slid open the door of the compartment. Scanning the six of us, he read aloud from an official-looking paper.

"Fräulein Strauss? Herr Cage?"

"Ja?" Litzi answered weakly. I shut my book, having just reached a scene in which the authorities were converging on the heroine at a small café near the Brandenburg Gate. Litzi nudged me with her foot.

"Ja," I answered.

"Come with me," he said in German.

"Why?" I asked.

"You are not to ask questions! Come now."

We reached for our bags but he waved us off.

"Leave those! Come now!"

He took me roughly by the arm and escorted us onto the platform, where more Vopos were waiting. Two took Litzi by either arm and headed across the cobbles toward a door on the right. My escort took me left, to a dim room where he flicked on a buzzing fluorescent tube, sat me down at a small table, then departed, shutting the door behind him. After waiting five minutes I opened the door, only to find two Vopos on guard.

"Back inside!" one shouted, but the door was open just long enough for me to hear muffled shouts from the room where they'd taken Litzi. The guards pushed me back inside and slammed the door. My spirits sank further when I heard the groan of a diesel engine and felt a rumble through the floor. Our train was leaving.

Maybe half an hour passed before the man in the brown coat entered. He shouted an order in an unfamiliar language—Russian?—and a Vopo brought a bottle of mineral water with two glasses. He poured some for himself, lit a cigarette, and watched me for several seconds. Then he addressed me in excellent English with a Prussian accent.

"That book you are reading, the one by the criminal CIA man, how did you select it?"

"You pulled us in because of that?"

"How did you select it?"

"It's my father's. I'm borrowing it. I liked the title."

"How many condoms did you bring?"

"*What?*"

"There are a dozen still in your bag. Were you planning to use them all?"

I shrugged, blushing in spite of myself.

"Or were you planning to conceal something in them and transport it back into the West in your stomach?"

"That's crazy." Did he really think we were smuggling drugs? Or were they going to plant some on us and haul us off to jail?

"Why else would you have so many for only two nights more?"

"They're cheaper in bulk."

He said nothing for a minute or two. He stubbed out his cigarette and lit another. I reached for the water bottle and he didn't stop me. It was a cheap local brand, gassy and harsh, but it calmed me.

"Your father, he is a diplomat?"

He gave special emphasis to the final word, as if it were a pejorative term, or an outright falsehood.

"Yes."

He smirked.

"In that case, you may think of me as a *diplomat* as well." He snorted under his breath. "What else does he like to read? More things like this Hunt trash?"

"You'd have to ask him. He's a collector."

"I am sure. What are his duties?"

"At his job?"

"Of course at his job. Do you know of any special duties?"

"No."

"You are sure of this? Do not lie to me."

"Yes. I'm sure."

"Has he not asked you to do his bidding while you are in the German Democratic Republic?"

"His bidding?"

"Observing things. Then reporting back to him, once you are home."

"He didn't even know I was coming."

"Yes, that is a useful story for you, I am sure." He smiled smugly. I've never been a violent person, but at that moment I wanted to lunge across the table and grab him by the neck. He stared awhile longer and then, as if he'd suddenly grown bored, he stood and left without a word. A Vopo reentered, took away the bottle, and shut the door.

I had no idea what had prompted his questions, which at the time only seemed bizarre. In light of recent events I now wonder if "special duties" was a reference to my father's courier errands. Had Dad been under surveillance? And why were they interested in my father's books?

The fellow in the brown coat must have concluded I had little to offer, because he never returned. Litzi was another matter. He spent the next ninety minutes grilling her. By the time she finally emerged, just after a Vopo escorted me onto the platform, she was hugging herself for either warmth or comfort.

"Are you all right?" I asked. I stepped toward her, but a Vopo held us apart. "Litzi, are you okay? Did he—?"

Sniffling, she shook her head as if to reassure me, but she looked pale and frightened.

Another Vopo brought our bags. I later discovered that the condoms were gone. They also took the Hunt novel.

They bundled us into the back of a rattling Wartburg that was idling in front of the station. The driver was a civilian in disheveled clothes. A second car followed us for a few miles, then peeled away toward Bad Schandau. Neither Litzi nor I spoke during the forty-minute ride to Dresden. We didn't know if the driver was a plainclothesman or some hack they'd hired off the street. He, too, remained silent. Now and then I glanced at Litzi, but she was invariably gazing out her window.

The driver dropped us at the Dresden Hauptbahnhof, more than two hours after we would have arrived by train. He sped away without asking for a fare, our gift from the German Democratic Republic. Litzi sagged into my arms.

"What did they do?" I asked. "Why did they keep you for so long?"

"The usual harassment," she said. "I'm an Austrian national with a Czech father, so they have to take their pound of flesh."

That was when I first learned that Litzi's last name hadn't always been Strauss. Her dad had chosen it after switching from Marek. He had grown up in Bohemia, a Czech national who'd fled to Vienna during the Second World War and then somehow managed to stay once the Soviets began repatriating all East Bloc nationals, just like they did with Harry Lime's girlfriend Anna in *The Third Man*. No wonder Litzi didn't like the movie.

"They can't deport him," I said. "Not now."

"Not legally, no."

"What do you mean?"

"I don't want to talk about them anymore. And I don't want to stay in Dresden any longer than we have to. I want to get to Berlin. *West* Berlin."

She refused to say more about the ordeal. I've always assumed she would eventually have loosened up over time, but my dad and I left Vienna three weeks later, so I never found out.

From Dresden, Litzi and I caught an early train the next morning to Berlin, and spent the day moping around its sights and its museums before boarding our reserved overnight compartment for Vienna. Litzi was still in too much of a daze for us to enjoy the ride the way we'd hoped.

Our families were furious, but they let us keep seeing each other during my final weeks in town. But the jolt of the experience cast a pall over our last days together, and even seemed to darken our correspondence afterward. For a few months we gamely lived up to our promises to write regularly, but never achieved quite the spark we'd had in Vienna. By the time I started traveling to the States to pick a college, we had stopped as if by mutual consent. Then we lost touch.

Now here we were again, seated in the Bräunerhof at the very table where we'd hatched our first big adventure. And damned if we weren't planning another one.

"You're sure you want to go through with this?" I asked.

"Of course." Neither of us was smiling now.

I checked my watch.

"Time to go."

"Moscow Rules," she muttered. "Hope that that doesn't mean we'll see the man in the brown coat."

"Oh, I hope it does. He owes me a dozen condoms."

She laughed, but only briefly. Then she tightened her grip on my arm.

13

Köllnerhofgasse was a bustling little street. Number 11 was the most run-down building on the block. The lock on the main doorway was broken, and the stairwell stank of mildew and pigeon shit.

In keeping with Moscow Rules, Litzi and I circled the block once in reconnaissance before entering, pausing several times to check for surveillance. The passage from *Smiley's People* had said the safety signal would be a pin "shoved high in the first wood support on the left as you entered." A yellow chalk line would indicate it was too unsafe to proceed. I looked left as we came through the entrance. A red pushpin protruded from the door frame just overhead.

But what did we do now?

"Check the mailboxes," Litzi whispered.

There were two rows of eight, each with its own buzzer. The locks were sprung on three. The name "Miller" caught my eye, written neatly in black ink for 4-B on an immaculate slip of paper.

"That's our man."

"Miller?"

"Brand-new card, and it's the name Vladimir used in *Smiley's People*."

"Nice work, Mr. Folly. Maybe that's how you should introduce yourself."

"As long as you use his girlfriend's name. Carolista."

Litzi made a face. I pressed the button.

We waited several seconds before the buzzer sounded to unlock the inner door.

In most big old buildings like this you hear a wide variety of noises as you make your way upstairs. Babies and televisions, dogs and stereos, an argument or two. Number 11 Köllnerhofgasse was as quiet as a tomb, and by the time we reached the fourth floor we were a little unnerved.

I knocked loudly. There was a flash of movement behind the peep-hole. Then the door swung back to the limit of a security chain. The smell of sweat and unwashed clothes poured through the breach. A short older man with unkempt black hair, late sixties probably, peeped out at us with a hint of fear in bloodshot eyes. He said nothing.

"Herr Miller?" I tried.

"That's what it says on the mailbox." His German had a heavy Slavic accent, probably Russian. "Is that all you can offer?"

"Vladimir Miller?"

He nodded. Some of the alarm faded from his eyes, and he shut the door to undo the chain. When he opened back up and saw Litzi, he blocked our way.

"The message said nothing about two of you."

"I didn't send the message. Did you send mine?"

I moved again to enter but he held his ground. I raised my voice so it would echo down the stairwell.

"Shall we continue talking with the door wide open, so that anyone below can hear?"

He glanced over my shoulder, scowling, then motioned us inside.

"Sit on the couch," he said.

We obliged him. He stood by an armchair with torn upholstery, watching carefully.

"You are not to move while I address you. You will do exactly as I say. Understand?"

Litzi and I looked at each other from opposite ends of the filthy couch, and when neither of us answered right away he produced a butcher knife from behind his back and rapidly approached me. I made a move to stand, but he was too quick, using his free hand to shove my chest and force me back into the seat.

"I said, 'do you understand?' " The knife blade was inches from my face, tilted downward.

"Yes," Litzi said from her end. "We understand."

He backed away, but only a few feet.

"Did anyone follow you?"

"Not that I know of."

"That is not a good-enough answer."

I shrugged.

"We checked several times," I said. "Moscow Rules."

"And you relied on *her*?"

"I'm not exactly a trained professional, or didn't they tell you?"

He wearily shook his head, but kept the knife pointed forward. It was rusty and stained, and probably dull, not that I cared to find out.

"Who is playing with my security like this?" he asked. "Do you know?"

"You'll have to ask your handler."

"My handler!" he said disdainfully. "He has been dead eleven years. These people now are never of any use except for themselves."

He paused, thinking over what to say, while I took stock of the room. The apartment was in the same shape as Vladimir. Plaster cracked, ceiling watermarked. The lumpy couch reeked of cat urine, and the upholstery was shredded along the back. No carpeting, just scuffed oak, with mouse droppings in the corners. The heat was off, and it was chilly.

Vladimir stepped to the window and flipped back a heavy curtain, which ejected dust into a pale band of sunlight. He looked down at the street in both directions, then dropped the curtain and came back to the couch, knife still at the ready. I glanced at Litzi, but she was watching Vladimir. I'm not sure what I'd expected, but it hadn't been anything like this.

"I assume you have some sort of message for me. For us."

"You are to tell no one of my location. They would pay good money to know it, but if you take their money you will be dead inside a week."

"Whose money?"

He waggled the knife and stepped closer.

"Don't treat me as a fool unless you wish to exit through the window."

Then he retreated to a far corner, where he knelt in a scatter of mouse droppings and, without turning his back, began working at a floorboard with the knife.

A scene from Len Deighton's *Berlin Game* flashed into my head—Bernie Samson, scolding a contact for hiding something beneath the floorboards, because that's where the searchers always looked first. Vladimir seemed to have run out of energy and ideas, an old spy at the end of his tether.

The board came free. He pulled out a small, clean envelope and stood unsteadily, then brought it to the couch and tossed it in my lap. When I moved to open it, he stepped closer and thrust out the knife in warning.

"Not here." The blade was inches from my nose, close enough to smell the rusty steel. "Anywhere you please once you've left, but not here."

"Okay."

"Tell your people it is from my own files," he said. "I knew someday there would be interest." He waggled the knife, flicking it across the tip of my nose as if he was scratching an itch. "If the wire transfer does not occur within three days, then I will come for you. For both of you. But if your clumsiness leads the others here first, then you can be certain that they will next come for you."

"Who are the others?"

He scowled as he had at my previous claim of ignorance. Then he slowly, achingly, raised the blade until it was touching the hair on my forehead. He flicked it sideways, scratching the skin and tossing my hair.

"Ask such a question again and I will shove this straight into your lying mouth." I listened to his breathing, trying to remain as still as possible and not daring to look away from his eyes. He slowly backed away, but only a step, and he continued to hold the knife forward.

"The wire transfer," he said again. "Three days, no longer."

"It will be done."

He smiled grimly but said nothing. Then he coughed and blew his nose on the sleeve of his free hand. I stood uncertainly, and Litzi followed suit. He watched wordlessly as we stepped toward the door. I was turning the rattling old knob when he spoke again.

"I have an oral message for you as well."

"Yes?" When I turned, he was grinning.

"Prague."

I paused with my hand on the knob.

"Prague what?"

"That is the complete message. Prague. Now leave. And if you see them before they see you, which I doubt you are capable of doing, then you had damn well better run like you have never run before."

His wheezing laughter followed us halfway down the stairs.

Back out in the street I looked up at Vladimir's windows and saw a curtain flick back into place. Maybe he was watching to see if we were followed. Maybe we should be doing the same.

"Where to?" Litzi asked. She brushed back the hair from my forehead and looked closer. "No blood. Only a very light scratch."

"We should find someplace to open this thing. I was about to suggest the Bräunerhof, but I guess we shouldn't be so predictable."

"Burger King," she said. I frowned. "Well, if you really don't want to be predictable."

"Lead the way."

There was a Burger King at Stephansplatz only a few blocks away, which explained why a Whopper banner was hanging from Harry Lime's house. A trio of punk-looking boys on skateboards nearly collided with us outside the entrance, but otherwise we attracted no apparent interest. We slid into a plastic booth that smelled of French fries. After a precautionary glance, I tore open the envelope.

No book pages this time. There was a pair of photo negatives, both in black and white.

"Looks like a document," Litzi said. "Two pages, or maybe two different documents."

At the top of each frame was a tiny blob that might be an official crest or logo.

"We need to get it developed," I said. "But we can't give it to just anyone."

I thought of George Smiley, and the negatives he'd discovered among the last effects of his Vladimir. He'd developed them himself, in the basement of his flat on Bywater Street, but I didn't have a clue about that sort of thing.

"I know someone at the Archives who can help," Litzi said.

"Do you trust him?"

"She. Yes. And she owes me a favor."

She got out her cell phone. The whole transaction took less than a minute.

"We have to hurry; she wants to leave soon."

The bonus was that I got to see where Litzi worked, because her office was just downstairs from the Prunksaal, the court library of Emperor Charles VI, a bibliophile's baroque paradise of patterned marble floors, ceiling frescoes, gilded woodwork, and floor-to-ceiling books, with an ample supply of ladders and stairways for reaching each and every volume.

"How did I ever miss this place when I was a boy?"

"It's not like you could have just walked in. And would you have been half as impressed when you were sixteen? I doubt there are too many Lemasters up there."

"Snob. What did our photo developer say?"

"She'll have our prints in forty minutes."

She gazed up toward the highest shelves, where someone on a ladder was carefully dusting a row of leather bindings.

"We're dinosaurs, aren't we?" she said. "Books are like Latin, the new dead language. Even most of the manuscripts I deal with have been digitized. So is everything that people write about them. Dust to dust, places like this. I should show you around before it all disappears."

She gave me the cook's tour, and we strolled companionably from shelf to shelf. The smell alone was intoxicating—all those pages, lovingly tended. Then her phone buzzed.

"Thanks. Be right there." She hung up. "Wait for me at one of those tables. If anyone asks, say you're with me."

She returned with a manila envelope and a magnifying glass and sat down next to me. She opened the envelope and pulled out two eight-by-ten prints.

"Oh, my," she said.

"It's all in Russian. Cyrillic characters. Do you have a translator?"

"Yes. But without knowing what it says . . ."

"Right. Not a good idea."

"There's a Russian cultural center near here."

"Not the one run by the embassy?"

"God, no. This one's private. I've been to their gallery. It's just around the corner from Vladimir, in fact. Artsy-craftsy types, very anti-Putin."

"Or so they say."

"Do you have a better idea?"

"Let's go."

She checked her watch.

"I'd better call first. I've got one of their cards."

She dug into her purse, but something brought her up short. Frowning, she pulled out an ivory-colored envelope, sealed, with nothing written on the outside.

"Did you put this here?" she asked, inspecting it carefully.

"No. But I recognize the stationery."

She turned it over and held it to the light. Her training in authenticating old manuscripts paid off right away.

"Gohrsmühle, if I had to guess, but from quite a few years ago. I'm not sure they make this anymore."

"I have a box of it at home. It's mine."

"Like the first one, you mean? You didn't tell me the paper was Gohrsmühle." She rubbed her fingers on the envelope the way a bank teller rubs a twenty to see if it's real. It brought a smile to her face. "Wasn't this the stationery you used for your letters from Berlin?"

"Very good."

"How can you possibly have any left?"

"I only use it for important correspondence."

"How do you think it got in my purse?"

"When's the last time you opened it?"

"Not at Burger King, we didn't buy anything. The Bräunerhof, probably, before we went to Vladimir's."

"Could Vladimir have done it?"

She shook her head.

"If he'd even come close to me, I'd have kicked out his kneecaps." Then her eyes lit up. "Those kids outside the Burger King, the ones on skateboards. One bumped me as they passed. His friends laughed."

"Really?" I was skeptical. "If my handler has started hiring off the street, then he's taking things up a notch, or just getting reckless."

"Maybe we should read the message."

She slit the top edge with a fingernail and withdrew a page of my stationery, folded neatly. He'd been using my Royal again. A page from a book was pasted on the paper, with a short message typed above it:

```
Deliver V's proofs ASAP
```

The page was another one from *Knee Knockers*, probably Dad's copy. I winced, feeling like someone who kept receiving severed fingers and toes from a kidnapper. We read the passage.

Boris arrived late to the Burggarten, but that was his style. So was sloppiness in general. With each step, the vodka bottle clanked against the key ring in his overcoat pocket. Eventually he grew annoyed enough by the sound to stop and move his keys to the opposite pocket, an occasion which of course called for another shot of vodka. He wiped his mouth on a sleeve and continued. Only when he came within a block of the dead drop did he actually begin taking proper precautions, an oversight which would be logged into Hartley's report as the Russian's "fatal error." The mailbox, at least, looked secure enough. It was a stone just to the right of a statue of Emperor Franz Josef I at the south end of the park, marked with a small slash of yellow chalk. Glancing around carelessly for onlookers, Boris slipped a small plastic bag from his trousers, lifted the stone, placed the bag underneath, then dropped the stone back into place. He took out a stub of chalk from his pocket and made a cross through the slash.

"So you're supposed to deliver these negatives?" Litzi asked.

"To a dead drop in the Burggarten. Where presumably someone will pick them up."

"Good thing we made prints. Sounds like he wants them right away. So what happened to Boris?"

"What?"

"In the book. It mentioned his 'fatal error.'"

"Oh." I swallowed. "Someone followed him. They waited until he was back at his apartment, then shot him in the face."

"Is everyone in these books shot in the face?"

"It was a common KGB tactic."

"Does your handler know you'd be aware of that?"

"Probably."

"I don't enjoy his sense of humor."

"Maybe he isn't joking. Where's that card for the cultural center?"

She searched her purse again and dug it out from the bottom.

"The New Moscow Cultural Center," she read. "Founded 1994. Art. Literature. Translations. Here's their number."

"Call them, then. Before I lose my nerve."

"Before we both do."

Now she looked as worried as I was. She punched in the number anyway.

14

The New Moscow Cultural Center looked like a shoestring operation. Its ground-floor offices were tucked behind a pharmacy and a kitschy souvenir shop with a window full of chocolate Mozart statuettes.

They'd been preparing to lock up when Litzi phoned, but the young man who answered grudgingly agreed to wait after she explained it was urgent. We decided to use fake names and pay in cash.

A buzzer opened the door. A few paintings, none to my liking, were propped on easels in the foyer. A man in his early twenties waited impatiently at a cluttered reception desk.

"You must be Feliks," Litzi said. "I am Mrs. Brünner. This is my friend from America, Mr. Norris. Thank you for waiting."

Feliks nodded gloomily.

"You have payment?"

"Certainly. How much?"

"Twenty euros per page."

Steep. Feliks had probably built in a gratuity for himself. I handed him the prints, but he refused to even glance at them until Litzi put four tens on the desk. He slipped the bills into his trousers and picked up the prints.

His eyes widened immediately, and he dropped the photos.

"Is this joke?"

"No," I answered. "No joke."

"Then you are crazy. Or maybe you are police."

"Neither."

He retrieved the bills from his pocket and handed them to Litzi along with the prints. She tried to give everything back, but he let the bills fall on the desk and shoved away the photos. As they oscillated to the floor he stood abruptly and disappeared down a hallway.

We looked at each other, wondering what to do next, and we were on the verge of giving up when a benevolent old face crowned with a snowy shock of hair poked out from the end of the hall. The little man who emerged looked like a forest gnome who had just crawled out from under a toadstool. As he drew closer he even smelled a little woodsy, like wet leaves on a trail.

"Please," he said, gesturing down the hallway. "Why don't we step into my office where there is greater privacy. Bring the documents with you."

He turned before we could answer, so we followed. His office was small but pleasant, with flowers in terra-cotta pots. A window overlooked an alley through the iron steps of a fire escape.

"I am Director Gelev. You seem to have upset young Feliks. May I get you some tea? I am afraid the coffeepot has already been cleaned for the day."

"No, thank you," Litzi said.

"None for me, either."

"May I see those papers, if you would be so kind?"

I handed over the photographed pages.

"Mm-hmm." He flipped to the second one. "Yes, I see."

He had the bearing of a doctor confirming a dire diagnosis.

"If it is not too much trouble, may I also see your identity papers?"

Litzi and I exchanged glances, then she reached for her ID card. I did the same with my passport. So much for fake names. He looked them over, then handed them back with a slight smile.

"You must excuse my precautions. Even with photographs of very old papers like these, the name of the KGB still carries a great deal of power, as you saw with young Feliks."

"These are from the KGB?" I asked.

"Did you truly not know this?"

"No. Although maybe I should've guessed from Feliks's reaction."

"May I ask how you acquired these documents?"

"I, uh . . ."

Litzi deftly cut in.

"I am an archivist at the National Library." She presented her business card. "People bring me all sorts of strange old items, thinking that I might have a use for them. Mr. Cage is an old friend who happens to be here on vacation. He brought them from the States."

Better than what I would've come up with, but Gelev immediately shot it full of holes.

"I know the National Library has budget strains, Miss Strauss, but does it no longer employ translators of Cyrillic?"

"I didn't want to use official resources on a friend's behalf. This seemed like a more . . . informal way to handle it."

"Of course. KGB documents. Very informal."

He turned to me.

"And you brought these from the States?"

"Yes."

"Did some émigré give them to you?"

"A friend of one, yes."

He raised an eyebrow and studied me further. Sweat prickled in my palms as if I'd been hooked up to a polygraph. He almost certainly knew I was lying.

"Very well. I will have them translated and return them tomorrow. I don't know what sort of price Feliks quoted you, but our standard rate is ten euros per page."

"I'm not sure I'd feel comfortable leaving them overnight. They're so old and everything."

He raised his eyebrows again. The photos, of course, were brand-new. My inclination was to snatch up the prints and leave. Maybe Gelev sensed that, judging from what he said next.

"Well, they do appear to be fairly brief. Perhaps I could go through them with you myself right now and tell you roughly what they say."

"Yes. That would work."

He motioned for us to pull up our chairs beside the desk. Then he took a pair of reading glasses from his shirt pocket, cleared his throat, and went to work.

"This first one is some sort of field report, from a man named Leo to another named Oleg. No last names are mentioned."

"Code names, probably," I said.

He eyed me over the tops of his specs.

"You are familiar with the working tactics of the KGB?"

"Well, no. But . . ."

"It is probably a safe assumption, all the same. The subject of Leo's memo is Source Dewey."

"Dewey? You're sure?"

"Yes."

So the KGB knew about Dewey. Were they using him, or stalking him?

"Go ahead."

"Apparently Oleg was in Moscow. Leo was not." He paused, running a finger along the lines of text. "'Dewey's movements proceed as expected. Mailbox delivery on nineteen seven.' He means the date, the nineteenth of July."

"Is there a year?"

Gelev scanned the page.

"Not in the report, but there is a filing stamp. Fourth of September, 1971."

"Thanks. Go ahead."

"'Mailbox delivery,' which you already heard. 'Pickup completed. Box empty on twentieth. As requested, contacts made at the following addresses on the following dates.' He lists them, there are several."

"How many?"

Gelev counted down the page with his forefinger, muttering in Russian beneath his breath.

"Three. Three names and three addresses. And they are not Vienna addresses, nor are they Moscow. Knowing both cities, I can say that with reasonable certainty. Would you like me to read them?"

We nodded. The contacts were first names only, meaning they, too, were probably code names. Karloff, Woodman, Fishwife. None was familiar. He then read the names of the streets, which I recognized right away, and I suspected Litzi did as well.

"The addresses are followed by more of the same. A reference to a mailbox delivery on the twentieth of August. Then someone checked to see that it was empty on the twenty-first. Then another delivery in early September, the first. Details such as that."

He paused, scanning toward the bottom.

"Ah, here is something different in the final paragraph. I will quote it as precisely as I can: 'Dewey has employed a new courier. I suggest we approach. On twenty-second of August I also detected possible surveillance of Dewey's network. Tactics are not those of our usual adversaries. Await your instructions on both matters.' And that is the end of the document."

"He doesn't mention a name for the new courier?"

Gelev checked again, then shook his head.

"No."

"Could I write down those translated names and addresses?"

"Certainly. Here."

He handed me a pen, then grabbed a sheet of paper from the feed tray of a printer. I wrote down the addresses as he read them back. One in particular stood out, and my reaction must have been noticeable.

"Have I said something to upset you?" Gelev asked.

Gelev would have made a great cop.

"No. I'm just a little keyed up."

"The KGB has been known to have that effect. Are you ready for the second document?"

"Please."

"It was also filed in September 1971, on the sixth of the month. This one is from Oleg to Leo. There is no subject label, but it seems to address several points. I will take them in order."

"Sure."

"His expense report for August is approved with one amendment. Payment to Source Nina not authorized."

"Nina?"

"There is no other explanation. Knowing what I do of Russians abroad, I suspect Leo was trying to get his boss to pay for some woman that he was . . ." Gelev glanced toward Litzi. "That he was seeing."

"Don't mince words on my account," she said.

"It is not my way to be coarse around ladies. I will continue."

He slid his forefinger to the next paragraph.

"There is discussion of what sort of car he should drive to the border the following week. Oleg suggests a Skoda that does not come from the embassy motor pool. Ah, here we go. 'Surveillance of Dewey to which you refer is possibly on behalf of Source Glinka, separate from your activities. Do not approach. Integrity of Source Dewey could be compromised.'"

"Glinka?"

"Yes."

"Any mention of Dewey's new courier?"

"That is the next and final item. 'Proceed with identification of

Dewey courier. Full vetting, but Dewey must not know. Report results immediately upon completion.'"

"So Oleg was concerned."

"It sounds that way. But, of course, this was almost forty years ago. Perhaps not enough concern for it to still matter."

"You're probably right."

Gelev put the paper down and took a deep breath. He seemed relieved, as if he had expected tales of torture, murder, or some other terrible secret.

I, on the other hand, was disconcerted. In the second memo, Oleg's reference to Dewey sounded downright cozy, as if they were allies, not adversaries. Although it was still ambiguous. And who were all these other parties spying on Dewey?

"Thank you," I said. "You've been a great help. Ten euros a page, you said?"

Gelev waved away the proffered bills and took a bottle of vodka from a desk drawer. He stood and fetched three tumblers from a shelf.

"There is no need for payment. It is just as well if there is no record of this transaction. But we must all have a drink, to wash away the memories of those old and bad times."

Litzi waved away the glass, but he poured her a shot anyway. The two of us sipped. Gelev knocked his back with a single swallow, then poured himself a second, which he finished before we were done. He set down his empty glass with a great sigh.

"You may count on my complete discretion, Mr. Cage. But as someone whose father spent seven years in the Gulag, I hope I may count on yours as well."

"Of course."

"Young Feliks, however, is another matter. When he becomes excited he tends to peep like a hungry nestling. So if you will pardon my rudeness, I must find out which café he has fled to before he tells half of Vienna about your visit. May I escort you out?"

Gelev frowned as he led us to the door, as if still working something over in his head. He paused after taking out his keys, then spoke again.

"I moved here many years ago, Mr. Cage, long before the difficulties of the Cold War were settled business. If indeed such things are ever settled. When I was younger I used to make a game out of spotting the

KGB men who came and went from this city. For Russians this was not difficult, partly because so many of them stayed at the same hotel, Gasthaus Brinkmann. As it happens, I was walking by it only yesterday, and recognized a man coming out the door whose face I had not seen in years."

He paused to let it sink in.

"KGB?"

Gelev nodded. The vodka was just beginning to bloom in rosy marks on his cheeks.

"Do you know his name?"

"Only what the émigrés used to call him—the Hammerhead—because of his massive jawbone, the great size of his skull. My older contacts say he is now pursuing business opportunities, so to speak. The words 'security consultant' have been bandied about. But even if he is employed by some Oligarch, it is only cover, if you ask me. Men like the Hammerhead know only one trade. And I find the coincidence of his reappearance with the arrival of these documents to be interesting, perhaps even disturbing."

"I agree."

"Yes, I can see that you do."

"Can you describe him a little more?"

"About your size, but thicker in the middle, maybe fifteen, twenty years older. Brown eyes. A full head of wavy hair, mostly gray now. But as I said, it is his jaw, the size of his head, that stands out. And a great slab of a face, red from vodka, with a wide mouth that never smiles but is often open, as if he were a landed fish gasping for air. It makes him look quite stupid, but I assure you he isn't."

"I believe you. We'll watch out for him."

"That is advisable, especially if you plan to keep those photographed documents in your possession."

Gelev locked the door behind us. We headed back onto the street, where he turned in the opposite direction without saying good-bye, as if eager to demonstrate to any onlookers that he didn't know us.

"Sounds like we're not the only ones in Vienna following old trails," Litzi said. "Maybe this Hammerhead is who Vladimir was watching for out his window."

We continued a few more steps in silence.

"Those street names in the documents," Litzi said. "I suppose you recognized them."

"They're all in Prague. I even knew one of the numbers, the address for Source Fishwife. It's an apartment building."

"The exact number?"

"I once knew it by heart. My best friend lived there. Karel Vitova."

"Do you think that he . . . ?"

I shook my head.

"At least a dozen families lived there. Not that the Russians would've thought twice about using a thirteen-year-old informant. But Karel never gave a shit about politics, and he hated the Party youth clubs. Even when the tanks rolled in, all he cared about was girls, cigarettes, and Jimi Hendrix."

"Do you think he'd know who it was?"

"If I could find him. He has to be in Prague. I could never imagine Karel living anywhere else."

"Prague. Like Vladimir's message."

"Maybe now we know why."

"The city where you stole my virtue."

"In spite of our nosy innkeeper."

"I never told you then, but she was really on our side. She confided to me one morning before you came downstairs that she was completely in favor of our trysts. It was the authorities she worried about. That's why she kept her books so carefully, especially where Westerners were concerned." Then, after a pause. "I could go with you again, if you wanted. If you didn't think I'd be in the way."

"In the way? Without you I'd still be waiting on prints from a drugstore. It's just that, well . . ."

"Yes, I know. Too dangerous for a girl."

"You know what I mean."

"If it's danger you're worried about, I'd be an extra set of eyes."

Her offer was appealing on many levels, but I could already imagine how disapproving my father would be.

"Why don't I sleep on it? We can decide in the morning. For now, we've got a mail drop to take care of."

Litzi slipped her arm through mine. We were about to set out for the Burggarten when an ambulance screamed past us up the street. Two blocks ahead a crowd was gathering, with everyone craning their necks from behind a police barricade on the corner. An officer pulled back the barricade to let the ambulance through.

"What's going on?" Litzi said.

"That's Köllnerhofgasse. You don't think . . . ?"

We hurried toward the corner, where the gawkers were staring up at the top floors of a building across the street—number 11. On the fourth floor the curtains of Vladimir's apartment were open to a view of a uniformed policeman with his back to the window. The ambulance was parked on the street below.

"What's happening?" Litzi asked someone up front.

"The cops came running in ten minutes ago. They pushed everyone back."

The policeman in the window turned to gaze down at us, then closed the curtains just as Vladimir had. A few moments later a murmur went through the crowd as two orderlies burst through the front door pushing a rattling gurney with a body beneath a sheet.

"Maybe it was an overdose," Litzi whispered.

"You think they'd call in all these cops for an overdose? And look at the sheet."

The top was bloody, up where the head would be.

"Shot in the face, ten to one."

"Shhh. People are listening. And look, just down the block, above the sign for the laundry."

I immediately saw what she meant. A security camera was trained on the doorway of Vladimir's building. If it was in working order, then our visit was on tape. As deserted as the building was, we might even be the only ones to have visited, especially if Vladimir's killer had been savvy enough to enter from the alley in the back. Assuming the victim was Vladimir, of course.

We waited a few minutes more on the off-chance that Vladimir might appear, perhaps in handcuffs. Then the ambulance pulled away. An officer came over to move the barricade. People began spilling onto the sidewalk as the crowd broke apart.

"We'd better take care of our delivery," I whispered. "The sooner the better under these circumstances."

We were just getting under way when my attention was diverted by a tapping sound from behind, an insistent rhythmic beat barely audible above the buzz of the dispersing crowd. I spun around, looking for Lothar, but saw only a shopkeeper who had just finished rolling up his awning. Maybe that was the source of the noise.

"What's wrong?"

"Did you hear it? That tapping?"

"What tapping?"

"Never mind. Let's get this over with."

"Then a drink, something stronger than wine. And tonight you're coming upstairs. Being alone in the dark isn't something I care to think about right now."

An hour earlier, that remark would have been thrilling. Right then it sounded more like the voice of necessity, and I could only agree.

15

So, danger had entered the equation, just as my father had warned. In its presence, I was surprised to find that I was worried but unflinching. Not brave or courageous, just determined, full of resolve. What the hell else was I going to do? Give up and go home? Back to an emptiness that, with Litzi at my side, I now saw with more clarity than ever?

But I must discourage you from expecting too much of me as events turn chancy. As Marty Ealing likes to say when assessing a potentially shaky client, let's review the particulars:

I am fifty-three, with no history of violence. My only recent acts of aggression have been verbal, usually while driving on the Capital Beltway. On the other hand, I am not a retiree with a beer gut, bad knees, and a colostomy bag. Regular running, plus a weekly game of basketball with other men past their prime, have left me in decent trim. A few years ago I even took one of those executive survival courses. Marty enrolled five of us, not out of concern for our safety but to suck up to a new client, a global security contractor that was getting bad press over its quick-triggered operatives in Iraq.

They taught us some stunt driving, various evasive techniques, a few handy physical moves like breaking a choke hold, escaping a wrist grip, disarming an attacker with a handgun—the very sort of stuff I'd probably never feel confident enough to try during an actual attack, although I guess you never know until the moment arrives. The one real fight I've witnessed in recent years, late one night outside a D.C. jazz club, had nothing the least bit practiced or choreographed about it. It was savage and elemental, probably the way any of us would fight if our life was on the line.

The best lesson the course taught me was that our most potent weapon is not a star knife or a Glock 19. It's our mind, our alertness, our ability to reason out and act upon clues of danger as they assemble in our midst. The same as it always was for Folly or Smiley, in other words. And in the mental department, at least, I have stored up all sorts of lore from my years of reading.

Eric Ambler taught me that the best way to sneak up a stairway is to stay to the sides, where the treads won't squeak. Lawrence Durrell let me know in *White Eagles over Serbia* that when you think you're being followed you should check the reflection in a shop window now and then to see who's behind you. Then there were le Carré's numerous descriptions of tradecraft, and Lemaster's many references to lessons learned at the Farm, the CIA's training facility in Virginia.

How ironic, then, that my first idea for decisive action came not from my favorite old spy friends, but as a result of my Capitol Hill work for Ealing Wharton. It popped into my head as Litzi and I bustled grimly toward the Burggarten, only a block from our destination.

"Time for a detour," I announced.

"But I thought—?"

"This way. Quickly. I'll explain later."

I led the way toward a computer store I'd seen the other day. There, in rapid succession, I purchased a cheap but fairly powerful laptop, a wireless battery-powered webcam, and a roll of black electrical tape. Duct tape would have been better, but this wasn't a hardware store, and we were pressed for time.

"Can you tell me what this is all about?" Litzi asked in the checkout line.

"Not here," I said, scanning the other shoppers. "Now all we need is a bottle of wine, a corkscrew, and two glasses. And chalk to mark the mail drop."

The drinking supplies were easily procured at a nearby *Weinladen*. Litzi slipped into an art supply store for the chalk.

"Now?" she asked, when we were within a block of the Burggarten.

"The gist of it," I said, "is that the best defense is a good offense."

"Translation, please."

"It's a cliché in American football. I'm adopting it as our strategy, if only to make me feel better. If we keep letting someone else call all the shots, we'll be setting ourselves up as easy targets for whoever killed Vladimir. So before I pick up another single literary bread crumb, I want to find out who's scattering them."

"And how do you propose to do that?"

"Better technology, for one thing. My handler's all about dead drops, book codes, and Moscow Rules, everything manual and on paper. That tells me he stopped learning new tricks around the time the Wall came down."

"That explains the laptop and webcam. But do you actually know how to use them?"

I did, only because of a dog-and-pony show I'd arranged for a congressional committee on behalf of a banker client last year. The committee was up in arms over ATM fees, so I proposed deflecting their anger by demonstrating one of the many fraud schemes that contributed to—but hardly accounted for—ATM operating costs.

The client sent me an ex-con who, in a riveting bit of C-SPAN theater, demonstrated a cheap rig that he'd once used to scam cardholders (and their banks) by stealing magnetic card codes and numeric passwords. A key piece of equipment was a wireless webcam, which he taped into place within view of the ATM's numeric pad. Another gizmo stole the info from the card's magnetic strip. He recorded everything on his laptop from a nearby parked car. Having watched him set it up, I knew every step. The only difference was that my surveillance target would be the dead drop. Litzi was impressed.

"There's the statue," she said. "How should we do this?"

"First we make sure no one's tailing us. Go to that bench, the closest one. I'll make a circuit of the park. If you see anyone watching me, call my cell phone and ID them."

"And then?"

"Maybe I'll follow him."

"Don't be stupid."

"Well, let's at least check."

The park wasn't exactly empty. A young woman was pushing a stroller past the emperor's statue, and two kids were on a bench maybe twenty feet away. A little farther along, an older man was feeding pigeons in the gathering darkness. My circuit of the premises, however, stirred no reaction from any of them. I returned to the bench.

"Let's wait for some of them to leave," I suggested. "Where are the negatives?"

"In my purse. 'Dead drop.' Not a promising name."

"We'll be fine."

The woman with the stroller left the park. The man feeding pigeons shook the last crumbs from his bag and walked away. The teens were still chatting. I had already spotted the rock with the chalk mark.

"Do you think someone has already been here to check?" Litzi asked.

"Maybe they stopped by on their way to Vladimir's."

"Don't say that."

She was right. I was giddy. A little cocky, even. Thinking that you're about to take charge of a situation can have that effect.

"Look," she said. "They're going." The teens were on the move.

"Okay," I said. "Zero hour."

I checked our flanks. A few people were still up at the far end, but in the evening gloom they wouldn't see what we were up to. I knelt by the bench and got out my gear.

"What's the wine for?"

"I've got the bottle and corkscrew. You hold the glasses. Anyone who sees us will think you're waiting for me to open it. Instead I'll be taping the webcam beneath the bench. Then we put the negatives under the rock, mark the stone, and leave."

I completed my work undisturbed. We crossed the park back toward Litzi's office.

"Now what?" she asked.

"Can we still get into your building at this hour?"

"At any hour, with my ID."

"Which side is your office on?"

"The opposite side."

"Too bad. Know anybody whose window faces the park? With a clear line of sight, it should be well within range for the camera signal."

"Lutz's office is on that side, and he never locks it."

"Perfect."

We entered the empty lobby and climbed the stairs. Everyone on her hall had gone home. Lutz had indeed left his door ajar. We settled behind his desk. I downloaded the necessary software, then clicked a few commands and watched the image come up on the laptop screen. Perfect. I switched off the image to preserve the camera battery, then turned on the motion-sensor function to activate the cam the moment anyone showed up.

"Now we wait."

"And if no one shows?"

"We go have dinner, then check the laptop in the morning. Any video will be recorded on the hard drive. We just have to make it back before Lutz does."

"No problem. He's a late riser."

"You sound like you know firsthand."

"Do you really want me to answer that?"

"No."

We waited an hour just in case, making small talk and avoiding the subject of Vladimir while I tried to assess Lutz from the stuff in his office. A photo showed him with a pair of teens, probably his kids, with no wife in sight. He was one of those ruggedly handsome Prussians with blue eyes and close-cropped hair. Probably younger than me. Far too early to feel this jealous, but there you go.

The camera switched on twice during the first half hour, triggered by passersby. It was getting almost too dark to see. After ten more minutes an image flashed onto the screen. Someone had stopped at the statue.

His back was to the camera, but he wore a dark overcoat and one of those loden alpine walking hats with the feather in the brim. The video was a little stuttery, and the lighting was terrible, but now the fellow was bending over, which meant he was probably lifting up the rock. Surely he would turn around at some point to check his flanks? But no, he only rose and continued on his way, leaving the picture without once turning his head.

"Shit!"

I scrambled down the hallway toward the back stairs, footsteps echoing in the empty building, then tripped an alarm as I shoved through a fire door at ground level. With 50 meters to go before I reached the Burggarten, and another 250 to cross the park, I peered into the gloom for any sign of movement, just in time to see someone in a long coat climbing into an idling sedan on Goethegasse, on the far side of the park. The door slammed, and the car accelerated smoothly toward the Opernring, where it turned left and disappeared.

"Shit! Shit! Shit!"

The only noise now apart from the traffic was the clanging of the alarm.

"Well, that was professionally done!"

It was Litzi, hustling up in my wake. She glanced back over her shoulder toward the National Library.

"Did you at least get a good look at him?"

"Didn't even get the make of the car, much less the tags."

"So much for your handler being too low-tech for his own good!"

"I better get the cam from the bench."

"*Scheise!*" Litzi exclaimed.

"What?"

"The laptop. We have to get it. Security will be all over the place by now."

"Should I come with you, take the blame?"

She shook her head.

"That would only make it more complicated. Fortunately I know the night supervisor. I'll think of something. Wait here."

I walked sheepishly back to the statue, untaped the cam, and stuffed it into my coat pocket, feeling like a chump. My pulse rate was finally beginning to slow down about the time the alarm shut off. I hoped Litzi wasn't in trouble, and I again questioned the wisdom of getting her involved. She approached a few minutes later, carrying the laptop. There was a puzzled look on her face.

"What's wrong?"

"Everything went fine. I made up something about hearing someone in the stairwell and trying to follow them outside. Let's just hope you don't show up on *their* cameras. But there's something new on the laptop."

"Probably me, from when I took down the camera."

"No. Before then. The prompt said *two* more videos had been saved."

We sat on a bench and I powered up. The most recent video showed my ghostly face looming right up into the camera, then the screen went blank. I clicked on the other video, which had been shot a few minutes earlier. A man moved into faint view from the right. He stopped in front of the statue and bent down by the rock with his back to the camera. Then he suddenly looked up, as if startled by a noise—probably either my running footsteps or the slamming door of the getaway car. His face came into profile. The poor lighting blurred his features, but the slouching wool hat was unmistakable, and when he stood I saw the cane in his right hand.

"I don't believe it. Lothar Heinemann."

He turned and went back in the direction he'd come from, vanishing from the screen.

The video stopped.

"You said he's a book scout?"

"That's what Dad called him. But from the look of things he knows more about my handler's movements than I do."

"This hunt is getting crowded. Maybe we should all meet for drinks at Gasthaus Brinkmann."

"Yes," I said, wondering if everyone was after the same thing.

"This only makes you want to find out more, doesn't it?"

I nodded. And it wasn't just the thrill of the chase, or even the frisson of danger. Danger is overrated, and I could do without it completely. The deeper appeal, I think, was that I felt as if I had fallen through a trapdoor and landed four decades in the past, and was now moving among the very figures that had once populated my Cold War dreams. Manning Coles was right. Spying was addictive.

Then I looked at Litzi, and sensed without saying a word that she was reading my every emotion. She shook her head.

"I'd like that drink now," she said.

16

Neither of us had the energy or inclination to deal with a maître d', a waiter, or even a menu, nor were we thrilled by the idea of sitting among strangers in a crowded restaurant, exposed and vulnerable.

"Why don't I make us an omelet?" Litzi said. "We've got wine, thanks to you."

"I thought you needed something stronger?"

"Wine's enough as long as we're under my roof, with all the doors locked."

I didn't have the heart to tell her how useless a lock was with this crowd, but I did see the value of being somewhere without a camera watching our every move. And that thought in turn gave me a new idea.

"Lead the way," I said. "But I need to make a detour."

"Nothing to do with 'the best defense is a good offense,' I hope."

"Shouldn't we use this webcam for *something*? It will only take a second."

She shook her head but didn't resist until a few blocks later, when she realized we were heading for the Gasthaus Brinkmann.

"The old KGB man? *He's* the one you want to spy on?"

"I need to see what he looks like, so we'll be able to spot him if he's following us."

"Oh, smart idea. Baiting the bear on his doorstep."

"Not his doorstep. The inn's. I'll mount the cam outside the gasthaus, then check the videos in the morning."

"Where will you put the laptop?"

I pointed up the block.

"There's a hotel across the street. I'll rent a room with a clear line of sight. Then I'll come by in the morning to see what turned up."

She again shook her head, but kept going. It was a quiet street, and there was a trash bin next to a sign for a bus stop only a few feet from the gasthaus entrance, which provided a perfect vantage point. I taped the camera into place within seconds without anyone observing us, and there was a front room available on the third floor of the hotel across the street, which I paid for with the Ealing Wharton Amex. Thanks, Marty.

"What happens when the trash man collects the webcam, or the chambermaid takes the laptop?"

"Maybe I'll beat them back here. Either way, nothing ventured, nothing gained. C'mon, I'm hungry."

Litzi's apartment looked pretty much how I'd imagined it. Tasteful, comfortable furniture with clean lines and vibrant colors. And books, of course. Loads of them—on shelves, in cabinets, stacked on end tables. The walls were hung with photos rather than paintings—not iconic scenes of Vienna, but out-of-the-way places I couldn't easily identify. In one, a much-younger Litzi posed among friends at a political demonstration.

"Where was this demo?" I asked, while she whisked eggs in a glass bowl. "Do I know any of these people?"

"Oh, that old thing." She looked back toward the skillet. "Just some election rally."

Maybe her former husband was in it, because she was quiet for the next few minutes. It made me a little gloomy for us. We'd come through the years psychologically intact, yet we were still fending for ourselves. It made me think of my father, another sole survivor.

"I'd better text Dad, tell him I'll be late."

Pulling out my phone, I paused and watched the movement of Litzi's hips as she swirled the eggs in the pan.

"How late will I be, do you think?"

She picked up right away on the significance of the question, and looked at me over her shoulder. Her eyes were no longer weary. The pan remained still above the flame, and she smiled, the same way she had when the innkeeper in Prague had first handed us our keys.

"The omelet's burning." I nodded toward the pan.

"Yes. Everything is."

I crossed the room and wrapped her up from behind. She slid the pan to the cool side of the stove and arched her back against me as I pulled back her hair to kiss her neck. I moved my lips to the skin beneath her ear, the nape of her neck. When she spoke her voice was husky.

"Tell him you'll be home for breakfast. I'm too lazy to cook for you twice."

She turned into my arms. Then she unbuttoned my shirt and pressed her lips to my chest.

"Those eggs will be cold by the time we eat," I said.

"Cold and burned. My new favorite way to eat an omelet."

We made our way to the bedroom, discarding items of clothing along the way, as if leaving a trail to find our way back. We finished undressing each other slowly, comfortably, eager but not in a hurry.

When you are single at a later age and are sometimes sexually inactive for long stretches of time, each reentry to the arena isn't always smooth, particularly when the women are several years younger. In my recent past there have been occasions when I've felt fumbling and unsure, like when I'm assembling one of those bookcases from IKEA, with their strange little parts that roll across the floor and the baffling instructions telling me to press male dowel A into female opening B, then twist until snug.

With Litzi, there was immediate comfort and familiarity, even though our bodies obviously weren't the same as they'd been at seventeen. We navigated our new topographies with confidence, with passion, and with the joy of our former selves. I remembered the taste of her skin.

Afterward she lit a candle and fetched the wine, along with the cold omelet, which was glorious, even the burned part. I was enchanted, content.

"So, which one of your book spies was the best lover?" she asked.

"Not counting James Bond?"

"He wasn't a lover, he was a cad."

"You sound like Dad. Oh, I don't know. Bernie Samson, maybe, from Deighton's books? He was pretty virile, or at least his wife thought so."

"His wife? So he was monogamous, too? Sounds too good to be true. Maybe Bernie could be your code name."

"Maybe not. His wife was working for the Russians. Although not really. It was very complicated."

She frowned, not caring for that, so I tried another one.

"There's Paul Christopher, from McCarry's books. Also monogamous. A poet, even. Top-notch lover."

"And what happened to his wife?"

"Run over in the streets of Paris by the KGB."

"Let's talk about something else."

"All right."

"How's your father?"

"Good question. I've upset him with all this snooping around. I have no idea how I'll explain what happened today, or if I'll even try. He's worried enough already, and he's pissed I've dragged you into it. I think he went to the embassy this morning to do some checking around of his own."

"I see him out on the town now and then. Always in very nice places. He's a man of genuine style. I've thought about going over to say hello, but I didn't want to embarrass him."

"You should definitely say hi. He's always liked you. And I wouldn't worry about embarrassing him. He's probably just out with one of his mystery women, the ones he never dared bring back to the house when I was growing up. I guess he thought I'd think he was being disloyal to Mom."

She shrugged.

"I wouldn't know. It never seems to be any one person."

"He's shy about all that, even now. It's probably why I always have to give him a few days' notice before a visit, although I doubt he'd admit it."

Litzi nodded, but didn't reply.

"What?"

"Nothing."

"You looked like you were about to say something."

She smiled uncomfortably.

"I know better than to get into the middle of something between a father and his son."

I let it go. We had more enjoyable things to do than discuss Dad.

We must've stayed up for another hour or so, and I woke up later nestled against Litzi's back. The room was dark and still. I was immediately alert, but this time jet lag wasn't to blame. I'd been startled by a noise from outside, a loud tapping from the street below. Now all was quiet.

Then there was a voice. A shout, or more of a hoot, followed by a peal of laughter. Young voices, not Lothar's or the Hammerhead's, so I relaxed. Just kids. Although, at my age, "kids" now seems to cover almost anyone up through their early twenties. Because how could any contemporary of my son's be anything but a kid?

There was another hoot, more laughter. They'd obviously been drinking, but they sounded harmless, and were soon well down the block. Yet something about them had unsettled me. What?

I realized they'd reminded me of the kids outside Burger King, the ones on skateboards who'd supposedly put the envelope into Litzi's purse as they bumped past us. I saw them again, a mental snapshot that now had the clarity that is only possible at such an isolated hour. And in my mind's eye I now saw clearly that they hadn't passed within five feet of us.

Then why had Litzi said they'd bumped into her? Was my memory faulty, or had she made it up? And if the latter was true, why? Unless she had been knowingly hired by my handler and had been in on this from the beginning. If that were true, she could've had the note with her all along, another item on her checklist of duties for the day.

I tossed in bed, angry at my doubt. It was that time of night when your thoughts can stray into all sorts of troublesome corners, and I wanted nothing further to do with it. But at least an hour passed before I could get back to sleep. In the morning I wondered whether to say something about it, but Litzi beat me to the punch.

"I've been thinking about those boys," she said. "The ones outside the Burger King."

"What about them?"

"Maybe that's not how the envelope got there. I'm not even sure they bumped into me. It might have happened sooner, or maybe later. I don't know what to think."

I was hugely relieved, although of course I couldn't say so.

"I wouldn't worry too much about it. Obviously someone found a way."

"Do you want coffee?"

"I'd better get to my father's before he leaves the house. And I want to check the laptop on the way."

"Oh, yes, I almost forgot. Back on the offensive!"

I laughed along with her. In the full light of morning the idea of catching the Hammerhead on video now seemed preposterous.

"What will you tell your father?"

"I don't know. As little as possible. The sooner I leave for Prague, the better."

"Should I start packing?"

"You're sure?"

"Only if you want me to. We said we'd sleep on it, and I slept on it very well. What about you?"

She caressed my cheek. I was happy she was coming, but the doubts of the night before hadn't completely dissipated.

"What's wrong?"

"Nothing. You really sure you want to do this?"

"Only if you are."

"Of course."

I said it brightly, but she tilted her head to scrutinize me for a moment, then leaned over to kiss me.

"It's all right if you change your mind, you know."

"No. Start packing. I'll check the train schedule and call from my dad's. We'll do it right this time. No men in brown coats."

And with that her face fleetingly darkened, a cloud that passed and was gone.

Out in the streets it was a gorgeous morning, leaves fluttering from the maples against a brilliant blue. Paperboys filled their news racks, and bakeries perfumed the air with the smell of warm bread and brewing coffee. Street sweepers tidied the last corners for the crowds yet to come, and the more ambitious café proprietors were already rolling down their awnings. My suspicions felt foolish. Maybe all of that "trust no one" gospel was getting to me, along with the residue of cynicism from my years at Ealing Wharton.

The thunderhead on this sunny horizon, of course, was Vladimir. The thought of his bleeding body on the gurney made me check again over my shoulder before I entered the hotel across from Gasthaus Brinkmann.

Seventeen video clips awaited me on the laptop. I was a little surprised there weren't more, given how many people were already out in the streets. In the first sixteen, men and women of all shapes and sizes flashed by, none matching Gelev's description of the Hammerhead.

As soon as the last one began with a large man emerging from the gasthaus doorway, I knew it was him. The iron jaw, the large head, the meat-red slab of a face, the windswept pompadour of thick gray hair. Gelev hadn't prepared me for his eyes. Brown, yes, but with an almost alarming intensity, probing and alert. When his gaze locked onto the webcam, I involuntarily flinched. He stopped and stared, tilting his head. Then he smiled sloppily, mouth agape, and he nodded slightly as if saying hello. He stepped forward, filling the screen, and reached toward me with a massive hand, its image distorted by its closeness to the lens just before the screen went dark. It was easy enough to imagine the rest, right up to the point when the camera's fragile orb must have collapsed in his powerful fist like an eyeball beneath a sledgehammer.

I checked the time signature on the video. Fifty minutes ago. If he'd been on his way to breakfast or a rendezvous, then he might be on his way back even now. I closed the laptop, a fluttery feeling in my chest like the one I used to get before big races against tough opponents.

Then I shook myself into action, briskly walking downstairs to drop the key at the front desk. I turned the knob on the front door before thinking better of it and heading for the back. I exited into an alley that took me to the end of the block, where I turned in the opposite direction from the Gasthaus Brinkmann, glancing over my shoulder every few feet all the way to Dad's.

Gelev was right. The Hammerhead didn't look like the sort of fellow you'd want to cross, and I told myself several times that he was almost certainly here on some other business than me.

Try as I might, I remained unconvinced.

17

When I opened the door of the apartment, relieved to be back on safer ground, Dad was standing over the stove making breakfast for two.

"Figured you were due to roll in soon. Hope you're hungry. Bacon's coming right up." He flinched from a spatter of grease, then laughed. "I always eat like an American when you're here."

"You don't have to, you know. I usually get by on yogurt and granola these days."

"I know. But something about having you back always brings it out in me. Maybe I'm homesick."

"You still get homesick for the States?"

"Almost any American does when he's been abroad long enough."

"I never did."

"Well, you never knew any other life. You'd feel it now, I bet, if you stayed away long enough."

It was an interesting thought. If you were to ask me where home was, I'd say Georgetown, not because I'd been living in Washington for years, but because that's where David was. Would it still feel like home if he moved away?

Seeing Dad at the stove took me back to so many mornings from our past. Throughout our gypsy tour of Europe, this was the one view that had never changed. Some families make it a point to always gather for dinner. Our time was breakfast. Toast, eggs, bacon, and coffee. The ritual reading of the daily papers, with Dad's running commentary and my persistent questions. Before we set out there was always a checklist for school—books? homework? lunch? Then he would see me to the schoolhouse door, even after I was old enough to get there on my own. Whether we walked, rode a tram, or, on rare occasions, took an embassy car, it gave us a chance to talk awhile longer. Nannies and sitters didn't enter the picture until the afternoon, and they were movable furniture, Dad the only constant.

So as I watched him now, spatula in motion—a far defter cook than Litzi, I thought with amusement—I experienced an overwhelming sense of landing at a safe harbor in a storm. Yet I couldn't avoid a feeling of mild regret as I noted his pronounced stoop, the age spots on his hands, the wispy hair. At seventy-eight, he is fragile, fading, and I know his few remaining years will fly by. I should spend more time here, and more time with David. The three of us should spend a week together sometime soon.

I carried the steaming platters of food to the table while he poured coffee. The paper was already folded next to the napkins. We tucked in.

"So I take it you've come from Litzi's?"

"We spent the day together. Very pleasant. We've decided to go to Prague for a few days."

"Prague. Interesting choice." He paused. "Have you enlisted her in your . . . investigation, for lack of a better word?"

"My research? She thinks it's fascinating. She has a few useful contacts."

"I'd be careful of those."

"Dad, she's an archivist at the National Library."

He shook his head but didn't reply. Then he opened his newspaper, his customary way of signaling for silence. It wasn't rudeness, it was our old routine.

"Goodness, the economy . . . Hmm . . . Looks like the U.S. midterms are going to be a disaster."

"More business for Marty Ealing, no matter what."

He peeped over the page.

"You sound like you're getting tired of him."

"I've been tired of him since day one. It's my tolerance that's running out."

He nodded, seemingly pleased, and turned the page.

"*Well*, now." Something had caught his eye. The pages shuffled as he pulled the story closer. After a few seconds, he lowered the paper and stared into space, concentrating. I bit into a slice of bacon.

"Tell me something. In this *research* of yours, has the name of a Boris Trefimov come up?"

"No."

He glanced back at the paper.

"Living on . . . Köllnerhofgasse?"

I swallowed. The bacon went down like a shard of tree bark.

"Why do you ask?"

"Well, there's this funny coincidence. Not ha-ha funny, but strange. I was at the embassy yesterday for a few odds and ends. Nothing important."

"No, of course not."

He noted my skepticism but didn't rise to the bait.

"Anyway, I was talking to Lewis Dean."

"And what does Lewis Dean do?"

"Oh, he's some sort of regional specialist." Whatever that meant. I made a mental note to look up Lewis Dean later in Dad's embassy directory. "While we were chatting, someone handed him a general information release that had just come in, a printout of an email alerting all hands to the presence in Vienna of this Boris Trefimov fellow, who apparently was wrapped up in some sort of smuggling ring that our people from Justice had an interest in. It gave his address and everything."

"Is that unusual?"

"Lew seemed to think so." Lew now, not Lewis. "Said it was almost like someone upstairs was letting it be known that Trefimov was there for the taking, because this sort of cable traffic—excuse me, this sort of *email* traffic, old habits die hard—always leaks like a sieve. He said it was as if someone had declared open season on the fellow. And sure enough . . ."

He showed me the story. Trefimov had been murdered at his apartment on Köllnerhofgasse. Beneath the headline was a mug shot of a younger, cleaner Vladimir.

"Someone killed him?" I asked, trying to inject a note of innocence. My mouth was dry, so I sipped coffee. Dad watched closely.

"You forgot to put milk in."

"So I did." I knew my cheeks were reddening as I reached for the milk.

"Not just killed him. Shot him in the face. The way the KGB used to do it."

"In *Smiley's People*, anyway." I couldn't resist.

"Yes. Poor old Vladimir Miller."

"Who sent the email?"

"Lew's people in Washington."

I wondered what to say next. I was wondering a lot of things, such as who "Lew's people" were, and which of them had released the information. Did Lew's people also know what Litzi and I were up to? Or the Hammerhead? Had one of them made the pickup at the dead drop? And was Dad privy to more than he was saying? Was he in fact baiting me? He seemed to have zeroed in on the story pretty quickly. Maybe he'd seen it before I arrived, and had been planning to spring it on me from the moment the bacon hit the skillet.

God, but I was getting paranoid. Mistrusting Litzi, now my dad. Maybe David would be next. Except I'd already done that, however fleetingly, when I'd wondered at Martin's if he had helped someone break into my town house.

"What else does the story say?"

"That Trefimov was believed to be a former KGB agent, stationed in Prague. Doesn't say when."

Early seventies, I could have told him. Code name Leo, most likely, reporting to someone named Oleg. Had to be. And I now wondered what the relationship had been between Oleg and the Hammerhead, or if they might even be one and the same, since "the Hammerhead" was just an émigré nickname. I nodded but said nothing.

"Lately he's been associated with organized crime. Human trafficking, drugs, and—now, this is interesting—peddling old KGB secrets, it says. Probably his own, don't you think?"

"Probably." My palms prickled with sweat.

"Here's something else. 'Police are seeking the whereabouts of a man and woman who may have visited the victim a few hours before the murder. A spokesman described their appearance as white, slender, middle-aged, modestly dressed, and of average height.'"

"That could be just about anybody."

"Not really."

My cell phone rang. I was so startled that I banged the table with a knee. I answered while Vladimir's photo stared at me upside-down from across the table.

"Yes?"

"Dad?"

"David! Good to hear from you. Isn't it kind of early over there?"

"Late, you mean? It's almost two in the morning."

"Is everything all right?"

"Actually, no. I'm at your place. And, well, I think someone's broken in. But I'm not positive, so I've spent an hour looking for other stuff that might be missing, and wondering if I should call the cops."

"Other stuff? What's missing? What makes you think somebody's been there?"

"Well, I know this'll sound, like, weird, but . . ."

"Just say it, son."

"Books. Three whole shelves, it looks like. Unless you took them with you, or boxed them up somewhere."

"No. I didn't. Which ones?"

"The ones I came looking for. Your spy novels. I was going to borrow Lemaster's *A Spy for All Seasons*, but they're all gone."

"Were the doors locked?"

"Every single one. Windows, too. And I don't think they took anything else. I've checked pretty carefully."

"Is there . . . Is there any kind of message for me?"

"On the answering machine?"

"No. This would be written. On the floor with the mail, maybe."

"Hang on."

He put down the phone. I listened to his footsteps. Dad, following the gist of the conversation, looked concerned, brow creased. His spotty hands rested on the table as if he was poised to leap into action. David came back on the line.

"No. Nothing. There was one thing earlier, but I'm not even sure it's worth mentioning."

"Tell me anyway."

"One of the books, a Lemaster, was open facedown on the couch. I assumed they missed it because you left it there."

"Which one? Open to what page?"

There was a brief pause as he stepped to the couch.

"*A Lesson in Tradecraft*. Page one-nineteen. Did you mark it up like this?"

"You know me. I don't mark them, and I don't bend the pages."

"It says 'Find his work' at the top of the page. Below, they've drawn lines around a paragraph."

"Black ink? Block letters?"

"How'd you know?"

"Read me the paragraph."

"Now? It's kind of long."

"Yes. Slowly, please."

"Okay. Here goes:

"Folly looked across the tearoom and recognized his old agent right away. Heinz Klarmann was a wiry man who, to judge from his bloodshot eyes, might have just emerged from some all-night competition—seven-card stud, boozing, computing prime numbers on an abacus; any and all of them seemed plausible. A tired brown hat slouched on his head like a deflated balloon, lending him the air of a failed artist. He looked more Bohemian than German, although the moment he opened his mouth it was plain to everyone that Klarmann was Berlin to the core. An elaborately carved cane which he tapped as frenetically as an SOS from a sinking ship helped disguise a slight limp of unknown provenance. Barroom scuffle? Child-hood illness? Drunken fall? No one knew, and Klarmann wasn't saying. All that Folly cared about was that once you gave him an assignment you could consider it done, no matter how many shots of Schnapps or doses of dubious pharmaceuticals Klarmann consumed along the way. The man was a mercenary at heart, and would always finish the job, a professional to the core. This is why Folly was forever worried that someday, somehow, some other service would steal him away.

"And that's it."

"You're sure there's nothing else? Flip the pages."

I heard a shuffling sound.

"Doesn't look like it. No, nothing. 'Find his work.' What does it mean?"

"I don't know."

"Does this have anything to do with that assignment you're on?"

"Possibly. Which is why I wouldn't advise you to stick around there any longer than you have to."

"Awesome. Should I call the police?"

"No. Just lock up when you go, not that it will do any good. Who else knew you were going there?"

"Nobody. Spur of the moment. I was up late studying for midterms and wanted something to read once I'm done. Unless . . ."

"What?"

"Maybe somebody overheard us at Martin's. When you told me to come by anytime."

"Doubtful. You should get some sleep if you've got a midterm. Don't worry about the house. Probably somebody's idea of a joke. It might even be somebody from my office. If they'd wanted to do real damage, they would've done it."

"Are you okay?"

"I'm fine. Doing well, in fact." I wondered how he'd react if he knew about Litzi, but this wasn't the time for that. "Your granddad's here. We're having breakfast. Want to talk to him?"

"Sure."

"But then get out of there and get back to your dorm, understand?"

"Yes."

"I mean it."

"I *know*!"

I handed over the phone, still a little worried for him, although it was a pleasure watching Dad light up as he asked about David's lacrosse and all his courses. Even as I fretted the passing seconds, checking my watch and motioning to Dad to move things along, I was already wondering why Edwin Lemaster had created a character that, except for the limp, was a dead ringer for Lothar Heinemann. Obviously it had been too long since I'd read *A Lesson in Tradecraft* or I would have remembered the Klarmann character the moment I laid eyes on Lothar. But now that I had the message, what sort of "work" of Lothar's was I supposed to go out and find?

Dad finally hung up and slid my phone back across the table. Then he watched me carefully.

"You going to tell me what that was all about?"

"I need a book first."

"Not another destroyed one, I hope?"

I went to the living room and brought back his copy of *A Lesson in Tradecraft*. Then I told him about the break-in and the message, and finished by reading aloud the passage from page 119.

"Lothar," he said. "He's turning up everywhere, isn't he?"

"I think he's following me."

"I wish I could say I was surprised. Surveillance is an old hobby of his. Although he used to reserve it for his competition. Whenever someone was getting items he wasn't, he'd follow them for days at a time to find out how they were pulling it off. Strange fellow."

"You always said Lemaster never wrote about real characters, that they were just novels."

"That's because you were usually asking about someone at the embassy."

I waited for more. Got nothing.

"This person who stole your books," Dad said. "If he's the one who ruined my copy of *Knee Knockers*, then he's been covering a lot of ground. He got you started on this mess, and now you're letting him use you to get whatever he wants."

"Maybe all he wants is the truth."

"We've both been around long enough to know that's bullshit."

He was right, of course. In Washington, "I only want the truth" has become the biggest lie since "Your check's in the mail."

"Okay. So maybe he has an ax to grind with Lemaster."

"Then it had better be a big one."

"What do you mean?"

"Look at who Ed's biggest fans and defenders are these days, or haven't you noticed? Pentagon brass, defense contractors. All those people he makes look like patriotic geniuses. I doubt they'd be happy if someone started implying they were spilling their best stuff to a proven traitor in the name of novelistic research. And you could say the same about everybody he ever worked for at the Agency. What else do you know about this fellow who's leading you on like this?"

"Pretty much nothing."

"What other passages has he marked up for you?"

"It's a long story."

"I have all morning."

"First you can tell me what you were really doing yesterday at the embassy."

"No, first we can go back to what we were talking about before the phone rang. The Vienna police, and their description of that slender couple, modestly dressed."

"Like I said, could be anybody."

"Look, son. I don't need to know everything you're up to. Maybe you think it's for my own good as much as yours. If anyone can understand that rationale, I certainly can. But from what I'm hearing, people are rather stirred up in certain quarters, and I'm concerned that you're the one who's stirring them up."

"Which quarters?"

"You can probably guess."

I sighed, feeling cornered. Then I decided to take the plunge. I would tell him everything, from the very beginning. At the rate he was going he'd know half of it by tomorrow night anyway. Maybe he would even be able to help.

I swallowed some coffee, collected myself, and began.

18

I went on for nearly an hour.

Dad frowned early and often, especially when I confirmed his sus-picions about our involvement with Trefimov, although he seemed even more upset by my account of the Hammerhead's discovery of my webcam.

"I can ask around about him at the embassy, if you'd like. Quietly, of course."

"Sure. Whatever you can find out."

"At least now I see why everyone's in such a tizzy."

"But why? This stuff was ages ago."

"It's like plutonium, son. One hell of a half-life, and lethal to the end."

"So who do you think's behind this?" I asked.

"Your handler? The obvious conclusion would be an old Agency hand, somebody with a grudge against Ed. Maybe even somebody from that damn funeral."

"Why not somebody from the book world? They know these novels inside out, and hasn't Lemaster changed publishers a few times?"

"At least twice, and never amicably. But, no, this is a spook."

"A spook turned author, then. Just like him."

"With what motive—professional jealousy? Even Ed would admit he's on the skids; why kick him now? If there's a wild card in all this, it's his personal life."

"Ex-wife?"

"Three. Complete unknowns. And God knows how many cuckolded husbands. That's his truly mysterious side. The inner Ed—his lovers, his enemies. No one I've come across has ever known a damn thing about any of that, so take your pick."

"Maybe Lothar knows. What do you think this message about him means when it says, 'Find his work'?"

"Well, Lothar's a book scout. His work is whatever he comes up with. First editions, diamonds in the rough. I suppose he could have found something your handler wants."

"You said he used to follow people. Who?"

Dad shook his head.

"I'm not even sure those stories are true. They might just be part of his legend. Lothar used to shoot enough smack to stay awake for five days running, and supposedly if he thought a competitor had a hot lead he'd pursue the fellow halfway across the continent. Then he'd crash and burn, and disappear for weeks."

"Could he have found something besides a book?"

"These antiquarian shops carry all kinds of stuff, especially the ones that were behind the Iron Curtain. Unless . . ."

"What?"

Dad bit his lip and looked down at the table.

"For a while, maybe twenty, thirty years ago, there was talk that Lothar was writing something. A spy novel, which was a nice irony. When I first hired him, he had no use for genre fiction. Thought it was all Bond and booze, a bunch of lightweights. Then he read a few of the good ones and something clicked. Fine by me, because it made him a better hunter. By the time he'd moved beyond my price range, he was keeping some of the better finds for himself. The word among collectors was that he had started writing his own magnum opus. Well, that certainly raised a few eyebrows. Remember, this was a fellow who knew Agency people firsthand. They'd hired him for his absolute discretion and his zeal for results—he was a lot like them, in those ways—but the idea that he might have started scribbling down some of his memories, even in fictional form, well, supposedly it spooked them."

"They asked him to stop?"

"I don't know. This was all second- and thirdhand. But he never published. For all I know there was never even a manuscript."

"Then what would 'his work' be, some kind of outline?"

"Or the whole thing could be a legend. You know how it goes with characters like Lothar. You tell a story about him and ten years later it's repeated back to you, twice as good as before. I will say this. If he *is* following you, then I'm worried for him. I'd heard he gave up that kind of thing once he got clean. I hope he's not back on the needle."

"Are you going to tell me who 'Dewey' really was?"

"Like I said, a code name. Never met him and never knew his true identity, much less his mission. If I was ever caught while making a delivery, I was supposed to say I was passing along a gift for a friend of the bookseller."

"Who gave you the cover story?"

"The same person who asked me to make the delivery. Ed Lemaster."

"Why?"

"Why me? Or why did I do it?"

"Both."

"You'd have to ask him the first question. As for the second, he wasn't just a friend. He was an employee of the United States government, and so was I. So when he requested that I become involved in what seemed to be a very minor role, I agreed without hesitation. It was my duty." He paused, staring off into space. "And frankly . . ."

"What?"

He smiled.

"I enjoyed it. It was pretty obvious it was part of some spy transaction, and considering everything I was reading at the time—he knew my tastes, of course—I was the perfect choice. Does that surprise you?"

"Not at all. Look at me."

"Except you're hunting Ed, not helping him."

"If that's what this is really about."

"I'd still strongly advise you to get out of this while you can, but I can't run your life, and if you're determined to stay in, then I'll do what I can to help."

"Thanks."

He nodded, but he wasn't pleased. I stood up from the table.

"And thanks for breakfast. For everything. I should pack. I'm moving on this afternoon."

"The sooner the better." He held up the photo of Trefimov. "It's probably a good idea for you to leave Vienna for a while."

"I'm planning to stop by Antikvariát Drebitko," I said. "One of their bookmarks was inside the parcel I picked up at Kurzmann's."

"Ask for Václav Bruzek, if he's still alive. That's who I always dealt with. And if you happen to wind up in Budapest, try Antikvárium Szondi."

"Budapest?"

"Just a hunch. Some of my Dewey errands took me there as well."

"How many years did you do them?"

"Six or seven. It ended when we moved to Berlin."

"Why then?"

"Well, Ed got out of the business not long after that. That was the main reason. But I was a little surprised he never had me do anything in Berlin before he quit. I always wondered if it might have had something to do with you."

"*Me?* How so?"

"You said Litzi's going with you to Prague?"

"Yes, but what does that have to do with—?"

"Be careful. I'd hate to see her dragged into all that sort of nastiness again."

"It's the EU, Dad. I doubt they're detaining people at the border anymore."

"I was thinking more about the aftermath. I'm sure it must have been difficult for her family or she never would've spied on me."

"*What?*"

The room seemed to tilt and blur, like when a lens comes loose in a camera.

"She spied on you?"

"Only once. Quite harmless, although I'm a little surprised she still hasn't told you. Maybe she never realized I'd figured it out."

"And this happened after our trip?"

"Right before you and I moved to Berlin."

"What did she do?"

I sat back down, legs wobbly. Packing could wait. Maybe the whole trip could wait.

"Oh, rummaged around a few of my things. Met a contact once or twice, probably to report what she'd found, which couldn't have been much because there was nothing to find. That was as far as it went, really. Like I said. Harmless."

"But why?"

"Her father was Czech. Strauss wasn't his real name, you know."

"That much she told me."

"I gather they must have threatened her in some way. It wasn't like they could have done much, but she wouldn't have known that, poor girl. The repatriations and kidnappings had ended by then, but that brand of insecurity dies hard, especially if you've ever been hauled in for interrogation. And they had other ways of getting back at émigrés. Planting embarrassing stories in the press, making it hard for them to travel. They must have ordered her to do them a favor before you and I moved away."

"How do you know?"

"She wasn't exactly a pro, and there were clear signs she'd been poking around. I've sometimes wondered if she *wanted* me to find out. So I reported it. Had to, I'm afraid. The fellow at the embassy who followed it up told me the rest. His people never took it seriously."

I didn't need to ask who "his people" were.

"Why didn't you tell me?"

Dad placed his hands on the table, fingers interlocked—the "wise counselor" pose that he had always employed when I'd done something foolish like blowing off an algebra exam, or failing to stand up for a friend.

"You were young and in love, and we were moving soon. And you never liked it when I intruded on that side of your life, which I quite understood. Everyone needs his privacy."

With the uttering of those words, the spirit of my mother was conjured into the space between us. I was sure Dad sensed it as well. But we let the moment pass, as always.

"Does this mean her name is still in some embassy file, or even at the Agency?"

"Oh, I don't know." He was uncomfortable now. "Maybe as a footnote."

It made me sorry for Litzi, but also for myself, unflattering as that sounds. This was the woman I had entrusted with everything, yet she hadn't leveled with me. And if she was willing to withhold that secret—well, you get the idea.

I stood to pack, although in some ways the trip was already ruined. Right or wrong, I could no longer trust Litzi.

"Don't take it so hard, son. Those were very different times, especially for families like hers."

"I'll try to keep that in mind."

19

Litzi stood at the far end of the train platform, striking a cinematic pose in an overcoat and a wide-brimmed hat, a suitcase at her feet. Her face lit up when she saw me coming, a lover's glow. Mine had flickered out at breakfast.

I greeted her with a dry peck on the cheek. Nothing felt right or comfortable, and she sensed it immediately.

"What's wrong? Has something happened?"

"Just a hectic morning. Took longer to pack than I thought, a few other things."

The words rang false and she eyed my small suitcase. Thankfully she didn't press the point. Our seats were reserved, and we had a compartment to ourselves. The first thing I wanted was a drink, but the cart wouldn't be coming by until we were under way. I'd been wondering for the past hour how to bring up the subject of her duplicity, and I was still pondering the question when I realized she was chattering away about something from the past. I only caught the end of it.

". . . that old wine bar just off the square, what do you think?"

"I'm sorry. I zoned out for a minute."

"I was just wondering if that old wine bar was still there that we went to before, the one right off the Old Town square."

I remembered it, a cozy little wine restaurant in a cellar with vaulted stone ceilings. At the time I'd been convinced it was the very spot where Sarah Gainham had set a key scene in her 1959 Prague novel, *The Stone Roses*. In the book, one of the waiters turned out to be not only a murderous Soviet spy, but also a woman.

"You spent the whole meal looking for cross-dressing waiters, as I recall."

I couldn't help but smile, which unfortunately made Litzi conclude I was back to my old self. The sooner I confronted her, the better. Maybe there would even be enough time for one or both of us to leave the train before it departed, if necessary.

"Look, Litzi, there's something—"

"What's happening?" she said.

She was gazing out the window, back toward the terminal. I turned and saw a column of policemen at a trot along the platform, six in all. Whistles blew. A porter hustled by our compartment, keys jangling. Litzi gripped my hand. It was an eerie replay of Bad Schandau, and once again the authorities seemed to be heading straight for us.

Footsteps thundered in the corridor. A policeman stopped at our compartment.

"Litzi Strauss and William Cage?"

"Yes?" I answered.

"Your passports, please."

A second policeman joined him, resting a hand on a holstered gun.

"It's them," the first one said. "You will both come with me, please."

This time I didn't have to ask what it was all about, but I did anyway for the sake of appearances. The answer was almost the same as it had been thirty-seven years earlier.

"No questions. Just come."

The big difference this time was the reaction of the passengers. In East Germany almost everyone had averted their faces, lest they be summoned next. Today's audience was raptly attentive. A small boy waved from a window until his mother yanked back his hand. An older man squinted at us above his reading glasses, then shook his head in disapproval. And in the last passenger car, at the second window from the rear, Lothar Heinemann sat watching me, eyes alight. As I was moving out of sight, he nodded slightly, as if to say, "See you in Prague—if you ever make it."

Then the train hissed and groaned and, with a massive lurch, began sliding away toward Prague without us. Litzi reached for me, but a policeman slapped away her hand.

"Two cars," one said. "They are to be interrogated separately."

Just like old times.

They sent a tag team to question me, two cops in civilian clothes in a room with all the expected trimmings—hard chair, bare table, harsh lighting, and a two-way mirror.

One cop was blond and short, a little pudgy, with the ruddiness of someone who spent a lot of time outdoors. He would have fit right in as a wurst vendor at the Hoher Markt. Heightening the effect was a mustard stain near the bottom of his tie.

The other one, who seemed to be in charge, was taller with brown hair and a downturned mouth, a sleepy cast to his eyes. He took his time getting started, sifting through a file folder as if it contained the world's most interesting material, while the shorter cop slouched in a chair with his hands behind his head. Other than the sound of pages turning, there was only the hum of the tube lighting. Two other plainclothesmen, one of them female, had taken Litzi to a room down the hall.

Finally the taller cop stood.

"Tell us what you were doing yesterday at number 11 Köllnerhofgasse at approximately four p.m."

"Visiting someone for an interview. I'm a freelance journalist doing a story for *Vanity Fair*."

I referred them to the letter of introduction, which they'd already found while searching my bag. They weren't impressed.

"Who were you visiting? Name and apartment number, please."

"I don't remember the number, but it was the fourth floor. The door was to the right as you came up the landing. The name was Vladimir Miller."

"Miller? No one by that name resides in that building."

"It was the name on the mailbox."

He looked at his partner. I couldn't tell what passed between them, but then the shorter one stood and produced a photo. It was the same one that had run in the newspaper.

"Is this the man you knew as Vladimir Miller?"

"Yes."

"So you did see him?"

"Yes."

He seemed surprised I'd admitted it so easily. The taller one spoke again.

"What was the purpose of your visit?"

"I told you. It was for a magazine story."

"Yes, but let's talk about the real reason. What kind of information were you there to collect?"

Now I had a problem. My answer had to be generic enough to match whatever Litzi said, but I certainly wasn't going to tell them everything and make this a bigger deal than it already was. For all I knew they might even charge me with espionage. But I didn't know how much Litzi would say. She would be living in Vienna long after I'd moved on (provided I was allowed to), and spilling my secrets might be the easiest way out for her. My only hope was to keep my answers as vague as possible for as long as possible.

"I had no idea what he was going to tell me. He invited us. Or invited me, anyway. Litzi was just along for the ride."

"He was a friend of yours?"

"I'd never even heard of him before yesterday."

"Of course. I'm sure you make a practice of dropping in on strangers."

"I told you, I'm a journalist, and he contacted me. I responded."

"Why did he contact you?"

"He didn't say why. He just indicated he had information for me, so he invited me over."

"For this so-called story of yours."

"Yes."

The pudgy cop spoke up.

"Invited you how? Personally? By telephone. By email? Be specific."

"He sent a message. A note. He said his name was Vladimir and that he wanted to speak with me."

"So this man who you don't know and have never seen before sends you a written invitation to come and see him, and just like that you oblige him?"

"That's how it works when you're a reporter."

They looked at each other. I got the idea they hadn't counted on these kinds of answers, and they were recalibrating on the fly.

"In addition to your duties as a reporter, and also as a Washington PR man for various wealthy interests—and we'll get to some of those in a moment—are you also in the same line of business as this man Vladimir, as you call him?"

"That's what he called himself to me. I didn't come up with the name."

"But you trade in the same commodities?"

"I don't know what he trades in."

"What was the topic of your discussion? Running arms to Afghanistan, or prostitutes to the Balkans?"

"Neither. We didn't discuss his business."

The shorter one snorted.

"This Vladimir, as you call him, was expecting a large wire transfer to arrive in his account very soon from the United States. I suppose you didn't discuss this with him, either?"

Now I had to lie.

"No."

For whatever reason—my gestures? tone of voice?—they seemed to sense they'd discovered a weak spot, so the pudgy one kept at it, leaning into my face and raising his voice.

"He said nothing of this pending transaction? You're willing to repeat that as fact to both of us?"

I had to brazen it out. What was it they said about interrogation techniques? That people look up and to the right when they're lying? Or was it down and to the left? I looked at the table, then thought better of it and looked straight into the detective's face.

"No. He said nothing about anything like that."

He smirked. The taller one shook his head, then slapped his hands on his knees and stood.

"This is useless," the short one said. "He's lying."

It seemed obvious what the next question would be. One of them would ask me what Vladimir *did* say. And how would I answer that?

"Have you ever heard of a book called *Petrovka 38*?" the taller one asked.

It caught me by surprise.

"Yes. It's by Yulian Semyonov."

"So you know this book?"

"I read it. Years ago."

"Tell me what you know of it."

I shrugged, still wary, but relieved that they seemed to have eased the pressure just when they'd backed me into a corner.

"Semyonov was a Russian who wrote Soviet spy novels during the

Cold War, although *Petrovka 38* was more of a cop novel, a murder mystery."

The word "murder" nearly lodged in my throat, which I'm sure they didn't miss. The taller detective reached into his file folder.

"Do you recognize this copy of *Petrovka 38*?"

I blanched in disbelief, not just from seeing the black silhouette of a stabbed body on the cover, with blood spilling onto the white background, but also because the upper right corner of the jacket was torn. It was my own copy, stolen from my town house in Georgetown, presumably along with the rest of my spy books.

"No."

"You don't sound very convincing. You don't look it, either. Your face betrays you, Mr. Cage. Are you quite sure of your answer?"

I looked down at the table and drew a deep breath.

"It resembles a copy I'm familiar with. But it can't be the same one, because that book is supposed to be at my house in Washington."

"Can't be? You mean the airlines no longer allow their passengers to carry books with them on transatlantic flights? And by the way, Mr. Cage, let us please dispense with this 'Vladimir' silliness, shall we? I am sure you are quite aware that the man's real name was Boris Trefimov, just as I am quite sure you were surprised to see this book only because you were expecting someone other than the police to find it at the scene."

"The scene?"

"It was at Trefimov's apartment, as you well know." He moved closer, thrusting the book under my chin. "It was found with his body, as you also well know, since you were the one who must have placed it there in his lap. And it was open to this very page!"

He flipped to page 13, and I saw the black ink right away, marked boldly around a paragraph near the top.

"I didn't take this book to his apartment, and I didn't see it while I was there."

Another snort from the sidekick. The taller detective put the book on the table and drummed the passage with a forefinger.

"Boris Trefimov could not read English very well, Mr. Cage, and this is an English translation, meaning this book would only have been left in his apartment as some sort of message for his superiors to find. But unfortunately for you, Mr. Cage, the police found the body first."

"I told you, I didn't—"

"Read the passage aloud for me, Mr. Cage."

"What?"

"I said *read the passage*! Aloud. For both of us. And for the tape machine."

"You're taping this?"

"It's procedure, Mr. Cage. Just think of it as a performance. Do it well and maybe you will receive a commission check from one of those audio book services."

He backed away to give me room. I cleared my throat and tried to keep my voice from shaking. I decided on a monotone to convey my emotional detachment, but after scanning the first few words I knew that would be difficult. The moment was surreal. Was I truly about to read aloud from one of my own stolen books to a Vienna detective trying to frame me for the murder of an ex-KGB agent?

"We are waiting, Mr. Cage. Your audience is on the edge of its seats."

"Right. Okay."

Before I could start, the page flipped of its own accord. I was about to turn it back to page 13, then stopped myself just in time.

"What's wrong now?" the taller one asked.

"It's a trick. You're trying to get me to put a fresh set of fingerprints on the copy. I won't do it."

"Oh, for God's sake!"

He briskly stepped forward, flipped the page back, then pinned it down with a pencil. I cleared my throat again. Out came Semyonov's words in my quavering voice:

"The bright beam of the searchlight cut easily through the night like a sharp knife through a slice of black bread. The night was split apart and they all saw the dead Kopytov. He was lying in a crumpled ball, a puny old man with big, peasant hands, which still looked as if they were alive."

The tall detective snatched up the book and shut it in one neat motion. Then he leaned down, breathing into my face. I was pretty sure he'd eaten a sausage for lunch. Maybe the shorter detective had sold it to him.

"A murdered puny old man with big peasant hands," he said. "Pretty fair description of Boris Trefimov, wouldn't you say?"

I shrugged.

"I wasn't there. I wouldn't know."

"Of course you were. You've already admitted as much."

"Not when he was dead."

He shook his head slowly and eased away from me. Then he held the book aloft like a backwoods preacher with a Bible, preparing to deliver some fire and brimstone. As he opened his mouth there was a knock at the door.

The tall man paused, book held high. Then another knock sounded, louder and more insistent, followed by a voice.

"Manfred?"

The door opened. Another stubby fellow who might have been the wurst vendor's cousin motioned the detectives out into the corridor.

"Both of you. Now."

"But—"

"Orders from the top."

Manfred shut the book with a snap, then left in disgust. The wurst vendor shambled out in his wake. They locked the door behind them. All was quiet, but my heart was leaping against my chest. I wondered if the tape was still rolling, or if there was anything more to see inside the book. Another marked passage, or a scribbled message. I listened for footsteps. Nothing. I pulled a handkerchief from my trousers and was on the verge of pulling the book toward me when I stopped abruptly, remembering the two-way mirror.

I looked at it, wondering who might be watching from the other side, and what they were thinking. In a halfhearted attempt to cover my blunder, I pretended to blow my nose, then stuffed the handkerchief back in my pocket.

A few minutes later the door burst open. It was Manfred, alone now.

"Get out of here!" he snapped.

"Where are you taking me?"

"Leave now! Leave this station house before I change my mind."

I couldn't believe it. I *didn't* believe it.

"I'm free to go?"

"I won't say it again!"

He was furious. I scrambled out of the chair and sidled past him. Out in the hallway I saw that Litzi had just emerged as well. She looked uneasy and pale, a flashback to Bad Schandau. Maybe Dad was right. Why hold her accountable for the desperate actions of a seventeen-year-old girl? We exchanged inquiring glances. Then a uniformed policeman approached with our suitcases and wordlessly escorted us to the main entrance.

As we stepped into the sunlight, I saw Dad approaching from across the street. His face was a mask of abiding patience.

"The cavalry's arrived," I said. "Let's get the hell out of here."

She nodded, still too shaken to do anything but agree.

20

"So how did you manage it?" I asked.

We were walking fast, eager to put as much distance as possible between ourselves and the police. Dad and Litzi had barely acknowledged each other, so I was feeling a little awkward.

"Manage what?"

"Getting us out of there."

"I didn't even know you were in there until the embassy phoned saying you were about to be released. I take it this was all about the dead Russian?"

"They thought I did it. They found one of my damn books in his apartment."

They turned toward me as if I'd jerked their heads on a string, faces incredulous.

"*Petrovka 38*," I added for Dad's benefit.

He shook his head but said nothing. A few feet later he stopped abruptly in front of a café and gestured toward the door. "In there," he said, as if it were a pharmacy with just the cure for what ailed us. "Now."

We followed without a word and took a table toward the rear. He ordered for everyone, reverting to full Dad mode as he dispensed the prescribed medicine—three shots of brandy on a tray. I have to admit, they were therapeutic. The first swallow eased our breathing. The second restored color to our cheeks, although Litzi still hadn't said a word.

"I suggest you take the next available train," Dad said. "Reprieves like this don't always last. While you're gone I'll do what I can to sort things out. And, by the way, hello, Litzi. Even under the circumstances, it's quite a pleasure to see you."

She smiled thinly, but some of the tension went out of her shoulders.

"A pleasure for me as well."

"She told me she sees you around town now and then," I said. "Out and about with your friends. I told her she ought to say hi sometime."

They looked at me as if I'd said something inappropriate, which made me too uncomfortable to continue.

"I would imagine she does," Dad said. "Vienna can be a pretty small place that way."

"Yes," she agreed instantly. "You are so right."

He'd slipped into German for Litzi, even though she was fluent in English. It doubled my eerie sense that somehow they were operating on a different wavelength from me. I noticed a quick exchange of glances, but couldn't decipher it.

"I, uh, saw Lothar Heinemann on our train," I said. "He was watching out the window as the police led us away."

This remark also turned their heads. In unison, of course. They were acting like brother and sister.

"I'm beginning to wonder," Litzi said, "if he was the same man who spoke to me in a bookstore a week ago."

Now it was Dad and me whose heads were yanked on a string.

"Lothar?" we said.

"Which bookstore?" I asked.

"Kuhnhofer, an antiquarian store just off the Graben. I was looking through a pile of old manuscripts and he asked if I needed help finding anything. I thought he worked there, then later I saw him leave with a bag of books in one hand and a cane in the other. He even recommended a title to me."

"Which one?" Dad asked.

She paused, trying to remember. We awaited her answer as if she were the Oracle at Delphi.

"I don't remember." She looked down at the last of her brandy. "But the word 'secret' was part of it."

"Genre title," Dad said. I nodded in agreement.

He swirled the last of his brandy, still deep in thought. Litzi and I swallowed ours, fully medicated now.

"I've been thinking about Lothar," Dad said. "It would be a mistake to regard him as a malign influence. If you ever manage to pin him down, he might even be able to help."

"All he's done so far is give me the creeps. Why was he on the train?"

"It's your handler that gives me the creeps. He certainly doesn't mind putting you in harm's way."

"True. But maybe he was also our guardian angel."

"It certainly seems that way. All the embassy knew was that someone had intervened on your behalf. They didn't know who or why."

"But why would he have someone plant the Semyonov book next to the body?"

Then I told them about the marked passage. Litzi seemed to shiver.

"I'm sorry if all of this is stirring up unpleasant memories," Dad said.

She nodded, smiling appreciatively. Maybe this was my opening to finally clear the air, with Dad along as a sort of mediator.

"Litzi, this morning Dad mentioned something about what happened after you and I came home from Berlin, right before I moved away."

Dad shot me daggers but I couldn't stop now. He lowered his head in apparent embarrassment as I plowed forward.

"He said it was no big deal, but how come you never told me that you'd spied on us?"

Litzi looked at me, then at Dad, who shook his head slowly.

"My fault entirely," he said. "I tried telling him it was harmless and understandable, but obviously that wasn't good enough for him."

"It's all right," she said. "I should have said something. I've always been ashamed of it. But I also have to say that if I had to do it over again I would not change a thing. You weren't in that room to hear what they said. Your father hadn't spent half his life telling you about those kinds of people and what they were willing to do."

"Really, Litzi," Dad said, "you don't need to explain. Bill was too young, too sheltered. He had his nose in too many books."

"Speak for yourself," I said, a little irritated with both of them.

Dad stood.

"I need to use the men's room," he said. "You two hash it out however you like, but you don't owe me any explanations, Litzi."

She seemed grateful for the gesture, and, counter to expectations, his departure helped dissipate the tension between us.

"Well?" I said. "What really happened back then?"

"You know the worst of it. They threatened my family. They talked about holding me in East Germany until my father agreed to repatriate. I never really believed they would do it, but the uncertainty is what finally gets you. That and the number of times they repeated it, over and over, in that awful little room in Bad Schandau. That terrible man and his stupid Russian sidekick."

"Sidekick? The German in the brown coat was the only one I spoke to."

"They swore me to secrecy about the Russian. I was never to mention him to you or your father. Not that he ever told me a name."

"They brought up my father with you?"

"He's mostly what they wanted to talk about, once they finished scaring me with threats and browbeating. And by then the Russian was doing all the talking."

"What did they want to know?"

"What he was like. Who he knew. They asked if I'd been in your house, what I'd seen there, what his habits were like."

"His habits?"

"How often he came and went. Especially at night. If he ever left through the back of his building. I told them I didn't know. 'Well, then, find out!' he said." She paused, picking up her glass, then realizing it was empty. "They asked me to go through his things."

"Jesus, Litzi."

"I told them I was too scared. I made up things about how mean your father was, and what a terrible temper he had. So they said to wait until I was alone in the house with you. I said my parents wouldn't let me be there alone. They laughed at that. The Russian said my parents also wouldn't want me to disappear one day from the streets of Vienna. So I said I would try."

"Was I ever that lucky, to get you all alone in my house?"

"Twice, remember?"

Now I did, especially the second time, when my dad had stayed out very late. I vaguely recalled that the evening had ended on a melancholy note, which I'd attributed at the time to my imminent departure. Now I knew better.

"When you went downstairs to steal us a drink from your father's liquor cabinet, I went out in the hallway to his door, and opened it. I went to the bedside table and poked around some books and papers, then I froze when I heard you coming back up the stairs. I couldn't go through with it. I hurried back and told you I'd been in the bathroom."

"What did you tell them?"

"I made up things, mostly. Mostly I talked about his books."

"What did they say?"

"I thought for sure they'd know I was lying, but they seemed very interested. They wanted to know which titles he had taken down from his shelves, and if any of the pages were marked. And then, a few days ago, you come along with all of these stories about the same kind of thing, books with marked passages and secret meanings. So of course I had to try and find out what was happening, and I can't help but wonder if this is why I was chosen."

"To help me, you mean?"

She nodded.

"Maybe it's even the same people," she said.

"The Russians? That doesn't make sense. My handler wants to find out if Lemaster was a double agent. The Russians would already know."

"Unless they were trying to find out if he was a faithful double agent, a *real* double agent."

Excellent point, and the possibility that it might be true cast everything I'd been doing in a new light. Even the Hammerhead might be my handler. Then, just as suddenly, the idea seemed ludicrous.

"I don't know, Litzi, using all of these old spy titles to lead me around just feels so, well, American, don't you think?"

"You don't think Russians read all those novels? You don't think they weren't going through every page looking for kernels of truth, just like you were?"

Another good point, which made my head hurt.

"I'm scared of all this, Bill. Especially after what happened to Vladimir. I love seeing you, love being with you again. But now it seems like too much, too far. Yet every time I think of quitting, or of not getting on that train to Prague, my curiosity becomes bigger than my fear, because this has become personal for me as well. And now you know why."

"So you still want to go?"

"From what your father says, it sounds like we'd better."

"Probably."

"But Prague won't be enough, will it?"

"Budapest, too, most likely. After that, who knows?"

"Then I had better phone my office to clear enough time. I'll have to come up with something good, I suppose."

Dad returned to the table, so she took her phone off to a corner where we wouldn't have to hear her lying to her bosses. He looked me over carefully, as if inspecting for damage.

"Everything all right between you?"

"Yes."

"Glad to hear it. You're a lucky man."

"I suppose I am."

"All the same, be careful."

"I don't intend to hurt her."

"I meant for yourself."

"I'm not sure how I'm supposed to take that."

"Just as well. I'm not quite sure how I meant it."

I was about to ask for an explanation when he held a finger in the air and reached into his pocket for a folded sheet of paper.

"Almost forgot," he said, glancing around to make sure we weren't overheard. He lowered his voice. "I talked to Lewis Dean at the embassy."

"The 'regional specialist'?"

"I asked about that Russian you described, the one you called the Hammerhead. He seemed to think it might be a fellow they used to keep tabs on years ago. They never knew his code name but called him Brass Tacks. They were pretty sure he worked for a Moscow hand named Oleg."

Leo's handler. And Leo, aka Vladimir, aka Trefimov, was now dead after having put some of his oldest secrets up for sale. I nodded and tried not to look alarmed.

"Lew checked some files for me. Dormant for ages on the subject of Brass Tacks, except for one item. They think that in the past year he went into business for himself with a bunch of other old hoods, calling themselves the Argus Consortium, which didn't show up on anyone's radar screens until this." He unfolded the paper, a photocopy of a *New York Times* piece from two months ago. "Take a look."

It was a brief story from the business section about new government contracts landed by Baron Associates.

"Isn't Baron Breece Preston's company?"

"Keep reading."

Baron had won two new U.S. contracts for intelligence services in Afghanistan and Colombia. Rough neighborhoods. Lucrative pay. The story estimated the total payout over the next six years would be $660 million, pending congressional approval. Then came the kicker. "The new contracts," the *Times* said, "cap a busy summer of expansion in which Baron also won a security contract in the former Soviet republic of Turkmenistan, as part of a joint venture with the Moscow-based Argus Consortium."

"Interesting," I said, trying not to show how worried I was by this alliance of two such disagreeable fellows, both of them apparently connected in some way—but how?—to the trail of old clues Litzi and I were exploring.

"Lew also said Breece Preston has apparently gone walkabout in the past few weeks."

"Walkabout?"

"Disappeared almost overnight from their Afghanistan operations center. Some cover story about a health issue involving his family, but no one's buying it, mostly because no one seems to know where he's gone."

"Wonderful."

"It's still not too late to get out, son."

"Actually . . ." I handed back the paper, ". . . it's beginning to sound like it is."

He grimaced and looked down at the table, but didn't disagree. He was about to say more when he looked up and broke into a smile for Litzi, who had materialized at my shoulder holding her suitcase. Dad stood. I did the same, although I felt a little shaky.

"All clear," she said brightly. "We'd better get going before they change their minds."

We said our farewells on the sidewalk.

"Best of luck, son." Dad gripped me fiercely. "I'm here if you need me. And don't forget to keep David apprised of your movements."

The three of us exchanged hugs. Then he went one way and we went the other. The weather was almost springlike, and to judge from her sunny smile, Litzi seemed to be shaking herself free of the ghosts that had been stalking her only minutes earlier.

I was the moody one now, not only worrying about who might be waiting around the next corner, but also wondering what Dad had meant by his cryptic warning about Litzi. I wondered, too, what both of them knew that I still didn't.

21

Folly's rule of thumb for safe traveling on the shadow side of the Iron Curtain was simple but maddening. Beware the Friendlies. This was especially true once you disappeared into the tumbledown gloom of the cities, where you were so easily observed, stalked, followed, every step measured and recorded for the daily tick-tock of the all-knowing watchlists and logbooks.

Your enemies, Folly reasoned, were far more reliable, predictably steadfast in their opposition. You knew where they stood, and planned accordingly. But Friendlies, especially the eager and daring ones who nonetheless managed to survive, well, how could you ever say for sure what accounted for their staying power? Was it their zeal to serve or their zeal to deceive? And, if you suspected the latter, how should you behave in their presence? How much weight should you give to their local rules of engagement? Folly took extra care never to turn his back on them, literally or figuratively, a caution he had lived by since his earliest days as a field man.

Yet, as with all such rules, there were painful exceptions, moments when his well-cultivated mistrust had nonetheless led to miscalculation, even heartbreak. He remembered in particular a Czech named Kohut, personally recruited, admirably rewarded. One fine October evening in Prague, Kohut lay dead at Folly's feet, his face obliterated by a Russian soft-nosed bullet. This unshakable proof of Kohut's loyalty had arrived just as Folly had become convinced of the man's duplicity. Such were the wages of vigilant mistrust.

How, then, was Folly ever supposed to make progress on enemy territory while operating under such careful constraints? Answer: He didn't. Not really. He only pretended to pick his way forward while in reality he was fighting a lifelong holding action against uncertainty and doubt.

As a field man, the pressures of this daily stalemate had finally driven him to a desk job. As a desk man, they were driving him to bedlam. So here he was, heading back into the field once again, bound for the deepest and oldest of the shadows from his past. And, like it or not, the old rules of caution were still in force.

Folly put down his newspaper and stared out the smudged window of the grumbling bus. The crossword lay unfinished in his lap, yet another set of enigmas beyond his capabilities. He saw that it was still raining, but the bus was at last approaching the outskirts of Prague, the very place where his formula had gone so utterly wrong.

Those lines of Lemaster's click-clacked through my head to the rhythm of the train as we rolled across Bohemia. The haunting words now seemed as relevant as if my controller had circled them in black ink beneath another message in his now familiar handwriting.

Litzi, my friendliest of Friendlies, had nodded off an hour ago as we glided past huddled villages and autumn pastures. As I watched her sleep, the train lurched and her eyes fluttered open. Her expression was blank, open to almost any interpretation, but I had already given up on the idea of operating under Folly's rules. Bedlam, indeed. Even with what I'd learned about her past, trust was the only option if we were to continue traveling together, so I squeezed her hand and watched her smile.

"Will it be as beautiful as it was before?" she asked.

"The better question is if we'll have time to notice."

Although it wasn't as if our Prague agenda was crowded. So far we had only two contacts—an aging bookseller and a boyhood friend. I was excited about seeing Karel Vitova. We'd tracked him down on Facebook, messaging him from Litzi's smartphone just before we crossed the border into the Czech Republic. He answered almost immediately, with a happy-face emoticon and a string of exclamation points, plus an address for an apartment just around the corner from where he'd grown up.

I'd met Karel around the time my dad began weaning me from the crowd of embassy kids at the American school. We'd done our part for assimilation by moving into an apartment clear across the river from where the other diplomats lived. Prague was the city where, at age twelve, I first began to run, inspired by the local propaganda for national hero Emil Zátopek, who had won three gold medals at the '52 Olympics, beating all comers in a grueling combination of the 5K, the

10K, and the marathon. An entire fitness culture sprang up around his legend, and I met Karel at a "Zátopek Movement" cross-country race for boys, where we finished one-two in a hilly romp through Petrin Park.

Karel's English was far better than my Czech, and he taught me the ways of the city. In return, I instructed him in American slang and pop music, which I might have had trouble mastering myself if not for my classmates at the American school, who'd spent far more time in the States.

It never occurred to me then that our friendship posed any risk for Karel's family—not until we visited the machine shop where his dad worked to deliver a lunch pail. Just inside the door, next to a counter where the manager sat, there was a clock and a wooden box, where the workers punched their time cards. Posted above it was a sign with underlined words and an exclamation mark.

"What's it say?" I asked.

Karel laughed.

"It's about you." He translated: "Timely arrival to work strikes a decisive blow against the American aggressors!"

I didn't think it was funny.

"Well, this aggressor's hungry. Let's get a sausage."

The manager, hearing our English, scowled and muttered a curse. We burst out laughing and ran into the street. Probably not the sort of thing that showed up well in his father's personnel file.

Litzi and I arrived at dusk with an hour to kill before meeting Karel for dinner, so we checked in to our hotel and walked through the Old Town. I kept an eye out for both Lothar and the Hammerhead, but as usual, Prague was mobbed.

The city's refurbished beauty bowled me over even as it dismayed me. When I was a boy the buildings were sooty and tarnished, grandeur in decline. Now every surface looked scrubbed, every brick repointed. But city boosters had overlaid it with neon, corporate logos, and all these tourists, so many of them that the locals looked like infiltrators, as beleaguered as when the Soviets were in charge. To make matters worse, there was a soccer match that night between the Czech Republic and Scotland, so the streets were filled with the blue plaid soldiers of the Tartan Army, Scotland's die-hard, drink-harder legion of fans.

We tried to take refuge in a *pivnice*, or beer pub, but all of them were thronged with Scots. Then Litzi spotted a promising oasis, a trim bar with red walls and enough bookshelves to furnish a small library.

"How wonderful," she said. "And it's called Bar and Books."

We settled happily onto a leather bench, but a single overpriced drink was all it took for us to see that it was more of a cigar parlor for the trendy than a haven for literary types.

"This is the future for people like us," she said. "Books as décor, something to put on the wall where you sip your whisky."

A man over her shoulder caught my eye. He stood by the door, attempting to project a casual air. Was it my imagination, or was he the same fellow I'd spotted reading a Russian newspaper outside the train station?

"Don't turn around," I said, "but tell me if you recognize that man by the door." I looked away to keep from making him suspicious. Litzi leaned back against the bench and idly scanned the room.

"Which one?" she whispered.

I turned. He was gone. An operative for the Hammerhead, or a product of my overactive imagination?

"Never mind. Let's go. We're due at Karel's in another fifteen minutes anyway."

The Old Town Square was pandemonium, an invasion not of tanks but of kilted drunks, peeing against the walls of sixteenth-century chapels and kicking soccer balls high in the air to land on the heads of the hordes below, like cannonballs from siege guns.

"Poor Prague," Litzi said.

We threaded our way toward Karel's.

"How many years has it been?" Litzi asked as I pressed the button for his apartment.

"Forty. We moved a couple of years after the Russians rolled in. Haven't seen him since."

The buzzer sounded. No sooner had we pushed through the entrance than a door rattled open two stories above. A shaggy head loomed above the railing, and a big voice boomed down the stairwell.

"My friend Bill! You are most welcome!"

I laughed appreciatively. Litzi and I hustled up the steps to find him grinning hugely with his arms spread wide. Karel had grown into a woolly bear of a man. His brown-gray hair was clean but uncombed, in contrast to the Trotskyite beard that he'd trimmed to a point. He wore a folksy sweater of thick wool and a threadbare corduroy jacket that draped him like a horse blanket. His eyes were the same sparkling blue they'd been at age fourteen, with a gleam that said he was still up for anything.

I introduced Litzi and he ushered us inside. Books and magazines were everywhere. Dust coated the screen of a small rabbit-ear television that barely postdated our friendship. Abstract paintings covered every wall.

"First things first," he said. He poured three amber shots of Becherovka, the local herbal liqueur, and passed them around.

"To Bill," he said, raising his glass, "who taught me to sing like John Lennon, party like Keith Richards, and sneak around like James Bond."

Litzi, who had never seen much of the Keith Richards side, seemed greatly amused. I grimaced at the medicinal bite of the Becherovka, but it released a flood of memory—two teen boys plotting their stratagems in alleyways and on riverbanks, with one eye out for parents and another for any available girl.

"To Karel," I said, "who taught me to run like the great Zátopek. For a lap or two, anyway. And who helped engineer my first real kiss."

He burst into laughter.

"She is married again, you know. Three times now!"

"And who was this lucky girl?" Litzi was enjoying our nostalgia.

"Karel's sister. She was sixteen."

"You were punching above your weight, old man. But she was willing, very willing."

"It was in that little courtyard near Maltese Square, the one with the funny statue of Saint George."

"The one you used to call Saint Lecher."

"Because of the creepy look on his face, like he was about to molest the dragon."

His sister wanted nothing more to do with me afterward. It turned out she'd only wanted to satisfy her curiosity about what it felt like to kiss a boy from the land of Elvis, Hemingway, and Radio Free Europe. The answer: Nothing special. I swallowed the last of the Becherovka, and couldn't help but shudder.

"Remember our first night of drinking this stuff?" Karel held up the green bottle, offering more as I held up my hand in refusal.

"What I remember better is the hangover."

From the street below, a chorus of singing Scotsmen carried up through an open window. Karel stepped over for a look, smiling down toward the cobbles.

"They're everywhere," I said. "Grown men with hairy legs."

"By dawn there won't be a drop of single malt to be found in the city."

"In the square they were all drinking pils."

"That's just to get their courage up. After the final whistle they'll need the real stuff."

"The square is a shambles," Litzi said. "Cans and bottles everywhere."

"Better than shell casings," Karel said. "Although not nearly as much fun to dodge."

Another glimmer of his old self. He gestured toward the door.

"Let us go and eat sausages and pig's knuckles! Unless you'd rather have pizza like the Tartans?"

"Pig's knuckles it is."

As we walked to dinner we caught up on each other's lives. Karel was teaching mathematics at a second-tier university and still listening to any new music from the West, now on an iPod. There was a Mrs. Vitova, but she had left the premises four years ago, when the last of their three children moved out on his own.

He took us to a cozy restaurant where most of the diners spoke Czech. But when Litzi insisted on a nonsmoking table, they ushered us to an empty room in the back, where the hostess had to switch on a light. They must have concluded we were tourists, even with Karel along, because the waiter brought us sweet red wine in shot glasses nestled on beds of dry ice in goblets. He poured water over the ice to make the goblets steam like cauldrons, then grandly announced in English, "Our special cocktail, on the house!"

We waited until he left, then burst out laughing.

"And to think when I was fourteen I could pass for local," I said.

"Because your Czech was perfect! By the time you left you didn't even have an accent."

"All gone now, I'm afraid."

"My parents were always very impressed by the way you tried to fit in."

"Tried? Locals used to ask me for directions. Same in Budapest, Vienna, and Berlin. Now, of course, even the cabdrivers can spot me a mile away. I'm thoroughly Americanized."

"Like half of Prague," he said, clinking his glass to mine.

Up to then I'd given little thought to how I might broach the subject of finding Karel's old address in a KGB report. I suppose I was counting on some sort of natural opening to occur. I was right, as it turned out, although I never would've guessed the nature of the opening.

"How are your parents?" I asked.

"My mother is very fine. She lives in the country with her dog and a vegetable garden, bad knees and all."

"And your father?"

"Dead. Eleven years. No, twelve. His lungs. Probably from all that dust in his factory. And the smoking, of course."

"I'm sorry to hear that. He was always very kind to me."

Karel smiled like a wolf.

"Your visits made him very happy. You were like an extra income for him."

"What do you mean?"

"He informed on you! To someone in the Interior Ministry. He would always do it the very next day, and tell them whatever you said."

I set down my drink, incredulous.

"Jesus. Did everybody inform on me when I was a boy? Why didn't you say something?"

"I never knew. He told me after you moved away. Being the son of a diplomat made you very interesting to them."

I shook my head. So much for all those fond memories.

"He *did* ask me lots of questions."

"Especially about your father. That was his assignment."

"Great."

"Each time he reported they gave him an American twenty-dollar bill. He would exchange it for a hundred and sixty Tuzex crowns, equal to eight hundred regular crowns, except you could spend them at those special shops for party officials. Remember when we saw him coming out of there once, with that bag full of soap and chocolate bars? You were so impressed."

"Yes. I do remember."

"It was as much money as a shop clerk would make in a month. He told me later that whenever you came through our door it was like a visit from Father Christmas."

Karel laughed heartily, although I found it a bit hard to swallow. Litzi smiled sympathetically, the other family spy from my past. Well, I had my secrets, too, and now was the time to unveil them.

"Did your dad ever mention any code names?"

"*Code* names?" Karel laughed. "Hey, I don't think it was *that* official. He was just a metalworker with a big mouth."

"So you never heard him mention the name 'Fishwife'?"

Karel began to grow uncomfortable.

"Bill, why do you ask me this? What do you know?"

Litzi looked down at her drink.

"Well, I found your address in an old KGB report a few days ago. Along with the code name Fishwife, which they must have assigned to your dad. As a regular visitor to the Interior Ministry, it was probably routine."

Now it was Karel's turn to look shocked and deflated, and I felt a twinge of guilt for striking back so heedlessly.

"Relax, it was ages ago, the seventies." The words seemed to bounce right off.

"A KGB report? You're sure?"

Karel's tone was grave. I suppose that even now, the idea of showing up on some ancient Soviet watchlist could pack a punch. He drained the last of the novelty cocktail, then peered into the empty glass as if deeply troubled.

"I'm going to need something stronger than this. Is that why you got in touch with me, just to ask me this?"

"No. Not the only reason. But that was part of it, yes. I saw the address on an old list of contacts, and it made me curious. It's part of some research I've been doing, following up on old stuff from my dad's life."

"Ah. I see. You are revisiting all of your old haunts, then?"

"Yes. Like Antikvariát Drebitko. Remember all those bookstores my father went to?"

"How could I not? Bookstores were dangerous places for Czechs, especially if they were known to sell Western newspapers on the sly. My father always told me to stay away unless I wanted to get a bad name with the police. Of course now all the old secret policemen run security firms for bankers and businessmen. But I remember nothing of any KGB people at our house. My father would have been too scared. These were small things he was doing, to help us get by."

"I'm in no position to judge him. That's not what I'm trying to do."

He nodded, but it was clear he wanted to move on to a more comfortable topic.

So we did, stiffly at first, and with the aid of a bottle of Frankovka—"a true Czech red," as Karel said. The mood eased, but we carefully avoided any further mention of our fathers.

Later, when we were all a little tipsy, he walked us to our hotel. As we prepared to say good-bye, I was convinced we'd weathered the storm. But my news must have still been preying on his mind. Just outside the entrance he stopped and raised a finger in the air.

"There *is* something I remember now." His eyes widened as he recalled the moment. "A visitor to our house. It really shook up my father."

"A Russian?"

He shook his head.

"And not a policeman, either. A foreigner. His Czech was terrible. I remember hearing him. My father sent me to my room, but I listened. No one else was home. He was a man who sold books. Or bought them, maybe. It wasn't altogether clear, but I know he had a big bag of them. Old ones, like your father used to buy. He was young, dressed like a hippie. To me he looked stoned, which I remember really astonished me. He carried a cane, although he seemed to walk just fine."

Litzi glanced at me. A coldness bloomed at the base of my stomach, turning all that wine into chilly slush.

"You never heard his name?"

"No."

"What did they talk about?"

"I don't know. I couldn't make out enough of the words. But the next day, when I wanted to go to your apartment, my father told me to stay away for a while. In a few more days, of course, things were normal, and I never saw this man again."

"His accent. Was it German?"

"Did you know him?" Karel looked surprised, even hurt, as if I'd been hoarding this secret from the beginning.

"I'm pretty sure his name is Lothar Heinemann. And if I had to guess, I'd say he's in Prague right now. He might even be watching us."

Karel wheeled around like a cornered bull, almost stumbling from all the wine. Litzi gave me a look that said I'd again been needlessly cruel, but our surroundings gave no cause for alarm. Drunken Scotsmen were still in abundance, along with an approaching phalanx of tourists lurching to and fro on Segways.

"Don't worry," I said. "It's me he's interested in."

Our farewell was subdued, and I felt bad for Karel. He invited us back anytime, but you could tell his heart wasn't in it. I should've kept my mouth shut about Lothar. I knew Litzi thought so, too, and she kept her distance as we crossed the lobby.

"Why Lothar?" she finally asked, as we wearily climbed the stairs. "He must have been more than just a book scout."

"My dad thinks he used to hunt down rare titles for people in the Agency. Maybe their arrangement was for more than just books. Otherwise the idea that he talked to Karel's dad makes no sense at all."

"Unless he was KGB."

"That's a sobering thought."

"Even if he was, you shouldn't have unloaded on your friend Karel like that. Czechs of a certain age are still haunted in a way you'll never understand."

Like her father, she meant. No wonder she was feeling protective.

"You're right. I'm sorry."

We were exhausted, and probably would have been asleep within seconds of entering our room, if not for the message that greeted us when I flipped on the light.

"Not again," Litzi groaned. "How did he find us?"

Another one of my Gohrsmühle envelopes was perched on the pillows like a complimentary mint.

"Who knows? More marching orders, I guess. Wonder which book he's torn apart this time?"

But this time there was only a folded sheet of stationery with a single typed line.

```
7 p.m., 22 Divadelni
```

"He must mean tomorrow," Litzi said. "Do you know the address?"

"Quite well." So well that I was stunned to see it again in black and white. "It's our old apartment building, where Dad and I lived. Down by the river, third-floor balcony on the left. I guess my handler is trying to make me feel at home."

I forced a smile, but Litzi didn't join me.

"I thought you weren't going to follow any more bread crumbs until you knew who was dropping them."

"It seemed like a good idea at the time."

"And now?"

"Maybe I should go back on the offensive."

"How?"

"If the next crumb is waiting at my old apartment, I ought to be able to think of something. I did live there for three years."

I lay awake for at least an hour, hectored by questions. Why did my handler want me to visit my old apartment? How had he tracked us down so quickly? And what could I possibly do to gain some—*any*—sort of advantage over his manipulation as this strange journey tunneled ever deeper into my past?

But my last waking thought was of the Lemaster passage that had hounded me throughout the train ride from Vienna.

Beware the Friendlies.

Easy for you to say, Richard Folly.

I fell asleep with Litzi in my arms.

22

Room by room, the bookstore known as Antikvariát Drebitko had spread like a termite colony. Over the years its sagging shelves had tunneled down hallways, eaten through retaining walls, and crawled into the windowless hideaways of three adjacent buildings along a cobbled alley in Prague's Old Town.

My father once compared browsing there to exploring an abandoned mine.

"If you go," he warned, "take a headlamp, watch for bats, and keep your eyes peeled for buried gems."

The proprietor in those days was a wiry, hard-bargaining Czech named Václav Bruzek, who had long ago given up on trying to sort titles alphabetically or even by native tongue, although he had separated fiction from nonfiction and had established chaotic ghettoes for subjects such as travel, history, politics, and biography. Most of the books were in Czech, but the English and German interlopers easily numbered into the hundreds, and the supply was often interesting enough to make my dad's foraging expeditions worthwhile. Dad had curried favor by giving Bruzek embassy copies of the *International Herald Tribune*, which boosted Bruzek's black market trade in forbidden newspapers. In turn, Bruzek tipped Dad to his choicest acquisitions.

"How does he sell those newspapers without getting in trouble?" I'd once asked.

"Who do you think his customers are, Bill? Party officials, secret police. The very people he needs to keep happy to stay open."

It was an early lesson in institutionalized hypocrisy, and the art of playing both sides against the middle. Such talents must have made Bruzek an attractive, yet risky, choice when Lemaster began setting up his courier network.

Back then, Bruzek had been in his late thirties. If he was alive, he'd be pushing eighty.

A bell jangled as we entered, summoning a thin fellow in his mid-twenties, shirttail out, a pencil tucked behind his ear. He worked his thumbs at a phone while managing to negotiate his way down crooked rows of tables and shelves.

"I will be with you in a moment," he said in perfect English. His phone twinkled as he sent the message, then he looked up with an air of inquiry.

"Yes?"

"I'm hoping to find Václav Bruzek. The elder, in case there's a junior."

"And you are?"

"An American journalist. My father was an old customer of Václav's in the late sixties. I'm writing a piece for *Vanity Fair* magazine about the old days."

He narrowed his eyes at the mention of the old days.

"My uncle doesn't talk much about those times."

So he was alive, at least, and this was his nephew.

"Do you know where I could find him?"

"He doesn't like unexpected visitors."

"Maybe you could ask him for me. My name's Bill Cage. My father is Warfield Cage. He sent me here."

His eyes flashed in recognition at the mention of Dad's name.

"I am pleased to meet you," he said. "I am Anton. Wait here."

He disappeared into the back. I listened for voices but heard only footsteps on a stairway, which soon faded into the depths of the store. Litzi surveyed the room.

"Wave to him," she said.

I followed her gaze to a security camera mounted near the ceiling.

"You really think he's watching?" I spoke out the side of my mouth.

"Of course."

She stared defiantly. I looked away. A few seconds later I heard footsteps. Anton reappeared.

"He said to come up. But not for long. His health is not the best."

We both started out across the room, but Anton stopped us.

"Not her. Just you."

"That's fine."

I said it a little too eagerly. Trust was definitely an issue, and the worst part was that I'm sure Litzi had begun to notice, so I tried to soften the blow.

"It will probably be easier to get him to talk if there's just one of us."
She didn't reply.

I followed Anton upstairs, then down a hall into the next building over, where we turned toward the back and climbed a second flight before again moving right and toward the rear. The scuffed old floors were warped and uneven, the air close and stale. At the end of the last passage the door opened onto a large room with a desk to one side and, at the far end, a daybed beneath a mullioned picture window overlooking a small green courtyard. Václav Bruzek was propped against a stack of pillows on the daybed. Papers were scattered in his lap, and a bowl of blueberries sat to his right. A cup of coffee, no longer steaming, sat on an end table atop a pile of books. The windowpanes were streaked and cloudy, and dead insects were scattered along the sill like knickknacks. I didn't know if Bruzek was lying down by choice or necessity, but his color was reasonably good, his hair was combed, and his eyes were clear.

Anton departed without a word, shutting the door behind him. Bruzek stared at me for a few seconds, then glanced toward the wall at the foot of the bed, where a mounted black-and-white video screen displayed Litzi, arms folded. I half expected her to wave. Her instincts for this sort of thing were a little unnerving.

"Who's the girl?" Bruzek asked. "She's certainly not American."

"Litzi Strauss, from Vienna." I felt an obligation to establish her credentials, so I added, "She's an archivist," but Bruzek seemed unmoved. "She's also an old friend."

He took another look at her, squinting now.

"Strauss like the composer? She's no Strauss. Bohemian is my guess." He dipped into the blueberries with a gnarled right hand and tossed a few into his mouth, talking as he chewed. "This was never your father's style, to travel in pairs. He did his own legwork. You have his eyes. His mouth, too. But obviously not his deliberation."

"What kind of legwork?" If Bruzek could skip the polite preliminaries, so could I.

"This is for a magazine, you said?"

There was a knock at the door.

"Enter."

Anton brought in a tray with two flowered china cups and a fresh pot of tea. He whisked away the old mug of coffee and set down the tray.

Bruzek poured two cups, which lured me across the room. I took a seat in a creaking office chair at the foot of the bed.

"Yes," I said. *"Vanity Fair."*

"Anton said you're writing about the old days, but that doesn't tell me very much."

"It's a story about Ed Lemaster. About his CIA career."

Bruzek raised an eyebrow as he stirred in a heap of sugar.

"Do you have a business card?"

"No, I'm a freelancer. But I do have a letter of introduction."

I got it out of my pocket. By now it was creased and wrinkled. Bruzek smoothed it in his lap, frowning at its condition in a way that only a keeper of old papers would do.

"If you plan on using this much longer you should have it laminated."

He handed it back. Then, with a grimace and a groan, he worked himself into a more upright position.

"Please help me stand. I would feel much more comfortable speaking to you from behind my desk."

I took his arm and helped him across the room to a ladder-back chair behind a huge mahogany desk. Behind it was a high wall of bookshelves, stuffed full and leaning slightly, as if they might fall at any moment. Someone needed to shim them up. Bruzek was light but still wiry, and once he was on his feet he was surprisingly steady. I retrieved his teacup.

"I'll be fine now. Pull your chair over."

We settled into our new positions, and I saw right away why he'd requested the move. His chair was set high, mine low. He was now looking down at me, a surprisingly commanding presence for a man his age. He placed his arms on the desk and laced his fingers together, a pose of patience and calm.

"Well?" he said. "I presume you have questions."

"Tell me how you first got to know Ed Lemaster. As a customer?"

"It was the mid-sixties, I can't give you an exact year. He was quite a collector. Still is, I presume."

"Did you know what he did for a living?"

"He never said."

An artful evasion, but Bruzek spoke again before I could follow up.

"Let's stop being so coy and genteel, shall we? I assume your father must have told you a few things or he wouldn't have sent you here, and if your subject is Ed Lemaster, then you're probably interested in his system for relaying messages. That was my only real role in his work. All those parcels for Dewey, correct?"

I wondered why he'd come to the point so readily—not that I was complaining.

"Who set it up?"

"I don't know."

"It wasn't Ed?"

Bruzek shrugged.

"Well, yes or no?"

"No. Not directly. It was someone acting on his behalf. Ed had introduced us a few weeks earlier, during a buying trip. The next time the fellow showed up, it was to talk about the setup, and how it would work. 'A friend,' that's all Ed ever called him, so I don't have a name. But he paid well and he paid promptly, and his instructions were simple and clear. Every delivery was always for Dewey, and I was always to call the courier to make the pickup. What happened afterward I have no idea. Who it went to? No idea. What purpose it ultimately served? No idea."

"Well, you must be able to recall something about this fellow. Was he American?"

"I don't know. I don't think so, but it wasn't clear."

"Oh, c'mon."

"I'm telling you the truth. He was fairly nondescript. He was well dressed but nothing flashy or very expensive. No labels or obvious brands. No watch that I could see. He didn't smoke, so there was no brand of cigarettes to give him away." Bruzek had obviously given this matter some thought, which made me inclined to trust his answer. "He always spoke Czech with me. Not as a native, but fluently. His accent was indeterminate, almost as if he'd gone to school in many different places while he was growing up."

Like me, I thought. Austrians always had trouble placing the accent on my German. Or, for that matter, like Bruzek, whose excellent English had a mixture of inflections, but sounded different from the way most Czechs spoke it.

"Was my dad the only courier?"

"No."

"Who else?"

"That information is not readily available."

"What's that supposed to mean?"

"It means that to be sure of its accuracy I would have to look it up, and I am not prepared to do so."

"Are you saying you kept records of these transactions?"

He scowled and picked a piece of lint off his shirt. He replied without looking up.

"Only because someone asked me to."

"Do you still have them?"

He flicked the lint away. We watched it drift to the floor like a tiny parachute.

"Do I look like a man who throws things away?"

Bruzek spread his arms to encompass the room, which in its clutter was a miniature version of the store. The high shelves behind him, I noticed, were filled with titles in all languages. Many looked centuries old.

"No," I said, "you don't."

"Not that any of the information I logged ever seemed important. Just dates and times, a few names and phone numbers, all of it recorded in a ledger. A chore for which I was never paid, by the way."

"You were supposed to be paid?"

"A substantial sum. That was the promise. Of course, if you would finally like to make good on this promise on behalf of your country, I'm certain I could arrange to acquire it for you."

"The CIA requested this?"

"That was my assumption."

"How substantial was the sum?"

"Calculating for inflation, I would put its current value at . . ." He looked at the ceiling while his mind ran the numbers. "At least five thousand euros."

"Out of my price range. But helping me with this story might make it easier for you to find a buyer."

He frowned, then got the gist of it.

"I see what you mean. By creating an embarrassment for them. A welshed deal to an important Cold War contact."

"Why do you think it was the Agency?"

He shrugged, uncomfortable with the question.

"Maybe it is not wise to talk so openly of these things, even now."

He pushed back his chair, putting some distance between us, and in doing so he bumped the shelves, which creaked and swayed alarmingly, a Babel tower of books that seemed ready to topple at the slightest touch. I instinctively braced my hands against the arms of my chair, ready to leap to safety. Bruzek smiled and didn't budge.

"No need to panic. These shelves have been like that for years, hanging over my head like the sword of Damocles. But the books are my children. They would never do me harm."

I tried to steer things back on track.

"Did Ed's 'friend' make the request that you keep the ledger?"

"No. It was done through another channel. A phone call."

"Wasn't that kind of risky in those times?"

"Yes. But the wording of the message was very vague."

"Did you recognize the voice?"

"No, no. Whoever the contact was obviously used someone else to make the call for him."

"How do you know?"

"Because the voice was that of a child. A boy. He must have been paid to deliver the message, and probably didn't have the slightest idea what it meant. He might even have done it for free. In those days, being requested by a stranger to place an anonymous phone call would have been too daring and exotic for any boy in Prague to resist. My own son would have done it. So it could have been anyone."

As Bruzek spoke, something cold and prickly began creeping up my spine, like a droplet of sweat defying gravity. When the sensation reached the space between my shoulder blades, I felt the hair stand up on the nape of my neck. I leaned forward.

"Do you remember the wording of the message?" I held my breath for his answer.

"Oh, yes. When that much money is mentioned, you don't forget the slightest detail. The call came to me at home. I was alone. It was a Friday, and my wife and son were at the cinema, some awful Stalinist film about the heroic fight against the Germans. This boy's voice came on the line sounding like he was trying not to laugh.

"'Václav,' he said—he never once used my last name—'Václav, you are instructed to keep a ledger of all particulars for all future deliveries.

Payment tenfold upon completion.' Meaning tenfold of my usual take for each transaction, that was my assumption. So of course I complied."

By now the coldness was creeping back down my spine.

"But no one ever paid you?"

"Because no one ever came to pick up the ledger."

"Would you show it to me?"

He paused again, shaking his head but not refusing. Then he grimaced, wavering.

"How about tomorrow?"

"I can see it then?"

"I'll have an answer for you. No promises. I must think about this. But I can tell you for sure tomorrow. Come after hours, seven o'clock. No, make it eight, after dark. These kinds of things should not be revealed by the light of day, don't you think?"

He stood slowly, and I did the same. At his shift of weight, the ominous shelves groaned and creaked. Or maybe I was just feeling the effects of what he'd told me.

"Shall I call Anton to show you out?"

"I know the way."

My steps on the narrow stairways felt stiff, wooden, as if I was descending into a dream. The feeling persisted all the way to the front of the store, where Litzi was still waiting and Anton stood behind the register. She must have read the emotions in my face.

"What's wrong?" she said. "What happened up there?"

"He has more information, but he wants a day to think about it. I'm—we're—supposed to come back tomorrow night at eight."

"What kind of information?"

"Details about courier transactions. Could be nothing, could be everything."

I withheld the biggest revelation, telling myself it was to keep Anton from overhearing. In retrospect, I'm not sure I was ready to tell Litzi, either, not until I'd had time to digest it.

Because I was the boy who had phoned Bruzek. I had read the message straight from a typewritten page that had been handed to me by a stranger who paid me fifty crowns. The stranger was no one notable, probably just a cutout. I had no idea who I was phoning, of course, and at the time I was convinced it was yet another of those small errands that had somehow been engineered by my father, in his role as a bit player on the fringes of CIA intrigue. Now I wasn't sure what to think.

We stepped into the street, where I was momentarily blinded by sunlight.

"What's our next stop?" Litzi asked. "Are you still planning to go on the offensive?"

I blinked, still emerging from the fog of disbelief.

"What? Oh, yes. Right. Later, if it's possible."

Deep memories, once they've been pulled from the muck, sometimes churn up enough old sediment to reveal other buried recollections, as long as you're patient. And by reliving that old phone call I had now remembered something else, an item that had probably been working its way to the surface ever since I'd seen my old address, 22 Divadelni, typed on a sheet of my stationery the night before. That, in turn, had just given me an idea for a possible preemptive action, a means of indeed taking the offensive.

"Where to, then?" Litzi sounded impatient, but now I had an answer for her.

"An old monument called Kranner's Fountain," I said. "I'm going to do a little illegal climbing, and you're going to be my spotter."

23

Kranner's Fountain with its grim medieval figures peered out at the Vltava River from a small park just across Divadelni Street from my old apartment building. Sixteen of the statues looked as if they'd walked straight out of *The Canterbury Tales*—an archer, a carpenter, a miller, a baker, and so on.

As a boy I had a prime view of them from our third-floor balcony, and they often featured in my dreams, climbing down from their perches after midnight to roam the square and beckoning me to join them.

My awestruck regard was probably what led me to boast to Karel one night that the creases and folds of their stone garments would offer the perfect hiding place for something small and valuable. At the time, the topic of spare keys was much on our minds. The Russians were poised to invade, and we took the threat personally. What if they seized our homes for billets? How would we retrieve all our stuff?

Dad had a spare, but he kept it in one of those obvious spots, beneath a flowerpot. Surely the wily Red Army would figure that out in no time. So I swiped it one day and had an extra copy made. Karel did the same at his house. Then, with conspiratorial excitement, we each came up with a hiding place, and mine was Kranner's Fountain—specifically, beneath the lower hem of the tunic of the horn-blowing hunter, whose face I could see in profile from our front window.

We cached our treasure by night. I crossed the dewy grass of the silent park and climbed ten feet up the marble barriers to the hunter's pedestal. Taking the key from my pocket, I groped above his right knee and glued it into place in the recess beneath the hemline with a U.S. commissary wad of Dubble Bubble, precious stuff in those benighted days of bad soap and scratchy toilet paper.

Was the key still there? Would it still fit the lock? Long shots. But if that failed I had the whole afternoon to come up with a Plan B.

First I had to figure out how to climb Kranner's Fountain in the middle of the day without attracting attention. As Litzi and I approached, several older women were walking their dogs on the gravel paths below. A policeman patrolled a nearby corner. But the most alarming sight was the statue itself. It was scrubbed clean of all the soot and grime that had blackened it when I was a boy, and if the cleaners had been thorough, then the gum and key were surely gone. Also, the fountain I'd climbed as a boy was dry, pumps broken. Now it was working. I'd have to get wet.

Another notable change, if inconsequential to my efforts, was that the city had recently restored the equestrian figure of Emperor Franz Josef I to the chamber atop the monument. He'd been missing in action for more than ninety years, ever since an inflamed citizenry removed him after declaring independence from the Hapsburgs. For those of you interested in portents and omens, this was the same Franz Josef I whose statue stood guard over the dead drop in Vienna's Burggarten. As Litzi put it, "By the time this is over, he'll have seen more of what's going on than that stupid webcam."

Litzi put our plan into action by asking the policeman for directions, keeping him occupied while I climbed over the low wall at the bottom, then soaked my shoes as I scaled the next one. I was stronger now than at eleven, but not nearly as agile, so I moved slowly in pulling myself up toward the base of the hunter, who looked younger than ever.

A woman walking a ratty dog came into view just below me. The dog began yapping and tugging its leash. She shook her head as I reached beneath the hem of the tunic.

Nothing.

She yelled in a snarl of Czech as I kept groping, feeling only the cold stone. Then my fingers brushed against something smooth and hard. I pried up a brittle corner with a fingernail and worked at it some more. By now the woman was lecturing me, and the dog was unrelenting. The rest of the gum came free so suddenly that that I nearly lost my balance. It looked slick and dark, blackened by soot, but the tip of the key poked from the end where I'd broken off the first piece. I stared down in triumph at the nattering woman, who turned away in a huff toward the policeman.

Hopping into the shallow water below, I looked up long enough to see that the woman with the dog had nearly reached the cop, who was still talking to Litzi. I was about to hurdle the final barrier when I spotted a man perhaps twenty feet to their right, lurking at the far end of the park and staring unabashedly at my efforts.

It was the Russian, the one from the train station and the gimmicky bar, still carrying his Moscow newspaper like an identity badge. He grinned, then nodded slightly before heading off in the opposite direction.

"You! Out from there!"

It was the cop, fast approaching and addressing me in English. Close on his heels was the woman and her yapping dog. She beamed as triumphantly as if she'd just pulled Franz Josef back off his perch. A worried-looking Litzi brought up the rear. I scrambled over the barrier, shoes squishing on the gravel. The key was in my right hand.

"What is the meaning of this!"

"My friend," I said, gesturing toward Litzi, "dropped her key in the fountain."

Litzi immediately began thanking me with flirtatious gratitude.

"Stupid me," she said. "I wanted to throw in a coin for good luck, but grabbed my key instead!"

The old crone, probably not understanding a word of the exchange, was now gesturing up at the hunter, no doubt describing what she'd seen me doing. But the cop, about our age, was paying more attention to Litzi. He looked back and forth between us as if deciding what to do. Then, perhaps to save face in front of the disapproving local, he told Litzi, "You must not throw coins into the fountain!"

"Yes, officer, of course."

"Sorry," I added. "It won't happen again."

He nodded sternly, then strolled away with his hands clasped behind his back while the dog continued to yap, complaining on behalf of its mistress. We scrambled away before he changed his mind.

"Do you think it still fits?"

"We'll find out at six o'clock."

My plan was to try the lock about an hour before the appointment. I figured it was too much of a coincidence that my handler would actually have had a contact living in my old house, meaning he would have made some sort of temporary arrangement. If so, whoever lived there would probably be gone by six, well before our contact showed up. Assuming there was a contact. Maybe there would simply be a message posted on the door.

"My worry now," I told Litzi, "is that we won't be showing up alone. While you were talking to the cop I saw the Russian, the one from the bar, watching me from the end of the park."

She glanced over her shoulder.

"He's gone now," I said. "But let's get a cab, take a ride to lose him."

"Unless he already knows where to find us at seven."

By late afternoon the wind was rising, blowing angry clouds across the rooftops of the Old Town and spawning zephyrs of litter and grit, as if determined to sweep every last tourist from the city. Tartan Army stragglers had to hold down their kilts, and each northerly gust carried the smell of rain. My feet, soaked from the fountain, were freezing.

I hadn't been inside 22 Divadelni since I was fourteen, and didn't know what to expect. The ambassador had never been thrilled by Dad's decision to live outside the diplomatic cocoon. To accommodate Cold War security concerns we endured monthly visits from sweeper teams that scanned every wall, floor, and ceiling with wands and beeping black boxes. They never found a thing. Dad nonetheless switched on the radio whenever we had company or made a phone call. Now, I was about to make the very sort of intrusion the embassy had always feared the most. If the key fit.

We arrived at the front steps right at six, watching our backs but seeing no sign of surveillance. A few raindrops were falling, the fat kind that precede huge storms, and the trees in the park were waving wildly. We took shelter in the vestibule. The floor tiles were scrubbed, and all the mailboxes seemed to be in working order, although my handler's minions had once again been playing with the name tags. A spotless new label printed with "CAGE" appeared in our old slot for the third floor.

We had no key for the downstairs door. We were hoping to get in by using the old trick of buzzing every apartment until someone let us in. But first we buzzed my old place, to see if the coast was clear. I tensed for a response, but the only sound was that of the rising wind.

"Good," I said. "Now let's get in."

On our third try there was an answering buzz from a second-floor apartment. We shoved open the door and climbed the stairs. A door on the second floor opened as we passed, and an elderly woman peeped through the slit.

"Sorry," I said breezily. "Forgot our key."

I couldn't tell if she understood, but she rammed home the security chain. We slowed down as we approached the third floor, and went the rest of the way practically on our tiptoes. I took out the key, then thought better of it and put my ear to the door, like a doctor listening through a stethoscope. I heard a faint buzz, like a refrigerator, but nothing else apart from a television downstairs. The lock looked encouragingly old.

"Here goes," I whispered.

Litzi bit her lower lip. I pushed the key into the slot.

It was a tight fit, stopping halfway in. I gave it a wiggle and slid it to the hilt. Then it wouldn't budge. Another wiggle, still no progress. Even as I fretted, a memory returned of a balky lock that often needed coaxing and just the right touch, but was I thinking of this house or the one in Budapest? I paused, took a deep breath to relax, but had no better luck on the next try. On the fourth attempt something gave way. The key twisted with a solid metallic smack as the deadbolt slid free.

I turned the knob. We were in.

The place smelled musty, and a little bit like garlic. No sign of anyone, but we moved carefully, Litzi following me through the door without a sound. I shut it gently behind us, then manually reset the lock. Only then did I exhale.

"I think we made it," I whispered.

"We'd better check the rooms first."

We did it together, Litzi lagging just behind me in case someone jumped out of hiding.

With all the gathering gloom outside, it was very dim inside, but we didn't dare switch on a light that could be seen from the street. Nothing looked familiar except the chandelier in the dining room. The décor wasn't at all to my father's taste. The furniture was modern, the artwork abstract. There was a state-of-the-art audio system and a big-screen TV with DVDs galore, but not a single book, nor even a newspaper or magazine.

On the coffee table, someone had left a set of keys atop some folded paperwork. One of the keys matched mine, and one of the papers was a pink carbon copy of a short-term rental agreement between someone named Jan Svoboda and one of those vacation lodging services that matches up tourists with willing local residents. The agreement was good for two days, until ten tomorrow morning.

"Svoboda," I said. "Definitely a Czech name."

The second page was a printout of a recent email exchange. My excitement built as I realized the meaning of its contents:

```
  From: kfresh62@dmail.com
    To: jsvoboda@cz1mail.cz.net
  Sent: Tuesday, October 12, 2010 10:23 PM
Subject: <Reply>Arrangements
```

Proceed as planned. I'll handle extra party. Bank code and payment procedure in attachment. Funds available upon confirmation of completion.

```
  From: jsvoboda@cz1mail.cz.net
    To: kfresh62@dmail.com
  Sent: Tuesday, October 12, 2010 09:47 PM
Subject: Arrangements
```

Appointment set, site secured, but worried about interest from new party. Please advise. When will payment be forwarded?

Finally, progress. I felt I had at last nudged back the curtain on my handler's identity.

"Svoboda must be our contact," I said, "which would make K-Fresh 62 my handler. Trace his email address and maybe we can come up with a name."

"Do you really think our contact is this sloppy?"

She was right. Leaving all this stuff out in plain view, even with the door locked, was hardly the mark of a professional.

"Wonder who the 'interested new party' is?"

"Surveillance?" Litzi offered. "Someone making sure he's doing his job?"

"Maybe. K-Fresh obviously didn't feel a need to tell him. We'd better memorize these addresses in case Svoboda makes us give his stuff back."

"I'll log them into my phone."

We searched the apartment again, this time checking under beds and in closets and cabinets. But it was soon apparent that everything else belonged to the residents. Whoever was meeting us must have come here only once to familiarize himself with the lay of the land. Presumably he had his own set of keys.

I looked in the fridge.

"Want a beer?"

"Stop," Litzi said. "We should get ready. He might be early."

No sooner had we moved back into the living room than we heard the downstairs door bang shut, followed by footsteps on the stairs, which rose in volume until they reached the third-floor landing. It was six-thirty.

"Quick, back in the kitchen."

I pulled the kitchen door nearly shut, watching through the crack. It was even darker there than in the living room. A key rattled in the lock, and I heard him wiggle it several times before he slid back the deadbolt. I moved out of sight as the door swung open, and we listened to his footsteps crossing the room. There was a rustle of clothing, then a beeping sound as he punched in a number on a cell phone. He coughed as he waited, sounding a little nervous. I heard the chirp of an answering voice, then our contact spoke in English with a slight Czech accent.

"Jan here. I am in place. I will call again upon completion."

The phone beeped as he disconnected. I pushed open the door and stepped into the room as quietly as I could. Jan had his back to me. I spoke to get his attention, poised to move quickly if he reacted badly.

"Hello, Jan. We decided to arrive early."

He started at the sound of my voice, then turned abruptly. We both reacted in surprise—he for obvious reasons, me because the man facing me was the so-called Russian whom I'd last seen watching us from across the park. Litzi gasped from her perch in the kitchen.

He recovered his composure first. When he spoke it was again in English, although this time the accent was Russian.

"I will not ask how you managed to arrive before me, but I am sure it must have involved illegal activity. The important thing is that you have come. Both of you, I see now."

Litzi came through the door.

"How come you speak like a Russian but have a Czech name, Jan?"

"It is a cover name, of course."

"I might have believed that if I hadn't just heard you on the phone, sounding completely different."

His face reddened, but he forged on after a slight pause.

"I speak that way on the phone also for cover, in case there is eavesdropping."

"Nice try."

"I have instructions for you." He stuck to his accent, brazening it out.

"You need to answer some questions first. Who is K-Fresh 62, and how did you end up working for him?"

Now he looked despondent, and a little panicky. His eyes darted around the room until his gaze settled on the coffee table, where he seemingly noticed for the first time that his things were missing.

"I pocketed your extra keys for safekeeping," I said. "Wouldn't want you to have to forfeit your deposit."

His cheeks turned a deeper red.

"So now if you could please answer those questions."

He set his jaw and stood a little straighter. Then he shoved a hand into his jacket pocket.

"Maybe first I would rather blow off your head."

I flinched involuntarily, which made him smile, but he kept his hand in his pocket, and I decided he was bluffing.

"You don't have a gun, Jan."

"Do you really want to find that out?"

"Yes, Jan. I do."

"Stop saying my name!"

"I will if you take your hand out of your pocket."

The fight went out of his eyes and he slowly withdrew his hand. Empty.

"I am supposed to tell you where to go next," he said, this time in his normal Czech accent.

"I'm fine with that. But not until you've answered my question."

"Look," he said, "and I am telling the truth when I say this. I don't know who this K-Fresh person is. I only know him through email. He's paying me, and he assured me this would be harmless. For everyone."

His capitulation was just pathetic enough to be believable.

"Including the part where you followed us?"

He frowned.

"Okay, yes. That also. I was supposed to make sure you saw me, and to carry the newspaper so you would think I was Russian. But there was never any question of doing you harm. I swear it."

"Did you put the message in my hotel room?"

He nodded.

"I bribed the chambermaid. She stood outside to make sure I didn't take anything."

"Where did you get the paper you used, and the envelope?"

"By overnight delivery. International."

"From where?"

"London. But there was no return address. Believe me, I was as interested to find out as you are."

"What did you mean when you said in the email that someone else had taken an interest?"

"Another man. I saw him twice while following you. At first he seemed interested only in you. Now I think he is after me as well, and I do not like it."

"Why do you say that?"

"Someone was in my apartment, going through my things, opening my mail. It's why I printed those emails, so I could erase them from my laptop. This was not supposed to turn out this way."

"Who is this man? A real Russian?"

"No."

"A German, then? An older fellow with a slouch hat and a cane?"

"No, no. He is American, I am sure of it."

"Sure of it how?"

"His clothes. The way he moves. Even his hair. No one in Europe wears hair like that except for motorcycle thugs."

Jan then proceeded to perfectly describe the haircut commonly known as a mullet. That, plus the rest of the description, perfectly fit Ron Curtin, Breece Preston's muscle.

My stomach went a little fluttery, and Litzi squeezed my arm. I tried to keep my voice even.

"When did you last see him?"

"This afternoon, when I left you in the park."

"Did he follow you, or stay at the park, watching me?"

"He stayed."

Oh, perfect. At least we'd climbed into a cab afterward. Maybe we'd actually lost him.

"So what is your message? What are my instructions?"

"The Cave. I am supposed to take you there. I was told you would know what I meant by that."

"I do."

"The Cave?" Litzi whispered.

"I'll explain."

"Then let's go," Jan said, turning toward the door. He seemed eager to get this over with, and who could blame him? But I wasn't ready to let him off so easily.

"You'll go first," I said. "We'll watch from up here to see if you're followed."

Jan emphatically shook his head.

"No! That isn't how I was paid to do it!" He clearly realized now—if he hadn't already—that he was in over his head. It was a feeling I could sympathize with. "In fact, there is no need for me to even go." He frantically pulled a set of car keys from his trousers and thrust it toward me. "Here. I will give you these now and tell you where it is parked. The other instructions will be waiting for you."

His eyes implored me.

"Jan?" I said it as calmly as possible.

"Yes?"

"Would you like your second set of house keys back, along with the lease agreement and the printed emails?"

"Yes." Quietly, meekly.

"And I'm sure you wouldn't be pleased if I emailed K-Fresh to tell him you were uncooperative and easily fooled, would you?"

He lowered his head, defeated.

"No."

"Then you go first, Jan. We'll watch from up here to make sure you're okay. If anyone follows you, we'll phone the police. All right?"

He nodded.

"Because we're the ones he's really after. Do you understand?"

Another nod.

"So get started. Then you can be paid, and that big ugly fellow with the American haircut will stop following you."

Jan left without a further word. Litzi and I moved to the front window and waited for him to appear downstairs. Darkness was falling, and the wind bent back the trees. I looked over toward where the Cave was, knowing that by now it would have eased into its own deep night.

24

"Tell me what the Cave is," Litzi said.

"See that dark area to the left of the park, over where the street dips below ground level and disappears, like it's going to tunnel right beneath the river?"

"Yes."

"There's an old storage area there, sort of like a cavern. It's usually locked up at night, but I presume Jan has a key. Karel and I used to play there. We'd jimmy the gate and run wild. It was always dark and damp, nothing much to see except empty beer kegs and a few parked cars, but we thought it was great and we called it the Cave. Winos always took dumps beneath the overhang just outside, so Jan better watch his step."

Once Karel and I had taken a flashlight. The flitting beam and the shadows it created had made the Cave even eerier. The most remarkable sight was the dripping far wall, a mossy embankment of stones that held back the river. In the deep silence you could hear the throb of the passing current.

"There he is."

Jan reached the sidewalk and glanced both ways. He looked vulnerable down there, an easy target, and for a moment I felt bad about sending him ahead of us.

"Who's that?" Litzi said, pointing to the right.

A figure had just emerged from the shadows and then stopped. In the light of the streetlamp I saw a flash of metal, which made me flinch until I realized it was a leash.

"Somebody walking a dog," I said. "A woman."

Not that women walking dogs weren't necessarily connected to this scheme, as I already knew firsthand. But this one soon took herself out of the picture.

Jan reached the end of the park, shoulders hunched against the wind.

He turned the corner and headed down the sloping cobbles toward the mouth of the Cave. No one else was in sight. More fat raindrops began to fall.

"Let's go," I said. "Wait any longer and we'll get soaked."

We caught up to him without incident. He was trying to scrape something off the sole of his shoe, and the opening stank to high heaven. Piles of human shit were coiled outside the gate, just like in the old days. The rickety chain-link cover of my youth had been replaced by a sturdy aluminum grid, but otherwise little had changed. From what I could see in the gloom there were still only kegs and cars inside, although now the models were Mercedes and BMWs.

Jan shoved open the gate.

"Here," he said, tossing me the car keys. "I'm not supposed to go in. The car is yours for one day only. Return it here."

The key fob had a Mercedes logo. When I pressed a button, a horn beeped and a set of yellow parking lights flashed from deep inside.

Jan turned to go, presumably content to leave the gate open for the rest of the night.

"Where are we supposed to take it?" I called after him.

He kept walking, hands in pockets as he rose briskly up the incline and disappeared to the right. I looked back at Litzi, who shrugged. We picked our way to the car, the dome lights showing the way. It was a Mercedes S450 sedan with German tags from Hamburg. But, as I later discovered, there were no ownership papers. There was a folder on the driver's seat along with a folded road map, a set of printed directions, and a hand-drawn diagram.

"For Mr. William Furse" was printed across the top of the directions.

"Furse?" Litzi said. "Is that a mistake?"

"Probably my code name for the evening. William Furse was a character in *The Double Game.*"

"And what became of him?"

"Nothing, thank goodness. He even showed up in a later book, still in one piece."

"How refreshing."

"Do you know anything about checking brakes?" I asked.

"To see if they're working?"

"Or if they've been tampered with."

She shook her head.

Neither did I. I got out anyway and crouched on the ground to peer beneath the car, hoping to see if anything looked cut, or leaky, or was dangling from the undercarriage. But it was too dark to see a thing, so I brushed off my knees and climbed back in.

"Well?"

"I'll try them out once we're under way. Maybe I'll go a little slower for a while."

"In Prague traffic that shouldn't be a problem."

I opened the folder.

The first thing I saw was a page from the le Carré novel *Tinker, Tailor, Soldier, Spy*. Written atop it in the familiar block lettering was a name, Valerie Humphries. Part of the novel was marked off below. The passage introduced one of my favorite of le Carré's minor characters—Connie Sachs, the crusty maven of records and research for British Intelligence. She was famous for her encyclopedic memory and attention to detail, especially with regard to anyone who had ever even winked at the KGB, or operated within their sphere of influence—including those chosen few who she enjoyed referring to as "Moscow Centre hoods." She drank heavily, played favorites, scorned the dolts who ran the Circus, and was thoroughly, girlishly devoted to the brilliant and beleaguered George Smiley.

Litzi read the paragraphs over my shoulder.

"She sounds like an alcoholic. Is that what this Humphries woman is like?"

"Maybe. Why don't you Google her? While you're at it, shoot a message to my father. See what he can find out about the email address for K-Fresh 62."

Litzi pulled out her smartphone and got to work while I studied the map and the directions, which pointed us onto a tangle of highways that led out of the city, then into the countryside before we were supposed to turn onto a dirt driveway from a rural road some forty miles northwest of Prague. Our destination was up in the hills where farmers grew hops for all that pilsner, and where their forebears had built castles like the one Kafka put in his novel.

The diagram depicted what seemed to be a farming estate, with a long, winding driveway that snaked past a barn and several outbuildings before reaching a rectangular house beside a pond. Presumably this was where we'd find Valerie Humphries. Whether she would be glad to see us was another matter.

"We're going to have to leave this cave before I can get a signal," Litzi said.

"At your service."

I turned the key. A hundred thousand euros' worth of German engineering hummed to life, answering the throb of the river.

"I hope old Valerie keeps late hours. The way I figure it, we won't get there until almost ten. Maybe by then one of Dad's buddies will have figured out who my handler is from that email address."

"How do you knows she's old?"

"Well, if she's at all like Connie Sachs . . ."

We eased through the open gate. At the top of the incline I rolled down the windows for fresh air. I glanced around for any cars waiting to follow us. Seeing none, I accelerated.

"You navigate," I said. Litzi picked up the map.

No sooner had we turned onto the boulevard alongside the river than the heavens opened, and within seconds, rain was sheeting the windshield. Even with the wipers at full tilt, the night was a watery blur. The brakes seemed fine. So far.

Traffic inched along in the downpour, but Litzi kept us entertained by reading aloud from an old *Newsweek* story from 1994 that she found online. Headlined "The Lady Takes Down a Tramp," it was an insider account of how a Humphries-led research team had helped expose the traitorous CIA agent Hamilton Hargraves. And of course the story couldn't resist comparing her to le Carré's Connie Sachs.

"Ninety-four," I said. "Twenty years too late for Jim Angleton. I wonder if she's old enough to have met him before he was sacked."

Litzi scrolled through the text.

"He's not mentioned. But the story says she was fifty-seven, definitely old enough."

"Meaning now she's seventy-three. Hope she still has all her marbles."

"Why send you to see her? Couldn't your handler have talked to her just as easily?"

"Maybe she's come up with something new that she'll only discuss in person. Or maybe it's just to further my education, so I'll know what to do next. As long as she's not another fake Russian, that will be an improvement."

The rain slackened as we reached the outskirts of the city, then fell harder as we eased into the darkness of the countryside. We missed a turn, getting lost enough that we had to backtrack ten miles, and by the time we finally pulled onto the gravel driveway it was nearly ten-thirty. The rural night was black behind its screen of rain, and the country lane was so rutted and mushy that once I nearly got stuck, fishtailing the rear wheels. Finally our beams lit the walls of a two-story stone farmhouse with a pitched shingle roof. There were four mullioned windows across the front of each floor, but only one was lit, downstairs and to the right. There was a separate garage with both doors shut, so we parked in the mush and sprinted for the door.

An overflowing gutter cascaded across the front. We took shelter on a small porch and I knocked loudly. An outside light came on, one of those yellow bulbs for keeping away bugs. A deadbolt slid back before the door eased free.

Any illusion I'd had of meeting a dissipated old drunk, gone to seed like Connie, was immediately dispelled. Valerie Humphries was in remarkable shape, her posture upright, every silver hair in place. But the real surprise was that I recognized her—she was the "Val" from the funeral on Block Island, the one who'd called Lemaster a "pariah" and had then been talking to Nethercutt's wife.

Fortunately, she didn't seem to recognize me, although she did inspect us both from head to toe. She wore a smart black wool skirt, a cream-colored blouse, and a string of pearls, the kind of older woman my father used to call "well preserved" when he was part of the embassy social scene. I would've wagered she dressed like this every night, one of those exacting personalities who demanded as much from herself as from those around her. As she looked us over, she seemed far less impressed with us than we were with her.

"I suppose you're Mr. Furse," she said, employing the code name.

"Yes. Sorry for the late arrival."

"Come in."

I introduced Litzi, but changed her last name to Hauptmann. Humphries raised her eyebrows at the first name, and I was pretty sure I knew why.

"No one warned me about you," she said to Litzi as she ushered us in. "I can't say that I enjoy these surprises, but I'm not the one who makes the plans, and never have been. I'd offer you coffee but the cook is asleep, and if I wake him there'll be hell to pay. Mine is undrinkable, so Burgundy will have to do."

"Burgundy would be generous," I said.

Especially since, with Connie Sachs, Smiley had to provide all the alcohol. The hard stuff, too, as an inducement to memory.

The room was comfortable, with low lighting, rich oriental rugs, and warm colors on the walls. There was a book on the couch that she must have been reading, with a Czech title. A scattering of crosswords and number puzzles were piled to the side—done in pen, not pencil. Maybe it was how she kept her mind sharp, although, as I was about to discover, her tongue could be sharper.

She picked up an open bottle of Burgundy from an end table along with a half-filled glass and led us farther into the house. We came to a sitting room with harsher lighting, white walls, and firmer chairs, as if she was warning us not to get comfortable. Then she fetched two more glasses from a sideboard and poured them full.

"Thanks," I said.

Even Dad, far more discerning than I, would have appreciated the vintage, which tasted dusky and complex enough to have some years behind it.

"How did you end up living here?" Litzi asked.

Urban Europeans were always curious about Americans who chose to maroon themselves in the Continent's outback.

"I married a Czech émigré who worked for the Agency. He always wanted to come back, and after the Velvet Revolution he bought property here. We came over after retiring. I suppose he thought he would become some sort of gentleman farmer. Two years ago he had a heart attack while riding his tractor. It kept rolling, clear across the farm and onto the highway, where it came to rest against an old poplar on the far side of the road. Blocked traffic all afternoon, or I might not have found out for days."

She spoke of it rather clinically, as if she'd just been reviewing his file, then she polished off her summation with a sip of Burgundy before turning to Litzi.

"I don't mean to be inhospitable, but when you've finished your wine you'll have to leave the house. I'm only prepared to discuss certain matters with people who I know have been cleared for the information, and I won't have you eavesdropping on me from some other room."

Litzi was incredulous. First she looked at me, as if this might be my doing, then looked toward the window, where the rain was still pelting down in the dark.

"You may use my rain slicker and hat," Humphries said. "They're in the closet by the door. You can borrow my Wellington boots as well." Litzi's expression changed from surprise to indignation. "If it makes any difference, there are horses in the barn, and you're welcome to visit them. I say that not just because the barn is warm and dry, but because you look as if you've ridden before."

Litzi tilted her head, reassessing this straightforward woman.

"You're right. I rode quite a lot as a girl." That was certainly news to me. "I'll be happy to visit your horses. They're probably friendlier."

"No doubt, my dear."

Litzi set down her wine and headed for the exit. Humphries waited while we listened to the creak of a closet door, the shuffle of a rain jacket, the squeak of boots. Finally we heard the front door opening to the sound of the storm. Then it shut with a rattle.

"Part of your cover, I suppose, but I can't say I approve."

"Excuse me?"

"The girl. And those ridiculous names you're using. Did they actually think I'd enjoy the joke?"

"The joke?"

"Oh, don't play stupid. Litzi was Philby's first wife. Furse was his second wife's maiden name." That was news to me. Lemaster's idea of a prank, perhaps. "But the less I know about you, the better. Besides, *he* sent you, didn't he?"

Was this a trick question?

"Who's 'he'?"

She smiled appreciatively.

"Good. Exactly how you *should* answer. And I certainly won't mention his name, either."

For the first time since I'd set out on this quest, I experienced the excitement of having at last brushed up against the source of it all. Not just an email address, but a direct and personal link. Humphries was apparently an old colleague of my handler's—at least that's what she seemed to think. She also seemed convinced that I was a CIA man. A professional, not a freelance. Meaning I had better start acting like I knew what I was doing, lest she get suspicious and clam up.

The rain came harder as a gust of wind shook the windows. I felt a pang of sympathy for Litzi, but it was time to get down to business.

25

"She's jealous, by the way, that girl you're calling Litzi."

It was an odd way for Humphries to begin, but I could hardly let it pass without comment.

"Jealous of you?"

She shook her head, frowning at the absurdity.

"Of you, and of what you know. But she must know things, too. You have to know at least part of the picture to be jealous of those who know the rest. And that's where your colleague is now. Her face was broadcasting it from the moment you walked in the door."

"And you know this how?"

"From more than forty years of observing other people just like her, in a business where what you knew defined your status. Reading files teaches you to read people, believe it or not."

"I'll keep that in mind."

I'd brought the folder from the Mercedes, which turned out to be a mistake. She reached over and nimbly snatched it from beside me on the chair. Opening it, she flicked through the pages and sighed when she saw the le Carré passage.

"Spare me the goddamned Connie Sachs crap, if you don't mind."

"But I didn't—"

"No sense in denying it. I can see it in your stupid mooning face, the star-struck look of the devoted reader who thinks he's finally found the real thing. Well, get it out of your head. The real Connie was some MI5 gal, Millicent Bagot. She died four years ago. Look it up, if that's what you're into. But I don't come from a book, and no one ever wrote me into one. Letting *Newsweek* write that load of PR rubbish about the Hargraves case was a mistake, but no one asked me, of course. None of the old Agency spooks who wrote novels even knew who I was, and that's the way I preferred it."

"And what did you know about them?"

"Most of the time I only knew them by their cover names. It helped me stay objective when it came time to evaluate their reports. I briefed a few of them, of course, on paper anyway. Supplied them with all kinds of useful items, which they promptly forgot the moment they were in the field, in favor of their so-called instinct. It's like when a crop scientist tests the soil to come up with the perfect formula for what to plant and how to tend it, only to have a bunch of stupid plowboys in heavy boots trample everything to mush, thinking they know better. Of course, later, when they're growing apples where they should have planted peaches, they bitch and moan when everything fails and ask why no one ever warned them. That's what it was like being in research."

She sipped her wine and smoothed her skirt, glaring at me as if I were another blinkered fool who would ignore her advice.

"So what have you been able to learn?" she asked. "What have you discovered?"

Whoa, now. Who was supposed to be getting information from this session, my handler or me? Was this going to turn into a face-to-face version of a dead drop, with Humphries reporting my latest findings?

"I'm the one who's here for information."

"Of course. But I need a reference point. For a researcher, context is everything. I'm not asking you to divulge operational detail, just fill me in on the big picture. And let me warn you now that I plan to be very tight when it comes to divulging actual names. Happy to give them when relevant, but there's no sense in being fast and loose unless it's warranted. The rules exist for a reason. Now, where do you stand?"

"Okay. Well . . ." I paused, collecting my thoughts. "I seem to be tracking an informational trail for some sort of courier network set up by Ed Lemaster back in the sixties, when he was an operative, on behalf of a source code-named Dewey, who may or may not have been known to, or even used by, the KGB. Its transit points were in Vienna, Prague, maybe also Budapest."

She nodded, seeming to approve.

"What's important is that you're familiar with the name Dewey. That's the key to the whole thing."

"And what, exactly, do you mean by 'the whole thing'?"

"Lemaster's betrayal, of course. His spying for the other side. Not that anyone who counted ever believed in it. I practically drew them a map at one point, X marks the spot, but no one ever picked up a shovel to dig for treasure. Maybe they were afraid of what they'd find. And for a change it wasn't just the field men who were playing the fool."

"Angleton, you mean?" I was guessing, of course.

"Yes, Angleton. Poor dead Jim. If he'd only listened to me and a few others, well . . ."

I couldn't help but recall that moment as a boy, when I'd encountered him on my bicycle as he tidied up in the wake of a murder. "Go home, son." That's probably what he'd be saying now. This time I wouldn't scare so easily.

"Is he at the middle of this?"

"Him and his people. And the two Russians, of course. Angleton's old pal Golitsyn, and his nemesis Nosenko. You know about that bloody mess, don't you?"

"Only what I've read in books."

"Books!" she scoffed. "They don't know the half of it!"

Historians had nonetheless written plenty about Golitsyn and Nosenko, especially with regard to their role in Angleton's ill-fated mole hunt.

"Golitsyn defected in what, the early sixties?"

"December of sixty-one," she answered. "The fifteenth. We didn't have much use for him at first, so he went over to help our cousins in London for a while. He returned in the summer of sixty-three, right after we'd moved into our new headquarters in Langley.

"Of course, you never would have known Jim Angleton's office was brand spanking new. Every square foot of space was already piled with paper. File folders were part of the décor, along with a whole row of safes. Kept his blinds shut, with a single lamp on his desk that left everyone but him in the dark. He'd hunch there like a miser with his coins, counting all the facts to make sure they added up."

"Was he already so paranoid?"

"Wrong word. The enemy *was* out to get us, and Jim knew it better than anybody. Once that bastard Philby burned him, he never recovered. Do you have any idea what it's like to work for someone who's so mistrustful, yet so brilliant? No matter what you said or did, Jim analyzed it to the last detail. As chief of research I was his main fact-checker, but that didn't mean I was above suspicion. Order the wrong damn thing for lunch at La Niçoise and he'd question you for ten minutes about your motives."

"But he trusted Golitsyn."

"Trusted him absolutely. Mostly because Golitsyn was just as suspicious of the Russians as he was. They both thought the Soviets were the world's reigning supermen when it came to deception."

"And then Nosenko defected?"

"Fourth of February, 1964. Golitsyn immediately pegged him as a plant, which was all Jim needed to hear. I believed it, too. Everyone in Jim's shop did. So Nosenko basically went into a hole in the ground out at the Farm."

"They kept him there awhile, didn't they?"

"Nearly four years. But it was never airtight. The hounds in the Soviet division managed to get their people in to see him. They were quite enchanted by Nosenko's stories, and when Jim heard they were feeding his tips to their field men, he was more convinced than ever that the Soviets were playing us for fools. The biggest problem was that Nosenko was directly contradicting Golitsyn, at least on some things. It was a threat to our worldview in Counterintelligence, so Jim mobilized for war. That's when he hired his three agents, the ones nobody was supposed to know about. They didn't even appear as a line item in our budget."

"And one of them was Lemaster."

"Code name Headlight. That was all I knew then, their code names. Headlight, Blinker, Taillight."

A lineup, it occurred to me, that could easily have been incorporated into a title for a John le Carré novel—*Blinker, Taillight, Soldier, Spy*—with only Lemaster's code name missing from the formula.

"Why 'Headlight'?"

"Jim rather liked the completeness of the set. Bumper to bumper, he had every signal covered, with himself at the wheel. It made things quite handy once the demolition derby of his Great Mole Hunt got under way. Because it was their job—their *sole* job—to verify Golitsyn and tear down Nosenko. Jim's very own truth squad. And it was my job, of course, to dot their i's and cross their t's, fact by fact. I was a busy woman."

She paused for a tiny sip of wine. Noticing my glass was empty, she refilled it. I had a feeling that even if we were to continue for hours she'd never empty hers. When information was being dispensed and discussed, she wanted to remain totally in control.

"So how did it go?" I asked. "Did the agents deliver?"

"For four months, nothing. Zilch. Jim was after me day and night. 'Find a lead for them!' Twirling his arms like some madman football coach on the sidelines. 'You've been tracking these Moscow hoods for years, can't you find them a single goddamn lead?' And those poor boys were working like dogs, of course, filing reports two and three times a week. But even I could see it was all garbage. Things we already knew, or from such dubious sourcing that it was completely unreliable.

"Then, in early sixty-five, Headlight struck gold. A man he met in Budapest. On a tram car, of all places, right as he was rolling across the Danube on the Margit Bridge. Source Nijinsky."

I was struck by the eerie symmetry of her story to Lemaster's version of how he'd come up with Richard Folly in Budapest in '67. Two characters, two strokes of fortune, both originating on the same tram line, two years apart. Maybe both were fiction.

"Nijinsky?"

"Like the dancer. Because he was so nimble. He had traveling papers for practically the whole East Bloc, the West as well. Headlight met him all over Europe. Everything he came up with made Jim smile. Finally, we had the confirmation we'd been looking for that Nosenko was a fraud, a plant, a cancer."

"What about Blinker and Taillight?"

"Empty vessels, at least for a while. Believe me, they weren't happy with the state of play. Headlight's star was rising. Theirs were in eclipse. At least until Blinker met a disenchanted Soviet diplomat at some falling-down resort on the North Sea, up in Rugen. They arranged for a meet on friendlier territory in Hamburg, where we got him for a full six hours at a safe house. Source Kettledrum. Very talkative, very much in the know. But not at all what Jim wanted to hear."

"He backed up Nosenko?"

"Not straight down the line. That was the beauty of it. Corroborated some things, but cast doubt on others. Whatever you thought of Nosenko, no one ever believed he was infallible. No defector ever was, which is why this source of Blinker's made such an impression."

"What did Angleton say?"

"That Kettledrum was a plant, of course. Golitsyn agreed. Perfect example of Soviet artfulness, they said. So they tag-teamed him, body slams week after week. Then, when one of Headlight's reports from Nijinsky shot him down as well, that was all Jim needed. They threw Kettledrum to the wolves."

"What do you mean?"

"They blew him to the Russians. Put out word that he'd been talking, but that we knew he was a plant. I think Jim wanted to see how quickly they'd snatch him back."

"Did they?"

"Sent him straight to Moscow on a chartered Aeroflot out of Schöne-feld-Berlin. Four days later we received a credible report he'd been executed. Not exactly the welcome home Jim had anticipated."

"Jesus."

"Well put. Kettledrum died for our sins. Not that it fazed Jim. His argument was, well of course they killed him! The better to fool us! No freedom-loving democracy would have sacrificed a good man that way, of course, not for simply doing his job. But these were the Soviet super-men who had to win at any cost! And with no congressional committees to look up their skirts they were free to play as fast and loose as they pleased. Our people in the Soviet division went berserk when they heard that, and Jim went berserk in return. That's when the real war began."

"With the Soviet division?"

"Worse, far worse. A civil war, right within our own tight little bor-ders of Counterintelligence. True believers versus the apostates. All the pitchforks were out. But of course Jim's was the biggest."

"Who opposed him?"

"Those names aren't relevant, and I think you know why."

Meaning one of them must have been my handler. I think.

"Which side were you on?"

"I stayed neutral. Records were an easy place to keep your head down. But for weeks nothing got done. Every report from Nijinsky and Headlight was hotly debated. The division was in gridlock. Finally even Jim knew there had to be either a truce or a resolution. He decided to settle it once and for all by summoning home all his agents—Headlight, Blinker, and Taillight. Each was to be fluttered under the most intensive conditions. Put up or shut up. Product testing at its finest."

Polygraphed, she meant. A lie detector. I'd seen the term "fluttered" in at least a dozen different novels.

"That's pretty extreme."

"Oh, it was, and it was quite a day when they all flew in. For three days everyone in CI was on pins and needles as the testing proceeded."

"And?"

"They all passed. Flying colors. Which to Jim only proved that Blinker must be KGB, because by then it was common knowledge how well trained their people were in handling polygraphs. Self-hypnosis, all sorts of tricks to equalize stress, whether you were lying or not. We tried to stay a step ahead of them, of course, but no one was ever sure if we were managing."

Where had I read all of this stuff about polygraphs? Now I remembered. *Orchids for Mother,* a 1977 novel. Based on Angleton, in fact. It even used his Agency nickname of "Mother" for the main character. The author was Aaron Latham, who like me had been a reporter at the *Washington Post*, although well before my time. Supposedly his portrait of Angleton was one of the deftest ever penned, in fact or fiction.

"So the whole thing was a bust?"

"It did produce one little oddity. Jim asked me to collect the records of their previous flutterings, to compare notes. In rounding up that material I came across a curious cross-reference in Headlight's file. Some episode involving a colleague in Belgrade who wasn't even with the Agency. And from way back in fifty-nine, before Headlight was even Headlight. Lemaster had only been aboard two years, and here he was mixed up with some brouhaha over tampered polygraph results."

The hairs on my neck stood up. Dad and I were in Belgrade then. It was the year my mother left us. And now I knew Lemaster had been there as well, long before Dad and he had supposedly become friends.

"Tampered with how?"

"The initial results indicated some sort of security breach, but apparently some junior diplomat had helped clean it up, or vice versa. The file didn't make it clear. Nothing all that unusual, I suppose. Fluttering was all the rage in those days, and it's never been infallible. But for whatever reason this other fellow intervened."

"Why?"

"The file didn't say. I tried checking with State, but they told me to fuck off. 'Personal and confidential.' Agency personnel people told us the matter was a moot point, because the test had been retaken with perfect results. But, well, I suppose now the implication is obvious. Maybe that was Lemaster's one weak moment, but some friend of his with better connections helped clean it up."

I tried to keep my voice from shaking as I asked the next two questions.

"Who was the junior diplomat?"

"His name is irrelevant."

"Was it Warfield Cage?"

She narrowed her eyes and slowly set down her wineglass, reappraising me.

"How did you come up with that name, Mr. Furse?"

"My methodology isn't relevant."

She very nearly smiled. Then, in an act that I took as a major concession, she fetched the bottle and poured herself a refill, although she of course topped off my glass as well. I needed it.

"I suppose I should take that as a good sign," she said. "Your work must be further along than I thought. Where were we?"

I concentrated, trying to regain my composure. No wonder Dad had always glossed over where he'd first met Lemaster. Had his actions helped a mole go free, and then thrive?

"We were still discussing the war. The believers versus the apostates."

"Yes. The showdown with the polygraphs. It took the fight out of everybody. Jim, too. Even Nijinsky's reports lost their edge. They were hazier, more tentative. As if he'd been spooked. Gradually Jim turned his attention elsewhere. Other suspicions, other targets. And we all know how that turned out."

"Badly."

"For everyone, Jim included. And that might have been the end of it if I hadn't found one last loose thread. A tiny one, barely showing. But when I pulled it, a whole row of stitching came loose, right there in the middle of Jim's favorite garment."

"Headlight?"

She nodded, pausing to collect herself for the final run. I sipped more wine. She put a hand to her glass, then pushed it gently away. Whatever she was about to tell me called for the utmost sobriety.

"It was a small thing." Her voice was quiet, but steady. "An old fil-

ing from some source of the Soviet division's, completely unimpeach-
able, mostly because for years the material he'd been providing at such
extreme danger to himself had, unfortunately, been quite unspectacular.
One of those poor souls who thinks he knows more than he does. But he
was occasionally useful for verification, so they kept him active.

"Well, one day I'm cross-referencing one of his filings with some
of our Prague material when I spot a throwaway item about a source
the Soviets were in contact with there and in Budapest. Code name
Dewey. Not much detail otherwise. Just a handful of dates and places
where Dewey had supposedly been active. No other mention of him
before or since, and its significance might have slipped right past me
if I hadn't just been reviewing the movements for all three of our field
men—Headlight, Blinker, and Taillight—for Jim's final postmortem on
our sad little civil war. One word caught my eye. 'Bookstores.' Apparently this Dewey fellow liked using them for meeting places, exchange
points. So did Headlight."

I leaned forward, watching her closely. She stared toward the corner,
into some faraway space.

"I took the few dates and places I had for Dewey and checked them
against the movements for our three lads. There were five points of
intersection, and every one of them was a match with Headlight."

"Did you show Angleton?"

"And have him explain that this was just Headlight's means of covering for Nijinsky? Or some diabolical plant by Nosenko? No. We were
being peacemakers by then. Love was in the air. So I took it very quietly to one of the generals on the rebel side. It raised his eyebrows, of
course. If it had been a month earlier, he would have screamed it from
the rooftops. But with the new truce mentality he proposed that we
keep it under wraps and try to build on it. We knew we'd need more
before we could ever take it forward."

One of the generals. Meaning my handler, most likely.

"And did you?"

She shook her head.

"We couldn't advance it, couldn't back it up. Besides, everyone was
still licking their wounds, and soon there was another in-house political
battle to deal with."

"The Soviet division again?"

She nodded.

"Flak from an old case officer of Headlight's who'd apparently been one of his first handlers back in Belgrade. Claimed all our digging around was raising hell with his old networks. Code name Thresher."

Hearing the name created a prickly sensation in my fingertips.

"Thresher? You're sure?"

"I wasn't cleared to know his real identity."

But was pretty sure I knew it. Breece Preston. Dad had mentioned that Preston and Lemaster might have worked together early on, but he hadn't known the nature of their relationship, or that the location was Belgrade.

Or had he? Those previous gaps in his knowledge now seemed dubious in light of the news about the fudged polygraph.

"Are you all right?" Humphries was peering at me in apparent concern.

"I'm fine. Just trying to keep everything straight. So, this flap with Thresher?"

"Yes. It made us more cautious than ever. Even if we'd been able to build a better case, I'm not sure how aggressively we could have pushed it."

"So the whole thing just went away?"

"You have to realize that by then Jim was on the verge of self-destruction, and Lemaster was starting to publish his books. In seventy-four they forced Jim out. It was not long after Lemaster quit. As soon as Jim left, the division quietly began calling in the rest of our field men. Blinker, then Taillight. Even if we'd been inclined to open things back up, there was no longer a pressing operational reason to do so."

She seemed almost ready to conclude, so I asked about some of the particulars of Vladimir's old memos while I still had the chance.

"What did you know about Source Leo, or code name Oleg?"

"KGB men. Leo was one of Oleg's travelers. Prague, mostly. A waste of time, usually. When he wasn't whoring he was usually drunk. Oleg sat back on his throne in Moscow and moved pieces across the board. Some people thought he was their Jim Angleton, hunting moles. Others were convinced he was running them."

"Did you ever come across the names Karloff, Fishwife, or Woodman?"

She furrowed her brow.

"No. Never."

"What about a Source Glinka?"

"That rings a bell." She paused, gazing off into the corner again. "Yes. From the early seventies. His name showed up in a single report, an intercept out of Leipzig. He was after someone named Pericles, who some of the boys on the Soviet desk were convinced for a while was a possible American mole."

"Pericles?"

"Jim dismissed it as rubbish. Not that it was much to begin with."

"Why did he dismiss it?"

"Why do you think? Because the only one of our own sources who ever mentioned the name was Nosenko. If there was anything more to it, then I never heard."

"So, after Angleton was gone, no more civil war?"

"Peaceful coexistence. And that's probably how things would have remained if not for that damned interview Lemaster gave in eighty-four. Some scribbler in Washington with an ax to grind."

This certainly explained at least one reason my handler hadn't told her my real name. That plus Dad's possible role. She obviously had nothing but disdain for the Fourth Estate, and for William Cage in particular.

"I've seen that piece," I said. "The one where Lemaster said he'd considered working for the other side?"

She nodded.

"It was like he was teasing us, telling us we'd missed our chance and would never catch him now. I always wondered what Jim made of it, but by then his health was failing, and by all accounts he still believed deeply that Nosenko was a plant. Then he died, of course. May of eighty-seven. I did hear something strange at his funeral. When the Agency went to clean out his house they found a signed copy of Lemaster's mole novel, *The Double Game*."

"Is that really so surprising?"

"That's not the odd part. Apparently Jim had scribbled all through it. Page after page, marked and annotated, with tabs and Post-its. Just like he would have done with a field report. Nutty, yes?"

"Yes."

"Unless he knew how to read between the lines better than the rest of us."

"So you think he was guilty. Headlight, I mean."

"I used to. Now? Some nights when I go back over everything in my head it never seems quite as damning. A few points of intersection on a map. Some unexplained coincidence. A source who was probably too good to be true. There was always something missing, and I could never decide what. And even if Nijinsky was a bad egg, I suppose Headlight could have been played as much as the rest of us."

"A victim of his own ambition?"

"Something like that. What finally prompted the reopening of this case, can you tell me? I have my own theory, of course. That damn funeral had to be part of it. An ill wind from start to finish, and a ghost in every corner." The Nethercutt funeral, no doubt, although I didn't dare mention that I'd been there. "But beyond that, what can you tell me?"

"Nothing, I'm afraid."

"Yes. Thought you'd say that."

Then she nodded as if I'd passed a security test, little suspecting that I wanted to know the answer more than she did.

26

Valerie Humphries rose from her chair, signaling that our interview was over.

"I'd better page your friend in from the barn."

She moved stiffly after all that time sitting down, and led me to an alcove near the entrance where there was an intercom with buttons for each outbuilding. She pressed one and leaned toward the panel.

"This is the all-clear, my dear. He's yours again."

We waited a few seconds for Litzi's response. She sounded out of breath.

"Someone just walked past the window out here."

"Oh, dear. How long ago?"

"A minute, maybe two."

Humphries seemed unnaturally calm. Both of them did, judging from Litzi's even tone. Hardly what you'd expect from a pair of glorified librarians with a stalker in their midst, out in the dark and the rain. I pushed the button to speak.

"I'm coming out there."

"Relax, dear," Humphries said. "We'll both go. I have a twelve-gauge, already loaded."

She opened a closet and indeed hauled out a shotgun.

"Grab that rain slicker. It was my husband's. A little short, but it will have to do. I'll take this old trench coat. Now how damn cliché is that?"

"You, uh, trained at the Farm, too?"

"Of course. Just because I ended up in records doesn't mean I wasn't properly prepared for anything."

She pressed the intercom button.

"Help is on its way, dear. Stay with the horses."

"Okay."

Humphries handed me a flashlight the size of a large salami.

"If anything moves, put the beam right in his face. I'll take care of the rest."

The rain hit us like a stiff wind, pelting our faces. Humphries locked the door behind us and kept the gun under the folds of her coat, leaning into the storm along the beam of light. Our footsteps slurped in the mud. Fallen leaves blew wildly across our path.

The barn loomed ahead on a slight rise, like a shipwreck on a reef. I was jumpy, looking everywhere, straining my eyes through the dark and the blowing debris for any sign of an intruder, especially a big American in a mullet.

"He's probably gone by now," Humphries said, sounding almost disappointed.

Litzi threw open the barn door as we approached. The flashlight lit her face. Considering the circumstances she looked pretty calm, although she was clearly glad to see us.

"Let's go 'round to that window where you saw him pass," Humphries said.

We slogged into high grass.

"Give us some light," Humphries said.

You could see a rough path near the barn window where someone had tramped down the grass. It led back toward the house, crossing the mud and then reaching a window that peeped in through the blinds toward the two chairs where Humphries and I had been chatting moments ago.

"Damned snoop," she said. She pointed to a large set of footprints in the mud at the base of the wall. She looked up at me and smiled crookedly.

"If I didn't know better, I'd say he might be your babysitter."

"Babysitter?"

She eyed me closely.

"They must think you're worth quite a lot if they're going to that much trouble, don't you think?"

"Unless he's here because he's after me. Or after you."

She laughed.

"Heavens," she said. "If that were the case, then we'd all be dead or tied up in someone's trunk by now."

She stooped. The footprints were beneath the eaves, so they were fairly well sheltered from the downpour.

"Well, the shoes aren't of a Russian make, I can tell you that," she said. "Although I suppose half the Oligarchs and their henchmen wear nothing but Italian loafers these days. All the same, he'll be gone by now."

"How can you be sure?" Litzi asked.

"I heard a car pulling away earlier, just before we buzzed you on the intercom."

I looked inquiringly at Litzi, who shook her head. I hadn't heard anything, either.

"Even with my old ears, when you live alone out in a place like this you learn to notice just about everything."

"Would you like us to stay the night with you?" I asked.

Humphries made a face.

"The cook is here. I can wake him in a pinch. Besides, I'm not prepared for company. There aren't even sheets on the guest beds."

"We can manage without them," Litzi said.

"No. No. Whoever it was didn't come for me. And when the quarry leaves, the problem will leave with it."

She smiled, but I said nothing as the rain dripped off my jacket.

"The two of you should be getting on. That bridge you crossed on the way in, five clicks from here? It often floods in rain like this. Getting washed into a creek would be a pretty unsatisfactory way to shake surveillance, don't you think?"

We went back inside just long enough to drop off the rain gear. As we said good-bye I couldn't help but notice that Humphries looked thoroughly invigorated. Even if she had to stay up half the night with the shotgun propped against the bed, she was enjoying herself.

"Watch yourself," she said before shutting the door. "If not for your own sake, then because you're doing this for all the rest of us who are no longer in the game."

We ran to the car, cranked the engine, and began rolling back through the muck toward Prague.

We were silent all the way up the narrow drive, keeping an eye out for anything that might jump out at us from the darkness. I was shivering from the cold and wet as we turned onto the smooth track of the rural highway, but the heater and the thrum of the tires on the blacktop soon calmed us. The creek was high, as Humphries had warned, but it wasn't yet flooding. Litzi smelled of hay, manure, and warm horseflesh, a comforting combination.

"How were the horses?"

"Beautiful. She has a good eye for them."

"Well, I knew the Viennese loved horses, but I never knew that applied to you."

"It happened after I knew you."

"You told her it was when you were a girl."

"It's complicated."

I let it go.

"Who do you think was snooping around?" she asked.

"The mullet, maybe? Or maybe someone checking up on us. Like she said, if he'd wanted to harm us he probably would've done it. It certainly would have been a convenient place to finish us off."

"Are we being fools?"

"Probably. Maybe that's part of what makes it interesting. Humphries obviously thought it was a blast."

"She does have spirit, even if she's a bitch. I hope she had useful information."

I briefed her on the basics but didn't mention my dad's involvement with the polygraph in Belgrade. I wasn't even sure how to ask him about it. Considering the timing, I was already uneasy about all the possibilities.

"What's wrong?" Litzi asked.

"I'm tired."

A midget-sized Opel with the dimmest of taillights was just ahead, barely visible in the rain. I braked and began looking for a way to pass, but we had reached a curvy section through a forest. A quarter mile later a big truck lumbered up on our rear, headlights blazing, horn sounding.

"What the fuck?"

I had to flip down the mirror to get the glare out of my face. I beeped at the car ahead of us, but it beetled onward. The truck lurched up within inches of our bumper.

"What's he doing!" Litzi shouted. "Do you think—?"

"I don't know! But there's nothing we can do about it now."

The Opel's brake lights winked as we approached another curve, and

I nearly rear-ended it. The truck responded with a groan and shudder, air brakes snorting as the damn thing actually tapped us, which nearly sent us sprawling, like a Chihuahua getting a love tap from a buffalo. I held tightly to the wheel as the Mercedes shimmied, then stabilized. The truck's headlights flooded the car.

"Who do you think it is?" I asked.

"Just drive," Litzi said. She looked pale and haggard in the glow of the dashboard light. We were too old for this. The truck bore down with another burst of acceleration, its engine throbbing in our ears. Just ahead on the right I spotted a gap in the trees—a small turnout, big enough for us but not the truck—and at the last second I wrenched the wheel right, hooking the tires off the shoulder into a slurry of wet gravel.

The truck blasted its horn in passing, heading off into the night after the hapless Opel. The Mercedes ground to a halt. I was exhausted. Litzi hugged herself and exhaled slowly.

"So maybe he was just an asshole," she said. "Your average lorry driver."

"Plenty of them to go around."

After a few seconds I tried turning back onto the road, but could only spin the front wheels in the mush.

"Shit!"

"We're stuck?"

I tried rocking the car back and forth between first gear and reverse, the way you do in the snow, but the tires only dug deeper. I shut off the engine and slumped in my seat in the sudden quiet.

"I'll have to dig us out. Right now I'm too tired to try."

"Why don't we rest awhile." She put a hand to my cheek. "It's probably the safest spot for miles."

The road was empty and quiet, and the rain had slackened to a drizzle. Drops from overhanging pines pinged on the roof like a distant drumroll, a martial lullaby. Litzi lowered her seat and curled up facing me. I opened the windows a fraction for fresh air, and instantly smelled the resin of the pines. Then I lowered my own seat and stretched out as best I could. I was almost instantly asleep.

An hour or so later I awakened to voices and the steady tapping of water on the roof. A flashlight beam veered into the car, and I sat up with a start, stiff and disoriented. Voices were speaking Czech, but the windows were fogged. I rubbed a hand on the windshield and saw a police car canted in front of us, blocking our way, not that we were capable of moving. Looking over my shoulder I saw a second police car wedged behind us. A cop was training his flashlight on our German tags. There was a sharp knock on the driver's side window, which awakened Litzi.

"What's happening?" she said groggily.

"Cops." I rolled down the window.

The policeman leaned down, smelling strongly of aftershave. He said something in Czech that I couldn't understand, so I answered in English.

"Sorry, I don't speak your language."

He sighed, then consulted with the other one, who took his place at the window.

"Your documents, please."

I fished out my passport and D.C. driver's license, hoping that was all he'd want. He inspected them carefully, then leaned down again.

"Auto registration papers, please."

Shit.

I made a show of searching the glove compartment and rifling through the map, then spread my hands in a plaintive shrug.

"I seem to have misplaced them."

He turned and spoke to his partner, which set off a flurry of activity. The flashlight beam went back to the tags, and the cops nodded as they spoke. One went to his car and got on the radio while the other one stood by my door, backing away a step and eyeing me closely. We were in trouble.

Litzi unlatched her door, and the cop on my side perked up like a soldier on alert. He dropped his right hand to the holster of his sidearm and shouted to his colleague.

"What are you doing?" I hissed.

"Let me handle this."

She slowly opened the door and stepped carefully into the night. Now both cops had their hands on their guns.

"Litzi, *what* are you doing?"

"Stay in the car." Her tone conveyed absolute authority and poise. Impressive, if unnerving.

The policemen approached from either side. They looked calmer now. She turned away from me and began speaking to them in a tone too low for me even to tell what language she was using. Within a few seconds the three of them were conferring with hand gestures and nods, like a committee meeting with Litzi presiding. The cop from the rear car returned to his vehicle and again got on the radio. I saw him speak into his handset, wait awhile, and then nod as he spoke again. He came back up front and took the other cop aside.

Their body language was interesting. A few shrugs, a sag of the shoulders, and a burst of animated movement. The cop who made the radio call seemed to be trying to calm the other one. All the while, Litzi watched patiently from a few feet away, arms folded. The first police-man then got into his car, slammed the door, and drove away in a spray of gravel.

The second one spoke briefly to Litzi and turned to go. He was about to get into his car when Litzi barked something that made him sigh and nod. He walked behind the Mercedes and, like a suspect under arrest, spread his legs wide and placed his hands against the trunk.

"He's going to push," Litzi shouted. "Start the engine and see if you can get us out."

Amazing. I did as she asked—why not, everything she was doing seemed to be working—and after a few seconds of heaving and rocking, the Mercedes gained just enough traction to crawl onto the shoulder.

Litzi shouted her thanks and hopped in. The cop wiped his hands on his trousers, got back into his cruiser, and drove away.

"That was miraculous. How did you manage?"

"I told them I was German, that it was my husband's car and you were my boyfriend, and that, well, it was a long story. But they believed me."

"German? What if they'd asked for your passport?"

"I'd tell them I left it at the hotel."

"What if they'd phoned the hotel?"

"Do you have any more questions, officer? It worked, didn't it?"

I wanted to believe her, but it didn't sound like the sort of half-baked story that would have passed muster with cops. But if I gave voice to those doubts, where would we be then?

"Okay. No more stops, though. Not until Prague."

Within fifteen minutes the rain stopped. Within half an hour the moon peeped through torn clouds as leaves blew across the highway. Litzi had hardly said a word.

"You don't trust me, do you?" she finally said.

"Why do you say that?"

"You didn't answer my question."

"I don't know what to think anymore. Even Valerie Humphries noticed something. She said you were jealous of what I knew, and that you must know something, too."

"That woman spent forty years being paid to be suspicious. What would you expect her to say? But as long as you're being suspicious about everyone, try starting with your friend Karel."

"Why, because his dad spied on me?"

"How did your handler know about the Cave, that place where the two of you used to play?"

I squeezed the steering wheel, not wanting to admit that the question had already crossed my mind.

"I don't know what to think about anybody anymore."

Even my father, I almost added, and Litzi seemed to realize I'd held something back. She lowered her seat and again curled up on her side, this time facing away from me.

I drove on toward Prague, alone with my worries.

27

The morning brought sunlight and a better mood. With nothing on our schedule until nightfall, when I was due to meet Bruzek at his bookstore, we slept late and awoke refreshed.

I went down to the lobby for a copy of the local English-language daily, then ordered a room service breakfast while Litzi showered. We moved the tray next to the open window, Litzi in her robe and me in a T-shirt and jeans. Whatever tension had existed the night before, a mutual calm now prevailed, and neither of us wanted to spoil it.

Litzi's phone beeped, and she smiled when she saw the message.

"From your father," she said. "Some friend of his ran down that email address."

I eagerly looked over her shoulder, but the news was disappointing. The messages from K-Fresh 62 had been routed via servers in Vienna and London from points unknown, and the identity was registered to a John Brown of New York, New York. An obvious fake who knew how to cover his tracks.

"So much for that lead," I said, gloomy again.

Litzi smiled and took my hand.

"We should do something fun this afternoon," she said. "Go off by ourselves somewhere, if only for a while."

"With only the Mullet for company? I'm not sure that's such a good idea."

She dropped my hand.

"Sorry," I said. "But I think we're running out of safe havens."

"No. You're right. If we go anywhere, we should stay in a crowd."

She shook open the newspaper and disappeared behind it. I poked at my eggs and toast while she ate her yogurt and fruit.

But the strong coffee was like a tonic, and as the caffeine kicked in it felt for a moment as if we were an old married couple, comfortably recuperating from a night on the town. Outside our window the eaves were still dripping from the storm, and we could hear pigeons in the gutter, fretting through the debris. Then Litzi set down her cup with a clatter of china.

"My God!" She dropped the paper onto our breakfast, staring at the page.

"What's wrong?"

"Bruzek is dead. Killed in his store, just after closing time."

She showed me the story.

"Murdered?"

"An accident, it says." She continued reading. "A shelf of books in his office. It fell on him. A relative—probably Anton, but it doesn't say—heard the crash and found him underneath, buried under all those books. Apparently the shelving struck his head. An ambulance was called, but it was too late."

I read the story. Two columns of type on an inside page, with a mug shot of Bruzek that must have been taken at least twenty years ago.

"Patricide," I mumbled in disbelief.

"What?"

"The books. He bumped into those shelves while we were talking, and they creaked and swayed like a big tree about to fall. But he told me not to worry. He said the books were his children, and would never harm him."

"How awful. For Anton, too."

"Do you think that . . . ?"

"Don't even say it. Maybe it really was an accident."

I shook my head.

"It's too much of a coincidence."

She pushed away the newspaper. Her eyes brimmed with tears.

"I have brought you nothing but harm," she said.

"Easy. It's not your doing."

"Isn't it?"

"Of course not."

Although it *had* crossed my mind that events had taken a decidedly dangerous turn almost from the moment Litzi and I had joined forces. I doubted she was to blame, but we did seem like an unlucky combination. Since our reunion at the Bräunerhof there had been two deaths, two close scrapes with the police, and a sighting of a stalker outside Valerie Humphries's farmhouse, plus all these people who seemed to be following us.

But why?

"These things we're tracking happened almost half a century ago," I said. "And the Soviet Union is dead and gone. What could possibly make it worth killing for?"

"Reputations are at stake. That's always worth something."

"Lemaster's? He wouldn't give a shit. It's not like they'd prosecute him after all this time. If anything, he'd get a sales bump from the publicity."

"There are such things as friends. Maybe he'd lose his?"

"He lives way back in the woods of Maine and keeps to himself. He hasn't given an interview in years. All those generals he talks to for his techno-thrillers would probably cut him off, but I doubt they're his type anyway. He's just using them, and to hear my father talk, that's how he's always operated."

"He didn't use you, did he? Quite the opposite."

"I'm not so sure anymore. From what Valerie Humphries said, he might have said all that just to taunt his enemies. It's got to be something bigger, something beyond him."

A knock at the door made us jump.

"Yes?" I called out.

A muffled voice replied: "Extra towels, sir."

Litzi got up to let him in.

"Don't!" But she was already opening the door.

I sprang from my seat and backed toward the window as the man entered. His face was obscured behind a stack of folded towels. I fully expected a gun barrel to poke out from the pile at any moment. Instead, he grabbed two towels off the top of the pile, put them on the foot of the bed, and left, shutting the door behind him. By then I'd backed myself into a corner and looked like a fool.

"Are you all right?" Litzi asked.

"Blame Eric Ambler," I said. "*Background to Danger.* There's a scene where someone tries to kill a man, and they get into his room by bringing extra towels."

She shook her head.

"Next you'll think *I'm* acting like someone in a book, and I'm guessing I won't like the comparison. The women in those novels don't come off very well, do they? No one ever seems to trust them. Just like with us."

I wanted to disagree, but couldn't. And she was right about the books, or a lot of them, anyway. I recalled Folly's string of faithless lovers, and Smiley's adulterous Lady Ann. The few women who were reliable seemed to either die or disappear, or descend into drunkenness like Connie Sachs. But instead of addressing Litzi's statement head-on, I chose the coward's way out.

"It's getting late," I said. "I should take a shower. Then we'll talk. Don't worry, we'll figure this out."

She nodded, but looked glum. I took one of the fresh towels and turned on the taps. As the hot water streamed down my face, I decided that, uncomfortable or not, I needed to start asking Litzi some tougher questions. In return, I'd open up a bit more myself. It might be awkward for a while, but it would put our minds at ease.

I must have been in there for ten minutes, letting the steam flush out my anxiety, and when I turned off the water, the only sound was the drip of the nozzle. I dried off, wrapped the towel around my waist, and stepped into an empty room.

Litzi was gone.

So were her bag and her purse.

All that remained from her was a handwritten note on hotel stationery, which sat in the middle of the bed like a dispatch from my handler. Before even reading it I threw open the door to listen for footsteps on the stairs, but there was only silence.

I sat on the bed, feeling that I'd committed the biggest blunder in years. Then I read the note:

I know that you do not fully trust me, and you are right to be this way. I am not yet worthy of your trust. So do not look for me, not only because you will not find me, but because it will divert you from what you must do to complete your work. Someday I will explain everything, but for the moment this is the best I can offer: "When she left him two years later in favour of a Cuban motor racing driver, she announced enigmatically that if she hadn't left him then, she never could have done."

Love,
Litzi

I recognized her signoff right away. It was from the opening pages of le Carré's first novel, *Call for the Dead*, a devastating summation of Smiley's faithless wife, Lady Ann Sercomb. I wondered where on earth Litzi had found it, which of course only made me wonder once again about what she really knew, and how much she'd been holding back. She was right about my mistrust. Yet somehow her worthiness now seemed less in doubt than ever, and I mourned her absence.

I called her cell phone, but there was no answer. I pictured her already seated on a train bound for Vienna, alone in an empty compartment with the sun in her eyes.

"Litzi" was all I could say, whispering her name like a blind man calling out for help. "Litzi."

28

For someone who had essentially been living alone for the past fifteen years, I felt surprisingly off balance as I headed to Antikvariát Drebitko shortly after midday. The hardest thing to get used to was the silence: no answering voice, no second set of footsteps marching in rhythm with mine. I missed her companionable warmth at my side.

There were trade-offs, of course. In the void of Litzi's absence I felt more observant, more alert, although for the moment it hardly seemed worth it.

The door of the bookstore was locked shut. A red "Closed" sign was posted in the window next to a handwritten notice in Czech, which presumably said something about a death in the family. A well-wisher had left a small bouquet of roses on the doorstep.

I looked up toward the windows on the second floor, but there was no sign of movement. I knocked anyway, hoping Anton might be around, but after a minute or two it was clear there wasn't going to be an answer.

It was time to leave Prague. The only question was whether to move on to Budapest as planned or quit this fool's errand of retracing a forty-year-old trail of evidence. By returning to Vienna I might be able to make things right with Litzi. Seen in that light, it was a choice between flesh-and-blood friendship and a pulp-and-dust spy hunt.

Then I considered those roses on the doorstep, already wilting in the midday sun. And it struck me again, as it had that morning, that if people were still dying over these supposedly stale leads, then there must be something alarmingly fresh and potent about them. I remained undecided as I set out for my hotel to pack, but by the time I'd stopped by the desk to pay my bill, I was leaning toward Budapest.

I opened the door of my room to find Lothar Heinemann waiting for me. He was seated in a chair by the window, appearing out of nowhere like a disheveled old elf. His cane was propped against the wall, and he had already helped himself to a tiny bottle from the minibar—a Scotch, maybe the last one in Prague now that the Tartan Army had skipped town.

I paused in the doorway. If I was going to run, now was the time. But who runs from elves? For all my indignation at Lothar's uninvited entry, his presence felt benign. So I shut the door behind me, and without uttering a word I headed for the minibar to pour myself a bourbon, neat. I sat facing him from the foot of the bed. When he seemed satisfied that I had nothing to say, he spoke.

"Three things you should know right away, Mr. Bill Cage. Item one. Someone else besides me watched you go into Antikvariát Drebitko yesterday, and after closing hours he returned, whereupon he entered the store by unconventional means, through a window in the rear courtyard. While it's still entirely possibly those bookshelves fell accidentally—they were damn well going to one of these days—I wouldn't bank on it, and I don't think the police will, either. Meaning you should probably leave town as soon as it's convenient."

"Who was it? Who did you see?"

"Item two. The man I saw, a rather large American with dreadfully styled hair, is at this very moment seated in a café directly across the street from your hotel, where he has just arrived along with a rather meaty Russian with some mileage on him, a fellow whose face and reputation—unsavory, believe me—I recall from many years ago."

"They're *together*?"

"Colleagues, by all appearances. In this matter, anyway. So if you do plan on leaving this establishment anytime soon, I'd advise you to exit through the back."

"But why would—?"

Lothar raised his hand like a traffic cop, cutting me off.

"Item three. You're better off without her."

"Oh, so now you're giving personal advice?"

"Under the circumstances, it seemed advisable."

"Well, now that I finally have you somewhere you can't run out on me, there are two more items you can add to your list. Four: Whatever happened to that novel of yours that was never published? Five: What the hell were you doing forty years ago when you went and scared the bejeezus out of Karel Vitova's father? Were you full-time KGB, or just doing errands for them on the side?"

Lothar laughed so hard that he wheezed. He swallowed some Scotch to tamp down a cough.

"Oh, my. You're still not adding things up to the right sums, are you? Even after all these days on the job. Which is one of the reasons I'm here. To help straighten you out."

"Imagine my relief."

"So you wish to know the details of my brief literary career?"

"Assuming that's what my handler meant by telling me, 'Find his work.' Also assuming you were the model for Heinz Klarmann in *A Lesson in Tradecraft.*"

Lothar smiled broadly and knocked back the last of the Scotch.

"Ed Lemaster's little tribute to me. He got a very nice dinner out of it one weekend in Tangier. Plus one hell of a deal on a rare first edition of Conrad's *The Secret Agent*, which I'd found in an absolute shithole of an Oxfam store in deepest, darkest Cornwall. Sold it to him for probably half of what I could've gotten from someone like your father. For that alone he should've put me in five more novels. But I can tell by the impatient look on your face that you're not interested in hearing about my greatest hits as a book scout."

"Why was your novel never published? And when you've answered that, maybe you can tell me why the man in the mullet has joined forces with the Hammerhead."

"No idea on the latter, although it's an excellent question. As for the former . . ." He slapped his hands on his knees and stood, more sprightly than I would have thought possible. "Let's discuss it over lunch. You need to leave before the police come around, so grab your bag and drop the key on the bed. On your way out maybe you should mention to the front desk that you're heading back to Vienna, for the benefit of all those people who will be stopping by to ask. After lunch, I'll get you started on a more roundabout route for Budapest."

"How do you know I'm going to Budapest?"

"We'll get to that. So what do you say?"

I said yes. How could I not? Then I packed, and followed his advice by mentioning to the desk clerk that I was catching the next train to Vienna. I exited the hotel in the back to find Lothar waiting in the alley, looking like a beggar as he leaned on his cane.

"Sausages and beer?" he asked.

"Sure."

"I know just the place. Ed used it once, in *London's Own*. Or maybe it was *Requiem for a Spy*. He killed a man there. Novelistically, I mean."

"It was *Requiem*. The waiter who got a fork through the eye."

"Yes, that's the one."

"Was it based on anything Ed ever did?"

"Lord, no! Ed is many things, quite a few of them disagreeable, but he has never been a killer except on paper. Nowadays, of course, he has no compunction about wiping out entire villages of destitute Muslims."

"He's playing to the red-meat crowd."

"Angleton would've seen that as further evidence of his innocence."

"So you know about all that?"

"Know about it? I was part of it. Why else would a simple old book scout take such an interest in your movements?" Lothar checked our flanks as we emerged onto a narrow lane at the end of the alley. He seemed so skittish that I wondered if he'd already spotted somebody.

"It's probably best if we dispense with any further shoptalk until we've reached our destination. Deal?"

"Deal."

Not that Lothar stopped talking. He remarked on just about everything in passing, from the increased number of Czech women wearing high boots and miniskirts—he heartily approved—to the proliferation of Franz Kafka kitsch in the local souvenir shops, which he scorned as hucksterism trying to look intellectual.

He stayed constantly alert, however—head swiveling, eyes in motion. He even refrained from tapping his cane, as if to maintain radio silence. A circuitous route led us to a beer joint where we descended to the cellar and took a table by a rear doorway onto a basement-level alley.

No sooner had we sat down and ordered—sausages, sharp mustard, and a pitcher of pils—than Lothar pulled out a small round silver case, unscrewed the lid, and dabbed a pinkie inside. It emerged with a frosting of white powder, which he snorted into each nostril. He briefly shut his eyes as his cheeks flushed. Then he smiled and put away the case. My astonishment must have been obvious.

"You disapprove?"

"Dad told me you'd cleaned up your act."

"Oh, I have. Smack was my downfall, and I'm off it forever. This is strictly for mood maintenance. Controlled doses, twice a day. No worse than a daily arthritis drug, or the little blue pill. Speaking of addictions, how'd you let her get away so easily?"

His mention of Litzi made me drain off half a glass of beer.

"Well?" he prompted. "Was it something you said?"

"More like something I didn't say. When I came out of the shower, she was gone."

"Just as well. She was on to you before I was."

"What's that supposed to mean?"

"Remember when we met? That bakery around the corner from Kurzmann's?"

"Yes." I had a feeling I wasn't going to like this.

"I told you then that a fine-looking woman was on your tail."

So he had. I'd assumed he meant the woman from Georgetown, whom I'd since forgotten all about.

"It was Litzi?"

He nodded, then frowned sympathetically. The beer sloshed coldly in my stomach as I considered the implications. But why should I believe Lothar? Maybe he was trying to mislead me.

"Bullshit."

"Call and find out for yourself."

"I've tried. She's not answering."

"I don't mean her mobile. Phone her office. Ask where she is, and how long it's been in the works. I did, just the other day. The answer was illuminating."

I wasn't ready for more bad news, but a creeping sense of dread told me it was unavoidable, so I retrieved her business card from my wallet and punched in the number for the Austrian National Library. Lothar polished off his first pint as he watched, then licked the foam from his upper lip.

A man answered on the fourth ring.

"Litzi Strauss, please."

"She is away on annual leave."

That didn't sound very much like the last-minute getaway she'd described to me.

"When will she return?"

"Two weeks more from Monday."

"Oh. Well, this is an old friend from the States. I'd, uh, heard she'd been called away on short notice, and I was concerned for her."

"No, no. Her vacation has been scheduled for quite some time. Would you care to leave a message?"

"No, thank you."

I set down the phone. *Scheduled for quite some time.* My handler must have arranged for her employment well in advance. If he had security connections, I suppose she would've been easy enough to find. As Dad had mentioned, she was probably still listed in some embassy file. For anyone who knew my background, she would have been the perfect choice for keeping tabs on my movements. No wonder I'd only had to deliver information once, by dropping off the photo negatives at a dead drop. Litzi had kept him abreast of everything else. The moment I started shutting her out, she quit. I should've heeded my earlier doubts. Instead, I'd kept on making a fool of myself. Maybe fifty-three was the age when, despite all your best efforts at maintenance and perseverance, everything began to crumble. Your knees, your waistline, your judgment. And now my optimism. If I'd hoped this enterprise would offer some payback for my previous mistakes, then the check had just bounced.

"Stop feeling so damn sorry for yourself. We've got a pitcher to finish. While you're at it, take the battery out of your cell phone, and next time you're out and about, buy a disposable one with a virgin SIM card. Your handler's tools are obsolete, and so are yours, including that silly webcam. That means every other interested party in this affair has the jump on you. And, believe me, they're out there, with encryption software, signal tracing, data mining, and satellite imagery. All you've got is a lot of quaint tricks from every novel you ever read as a boy. If you're going to keep doing this, then you'd better start playing by newer rules than your handler's."

"I just hope my handler's working for the right side. Sometimes I think he might even be working for Moscow."

"Now that's a laugh. Don't worry, he's American to the core."

"How do you know so much about him?"

"Because he was my handler, too, once upon a time."

I almost choked in midswallow. Lothar watched me wipe the beer from my chin while the news sank in.

"The Agency hired you?"

"It was a contract job. To track down this courier network Ed had supposedly engineered. A renegade transaction from start to finish. That's why your movements intrigued me from the start, and why I've been following you ever since. I want to know why history is repeating itself. The same deliveries. The same contacts. The same old people doing the same old things they used to do, except now there's no one left at the end of the line to receive all those messages that were once handled with such exquisite care."

"No Dewey, you mean?"

"No Dewey, and no super-paranoid Jim Angleton hovering over everything like a malign cloud, although I'd wager his ghost is watching us with great perturbation."

"Who is he, then?"

"Our handler?"

I nodded. He laughed.

"That's the sort of information that must be earned. And you're a long way from earning it."

"You said you were here to straighten me out."

"To a point. I want to help *you*, but not the jackass who's running you. So for the moment I'm taking baby steps and watching your back. When I'm able to, of course. I still have my own affairs to attend to."

"I guess this is how you know I'll be heading to Budapest next."

"Antikvárium Szondi. Except it's no longer on Corvin Square. Try the row of bookshops along Museum Boulevard. I tracked you there once, when you were just a boy."

"Me?"

It was an odd sensation, imagining a much younger Lothar shadowing a much younger me along mysterious streets that had gone fuzzy in my memory. It stirred an odd lightness in the hollow of my chest. Then skepticism took over.

"My father said he never used me for Dewey deliveries."

"Never knowingly. In that sense he's telling you the truth."

"How would he not know?"

"The name Dewey wouldn't even come up, although I think it's the only code name the Agency ever got wind of, and Lemaster wouldn't have made the request. Your dad probably thought he was doing a favor for the bookseller, or for some other friend. By the time this network was operating at its peak, people were doing things on Ed Lemaster's behalf without the slightest clue of who they were assisting. That was the beauty of it. Even your friend Karel's father made a delivery once."

"Source Fishwife. Is that why you spoke to him?"

"Posing as a security policeman, of course. I think he was convinced I was with the Russians. Even with my German accent, in those days all you had to say to a Czech was 'secret police' and they would tell you anything. At one point Ed's network got so busy that I even asked poor old Bruzek to begin keeping a ledger of related transactions. Not directly, of course, that would've blown my cover. So I chose a cutout, who in turn paid a certain young boy whom I had selected in advance to make the phone call, repeating my message word for word."

Lothar smiled as he watched that sink in.

"So you used me, too."

"How could I resist? You were an absolute star of a courier. Reliable, punctual, rain or shine. And tireless on the cobbles, like Zátopek. Over in Buda once, you scampered up that steep hill by the tramway so fast that it damn near killed me. But of course I had vices then. And I was smoking, a pack a day."

"I'm so relieved you gave up your vices. What made the Agency desperate enough to hire a drugged-out book scout?"

"They were less desperate than you think. I'd trained for the game once, which I'm sure they knew. I just never made it through finishing school."

"The Farm?"

Lothar shook his head.

"MI6. They needed Germans in those days, especially Berliners. So they took me up to Hamburg and taught me all kinds of tricks, plus a lot of hocus-pocus. As someone smarter than me once said, they crammed two weeks of intense training into three months of crashing boredom.

"And, let's face it, landing a top-notch book scout was a plus for them. They were already pretty sure this courier network was being run through a string of antiquarian shops and sellers, which meant I was equipped with the perfect contacts and the perfect cover. On both sides of the Iron Curtain. And I was already acquainted with Ed and his literary shopping habits."

"Then why does our handler have me retracing your steps?"

"Because I never filed my report. Not the final one, anyway, the one with the best stuff. I was deep into smack by then, and not the most reliable fellow about dead drops and deadlines. So, at some point after I'd been AWOL for a week or two, he'd had enough. Traveled clear across the Atlantic to fire me, then demanded to see all my work. I told him to fuck off and vowed he'd never get a single line out of me unless I was paid in full, plus a bonus—my habit was quite expensive by then—and, well, he answered in kind. He must have thought I was bluffing."

"But you weren't?"

"Not in the least. But by the time he realized that, his grand inquisitor, Jim Angleton, had been sacked and Lemaster was a best-selling author already out the door. So everything sort of faded into the background. Until now, for whatever reason, when our dear handler seems to be giving it one last go and has anointed you as the new Lothar. From what I've seen of your work, I can't imagine why."

"Join the club. Neither can I."

"You're cheap. That's one thing. That fake Russian he had following you ought to tell you something about his limited resources. I suppose he also appreciates that you know the books inside out. Otherwise you're completely unqualified, meaning he's desperate."

"Well, if you really want to improve my job performance, just brief me on what you found out."

"Why? So you can give him everything, free of charge? Besides"—and here he smiled coyly—"all that information is readily available in painstaking detail. You need only read it."

He let me consider that for a second. After another swallow of beer, I had it.

"Your novel. You put everything into your novel."

"It seemed like the best way to bring it to life. If he wouldn't pay me, then I'd give it to the world, which could reimburse me copy by copy. I found a small press in Frankfurt that was very eager to publish. A shitty advance, but hopes were high."

"What happened?"

"What do you think? Some asshole in Langley got wind of it before the ink was dry on the galleys. Even in the early seventies it wasn't all that hard for the Occupation Powers to quash something like that if they deemed it sufficiently dangerous. They even broke into my apartment. Took every copy of my manuscript, and of course back then there were no CD-ROMs or memory sticks."

"But you said there were galleys."

"Very good. You *do* pay attention."

"How many?"

"Twenty-five. As I said, it was a small press. They only printed enough for reviewers at a select cadre of German dailies and magazines, but the copies had all been mailed out the day before the order came down, so my publisher sent out a recall notice."

"Were they all returned?"

"Twenty-four were. But in Heidelberg some enterprising subeditor with a habit worse than mine had already sold it to a secondhand dealer, along with a boxful of other publisher freebies. He was so pharmaceutically addled that he couldn't remember who'd paid him. And by then, of course, the Agency's single best source on how to track down obscure book titles—*the* one person who might have found it—was persona non grata."

"You."

"Of course."

"So you still have it?"

"Absolutely not. I knew my apartment would be the first place they'd look, and the one place they'd keep looking, year after year, or until they got tired of rifling through my shelves and pulling up floorboards. I decided it would be far safer in its original location. Or, rather, the location where it ended up, a few harmless transactions later."

"You bought it back, then resold it to some more obscure vendor."

"I made special arrangements, let's put it that way. Sometimes it's safest to hide in plain sight."

"Well, that's a big help."

He shrugged, unmoved.

"It's not somewhere you've never been, I will say that."

"Seeing as how my dad must have dragged me into a zillion bookstores all over Europe, I'm not sure that's a big help."

"Then you'll have to think like a book scout, that is, like a spy. Or, at least, like the only kind of spy that seems to appeal to you and me—the old-fashioned kind. Low-tech and low to the ground, surviving on his wits. And I promise you this. If you do find it, come to me first, and I'll tell you his name."

"My handler's?"

"*Our* handler's. Then you'll know why you should never hand him the information."

"So, two people are dead, and you're making a game out of it, too?"

"You've read the books. When has it not been a game? And when have the stakes ever been anything other than life or death?"

"Tell that to Bruzek's nephew, Anton."

"Poor old Bruzek. A greedy bastard, but he didn't deserve that. Got a little careless in his old age, I suppose."

"Then why haven't they killed me? God knows I've been careless at times."

"At times? Don't flatter yourself. They don't *want* to kill you. Not yet. Because they want you to succeed. They're after the same thing you are, and they're hoping you'll lead them to it. Finding it is what will put you in mortal danger. Unless of course you lead them to something in the meantime that will allow them to figure it out for themselves. Then you'll be equally disposable."

"How will I know what that is?"

"You won't. Which reminds me, you still haven't removed the battery from your phone."

I pulled the phone from my pocket and grudgingly popped out the battery.

"Here's something else I don't understand," I said. "Why does this all have to be so damn complicated? The clues, the step-by-step instructions. Why can't my handler—our handler—just tell me what he knows and what he wants me to find out?"

"Oh, c'mon. That's the nature of the business. To hoard information and only dole it out on a need-to-know basis. To keep your operatives in the dark for as long as possible, if only to limit your own vulnerability. I always used to laugh whenever some stupid book critic complained about how byzantine Ed's plots are, or whined that they had to peel away the meaning layer by layer, like an onion. If they only knew. The real thing is twice as complicated. And the layers? More like those fragile ones on a Greek pastry. The instant you try peeling one away, it crumbles in your fingers, until eventually you're left with nothing."

"That's the way I feel about Lemaster sometimes, like he's crumbling away to nothing. The more I find out about what he did, the less I learn about him."

"You and everyone who knew him. For Ed, the best part of every relationship was the courtship. He enjoyed luring people into his orbit, and he had all the necessary tools—intelligence, wit, charm. Warmth, to a point. But his real knack was for knowing which piece of himself to put forth for your initial inspection. With your father it was his fascination with books. With me, our brand of Continental politics, the way we saw the world. But it was like he had a built-in thermostat, set to switch off whenever a friendship warmed to a certain level. You'd realize all of a sudden that he'd gone cold on you, even though he was still taking everything you had to offer."

"Sounds like part of his tradecraft."

"Possibly. But I think it came naturally. Maybe it's the only way he knows how to be."

"What piece did he give you? You said politics."

"I was going through my 'Don't trust America' phase, and Ed played right along, even though he knew I was aware of what he did for a living. He wasn't too thrilled with what his country was becoming. The longer he stayed overseas, the more he became a European."

"That sounds more like my dad than somebody who'd write those flag-wavers he's been churning out lately."

"Nobody was more surprised than me when Ed moved back across the water. And those recent novels?" Lothar shook his head.

"You think he does it to steal their secrets?"

"Possibly. Or maybe it's just how he entertains himself now. Gain their trust, find out how they live, work, and play, then write them as caricatures while making a bundle into the bargain."

The remark reminded me of what Lemaster had told me about the appeal of being a double agent—"to just walk through the looking glass and find out how they really lived on the other side—well, isn't that the secret dream of every spy?"

Had that been more than just a motivation for spying—his blueprint for life, perhaps? I was silent for a moment. So was Lothar. Then he downed the last of his beer, licked his lips, and leaned across the table.

"Down to business. Now that you're no longer carrying a homing beacon in your pocket, here's how I would like you to proceed to the train station. After the way you've been blundering about, maybe a sudden burst of old-style tradecraft will actually catch them by surprise. If so, it might buy you a day or two without pursuit. With luck, that's all you'll need."

He proceeded to outline a complicated sequence of tram rides, switched taxis, and brisk walks through crowded stores that would eventually take me to the train station. Then he checked his watch.

"You can still make the three-seventeen." He handed me the plainest business card I've ever seen. No name, no title, no address. Just a number for a cell phone, written across the middle.

"To be used only in an emergency," he said. "Ask for Heinz."

"As in Klarmann."

"Good. You're not completely hopeless."

He put a few crown notes on the table, then picked up his cane and stood to leave.

"Your life as a more polished operative, of the sort that might once have made Richard Folly proud, begins now," he said.

I gathered up my bag, checked the bill to make sure he had left enough for both of us, then turned to say good-bye. But Lothar, who had been playing at this far longer than I, was already gone.

29

I hadn't been to Budapest since I was eleven. My three years there were like a mirage, quivering on the horizon of that long-ago era before girl-friends, running, and the imaginary worlds within Dad's books.

It was the one European home that initially felt foreign to me, prob-ably because we moved there after our two years in Washington. To a kid fresh out of America the city was old and oppressive, smelling of coal smoke and cabbage. The cars were clunky. The boys wore boxy shorts and bad haircuts. Television flickered with unfamiliar faces speaking a harsh new tongue, and none seemed half as welcoming as Jackie Glea-son or even Ed Sullivan.

In my only memory from our first week, I am wearing a cherished coonskin cap straight out of Disney. Dad and I are waiting for a tram when a foul odor blows up from the street, and I wrinkle my nose in disgust.

"The sewers," Dad explains. "They're very old here."

As I grew familiar with these gusts of ill wind in city after city, I came to regard them as the labored breath of Europe's past, struggling up from its mass grave beneath the streets. When I told this to my father, years later, he turned pensive.

"Budapest cast a shadow over you before we even got there. You were born in Vienna the week the Red Army rolled into Hungary. Our embassy was the main listening post, and everyone was devastated. We'd egged the poor bastards on, then none of us lifted a finger to help. That's when it finally sank in that, in Europe at least, all the fighting from then on was going to be done by spies and propagandists."

And, as I know now, Budapest was where I began my career as a cou-rier for Edwin Lemaster. My unwitting father saw those errands as a chance for me to earn pocket money while building up family goodwill at stores where he loved to browse. I wondered if they'd still be happy to see me.

The train stopped briefly in Vienna on its arc toward Budapest. I toyed with hopping off to look for Litzi, and took out my cheap new cell phone to call her before deciding against it. I played peek-a-boo awhile with a toddler in the next row, smiling as he squealed in delight. His beautiful Earth Mother mom took great joy in him, and I was glad Litzi had been spared this scene of maternal bliss. I missed her, then was angry with her. I again took out my phone, this time to call David. But by then we were deep in farm country and the signal failed.

After reaching Budapest well after dark, I caught a subway to the stop nearest Antikvárium Szondi and found a room in a small hotel. No one seemed to be following me yet, and to maintain my new advantage I holed up for the rest of the night, eating next door and retiring early. In the morning, after a cold breakfast and a pot of coffee, I set out for the bookstore. I arrived just as an older man who seemed to be the proprietor was cranking down the awning.

"Mr. Szondi?" I said, without even a clue as to whether he spoke English.

"Béla or Ferenc?"

"Whoever's in charge."

"Neither. Ferenc was until he became too ill. Béla took over a few years ago, but he sold the store to me last month. I am sorry if you have been inconvenienced."

He folded away the crank handle, then squinted into the sun to observe me better.

"I am Andris László. And your name, sir?"

"Bill Cage. I've come over from the States."

A look of mild concern flitted across his features.

"I was not expecting you so soon, although I suppose nothing should surprise me after what has been happening lately."

"You were expecting me?"

He looked up and down the sidewalk, then back at me.

"Please come inside. I have something for you."

He went behind the register and reached beneath it for a small parcel, book-sized, wrapped in butcher paper. Just like the good old days, although this fellow didn't seem familiar with his role. There was no writing on the outside except the price, which was about the same as I'd paid in Vienna once you converted it to forints.

"It's the way old Ferenc used to wrap everything," László said. He seemed to be watching me closely. "They stopped using paper like that years ago."

I paid the amount. He seemed reluctant to take the bills.

"Can you tell me how this reached you?" I asked.

He gave me a long look, then called out toward the back of the store. "Lukács!"

A harried-looking teen scurried out from the back, pushing curls out of his eyes. László barked an order in Hungarian, handed Lukács the register key, and came out from behind the counter.

"Apologies for my rudeness, Mr. Cage, but this has been a strange business altogether, and I have been uncertain as to how I should deal with you when the time came." He held out his hand in greeting, an American sort of proffer. I shook it firmly. "We should go somewhere to talk, especially if you intend to meet with the Szondis. No one should do that unawares."

"More trouble than they're worth?"

"The older one, Ferenc, no longer has his wits about him. His son, Béla—well, that is not a topic to discuss here."

László said something more in Hungarian to the younger man, then led me outdoors, where he again looked in both directions.

"You have come here alone?"

"Why do you ask?"

"Others have been inquiring about you. It started a few days ago. Three different men, each acting as if he was your friend. But . . ." He shrugged, uncertain.

"Three? Was one of them a scruffy-looking German, maybe a few years older than you? Floppy hat, carries a cane?"

"No. But if I didn't know better I would say you are describing the book scout Lothar Heinemann. I am told he was once a regular at this store."

"Once?"

"He was banned by the Szondis, but I do not know why. If you see him, you must tell him he is again welcome at Antikvárium Szondi."

"I doubt he knows the store has changed hands. He certainly didn't mention it to me."

"You have seen him?"

"Just yesterday, in Prague. He sent me."

Lázsló shook his head, more confused than ever. He said nothing further until we reached our destination a few blocks later, the elegant Café Central, with windows facing onto both sides of a fashionable corner. Its chandeliers, high ceilings, and L-shaped floor plan stirred a memory from a long-ago Saturday with my father—him with his coffee, me with hot chocolate, both of us sipping to a morning serenade of chuffing espresso machines and the rustle of foreign newspapers.

It was too late for breakfast, too early for lunch, and there were few customers. We took a corner table in the smaller wing.

"My dad used to bring me here, but I don't remember it being this fancy."

"They have done many things to make it look nicer. Some of the older customers do not like it as much now. It feels too prosperous, too safe."

"Too safe?"

"Look around. You can tell the ones who came in the older days. See how they bend so low across the table that their heads nearly touch? This was where you would come to talk about things that could not be said in other places, as if you could hide the words in your cigarette smoke, or in the milk on top of your coffee. Secret policemen were here, of course, watching from behind their newspapers. They would be the only ones daring to read some banned periodical, hoping you might ask to borrow it so they could note your name and face. Maybe that is why I brought you here, because I am not yet certain I should help you. Not yet certain I should even be talking about these things." He smiled uneasily. "Could it be that you are like those policemen, offering something I shouldn't accept?"

"I hope not."

A waiter took our order. When he'd gone, Lázsló fretted with his hands, as if unsure where to begin.

"You mentioned your father. Was his Christian name Warfield?"

"Yes. He lives in Vienna now. We were here from sixty-four to sixty-seven. We moved away when I was eleven."

"I was nineteen then. My uncle used to talk about him. Your father, I mean." He seemed to choose his next words with care. "He said your father was . . . a grand figure, a special man."

"That's kind of him."

I wondered what Dad could have done to inspire such a description, but László didn't elaborate. He again looked down at his hands, then put them in his lap.

"You were going to tell me about the Szondis," I said. "Where would I find Béla?"

"They have a very fine house on Corvin Square, near where their shop used to be. It has an elevator, even from the old times. The house with blue trim. It will be easy to find."

"I take it they've done well for themselves."

"They are the kind of people who always do, no matter who is in power."

"You don't like them."

He shrugged and took out a pack of cigarettes.

"It is not a matter of like or dislike. It is a matter of trust or mistrust. The transaction with the store, it seemed very regular. Friends advised me against it, but the price was fair, the terms reasonable. A week after I moved in I began noticing that many of the better items had been removed, including an entire locked bookcase that I am sure had been there during the sales inspection. I complained, of course, but what could I do? One can only deal with people like the Szondis from a position of advantage."

"They're well connected?"

He smiled grimly, cheeks puckering as he inhaled aggressively on his cigarette.

"Connections, money, muscle. You will see. Unless you approach them from a position of greater leverage, they will either shrug you off or find a way to make use of you. May I ask what your business is with them?"

"I'm not sure I know. I want to ask about things that took place a long time ago. Book deliveries, like this one." I held up the wrapped parcel. "My father was an old customer."

"From sixty-four to sixty-seven, you said?"

"Yes."

He thought about this for a second, blowing smoke toward the ceiling.

"That's when they began to make their fortune, or so I am told. I was only a boy, but my uncle was in the business. Perhaps I should explain how things worked for booksellers then, and how things worked for the Szondis."

"I'd be grateful for that."

"The mid-sixties was a time of reform, of hope. After fifty-six it sank in that the Americans were never going to come to our rescue, so people settled in as best they could. As people accepted this reality, production improved. So did the economy. We called it peaceful coexistence."

"My father used to say Budapest was the best posting in the East Bloc. Americans from Warsaw and Bucharest used to come here to relax."

"You still had to be careful here, but even in the arts things began to ease up. In literature, important works were finally being translated into Hungarian—Kafka, Sartre, Beckett. Of course, if you wanted to buy new books, there were only the state stores. But some antiquarian shops were still privately owned, like Ferenc Szondi's shop on Corvin Square.

"People then were always looking for ways to raise cash, and he offered to buy their old books. His son Béla became an appraiser, and it was a gold mine for them. People had no choice but to take the prices they offered. They built up a huge private library. That is when they bought their house, with its elevator and rooftop terrace."

"I gather they knew a lot of embassy people."

László nodded.

"Ferenc took up the bourgeois sport of golf, so that he could meet the diplomats of all nations. They played on a small course in the Buda hills. Béla played tennis on Margit Island, even though he was known mostly for hitting the ball over the fence."

"Dad used to go there. Both places."

"And of course diplomats could buy the kinds of books that the state stores weren't even allowed to display. So could well-connected people from the Party. The Szondis could sell those books because they had friends in high places."

"They were collaborators?"

"There has always been talk that they were informants. In the early eighties, Ferenc was caught smuggling fifteenth-century manuscripts to West Germany. But instead of his being punished, it was hushed up. What does that tell you?"

"Didn't that hurt them when everything finally changed?"

László smiled ruefully.

"With enough money you can avoid the trouble that others are susceptible to. The Szondis rebranded themselves as businessmen who had craftily outlasted Communism. Béla became a patron of the arts, a donor to charities. If you have a cause, Béla will lend his name. But if you run afoul of one of his business concerns . . ." László shrugged.

"So their past has never caught up to them?"

"A few people have tried to hold them accountable. But apparently the Szondis have seen to it that nothing remained on paper. The last person who dared to question their earlier conduct ended up with a million-forint judgment lodged against him in the courts."

So this was the family my father had let me run errands for, errands that had been part of Ed Lemaster's courier network. Now here I was preparing to meet Béla, with no idea of what he might be willing to tell me. Not much, according to László, unless I could come up with some sort of incentive.

"You think I am exaggerating," László said. "I can read it in your eyes."

"It's not that. It's just that, well, I work in Washington public relations. I'm used to dealing with the lowest of the low, if you know what I mean."

"So your clients in Washington, they often send enforcers around? To make threats, or to slash the tires on your car? Or worse, perhaps?"

"Well, no. I thought you said they filed lawsuits?"

"That is one of their methods. Those three men I mentioned, who came asking for you. One of them works for the Szondis. A handyman."

"A leg breaker?"

"Here, I will show you."

László put his cell phone on the table and punched in a few commands. A newspaper website popped onto the screen, with a photo of Béla Szondi at a ribbon cutting for a new children's health center.

"The man to Béla's right."

The shot was in profile. The fellow indeed looked like a rough customer—a human bowling ball draped in a black wool coat, with close-cropped hair, the unsparing eyes of a shark. The kind of man you'd instinctively give a wide berth to in the street.

"Would you like to see pictures of the other two men as well?"

"They were also in the paper?"

"No. But when they came into the store I had Lukács come and wait on them while I pretended to make phone calls. I took their photos with my phone."

"You're very good at this, Mr. László."

László took the compliment in stride, then clicked to the photos. The first was a shot of Ron Curtin, mullet and all. The second was his apparent new ally, the old KGB man whom I knew only by his nickname of the Hammerhead.

"You know them?" he asked.

"Somewhat. And they're not friends, in case they come asking for me again. When were they here?"

"Five days ago. One came in the morning, the other in late afternoon."

So, not only had they been following me, at times they'd been a step ahead of me.

"Thanks," I said. "You've been a huge help."

He waved away the praise.

"I will erase these now. I kept them for you to see, but I do not wish to keep them any longer."

"Understandable. You said you also know about Lothar Heinemann. I was wondering, though, if you'd ever come across his book. It would be in the form of a galley from a small press in Frankfurt. An Advance Reader Edition, I believe they call them now."

"Lothar is an author?"

"This would've been years ago. Early to mid-seventies."

László shook his head.

"I only know him as a collector, a procurer, and quite an outstanding one. He has a nose for these things. I was not aware he was ever a writer. This book, it would be of great value?"

"Not to most people. But it would be to me."

I handed him one of my Ealing Wharton business cards. I considered scribbling the number for my new cell phone, then thought better of it.

"Shoot me an email if you spot it."

"Of course."

László seemed relieved to be back on the more familiar ground of bookselling. It reminded me of the parcel, and I put it on the table.

"How did you end up with this?" I asked.

His face darkened. He reached for his cigarette.

"Someone dropped it through my mail slot last Sunday. I found it early Monday. A small note was attached saying to hold it for you. There was no name, no address, no number. I didn't know if you would be here in days or months. Or ever. Then, when all those men came calling, asking about you, well, I didn't know *what* to think. Do you know what is inside?"

"A book, if it's like the others. Probably with a message. Should I open it now?"

László waved away the idea.

"I think my involvement has gone as far as I would like. In fact . . ." He checked his watch. "Nothing personally against you, of course. But I should return to my store."

He rose from his chair, as if worried I might open the package anyway. I stood, too. In parting, László offered another handshake. I watched through the plate glass as he emerged outside. He peered up and down the street before setting out for his store.

László's caution was contagious. I found myself scanning the café for Szondi's thug before I opened the parcel, and I held the package beneath the marble table as I tore open the butcher paper. As expected, there was a book inside. It was marked in two places.

The title, *Night of the Short Knives,* was pretty obscure nowadays, a 1964 novel about spies in the corridors of NATO military headquarters. The author, J. Burke Wilkinson, was quite familiar to me. He had come to our house in Vienna with his wife, Franny, for a small dinner party, probably around seventy-one, when I would have been fifteen and my father was in his late thirties.

Wilkinson, who'd served earlier in the State Department, was twenty years older than Dad, but it was easy to see why they'd hit it off. They were the product of the same schools, the same circles. They even spoke the same form of expat English, an erudite blend of British and American slang.

Wilkinson was a wonderful raconteur, with great material. He'd been a schoolboy classmate of spymaster Richard Helms, and a Cambridge contemporary of Kim Philby's. Later in Paris he knew Hemingway, Waugh, and Gertrude Stein. In addition to his novels, he'd written a biography of the spy novelist Erskine Childers. It was from Wilkinson that I learned the extraordinary news that Childers, a late convert to Irish nationalism, had himself been hanged as a spy.

That long-ago evening had made quite an impression on me, and as I read the marked passages, Wilkinson's words rose to me in the gentlemanly cadences of his dinner table conversation. It felt as if he was sitting next to me, dressed in pinstripes and holding a glass of Dubonnet, which helped turn his prose into a personal warning of clear and present danger:

> *In novels about spies everyone watches everyone else all of the time. The man lighting a cigarette at the next table is always something more than he appears to be. No luggage ever remains unsearched. The car behind the car knows its distance and keeps it. Thus the dangerous moment is the time when nobody is watching, for that means the other side knows exactly what you are doing and doesn't need to search and follow. Then is the time to beware.*

I paused to again look around the café. No one was paying me the least bit of attention, which of course I now took as a bad sign. I wondered if my handler was also beginning to feel the heat, wherever he was.

The page for the next passage was marked by a business card for a local laundry on Kiraly Street, with the words "3 p.m. today" written at the top. The marked paragraphs of the book described an operative walking into a laundry to ask the attendant if a shirt could be cleaned and pressed within two days. The attendant said yes, then gave the operative a yellow slip of paper, which carried the operative's marching orders.

So there was my schedule for the afternoon—a trip to the laundry at three, followed by a visit to the Szondis' house on Corvin Square. From what László had told me, I was now expecting Béla Szondi to blow me off, no matter how faithful a customer my father had once been. I couldn't say that I'd blame him, seeing as how the last bookseller I'd sought help from now lay dead in Prague.

With those thoughts in mind, I surveyed the café's customers a final time before leaving. None was a likely suspect for a tail, and none left the café when I did.

According to Mr. J. Burke Wilkinson, it was time to beware.

30

By shortly after three o'clock I had the leverage I needed to confront Béla Szondi, thanks to my transaction at the laundry. The attendant, a man in his sixties with the droopy eyes of a bloodhound, took my request in stride, which made me suspect he had done this before. I handed him a dirty shirt, figuring I'd never see it again, then asked pointedly—bad tradecraft, probably—if it could be cleaned and pressed within two days.

"Of course," he replied, not batting an eye. "The shirt you brought last week is ready." He handed me a shirt box, which I carried away like a satisfied customer. I didn't open it until I was back at my room.

Inside were three pages of a CIA report from December 1983, written by the Vienna chief of station, Stu Henson, yet another figure from the Nethercutt funeral. The first page, the report's cover sheet, explained that this was an assessment of top-level government collaborators and informants in Budapest. Also included were the report's seventh and eighth pages, which described the activities of Ferenc and Béla Szondi over a twenty-year span. To me the info was trivial—unfamiliar contacts, small-bore episodes. But to the Szondis and their victims it would be explosive reading. With Hungary's security archives sanitized, this was the last available proof of their duplicity.

To my surprise, the pages were originals, not copies. This suggested that some sort of deal had been arranged between my handler and the Szondis, with me as the middleman. Presumably my handler wanted information in return. The question was how to get what I wanted without running up against their enforcers.

To clear my head for the task at hand, I set out on a good, hard run for only the second time since I'd arrived overseas, which reacquainted me with the city without having to worry about surveillance. Runners could blow through stoplights, veer into parks, and go the wrong way on one-way streets. It would take a team of dozens to keep track, and if my pursuers employed that many people, then I was doomed anyway.

I stiffly jogged a few blocks before hitting my stride on Váci Street, the city's most touristy boulevard. Then I wound my way toward the Basilica of St. Stephen, dodging photographers' tripods and a trio of drunken young toughs waving wine bottles like batons. The streets began to feel familiar, and when I cut west toward the Danube I spotted the apartment building where Dad and I had lived with other embassy families.

It was a hulking place, seven stories high. As in Prague, we had a balcony with a riverfront view. Next door, in a small park that buffered the apartments from the fortresslike Parliament, I saw the spindly statue of the stooped national hero, Károlyi Mihály. My American friends and I had thrown snowballs at him with impunity, even when the police were watching. Trotting along the Danube, I remembered how we'd also mocked the lyrics to the Strauss waltz. "So clear and blue, we sing to you" became "So cloudy and brown, you stink so we frown." Embassy brats, drunk on immunity.

I was winded after a mile, but by the time I was working my way back to the hotel I was loose and warm, lungs wide open, so I finished with a head of steam. Now I was ready. To hell with damned Wilkinson and his warnings. Filled with endorphin bliss, I showered, picked a location for a later rendezvous, then set out for the Szondi house in Corvin Square on the number 2 tram to the Chain Bridge. The crenellated walls of the castle loomed above, but my destination was below it, along the face of the hill. I reached the yellow brick lanes of Corvin Square, easily found the house with blue trim, and knocked at the door.

The rumble of plodding footsteps sounded from deep within the house, followed by the clank and lurch of an elevator. The door opened on the jowly face of a man with swept-back black hair, almost certainly dyed. His aftershave smelled like mint. Smug. That was my first impression.

"Ye-esss?" he asked slowly in English, in a manner that reminded me of the shady Dr. Winkel in *The Third Man*.

"I am Bill Cage, the son of Warfield Cage. Are you Béla Szondi?"

"Ye-esss. What is your business?" He showed no sign of having recognized my father's name.

"I'm hoping you can tell me a few things about some very old trans-actions, all of them involving a customer named Dewey. I don't wish to intrude on your privacy, so naturally I'd keep anything you told me confidential."

"I am sorry you have come such a long way for such little satisfaction, Mr. . . ."

"Cage."

"Ye-esss. Cage." He was already inching backward and pushing the door forward. "But for me the past is a closed book. My memories are too vague to be of any possible use to anyone. So I will bid you good day, sir, and wish you health."

The door whined on its hinges. I pulled the pages of the report from my lapel pocket and thrust them into the shrinking opening, hoping that the CIA letterhead would catch his eye.

"This might help refresh your memory."

I yanked back the papers to keep him from slamming my arm in the door.

The door stopped, inches from shutting. I spoke into the gap.

"It's a report detailing your work for the Communist regime."

The door slowly reopened. Szondi eyed me disdainfully, then looked to either side, as if checking for eavesdropping neighbors.

"This kind of baseless gossip has been raised before, but if you claim to have some sort of forged proof, then it is probably preferable to dis-cuss it in private. Why don't you step inside." He stepped back to let me through.

"I'd prefer to meet somewhere out in the open. Just the two of us. I'd also prefer if you could offer something of value in return."

"By value, do you mean—?"

"Information. I'm not interested in money." His posture relaxed a bit, now that he knew I was within his price range.

"Then we might be able to reach an accommodation, even though, as I said, I don't believe those documents of yours can possibly be authen-tic. Still, a nuisance is a nuisance. May I see them again, please?"

"Later. When you have something for me to inspect."

He paused, the wheels turning, then nodded.

"Now that you mention it, I might have something with regard to those Dewey transactions that could be of very great value. I might be willing to part with it in exchange for your materials. Only so that I may further investigate their provenance, of course."

"Of course."

"Then let us meet, just as you wish. There is a small café, very private, where—"

"I already have a location in mind. And you have to come alone."

He frowned.

"I must protest such conditions. The item I propose to bring is of such intrinsic value for collectors that I would not feel secure carrying it without my usual escort. Many people in Budapest are aware that I am a wealthy man, and as I have become old and frail I have made it my habit to always be accompanied."

He didn't look frail to me, and I wasn't interested in meeting his thugs.

"Your choice," I said. "If you'd rather not, I'm sure there will be other interested parties."

He sighed, not pleased.

"Very well. Name your location."

"The Panorama Café, at the top of the hill. One hour from now." I didn't want to give him too much time to plan. "Bring the item you mentioned, and be prepared to talk about what you remember."

He didn't look happy with my choice, but after a second or two he nodded.

"Who are you working for, Mr. Cage?"

"Myself." A mistake. I realized it as soon as Szondi smiled warmly in response.

"Good. I prefer to deal with people one on one. I will arrive alone, as you ask, and will trust you to do the same. The Panorama. One hour."

He smoothly shut the door. A moment later I heard voices, then subdued laughter, followed by the clank and whine of the elevator.

I wasn't happy about the laughter.

31

The Panorama Café was directly uphill from Corvin Square, at the south end of a turreted stone fortress known as the Fisherman's Bastion. It offered spectacular views across the Danube, back toward Pest. I walked directly there up a switchback of stone stairways through the trees, then settled in with an overpriced pot of tea delivered by a gloomy waiter. Three musicians dressed as nineteenth-century peasants were playing traditional music on a violin, string bass, and hammer dulcimer, the perfect soundtrack for what I hoped would be a sinuous tale with Ed Lemaster at its center.

Szondi arrived twelve minutes late. He came from the other direction, approaching across a small plaza with a statue of St. Stephen. He already looked impatient, then had to pause at the entrance to wait for some Italians to shoot a family photo. Two children bumped him as they ran squealing toward the statue. Szondi brushed away their essence from his right sleeve. A coat was slung over his left arm, and he appeared to be carrying something beneath it. I gestured toward the other chair. He glanced toward the musicians in apparent disdain.

"I hate this sort of kitschy screeching. A bigger cliché than a bowl of goulash. If I could, I would shove them from the parapet."

"I kind of like it. What did you bring for me?"

"Do you have the papers?"

I flashed open my jacket, showing the folded documents in the lapel pocket. He nodded, then pulled the edge of an old book from underneath the folded coat. He let me see it just long enough for the title to register—*The Great Impersonation*, one of the better novels of Edward Phillips Oppenheim, a prolific British novelist from the early twentieth century. Dad had five of his books.

"My father has a similar copy," I said. "I never thought it was all that rare."

"Rarity is not the reason for its value. Why don't I inspect the papers you brought? Then, if I am convinced they are of sufficient quality as forgeries, I will consider exchanging this book."

"You still haven't told me its significance."

"This copy was meant to be exchanged by one of Ed Lemaster's couriers as part of a Dewey transaction. Long ago it came to me wrapped in butcher paper, and I was prepared to follow the usual routine: the phone call, the drop-off, and so on. I am sure you know. But it was never delivered."

If he was telling the truth, the book was indeed valuable.

"Why do you still have it?"

"I was never comfortable with the arrangement. I came to feel I was being taken advantage of."

"Weren't you being paid?"

"Not sufficiently. I made that known."

"To Ed Lemaster?"

"To the usual contacts. I did not know their names, or even their nationalities. I only knew from an earlier visit, when the arrangement was first conceived, that Mr. Lemaster was part of it. My participation began as a favor to him, as a valued customer of mine. Later, I learned enough about the network to make me uneasy."

"So you tried to jack up the price?"

"You mischaracterize it, of course. I asked for fair compensation."

"And?"

"My request was refused. But by then a new parcel—this one—had just arrived through the usual channels."

"So you opened it, hoping to find out what all the fuss was about."

"Yes."

"And found the Oppenheim book inside."

"This very copy."

The ends of my fingers tingled. I'd reached the end of a vitally important thread. If I swapped the papers for the book, I might get out of here in time for the evening train to Vienna.

"So I take it Lemaster didn't agree to your asking price."

"Regrettably, no. So I decided to keep the book. As insurance."

"Against what?"

"Against this very sort of day. Of course, in those times I always expected that any trouble would come from someone threatening to expose my dealings with the West."

"You were convinced this network was for the West?"

"Of course. Why would I have thought otherwise? Say what you will about those forged documents, I was a good patriot for the resistance, and this proves it."

"Or maybe you were just willing to take money from anyone, no matter whose side they were on."

"You embassy people." His words dripped with disgust. "You lived in such a bubble. Your secrets made you feel safe, but they also made you fall in love with the idea that you were virtuous. All secrets are dirty, Mr. Cage. No one who handles them remains clean."

"How come Lemaster never demanded the book back?"

"He did. I told him I had destroyed it, that I had thrown it into the Danube."

"He believed you?"

"What choice did he have?"

"What did you find inside the book?"

"If I answered that question, then the book would lose much of its value."

"Then let's trade. Yours for mine, right here."

He smiled, which told me I'd proffered too quickly. Béla Szondi was an old hand at manipulating overly eager customers.

"It is not that simple. And I certainly would not make the exchange here. For all I know you've alerted the police, or the newspapers. That Italian shooting snaps of his family might be some hack for *Magyar Hírlap*, ready to put me on the front page: *Respected Antiquities Dealer Caught Covering Up His Past*."

"I doubt it would say 'Respected.' But I could probably arrange for a story like that if you don't want to go through with this."

"I am not opposed to doing business with you. But I must first be able to examine the documents, and I will only do that where there is more privacy."

I was wary, figuring he meant to maneuver me into a car or a house. "Where?"

"Not to worry. Only a few feet from here. Just below, on the very stairs you probably climbed to come here."

The stairway was out in the open. I tried to remember if there had been anything iffy about the switchbacks and terraces along the way, and came up empty.

"Shall we complete this transaction or not?" he said. "If not, I can always throw the book into the Danube for real this time."

"Let's trade."

"You are a shrewd bargainer, Mr. Cage. One of the better ones I have dealt with."

Meaning I'd probably been a chump, but right then I didn't care.

"Let us retire to the stairway, then."

He stood. I reached for my wallet to pay for the tea, but Szondi stayed my hand.

"Please. You are my guest." He laid a pair of bills on the table. "After you."

"No. After you."

He smiled a bit too broadly, then nodded.

"I take no issue with a man who wishes to be careful. I admire it, even."

We left the café and walked to the stairs. Szondi flinched as a tourist camera flashed in passing. I lagged back a few feet, which he didn't seem to mind. Two flights down, Szondi came to a stop just as the beefy fellow whose photo László had shown me loomed into view one flight below. He poked a gun barrel from inside his black jacket and smiled crookedly. I stopped, ready to beat a retreat, but when I turned I saw that a second armed thug was trotting down the steps toward us in Szondi's wake.

"Keep going, Mr. Cage," Szondi said. "Just awhile longer now and it will all be over."

I wasn't thrilled with his wording. I looked around for help but the stairs were deserted. Soon they would kill me, perhaps within seconds. I felt certain of that. On the next flight down the first thug stepped off the stairs toward the stone wall that buttressed the hillside.

"Keep following him, Mr. Cage."

He disappeared beneath the stairway into an alcove built into the wall. My heart was beating way too fast, and I was trying not to show fear in my face or gestures. It was time to make a move, or just run, but there seemed to be no opportunity for either. The thug behind me grabbed my right arm and led me up into the alcove, which stank of urine and damp trash, and as soon as we were inside I belatedly realized that any hope of escape was now gone. The two thugs moved to block the exit, with Szondi between them. This was where they would do it.

"Hand me the papers, please. Put them on the ground in front of you and back away."

Szondi kept his distance, which was a bad sign. I held on to the papers.

"Put the book down first," I said. "You can slide it over to me."

"And then find out later that the papers are fake? Even if they're real, how do I know you haven't made copies? We'll have to search your room, of course."

"Then why don't I take you there now?"

"We know where you're staying. I'm sure we'll be able to find the key after we're finished here."

Szondi smiled as the import of his words sank in. The thug on the left leveled his gun at me. I rose on the balls of my feet to make a dive for it, and was about to answer when a woman's voice barked an order from somewhere out in the open—an order that made both thugs freeze. I lost my balance, dropping to my knees on a slurry of wet newspapers and broken bottles, then scrambled to my feet just as Litzi stepped into the opening behind Béla Szondi.

She said something more. This time the thugs dropped their guns, which she kicked out of the way. They backed up a few steps and put their hands on their heads. Her next words were in English.

"Come out of there, Bill."

"Gladly." By now my heart was going a hundred beats per second, but I still had enough of my wits about me to remember what I'd come for.

"Tell Béla to give me the book."

This brought a sneer from Szondi, who seemed far less intimidated than his hired hands.

"You cannot speak to me directly, Mr. Cage? You let a woman do your talking for you?"

"Drop the book," I said. "Then back away."

He opened his hand. The book came open as it fell, pages fluttering, and landed facedown in the muck. Even under the circumstances I couldn't help but wince.

I stepped over toward Szondi to retrieve it.

"Wait!" Litzi said.

Too late.

Szondi pulled a gun, and now I was directly in his line of fire, and shielding him from Litzi. But even as the barrel rose level with my stomach, a wonderful thing happened. Instantaneously, with barely time for a thought, I reacted just as I'd been taught to on that long-ago afternoon when I took the executive survival course, courtesy of Marty Ealing.

My move was from "Lesson Three: Disarming an Attacker." My left hand shoved aside the barrel while my right clamped his forearm and twisted it until he cried out in pain and opened his fingers. The gun fell, right on top of the book, and I shoved Szondi onto his ass into the filthy muck. I grabbed the book, then the gun, and backed away.

The two thugs, apparently far smarter than their boss, hadn't moved a muscle.

"Nicely done," Litzi said. She looked even more surprised than me. Then she pulled a roll of duct tape from her shoulder bag and tossed it to me.

"Tape those two to that pole by the entrance, back-to-back," she said.

She motioned the thugs into position, and they seemed in no mood to test her resolve. My hands were shaking as I started unpeeling the tape. Had I really just done that? As I taped the men into place I glanced at Litzi. I'd never seen this look in her eyes—neither rage nor menace; instead, a cold resolve. If either thug had even wiggled a toe, I'm positive she would have shot him. And where had she gotten a gun? Being someone who generally doesn't know a Glock from a glockenspiel, I couldn't have told you its make and model. But it was compact and tidy, and black as the night. It fit so comfortably in her hand that it might have been made especially for her.

I kept pulling the tape free with a ripping sound, then wound it around the thugs' arms and midsections, pinning them together back-to-back with the pole in between, seven loops in all.

"Get up," she said to Szondi. "Keep your hands where I can see them."

I then taped Szondi to another pole, eight loops for him.

"That's enough," she said. "They'll be able to get out soon enough, or else someone will hear them down here. But by then we'll be gone." Then she spoke one last time to Szondi.

"If you try to have us followed, these documents will be in tomorrow's newspaper. A reporter I know is already standing by with copies, and if he doesn't have an all-clear from me by six o'clock then he's going to print them. Understood?"

He nodded. No more smiles.

Then we left. Just like that. Me and my trusty old girlfriend, who I'd once fancied needed my protection from the bad old East German *Volkspolizei*. The quiet archivist, my Marian the Librarian with nice legs, sensible glasses, and the maudlin backstory of an expired biological clock. The woman who, when she was seventeen, had been too timid even to do a decent job of spying on my father, yet she had apparently been in league with my handler from the beginning.

But under the circumstances, how could I be anything other than ecstatic to see her, even though she was packing heat and speaking the local language like a native? I kept glancing at her as we briskly descended the stairway toward the river, but she looked straight ahead, as businesslike as ever. By the time we reached the bottom my pulse had nearly returned to normal, and the evaporating sweat on my back was prickling like dried seawater. Glancing over my shoulder, and seeing no one in pursuit, I finally judged it safe to talk.

"I didn't know you spoke Hungarian."

"I don't. I practiced three phrases: 'Drop your weapon.' 'Hands on your head.' 'Don't move or I'll shoot.' I'm not sure what I would have done if they'd talked back or resisted."

"Shot them? That's what they seemed to think."

"It's what they were supposed to think."

"I get the idea you've done this before."

She shook her head.

"Only in training."

"For the Agency?"

"God, no!" She frowned at me.

"Austrian Intelligence? And please don't say KGB."

This at least got a laugh, a flash of the Litzi I thought I'd always known.

"The Verfassungsschutz. The federal internal security police, but it was ages ago. I'm an archivist now, well and truly. Professionally, I don't even live in this century anymore, or even the last one."

"An archivist with a gun?"

"On special loan. At midnight tonight it turns back into a pumpkin."

We headed for the bridge, blending back into the flow of pedestrians and bicycles.

"Is that all you're going to tell me?"

"What more do you want to know?"

"All of it, if you don't mind."

"Saving your skin isn't enough?"

"No."

She smiled again. Every time she did, I inched a little closer to being able to see how these two Litzis might actually coexist. It wasn't as if she'd become this way overnight. We'd been apart for thirty-seven years. No doubt she had changed in all sorts of ways. Up to now my view of her had been clouded by nostalgia. Now I finally beheld her as she really was, a woman of experience, a woman with a past.

"I was only in for three years," she said. "They recruited me during my last year at university. Since then, I've only done the odd errand here and there, a few favors during manpower shortages. But never anything serious, and nothing even close to dangerous."

"So you were, what, twenty when you volunteered?"

"Twenty-one, and I didn't volunteer. They approached me. Apparently they got my name from someone at your embassy."

"Dad was no longer in Vienna by then."

"I'm not saying it was your father. But they knew all about our little trip and how I'd been threatened by the Vopos and, by implication, the Soviets. Knew it right down to the name of the little town where they pulled us off the train."

She stared at me longer than necessary as we moved onto the bridge, to the point where I almost felt compelled to deny any involvement. Then she looked straight ahead and resumed her account.

"They told me they could ensure that nothing like that would ever happen to me or my family again. No more threats. But first they needed my help against 'those kinds of people.'"

"Russians, or East Germans?"

"Leftists in general. More to the point, the RAF."

The Red Army Faction, she meant, the organization of ultra-left, ultra-violent young people—half of them female, oddly enough—who had operated in Germany from the late sixties to the turn of the millennium. Known originally as the Baader-Meinhof Gang, its members had been implicated in shootings, bombings, kidnappings, and robberies, a reign of terror across three decades that peaked in 1977 with a string of abductions known as the "German Autumn."

"I thought the RAF was strictly German?"

"It was, but in late seventy-seven they came into Vienna and kidnapped a millionaire on his doorstep, and I think the authorities went a little crazy. For a while they were convinced that every little bunch of campus lefties was going to metastasize into the next RAF cell, and that's where I came in."

"You were undercover?"

She nodded. "I was supposed to infiltrate them. Some ultra-left group at my university."

"How did it go?"

"Fine, for a while. But it ended badly."

"Meaning what?"

"Meaning, badly enough that they let me quit, then helped me find a job. They kept my involvement a secret. Even my husband never knew. To him I was just Litzi the sensible librarian."

"I understand his point of view."

She was quiet for a while as we negotiated the crowds on the bridge. I wondered what she meant by "ending badly." In disgrace? Betrayal? Death? But by the time we'd crossed the Danube another question had occurred to me.

"Was this job—the one involving me—just another 'little favor' they asked you to do?"

She didn't answer right away.

"As far as I know."

"So that story you told me about the fat man in the seersucker, the character right out of Ambler, it never happened?"

"They told me to tell you that. I had no idea why until you showed me the description in the book."

"Did you know it was going to be me at the Bräunerhof?"

She shook her head emphatically.

"They had me tail you from your appointment earlier that morning at Kurzmann's, the bookstore. A man with a brown paper parcel—that's the only description they gave me. I was supposed to keep my distance until the rendezvous, and I wasn't close enough to recognize you until you came out of the phone booth. Obviously they had good reason to pick me, but I'm sure they wanted my surprise to be genuine."

"It definitely fooled me."

"I wasn't trying to fool you. Not about that. I was thrilled to see you, but I hated the idea of deceiving you. Hated it. That night after you left my apartment I sent word that I wanted out."

Before we slept together, in other words. For some reason that mattered.

"They refused?"

"They said I could quit, but only if I stopped seeing you. I was supposed to be there to protect you, to watch your flanks."

"And to report my movements."

She shut her eyes, then nodded.

"Yes. That, too. And when I saw that the work was becoming dangerous, too dangerous for me to control, then I quit, in the hope that you would quit as well. But when you didn't, well . . ."

"You continued following me?"

"Yes."

"Under whose orders?"

"No one's. I went AWOL. Threw away my phone, stopped checking in. I took certain measures in Prague to ensure I wouldn't be followed, then came here on a bus. I guessed that you'd stop at Antikvárium Szondi, and that's where I picked up your trail."

"Where'd you get the gun?"

"An old contact. It's like any other kind of business. Half of it is connections and calling in old favors. Even after people get out they always keep a hand in, whether they want to or not."

"Like Breece Preston?"

"Yes, like him. The Hammerhead, too."

"Why would the Verfassungsschutz be running this show?"

"I doubt they are. I'm just a resource they're lending out. Like I said, connections and favors. I have no idea who your handler is, or who he works for, but obviously he has friends over here who still owe him."

"So do you."

"What do you mean?"

"The Vienna police, for one. It wasn't my father's connections that got us released, was it?"

"I made a call. Or asked them to make one. They did it because they recognized the number right away, and knew they would be in trouble if they ignored it."

"Is that the same number you gave to those Czech cops, the other night in the rain?"

"Yes."

"Handy."

"You do what you have to. But today I was working for you only. And now I want you to quit. You've seen where it leads. Two people are dead and you would've been the third. We can change hotels, then leave on a bus in the morning. We'll switch routes in some market town, then cross the border where they won't expect us."

"You really think the Szondis will try something?"

"They're the least of your worries. Two other people, minimum, were following us in Prague, including the big American with, what did you call it?"

"A mullet. And I know they were. Lothar told me."

"Lothar." She rolled her eyes.

"I wouldn't take him lightly. He's had some of the same training you had."

"That's not what I meant."

"You don't trust him?"

"How can I trust him when I don't know who he's working for?"

"You could say the same about yourself."

That stopped her.

"You're right. You could. Another good reason to quit. But fortunately you don't have to. I took the liberty this morning of giving notice for you. By now your handler will have received word that we are off the case."

"*Took the liberty?* That's an understatement!" I stopped on the sidewalk, furious. We must have looked like an old married couple, quarreling in public. "I really *do* thank you for saving my ass, but I'd like to make my own decisions if you don't mind."

"Someday you'll thank me. So will your son, and your father."

"And Edwin Lemaster."

"What of it? Do you even know him? Much less know what he really did or didn't do for his country?"

"Or some other country."

"Some other country that no longer exists. If anyone knows the emptiness of actions carried out in the name of country, it's me. Everything I ever did for a nation, or an agency, or for some bureaucratic overlord is ashes to me now."

"You said it ended badly."

"I also said this is not the time to discuss it. There are bigger questions. Like, did you ever stop to think that your handler—*our* handler—might be ex-KGB?"

"Lothar says otherwise. He worked for him, too."

"Then maybe Lothar was also duped."

It was a crazy idea, and probably a scare tactic. But the scariest thing was that it was possible. Another layer of that Greek pastry Lothar had talked about crumbled before my eyes. For all I knew, Lemaster might even be the one who was running me in circles, finally getting his revenge on the reporter whose ambush had brought on his decline. He certainly would have known that curiosity was my fatal weakness.

Maybe Litzi was right about quitting. At the very least, it was an opportune time to leave Budapest. We could return to Vienna, where her connections—and Dad's—would offer the greatest protection. Then, with the Oppenheim book in hand, I could decide in relative tranquillity whether to continue.

"All right, then."

"You'll quit?"

"For now."

"Let's get your things. I'm registered at a more secure location. By this time tomorrow we'll be back at your father's."

"And then?"

The question covered more ground than this spy chase of ours, and we both knew it.

"I don't know," she answered. "We'll talk about it later. In complete honesty."

"Did they train you on that as well?"

She didn't care for the question. I hadn't expected her to.

32

We settled into our new digs, a tiny inn that Litzi chose for its front and rear entrances and the desk clerk's striking lack of curiosity. He requested neither passports nor true identities.

Her checklist apparently didn't include cleanliness. The bedsheets smelled like the stairwell, and the bathroom looked like an art installation celebrating a century of rust. But after locking the rickety door I finally felt secure enough to get out Szondi's copy of *The Great Impersonation*.

Author E. Phillips Oppenheim had never been a spy, although he worked for Britain's Ministry of Information. Hardly anybody today has heard of him, even though in the 1920s he was famous on both sides of the Atlantic. He made the cover of *Time* magazine, and wrote more than a hundred novels. Yes, a hundred.

The Great Impersonation was probably the most popular, but by the time I tried to read it in the early seventies it was badly dated. I didn't make it past the first chapter, mostly because the characters kept saying things like "By Jove!" and "Ripping of you, old chap!"

Now, as I flipped through the pages in search of a message, those "By Joves!" kept winking up at me. I found nothing in the text. Then I slid my fingers along the clothbound cover and peered down the spine for any sign of an inserted note. No success there, either. Maybe the courier network had used a book code and sent the key by separate channels. That would explain why Lemaster took it in stride when Szondi kept the book.

Litzi, watching me, shook her head in disapproval.

"You're out of that now, remember?"

"There's nothing in here anyway."

"Give it to your father, then."

"He's already got a copy."

"Sell it on eBay."

"Maybe we could trade it for dinner. I'm hungry."

"Stay here. There's a takeout place down the block."

After she left I realized I was also craving a beer, but Litzi no longer had a cell phone, so I went in search of refreshment, hoping to make it back before her. I did, but on arrival I was greeted by yet another sealed envelope that someone had shoved beneath the door. So much for the idea that we'd covered our tracks.

Feeling vulnerable again, I set aside the beer and ran downstairs to the desk, where I discovered to my irritation that the clerk's no-questions policy extended to visitors and would-be thieves.

"No see anyone," he insisted in broken English, hands in the air like a suspect. When I continued to harangue him for information he went into his small office and shut the door. I hustled back upstairs, hoping to take care of business before the newly bossy Litzi returned. I took the envelope into the bathroom, shut the door for privacy, and slit it open.

The format was familiar enough—single sheet, typewritten, with a torn-out book page pasted below—except the paper wasn't my stationery, and the typing hadn't been done on my Royal. The deviations from the pattern made it feel like a rush job. Or maybe somebody new was issuing orders.

"I sense that your interest is waning," the message began. "This will get you back on track. Think Belgrade 1992."

Below was a street address in Pest near the Keleti train station, followed by the words, "Visit anytime. You're expected."

The reference to Belgrade '92 naturally piqued my interest, since that was the point at which my journalistic career ran off the rails, thanks to the denied visa. I expected the book passage to be something about dashed dreams or pouting young men.

It was far more cryptic. The page was from le Carré's *A Perfect Spy*, my favorite of his non-Smiley books. It was the tale of Magnus Pym, a Philby-style mole whose father was a charming con artist. Le Carré supposedly wrote it as a sort of personal exorcism, unloading his emotional baggage over his own dad. In that sense, at least, Magnus was the author's alter ego. But in another way he was more like me—an only child raised by a single parent, the product of an insular upbringing in which father and son were almost always on the move. The marked excerpt was a mere sixteen words.

Love is whatever you can still betray, he thought. Betrayal can only happen if you love.

I was still trying to figure out what that could possibly have to do with Belgrade '92 when I heard Litzi come back into the room.

"Bill?" She sounded worried.

"In the toilet. Be right out."

"You went out for beer?" She'd found the six-pack on the bed.

"Sorry, I was thirsty. Tried to catch you on your way out."

I folded the message into my pocket, then flushed the toilet and ran water from the tap. When I opened the door I saw that she, too, had picked up some beer.

"You shouldn't have left. I doubt the desk clerk is very vigilant."

"You're probably right about that."

"What's wrong?"

"Nothing."

"Your face doesn't look like 'nothing.' Did something happen?"

"Everything's fine."

She watched me a few seconds more. I considered telling her about the message. But it was more personal than the others, and it troubled me for reasons I couldn't yet explain. The part about love and betrayal might even be referring to her, so for the moment I kept it to myself. If she was still hiding details of her career with the Verfassungsschutz, why couldn't I hide this? But the main reason was that I didn't want to have to explain what had happened back in '92, or, rather, the aftermath, which I'd handled so poorly.

The food was Chinese, and tasty, and the atmosphere grew more relaxed as we stuffed ourselves with dumplings and garlic chicken. By the time we finished, the room smelled of grease and soy sauce, and we'd downed four of the beers.

We watched some Hungarian television on a wavering black-and-white tube, then packed for an early getaway, brushed our teeth, and climbed into bed. There was no question of sex. Each of us was exhausted, worried, and, more to the point, too wary to make a move. Still, when she rolled up against me later in the sag of the narrow bed, I placed a hand on her waist and snuggled closer. It was a start. But toward what?

I awakened hours later, when it was still dark. The words of the message were still tumbling around in my head. I slipped out of bed and stood barefoot by the window, listening to the night for any sound of movement. I took the note from my trousers, unfolded it as quietly as possible, and reread the quote by the light over the bathroom sink.

Whose betrayal, I wondered? And whose love? And how was any of it relevant to the task at hand, or even to Belgrade '92? If the note had made any sort of demand upon me, ordering me to appear at a certain time, say, or by a certain deadline, I probably would have defiantly ignored it. But by leaving things open-ended—"Visit anytime. You're expected"—my handler had turned the request into an enticement, a lure, and as I pulled on my trousers I surrendered to its power.

I shut the door behind me with a tiny click. The innkeeper was gone from his darkened post. When I reached the street I took out my map of the city. Trams and subways weren't running at this hour, but my destination was only about a mile away, so I set out on foot. Every step echoed in the empty streets, and for blocks I stared cautiously into the depths of every shadow. As I eased into a rhythm, my nervousness abated. Clearly I was alone.

The address was a house, a crumbling three-story Hapsburg fortress built of stone, with grand dormers, a spired turret, and a pitched slate roof. I rang the bell, but there was no sound in response, so I knocked loudly, then began counting the seconds beneath my breath. At eleven I heard footfalls on the stairs. The only other sound was the hum of a streetlamp.

Someone was coming, a heavy but uncertain tread, like a man leery of falling. Old, I guessed. A key rattled and clicked. The door opened just enough for an eye to peer out at me from a face full of folds and wrinkles. The door swung free.

With Belgrade as a point of reference, I recognized him right away, even after eighteen years. He looked as grumpy and disagreeable as ever.

"Cage," he croaked. "Inconvenient as always."

"The message said anytime." My voice misted in the autumn chill. "I decided to take you at your word."

"*I* didn't write that."

He glanced up and down the street, then motioned me inside.

"You'd better be alone."

"As far as I know."

He wore a white silk robe and felt slippers. He didn't offer a hand in greeting, which was just as well because I wouldn't have taken it.

"You do know who I am?" he asked.

"Of course. Milan Bobić."

Bobić had been the press spokesman for the Yugoslav Foreign Ministry. He was the official who, after days of testy wrangling, had finally marched me into a conference room and explained that my visa request had been denied. The decision, he emphasized, was final and irrevocable, and no manner of appeal or pleading would ever make it otherwise. To my mind, Bobić embodied the beginning of my end.

The *Post* protested the decision, but recalled me from the field and sent a more acceptable candidate. The following week I sat down with my wife, April, to say that, until I had a chance to regroup professionally, perhaps we'd better postpone our plans for starting a family. At least by one year, preferably two. That's when she told me she was pregnant with David. He was the greatest gift of my life, and at the time I treated him as a millstone, an ambush. As I said before: Beware the thwarted man, particularly if he is in his mid-thirties and is already gazing off with trepidation toward the bitter end. I acted like an immature ass, spoiled and undeserving, and now here I was back at the source, although I suppose I'd known for all of these years that the real source of the problem was me.

Bobić sat me down in his kitchen, which smelled of onions and old plumbing. He flipped on a ceiling light, squinted, then retrieved a bottle and two glasses from a cabinet and set them on the table.

Slivovitz, of course, the Balkan plum brandy that had lubricated more than a dozen years of war and revolution, and entire centuries of aggrievement.

"Drink first, you will need it." He didn't forget to help himself.

"What are you doing in Budapest?" I asked.

"When Milošević fell, Belgrade was not the right place for people like me. So here I am. All those cowards who came here during the war to dodge conscription are now back in Belgrade, pretending to be true Serbs. I should have waved to them as we passed at the border."

"What do you do now?"

"It is too late for a chat. Drink."

I polished off the brandy in two swallows, a cheap store-bought brand that was about as smooth as sulfuric acid. He poured another shot.

"You will need them both." A grim nod of certainty, but I shook my head and pushed away the glass. He shrugged, drained it himself, then stood and went to a desk in the hall, where he slid open a drawer. He walked back to the table holding a folded paper in his right hand.

"I understand, Cage, that you and your father are both collectors. I am as well, especially of items that are likely to appreciate in value."

He handed me the paper, then remained standing as I unfolded it and began to read. It was a letter, dated March 11, 1992, on the official stationery of Wallace Vandewater, Assistant Secretary of State for European Affairs, U.S. Department of State.

The letter was only two paragraphs, four sentences in all. Mr. Vandewater certainly got straight to the point:

> *Dear Mr. Bobić,*
> *We respectfully request for reasons of national security that the application for a residence visa filed with your country by Washington Post correspondent William D. Cage be respectfully but firmly denied. By necessity, our rationale for this request must remain confidential. On the same grounds, we further request that the reason for your denial not be revealed to Mr. Cage.*
> *I trust this will be our only correspondence on this matter.*
>
> *Respectfully yours,*
> *Wallace Vandewater*

He signed it with a flourish, like a literary autograph dashed off in a great hurry so that other fans wouldn't be kept waiting. I'd never met Mr. Vandewater, but I did know his top deputy at the time, Warfield Cage. My father went to work for Vandewater in 1991, after the State Department finally called him in from the field following thirty-six years of diplomatic service. He remained at the job until 1998, when he retired to his favorite city, Vienna, the birthplace of his son.

At first, I wasn't sure what to feel. Shock, of course. Dismay and grief, naturally. Collectively they hit me hard enough to stir up the first wallowing surge of nausea, which I fought down by drawing a deep breath. My chest felt tight for a second or two, but I was certain that anger would soon make me capable of breathing fire, even though at the moment a huge boulder of bewilderment was blocking its path.

I reread the letter, looking closely, even desperately, for any sign that a mistake had been made, or that Vandewater's intent had been misconstrued. Missing that, I hoped to discover signs of a forgery, a ruse.

But as a diplomat's son I'd seen these kinds of letters many times before, on this very grade of official stationery. And as badly as I wanted to find something amiss, everything was in order. The only item that might be in doubt was whether Vandewater himself had written it, because I knew from Dad that these sorts of chores were often handled directly by deputies, who added their bosses' signatures with an autopen.

Is that what my father had done? Was he in fact not just a willing participant but the instigator? And why? *National security?* The idea was preposterous. I was a journalist then, period. Ambitious and curious, yes, but only a scribbler. I didn't keep secrets, I exposed them. Why had I been the object of this outrage?

I needed another drink, but when Bobić anticipated me by pouring a glass, I refused to give him the satisfaction.

"There is more," he said. "As I told you, I am a collector."

He handed me an old report of some kind, but it was typed in Cyrillic characters—either Russian or Serbian—and I couldn't read a word of it.

"Is this in Serbo-Croatian?"

"Serbian. It is from an ambitious young employee in our Foreign Ministry in 1959, Ivo Marković. His job was to coordinate electronic and visual surveillance of Western embassies. Would you like a translation?"

"Probably not, but go ahead."

1959. The year of the polygraph that Valerie Humphries told me about. The year that Dad and Ed Lemaster must have first crossed paths, and probably Breece Preston as well. The year my mom left us, then died on a high road in Greece.

"Apparently your father became involved in some sort of dispute. 'A flap,' I believe they called it."

"Flap" had always been CIA slang for a screw-up.

"Over what?"

"It is vague. Marković could not recover every detail. But it was serious enough that a polygraph machine was used, and its results were debated, then suppressed. The other figure in this drama was a young embassy functionary whom we had already identified as an employee of the Central Intelligence Agency. He is known now as a great author."

"Edwin Lemaster."

Bobić nodded.

"Marković determined that some sort of indiscretion had occurred."

"Indiscretion?"

"A security lapse. Potentially a serious one. Apparently there was great worry in your embassy of public embarrassment, even scandal, but Marković concluded that your father was able to keep it under wraps."

Just as I thought.

"So this was something Lemaster had done?"

"The evidence was not clear on that point. All that Marković knew for certain was that one of their careers was briefly in the balance, then saved. A salvage job. I believe that was the term he used."

Meaning Dad had either covered for him, or had coached him on how to beat the machine on a second try.

"What else?"

"Well, don't you see the link?"

"The link?"

"To what happened in ninety-two. Ivo Marković—do you not recognize the name?"

Now I did, even though I'd done my best to erase every memory of my brief time in Belgrade.

"He was at the Foreign Ministry," I said. "One of the Milošević people."

"A top deputy. Had you been installed as a full-time correspondent, you would no doubt have sought to interview him. And when your name came up for a visa, he was the one who remembered this affair from the 1950s. Being a collector himself, he quickly produced a copy of this old report. Your father, no doubt, became aware of its existence."

"So he had me blackballed?" I was incredulous. "Some minor embassy cover-up for a CIA man led him to engineer *this*?"

"You must understand. The Western media were completely against us. We were using all leverage at our disposal to change that. If you had worked in Belgrade, I am sure that this would have been used to try to influence you. Your father's past would have been exposed. And with it, Mr. Lemaster's."

I didn't buy it. Or at least not until I considered a further possibility: What if, by covering for Lemaster, my father had enabled a budding double agent to flourish and grow? And what if, by 1992, even Dad suspected as much? Darker still, what if he'd then become part of Lemaster's campaign of deception, which would have made him even more vulnerable to the release of those old secrets from 1959?

A real Joe. That was how Lemaster had described Dad on the day of our interview. "Joe" was British espionage slang for "agent," as I knew from my reading. A few days ago Dad had sworn point-blank that he'd never worked for the CIA, and I'd believed him. Maybe I should have asked instead if he'd ever worked for the KGB.

"You see it, do you not?" Bobić said it with a note of triumph. "I can tell by your eyes. It is true. He worked against your interests in order to protect his own."

That was indeed the nut of it, a painful truth that landed like a knife at the bottom of my gut. And what of my mother, who had left us that very year? Had Dad's duplicity driven her away? She might even have discovered details that Marković hadn't known, so she'd run off to Greece to be killed in an accident. Assuming it was an accident. Because Breece Preston was possibly in the mix as well, in some way, shape, or form. What did I truly know about any of those events, other than my father's version?

A chain reaction of doubt and worry built toward critical mass, fueled by slivovitz. I stood shakily from Bobić's table. His air of satisfaction sickened me. I wanted out of there. Now.

"You must think about these things, then act upon them," he said smugly as he followed me to the door.

As I reached the silence of the streets, I thought I heard him laughing. Like Szondi, I thought. Like all of Budapest, it seemed.

33

While walking back to the inn it occurred to me that, like it or not, my handler had achieved the desired result. I was now determined to see this through, no matter how dangerous. If vengeance was his goal, then he had chosen the perfect vessel for delivery.

The quest had begun for me as a means of renewal, perhaps even redemption. It had turned into something far uglier—a means of retribution—and I felt powerless to stop it. It was still dark when I returned, but Litzi was awake and dressed, and fretful with worry.

"Where *were* you? I thought they must have taken you."

"I was finding out the truth about my father."

That caught her short.

"It doesn't seem to have made you happy."

So I showed her the documents and told her the two Belgrade stories, beginning with my downfall in the early nineties, then working my way back toward the so-called "flap" involving the cover-up of a failed polygraph.

To my annoyance, Litzi was not particularly sympathetic. She listened with an air of growing impatience, and by the end she was rolling her eyes. Just as I was finishing, she could no longer contain herself.

"No, no, *no!* You see it, but you don't see it. Or maybe you've known all along but *refuse* to see it. Or maybe I just think that because I know more than you."

"What do you mean?"

She shook her head.

"I shouldn't be the one to tell you. This is between you and your father."

"I'll manage that all right, the moment we're back. With everything I've learned, he'll *have* to come clean. At least now I know why he didn't want me to pursue this."

"You have it backwards. Yes, he was behind the letter. That's clear enough. But the only person he was really betraying was himself. Don't you see?"

"No. I don't." She watched me closely, as if deciding whether my bewilderment was genuine. Then she took my hand, more in the manner of mother to child than woman to lover, and she spoke very gently.

"That time that I spied on him, when you were seventeen. Remember that I told you I went into his bedroom, but didn't find anything worth reporting?"

"Yes."

Her tone was grave.

"Well, I did find something. I never reported it, because it had nothing to do with his work. But I am almost sure your father knew I'd seen it."

"Go on."

"It was an address book. A little black book, people call them, with names and numbers. It was sort of a diary, too, with notes about the people. It was very personal, very intimate. All of the names were men. It was his life, his *secret* life, but it had nothing to do with spies or spying or even your precious Ed Lemaster. Do you understand me now?"

I nodded, floored. Then I thought some more. Everything I'd been seeing was now standing on its head.

"The polygraph," I said. "Bobić said they weren't sure which one of them failed it. Do you think it was Dad?"

"Of course. It was the question they always asked in those days, whether you were going into intelligence or sensitive diplomacy. They even asked me when I was vetted for the Verfassungsschutz: 'Have you ever had a homosexual experience?' Heaven help you if you got it wrong."

"Unless you had a young friend in the CIA who could help you clean it up."

"I suspect he also coached your father on how to beat it on the second try."

"That also fits with what Humphries told me."

"She mentioned the polygraph?"

"Sorry. I didn't want to tell you. I was too ashamed. I thought my father was protecting a mole."

"He was protecting himself. And Lemaster helped him."

For a fleeting moment I felt I'd been set adrift. A sigh welled up in my chest, and I exhaled slowly. My face felt hot, the heat of shame—not for Dad, but for me, and for everyone else who had never really known him. We were the reason he'd kept living a lie, year after year, in city after city.

The letter in '92? Yes, it was an outrage, a dagger in my back. But by then the stakes must have seemed higher than ever. He was a ranking official, and Lemaster was an esteemed novelist. Why risk both their reputations, especially when he probably figured his son was strong enough, smart enough, talented enough to handle such a setback?

Other things began to fall into place.

"Those men we used to meet when I was younger. I always thought they were spies."

"I think I've probably seen him with some of those men."

"When you've seen him out on the town?"

"He always gives me a certain look, a look of understanding, and of thanks."

"For keeping his secret."

"Because he always kept mine. He never told you about my years with the Verfassungsschutz, and I'm sure he must have heard."

No wonder he'd been reluctant to tell me about his friendship with Lemaster. I remembered the excuse he'd first used, right after the story came out in the *Post*: "There were security issues." Yes, there certainly were. Some very sensitive and personal ones.

It also explained why he'd always preferred to live outside the embassy community.

"We should leave soon if we want to catch the early train," Litzi said. She glanced out the window, and I saw that the first light of dawn was up, coating the rooftops in gold.

A new day was here. A new age entirely.

34

As we boarded the train, I thought of all the men before me who'd been dispatched on grim missions to confront double agents with evidence of their duplicity. There was Nicholas Elliott, sent all the way to Beirut to try and wring a confession out of old pal Kim Philby. Le Carré's Smiley, hiding in a dreary London safe house, listening through the walls as colleague Bill Haydon implicated himself to a Russian. Deighton's Bernie Samson, meeting up behind the Iron Curtain with his wife, of all people, as she confirmed her defection to the Soviets. And poor old Folly, seated stiffly in a Vienna café, watching from behind a newspaper as his lifelong friend Don Tolleson came a cropper.

Now there was Bill Cage, pseudo-spy and snooping son, the man who hadn't known when to quit, on his way to at last seek the truth from his dad, who had fooled him for a lifetime. I realized then that each of us, in his own way, had been on a mission of love. Folly even emerged from behind his newspaper long enough to shake Tolleson's hand, for God's sake, a gesture I'd never understood until now. The words of Magnus Pym told me all I needed to know.

Love is whatever you can still betray, he thought. Betrayal can only happen if you love.

The biggest difference between those other fellows and me was that the rivalries of the Cold War had eventually amounted to nothing—a tired whimper of resignation beneath a fallen Wall and a few toppled statues. But how would the long stalemate of secrecy between Dad and me end? In anger and division? Hope and reconciliation? I wanted the latter, of course, but it would be a few more hours until I found out.

As always, he was standing in his open doorway as I stepped off the elevator. I'd phoned ahead from the bahnhof saying we needed to talk, and I could tell from his somber expression and folded arms that he knew this was important. I put down my bag as soon as he shut the door. Then I cut straight to the heart of the matter.

"I know about Belgrade. Both times, yours and mine. And I know why you felt you had to do it."

He paused to absorb the news, but he didn't look surprised.

"I suppose Litzi was able to fill in some of the blanks. She's certainly seen me around with my friends enough."

"She mentioned that."

"And there was that black book, once upon a time. I've always been grateful for her discretion."

"Is that why you returned the favor? You must have heard later when she was recruited."

"How much did she tell you about that?"

"She said it ended badly, but she didn't say how badly."

He nodded, but offered no more. I wasn't sure whether to be touched or infuriated by their continuing delicacy with each other's secrets.

"So what about you?" he asked. "Where do I stand with you?"

His expression was stoic, but his posture suggested he was bracing for a blow. Maybe that's why he seemed surprised when I gripped his shoulders and embraced him. I felt him sag in relief. Then he gave me a fatherly squeeze, the kind he'd always had in reserve whenever I'd needed one most. For all of the subjects we had avoided over the years, he had never once ducked me in a time of need. I certainly couldn't make that claim with regard to my own son. He sobbed only once, more a gasp than a cry, and when we broke apart his eyes were dry.

"I ruined things for you," he said. "For your mother, too. As good as killed her."

"That's why she left?"

"How could she stay, once she knew who I really was? She was planning to come back and get you. We even discussed the possibility of some sort of marriage of convenience, which was pretty much what we already had. We eventually agreed that she would travel for a few weeks to think about it, to sort things out. Then she would take you off to Boston, where her parents lived. You'd go to school there, and spend summers with me. So off she went. She'd always wanted to see Greece. Then she got on that damn bus."

He went to a desk, where he unlocked a narrow drawer and pulled out a yellowed clipping from an English-language newspaper in Athens. Seventy-nine people in all, including four other Americans. The driver had been drinking.

"I cost you your mother. I've never forgiven myself for that."

"You weren't driving."

"Might as well have been."

"And you didn't ruin me in ninety-two. You just gave me a handy excuse for me to do it myself."

"I think we could both use a drink."

I smiled, because that had always been his generation's answer for everything. Angleton's martinis, Folly's Manhattans, and Dad's whisky, although for the moment alcohol seemed as good an elixir as any.

"Then we'll have a long, long talk. Let's sit in the living room."

He poured two whiskys, neat, and we pulled up our chairs like a pair of old soldiers at a regimental reunion, knee to knee beneath his book-shelves. We covered all sorts of ground, awkwardly at first, then with a growing sense of ease.

Yes, he had failed a polygraph in Belgrade in '59, derailed by the obvious question. Yes, a young Ed Lemaster had helped him smooth it over, first by calling on his Agency connections who administered the program, then by coaching Dad to handle the questioning better the second time around.

"Here's how naïve I was then," he said. "I didn't even know he was CIA until this came up. Of course, afterward I was indebted for life. Maybe that's what he was counting on. So when he came to me years later to ask for a few little favors, who was I to say no?"

Dad did seem surprised—alarmed, even—when I told him how extensive Lemaster's courier network eventually became, with far more code names and far more couriers, me included.

"*You?*" he said. "Those errands I had you doing for those booksellers? My God, what a fool I was."

His face darkened when I told him of the network's apparent Moscow connections.

"Did you ever suspect he might be working for the other side?" I asked.

He thought about it for a second between swallows of whisky.

"Let me put it this way," he said. "Did you ever suspect me? Of being the way I am, I mean?"

"Maybe at some level. Especially when I was older, after college. I guess I did wonder why you always wanted a few days' notice whenever I visited. I looked in your closets once, thinking I might find a whole row of dresses for some paramour."

He smiled.

"Looking in closets. That alone should have told you something. It's one reason all those books always appealed to me. Spying, duplicity, cover. Intelligent men leading two lives at once. It was everything I was doing, except in their versions it was more glamorous and exciting, even noble. Although not so much in the Folly and Smiley books. They were more like me. Nobility itself was the fiction."

"Why didn't you just tell me?"

"It was like any secret, I suppose. The longer you keep it, the bigger it grows. Before long, coming clean is no longer an option."

"I would have understood."

"Really? I'm not so sure."

"What's that supposed to mean?"

"Oh, you're quite enlightened about it now, of course. Anyone with half a brain is now. But you should've heard the things you used to say with your friends growing up. Fags, queers, and all that."

I blushed. "I was awful."

"Son, you were a boy, with all of a boy's stupid biases and insecurities."

"Still, you should've told me to shut the hell up."

"I did give you the occasional lecture on tolerance. But I never wanted to get too specific—might've blown my cover. Besides, it wasn't like you were in danger of becoming a skinhead." He turned somber, looking off into space. "I should've told your mother from the beginning. Our marriage was a career move for me, a camouflage. Although then we would never have had you. And with no you, there's no David."

He seemed the most uncomfortable when talking about the letter he wrote in '92.

"When I heard you were going abroad I was thrilled. You were perfect for the job. Then Marković sent me a letter. He said it would be a shame after everything that happened in fifty-nine if my son were to create further problems for him and his country. He wanted me to assure him that you would write favorable stories. He had no idea of how a free press functioned, of course. I believe he was convinced that I really could influence what you wrote, not just because I was your father, but because of my position at State. I knew that was insane, so I sent the letter. I told myself it was to protect your integrity, to protect you from embarrassment, but it was really just to protect me. Then, when things fell apart so badly in your life, well . . ."

His words trailed off.

"I was nearly thirty-six years old, Dad. Old enough to fend for myself."

He shrugged, and for a while we were silent.

"What will you do now?" he finally asked. "Are you finished with this business?"

"I don't know. I need to think about it. Unless Lothar's willing to help, I'm not sure there's much more I can find out anyway. But one thing's still bothering me. Why is Breece Preston so interested? I didn't want to scare you, but his man Curtin has been following me across Europe."

Dad was ashen. He poured himself a refill and shook his head.

"Well," he finally said. "He and Ed did work together in Belgrade."

"I was wondering if you knew that. Bobić mentioned it as well."

"One thing people say about Preston is that he's always a pro about covering his ass whenever he fucks up. Maybe this is an example. A few hundred million in government contracts would certainly seem to make it worth his while to stop you, if he thinks you might find something damaging. Quit while you're ahead, son. Better still, quit while you're alive."

"Like I said. I'll think about it."

Litzi joined us for dinner that night, a subdued affair of cold cuts and beer. The three of us seemed listless and spent. But after coffee the conversation gained momentum, and I detected an odd chemistry of collusion still at work between Litzi and Dad. Every time I looked up from my cup it seemed they had just shared a glance, a nod, a significant gesture of solidarity, even sympathy.

"What is it between you two?" I finally asked. "You're like a pair of identical twins, passing thoughts back and forth right over my head. It's rude and it's pissing me off. And I hope I made that sound like a joke."

"You didn't," Litzi said, "but I understand. Our conspiracy of silence was completely unfair to you, but it was never about fairness, or even about you. I was loyal to your father's privacy because he was loyal to mine."

"About your work for the Verfassungsschutz?"

"Not just the work. The consequences." She turned toward Dad. "You've always known, haven't you? There must have been some kind of report afterward."

He nodded gravely.

"You don't have to tell him," Dad said. "It's got nothing to do with him or me."

"That's why I want him to know. Because it concerns only me. I hid it from my husband for eleven years of our marriage, and it's one of the reasons he left. He always knew something terrible was getting in our way, but he never figured out what it was, and then he stopped trying. If Bill and I are to continue as friends, he should know." She turned to me. "Will we continue to be friends?"

The old Litzi Strauss bluntness was on full display, as endearing and unnerving as ever. I couldn't possibly say no.

"Something more than friends, I hope."

Then she told me her story, one last painful disclosure to cap a tumultuous day.

Making friends with the so-called radicals among her fellow university students had been easy enough. She liked them, even though she found their politics uncomfortably strident. They liked her, too, and quickly came to trust her. As time passed, her reports to the Verfassungsschutz grew shorter and less detailed. Her handler complained, and so did her handler's bosses. She asked to be released from the arrangement. Not without results, they said. They threatened to expose her.

Then she came up with something big—urgent word that a young German woman on the run, an actual member of the Red Army Faction, would soon be passing through Vienna, and needed safe harbor for one night only. Litzi found out the date and location, and passed them along. The result: a botched raid in which the German fugitive opened fire on the police. She was captured, as were two young women living at the house. But a third woman, new to the group and a friend of Litzi's, was killed in the cross fire.

The campus group scattered in the wake of the tragedy, which provided Litzi with the perfect out. The government found her a job, and for the most part left her alone. But the image of her bright young friend followed her wherever she went.

"When I couldn't conceive a child, I knew it was part of my punishment," she said. "We tried clinics, fertility drugs, in vitro. Nothing worked. We even discussed finding a surrogate, but I knew I'd never be able to use another young woman for my own benefit, not again. And when my husband sensed my heart was no longer in it, well . . ."

She shrugged, as if trying to slough off the intervening years in a single gesture of surrender.

35

I walked Litzi home well after midnight, but didn't stay. Both of us felt that my proper place that night was under my father's roof. Too restless to go straight home, I detoured into twisting lanes and alleys through the heart of the city. Even there, Vienna was never completely at peace. The troubled and the restless were forever on the prowl, shoulders hunched. Car wheels hummed out along the Ring, and the legions of surveillance cameras gazed eternally from on high.

I ended up on a narrow street I remembered from my teens—playing soccer with friends, the ball bouncing wildly off walls and door fronts, skipping crazily on the cobbles. At the end of the block was an old bookstore that had once been a favorite of my father's, smaller than Kurzmann's but in far better shape. I recalled the fussy old proprietor, who'd had little patience for fidgety boys, although the shop itself had been a wonder, with a richer concentration of treasure than most of Dad's haunts. By necessity, probably, since its holdings were crammed into a single square room with only a tiny office in the back.

I peered through the picture window into the gloom of its high shelves. A streetlamp lit the view. A tapping noise made me whirl around, but it was only water dripping from a downspout. I read the familiar name painted on the plate glass: Der Flügel, German for "The Wing." Then I noticed something that had never registered before. Beneath the name was a tiny drawing of a piano. *Flügel* was also slang for a grand piano, because of its winglike shape when viewed from above.

In the middle of a busy day, with people and cars hurtling by, I doubt my mind would have been focused enough to make the connection that occurred next. But in the calm darkness of two a.m., the tiny piano stirred up an old name from deep in the readings of my past: Max Flügel, nickname Das Klavier, or the Piano.

He was a minor but remarkable character who first appeared in

Lemaster's *A Lesson in Tradecraft*—Flügel, the can-do fixer who ran a safe house in Hamburg. He also had another distinction, if my memory was correct. He once had an encounter with Heinz Klarmann, the free-lance operative modeled after Lothar Heinemann.

Now the store had my full attention, especially as I recalled Lothar's cryptic words about where he'd stashed the last remaining copy of his unpublished novel. It was hiding "in plain sight," he'd said, and if I wanted to find it I had to "think like a book scout, that is, like a spy."

I checked the store hours posted on the door. They opened at ten a.m.

When I got back to Dad's I pulled down his copy of *A Lesson in Trade-craft* and found the following exchange, set at Flügel's safe house in Hamburg. It comes just after Heinz Klarmann's narrow escape from a would-be assassin:

Klarmann stood a few feet inside the entrance, dripping November rain-drops on the tatty carpet. He'd already tracked mud onto the floor, and Flügel watched from the end of the hallway in obvious disapproval, shak-ing his head and clicking his tongue.

"Shoes off, if you please!"

Klarmann grumpily complied.

"That jacket as well. Use the hook by the door. The filthy hat, too."

"So is this to be the dockage fee for safe harbor? Perpetual attack by an anal-retentive key holder? Perhaps I should take my chances with the Russians."

"Your life, your call. My house, my rules."

For a moment Klarmann hesitated, as if actually weighing the option. Then he frowned and shrugged off his jacket, grumbling all the while. But he left the hat in place, and Flügel held his tongue even as Klarmann walked defiantly toward the stairs, the soggy hat dripping as regularly as the ticking of a clock.

And there you had it. A fussy proprietor named Flügel offering "safe harbor" for Lothar Heinemann's alter ego. One didn't even have to think like a spy to make this connection. Certain that I was on the threshold of discovery, I slept soundly.

In the light of morning I was more uncertain about my epiphany. It felt like a stretch, mere coincidence. But it was still intriguing enough to check out. I took precautions to keep from being followed, by boarding a series of trams and buses, then doubling back until I strolled up to Der Flügel shortly before 10:15. The door rattled open. No need for a bell in a shop this small.

An older man with wisps of hair plastered across a shiny scalp nodded to me from a stepladder. He was shelving books in the Mozart section, which took up half a wall.

"*Guten Tag.*"

I replied in kind and went straight for the fiction. The books were neatly alphabetized by author. Several nice finds leaped out at me, but when I reached the *H*'s there was nothing by Lothar Heinemann; the volumes jumped directly from Heinrich Heine to Hermann Hesse.

I checked a few other categories—Local Interest, European History. No luck. So much for my moment of inspiration. I cleared my throat. The fellow on the ladder responded immediately.

"Are you looking for something special?"

"Do you have anything by Lothar Heinemann?"

"The book scout?" He looked flabbergasted. "*For* him, you mean?"

"No, *by* him. A novel in galley form. I don't know the title."

"I wasn't aware he had written a novel."

"It was never published."

"Ah! That explains it, then. We do not deal in manuscripts. Oh, begging your pardon, we do not deal in *unpublished* manuscripts. We do, however, have a very limited collection of manuscripts, three or four by some German authors. But those are kept under lock and key in our special collection. Although I'm certain none were written by Lothar Heinemann. But if you would like to check for yourself, I can obtain the key."

"Sure," I answered halfheartedly. "Where's the special collection?"

"In the office. But we must proceed quietly. Herr Ziegler has not yet had his coffee."

I thought he was joking until I noticed his look of trepidation. He fairly tiptoed toward the office in the back, where he put his ear to the door, then knocked lightly.

"Herr Ziegler?"

"Yes! What is it?" A snarl from within.

"A customer wishes to browse the special collection."

A loud sigh. Then the creak of an office chair. The door swung free. Herr Ziegler glared at us as if we'd interrupted the world's most indispensable work. Balance sheets and order forms were fanned across his desk, but so were the football pages of the *Wiener Zeitung*, next to a steaming mug of coffee and a half-eaten slice of strudel. He was tall, thin, and imperious, a weathered strip of jerky with watery blue eyes.

He gestured for us to enter, then barely moved out of our way. The clerk walked crabwise to keep from bumping him but I brushed on past, heading eagerly toward a glass-fronted bookcase along the far wall. The clerk fumbled with a set of keys, then unlocked the bookcase and pointed toward the bottom.

"The manuscripts are down there, as you see."

But I was already looking at the fiction titles. As with the books in the rest of the store, they were in alphabetical order. Novels filled the two top shelves. I quickly scanned the *H*'s, but saw no Heinemanns. I checked again to make sure. Nothing.

Any remaining optimism from the night before was now gone, and I was about to turn away when I spotted a blank powder-blue spine— the very sort of cheap cardboard jacket often used for prepublication galleys. It was in the wrong part of the alphabet, but I pulled it out anyway. Title and author were printed in block letters on the plain blue front.

Der Kurier
Heinz Klarmann

Of course. Now it seemed obvious. A pen name stolen from his alter ego. Just enough of a tweak to throw off any searchers who inquired by telephone, which was probably how my handler would've worked to save time, proceeding store by store across Europe.

"Do you have any titles by Lothar Heinemann?"

"No, sorry."

Even if someone had checked in person, they would've had to breach Ziegler's inner sanctum, and even then they would've been greeted by a blank spine shelved with the *K*'s.

"Sir, don't you want to see the manuscripts?"

The poor clerk was down on his knees with a small pile.

"I'd rather have a look at this," I said. "Can you tell me what the price is?"

Ziegler, having returned to the sports pages, wasn't paying us a bit of attention. The clerk stood awkwardly. He took the book and flipped open the cover to the inside page where the price should have been, scribbled in pencil.

"I've never understood why we keep this old thing," he said. There was no marked price, so he flipped to the back.

"Well, I'd definitely like to buy it."

Or, short of that, maybe I'd snatch it straight from his hands. That's how eager I was to begin reading. If it even came close to living up to Lothar's billing, then I had just discovered the key to everything. At the very least, Lothar would now have to reveal the name of our handler.

"Herr Ziegler," the clerk said in a begging tone, "our customer would like to buy this volume, but, well, I can't seem to find the price."

Ziegler sighed and looked up from his paper, peering above his reading glasses.

"Which volume, Klaus? You'll have to actually *show* it to me."

Klaus raised the pale blue cover into view. Ziegler's expression instantly changed to one of alarm.

"That's not for sale! It's not even supposed to be available for inspection. Put it away at once!"

I snatched it out of Klaus's hands as they both gasped. Ziegler seemed to take notice of me for the first time. He smiled tightly and extended a long, thin arm.

"As I said, sir. That book is not for sale. So, if you please."

"Are those Lothar's standing orders?"

His mouth opened. His eyes narrowed.

"Who are you?"

"Bill Cage, Warfield's son. I'm a friend of Lothar's."

"So you say."

"Call him. He'll vouch for me."

Ziegler seemed uncertain of what to do next, so I got out Lothar's business card, the one with nothing on it but a number.

"Here's his mobile number, in case you don't have it."

"Of course I have it! It's Lothar Heinemann, for God's sake!"

"Then call him. Tell him Bill Cage is in your shop, and that I've found the book."

Ziegler eyed me again, then morosely picked up the phone. He was not accustomed to following orders, and he was grim as he punched in the numbers.

"Heinz, please . . . Ziegler at Der Flügel . . . Yes, Lothar. There is a man here, Bill Cage. He has, well . . ." Ziegler cringed like a boy with a bad report card. "He has found your book."

Lothar's laughter was audible across the room. An expression of immense relief spread across Ziegler's face. He propped his elbows on his paperwork and puffed his cheeks as he exhaled. He gestured for me to come forward, then put his hand over the mouthpiece.

"He wishes to speak to you. If you will just hand me the book first."

I grabbed the receiver but held on to the book. Ziegler grimaced but didn't fight back.

"Is that really you, Cage?"

"You owe me a name."

"Of course. I'll pay in full."

"Where are you? When can we meet?"

"Berlin. Regrettably, we'll have to do this by telephone. But you must read the book first."

"You'd better tell Ziegler. He seems inclined to keep it."

"He *will* keep it. You're going to read it there, in his office. That book is not for sale, not even to you. How long have you been in the shop?"

"No more than fifteen, twenty minutes."

"When an hour has passed, they're going to come looking for you, to see why it's taking so long."

"Curtin?"

"Him or the Russian. Perhaps both. They'll have guessed why you're there."

"How do you know I haven't lost them?"

His laughter this time was more of a wheeze.

"Listen, Cage. You're in for a very long day. There is still a fifty-fifty chance that no harm will come to you, but only if you follow my instructions."

Did I believe him, or was he just trying to scare me?

"I want you to put Ziegler back on the line so I can make the necessary arrangements. He will piss and moan, but he'll get the job done, and when he hangs up he's going to tell you what to do next. But I don't want you doing anything further—*nothing*, do you hear me? not even take a piss—until you've finished reading it. Then I want you to call me. From the phone at Der Flügel, not from your own. That's when I'll give you the name. Understood?"

"That could take hours."

"My prose isn't that bad, Cage. It's the only way this will work. If you leave the store before then, with or without the book, then I promise you'll never get a chance to even read page one. You must trust me on that."

"Okay."

"Good. Give the phone to Ziegler. Is that fool of a clerk Klaus there?"

"Yes."

"Then pray to God he doesn't handle the arrangements. Good luck, Cage. And happy reading. I hope I'll be speaking to you again."

I handed the phone to Ziegler, who by now was very grave in manner. He said little as Lothar talked to him other than the occasional "Yes," nodding all the while. A few minutes later he hung up. The first thing he did was order Klaus home.

"On your way out, put the 'Closed' sign in the window. I'll write a note explaining to our customers that there has been a family emergency."

It reminded me of the note in the window at Antikvariát Drebitko, which didn't seem like a good omen, but of course neither Klaus nor Ziegler knew about that. So Klaus merely nodded, seeming relieved to be escaping a situation that had suddenly turned tense and serious. Ziegler waited for the office door to close before addressing me. He took a set of keys from a drawer and put them on the desk.

"This is my spare set. You'll need to lock up when you're done. Then I want you to put them into this envelope and drop them back through the mail slot. Do you understand?"

"I'll be locking up?"

"*Pay attention*, will you?"

"I understand. I'll lock up, then put the keys back through the mail slot, inside the envelope. Where will you be?"

He shook his head, as if that wasn't relevant.

"This is the most important part, so listen closely. You are not to take any notes. None. When you are finished reading, you must move the filing cabinet away from the wall. This one here." He tapped it. "Okay?"

"Okay."

"Behind it you'll find an opening to an old coal chute that used to come into the building from the alley in the back. Drop the book into the chute. Don't worry about its condition, just drop it there and then slide the filing cabinet back into place, do you understand?"

"I understand."

"After you've done that, you will let yourself out of the store as previously instructed."

"Okay. And then?"

He threw his hands in the air and shook his head, as if to say that was none of his business and never would be, no matter what happened to me. It wasn't exactly reassuring, but by then I was eager to begin reading.

"If you are quite clear on all these matters of procedure, then I will leave you to your work. Good-bye."

He departed in a rush. Moments later I heard the lock smack home on the outer door. All was silent. It was just me and the book. I sat down at the desk and turned to page one. The book was in German, of course, but here's the rough translation of Lothar's opening paragraphs:

On this particular Wednesday in Budapest, the spy known as Headlight had decided to employ a different sort of courier. A boy, no more than ten years old, and an American at that. He was one of the privileged specimens from the embassy, although you never would've guessed it from his loose and ungainly brown shorts, which were just like those worn by all the grimy locals that numbered among his playmates.

He was an intelligent boy, the American, and carefree in the way that only an outsider could be in this capital of closely held secrets. Yet there was something inherently wary in his gaze and demeanor, as if life itself up to now had been one long covert action. In other words, he was the perfect choice for the task at hand.

Well, Lothar certainly knew how to start things off. Not only was I hooked, I was already oblivious to any thought of the forces that would soon begin gathering outside the walls of Der Flügel, waiting impatiently for me to emerge.

Even if I'd been aware, I'm not sure it would have slowed me down. This was the first spy novel I'd read since the Wall had come down, and for all I knew it might be my last. So I sure as hell was going to make the most of it. I turned the page, eager for more.

36

Lothar was a fine storyteller, and if not for my urge to wring the significance from every detail, I would gladly have surrendered to his narrative powers. His tale briskly wound its way through all the cities I'd once called home. The names of his characters were easy enough to decipher: Earl LeGrange for Ed Lemaster. Jeff Anderson for Jim Angleton. Bartlett Pierce for Breece Preston. Warren Cave for my father. And me, of course, appearing simply as the Boy.

But Lothar's most daring stunt was that all the code names were as real as the locations in which they operated: Headlight, Blinker, Taillight, Nijinsky, Dewey, Oleg, Leo, Thresher, and quite a few more. Somehow, through all his footwork, the indefatigable Lothar had tracked down everyone, Russians as well as Americans.

As their deeds unfolded, it became clear that only Headlight, or Lemaster, was ever certain at any given time about what both sides were up to. But which one was he working for, and toward what end? Lothar's art was that you weren't sure, even as Headlight played both sides against the middle.

The McGuffin, or plot point on which the book hinged, was the question of whether the CIA would be able to keep the Soviets from getting their hands on a copy of NATO's contingency war plans for central Europe. It was one of the novel's few weak points, which led me to believe that Lothar had made it up. In fact, it was fairly easy to spot the moments when he was winging it, or finessing gaps in his knowledge. His prose may have been powerful, but his powers of invention were weak. This told me that however thoroughly he'd penetrated the operations of both sides, he had never uncovered any of the actual secrets they were trafficking in.

The Lemaster courier network he described was a complex feat of espionage genius, a multilayered structure in which secrets were passed within the covers of old espionage novels. In one of its more clever touches, the rarest books were used for passing the most important secrets. Was that Lothar's creation, or Lemaster's?

In Lothar's version, at least, the information was passed by using book codes, with the code key being sent via separate channels, much as I'd already guessed. But here, too, the device felt unconvincing, which made me suspect Lothar never actually got his hands on a code key. On that point we both seemed to be guessing.

Lothar kept things interesting by setting up a series of close scrapes, and by showing the machinations of the rival spymasters as they tried to pinpoint what Headlight was really up to—Angleton in Washington, Oleg in Moscow. At various times both were convinced that they were getting the best of their rivals, only to believe in the next minute that they were being bamboozled.

Lothar let the reader go back and forth this way until the final twenty pages. In the climactic scene, Headlight passes the coveted NATO report to his Soviet handler in a meeting at a Vienna café—the Bräunerhof, by God, with Headlight initiating the exchange by entering the very phone booth where Litzi and I had recently reunited. He places a coded call, walks to the newspaper table, and slips the report inside a copy of the German newspaper, the *Frankfurter Allgemeine Zeitung*. He then leaves the café just as his Soviet handler takes the newspaper back to his own table and slips the report inside a briefcase.

So there it was. In Lothar Heinemann's judgment, Lemaster was a Soviet double agent.

Even after days of believing that this might well be the case, the news hit me harder than I would have expected. I sat there remembering the Ed Lemaster of twenty-six years ago, swirling wine in his glass and teasing me with his talk of having contemplated betrayal.

But had Lothar really witnessed such a decisive moment, or had he surmised it from his threads of evidence? Even if the former was true, had he really known the details of the item Lemaster placed inside the newspaper? Was the betrayal genuine, or had Lemaster been passing a clever bit of disinformation?

Lothar left unresolved the question of whether Lemaster's first CIA handler, Breece Preston, had been in on the scheme or merely a dupe. Not that Preston would have appreciated either interpretation. Either way, he didn't look reliable enough to entrust with millions of dollars to spy for your soldiers.

While Lothar's verdict on Lemaster was clear, to me the jury was still out. And this was hardly the sort of "proof" I could publish in a magazine story, especially since I wouldn't even be leaving the store with Lothar's book. But at the very least, especially if Valerie Humphries's account was accurate, Lothar's findings showed Lemaster had been far cozier with the Soviets than his Washington handlers had ever realized or sanctioned. If he wasn't a double, then he had run one hell of a rogue operation.

But the book's most diabolical section, as far as the CIA would have been concerned, was the acknowledgments page in the back. Each and every Agency operative portrayed in the book was thanked by name. All you had to do then was match their initials to those of the characters in the book to fill out the entire covert cast. No wonder the Agency had intervened to stop publication.

My handler would no doubt be pleased by these findings, which made me all the more satisfied with the idea of withholding them from the manipulative son of a bitch. And now I would finally learn his name.

I checked my watch. It was 7:43 p.m., dark by now, and I was hungry, thirsty, and needed to pee. I picked up Ziegler's phone and punched in Lothar's number. He answered right away.

"Heinz?"

"You're finished?"

"It's impressive."

"The prose, or the contents?"

That's when I realized that even after all this time, Lothar had retained his authorial vanity. The CIA had not only bottled up his secrets, it had also deprived him of his literary moment—reviews, reaction, and, most important, readers. Lothar, who practically lived in bookstores, had never once seen his own work on a shelf or a display table, tucked in among his favorites. So now he was eager to hear at last from his one and only patron.

"Both. Best thing I've read in years."

"Well . . . it has its problems, of course. But I'm gratified to hear you say it. Truly."

"You seem pretty sure he's guilty."

"As sure as you can be in this business. Meaning not very."

"But you were winging it on the book codes, weren't you?"

"An educated guess. Our handler was always convinced that there must be something about the books themselves that held the key, but I never found it."

"You promised me a name."

"Try page one-nineteen. I believe you've already met him, however briefly. But don't say it over the phone. By now I doubt we're the only ones on Ziegler's line."

I thumbed quickly to the page, running my forefinger down the column of type until I saw the name Gil Cavanaugh, an assistant to the Angleton character. I was pretty sure I knew who that was, but checked the acknowledgments page, and there it was: Giles Cabot.

I thought back to the funeral on Block Island. Wils Nethercutt, the deceased, and his neighbor and onetime Agency rival, Giles Cabot, confined to a wheelchair even as he faced down a menacing Breece Preston. A perfectly logical choice, but nonetheless amazing. I'd been strung along across half of Europe by a frail invalid who must also be a bookworm. At least I knew where to find him.

"Do you have it?"

"I do. Thanks to your acknowledgments page."

"A cheap shot at the Agency, but I couldn't resist. The bastards owed me. Still do. Now for the hard part. Follow Ziegler's instructions to the letter, but once you leave the store I doubt you'll be going very far. I just hope that the right people get to you first."

"Is that a guess, or do you know something?"

"A little of both."

From out in the store I heard the sound of smashing glass.

"You're right. Someone's just broken in."

"Get moving, Bill. Finish the job, then run like Zátopek. *Now!*"

I slammed the receiver and moved quickly to the file cabinet and wrenched it away from the wall. Footsteps pounded through the store. The doorknob rattled. I knelt and reached behind the cabinet, pulling the handle of an old metal flap hinged at the bottom, which opened onto a coal chute. I tossed in the book, wincing in spite of myself as it banged and tumbled. As I peered into the darkness of the cellar I thought I heard the scrape of leather soles below. The flap thumped back into place. I stood and shoved the cabinet back against the wall, then had just enough time to move back behind the desk before the office door splintered open with a crunch of shattered wood. Two men rushed me. One pinned my arms behind my back while the other shouted in heavily accented English, "The book. Where is the book?"

I'm not quite sure where my answer came from, probably some old paragraph from a long-ago rainy Saturday, author unknown. But it made all the difference.

"It's in a burn box in the corner." I nodded toward a shelf where Ziegler piled his old newspapers. "It's set to activate in two minutes."

A burn box is a spy device. You throw your secrets inside and lock it up. If anyone comes to take them, you push a button or punch in a number to incinerate everything inside before the enemy can retrieve a single scrap. My assailants knew this as well as I did, and my words created such an alarming sense of urgency in both of them that for a single decisive moment they forgot all about me and rushed toward the corner.

I darted out the office door toward the broken glass at the front of the store. They were still shouting and thrashing around as I stepped into the cool Vienna night.

Free. But for how long?

Looking left, I saw a van twenty yards away, engine running, passenger door opening. I set off in the opposite direction, giving it everything I had, all of the old Emil Zátopek effort and drive. But even the great Zátopek was a distance runner, not a sprinter, and I was merely a desk-bound flak with fifty-three years on the odometer. They caught me in half a block, a man on either side clamping onto an arm just as a second van squealed to the curb beside us.

Breathless, I expected them to toss me inside. Instead, my escorts nimbly turned me back toward the first van, which was gunning toward us in reverse, straight down the sidewalk, its panel doors open. Behind me I heard the second van back on the move, and voices shouting in Russian. Some sort of brutal competition was under way, and I was the dubious prize.

My shoulder slammed against the floor of the first van as my two escorts shoved me inside. Both tumbled in with me, and everything went dark as the doors slammed shut. I heard the grunting of bodies landing atop me, the grind of the revving engine, the muffled shouts of our pursuers, and the thump-thump of the tires as we roared back onto the street across the curb. Then a drumroll across cobbles, another shout, followed by the shriek of a siren and heavy breathing from above. A needle plunged into my buttocks.

"Ow!"

I was about to say more when the world disappeared.

37

"How many fingers?"

An older fellow with gin blossoms and yellow teeth asked me that question. His face was only a foot from mine. He wore a gray pin-striped suit, tie loosened at the neck.

"Three," I answered. I was groggy, just coming around.

"How many now?"

"Where the hell am I?"

"He's fine," a second man said from somewhere behind me. I twisted in the chair to see him but couldn't turn more than a few inches because I was strapped around the waist and chest. My hands were bound at my sides, and my feet were bungee-corded to the legs of the chair.

"What the fuck is happening?"

"See? That stuff wears off in an hour, then it's gone in seconds. Just like I told you."

An hour. Then it must be close to nine p.m. I had a headache, but the guy was pretty much right, because I seemed to be thinking fairly clearly. I looked around at what I could see of the room. Small and antiseptic, somebody's office. An American flag in the corner and a picture of the president on the wall. It didn't look like the sort of place where someone would beat you, waterboard you, or hook up your genitals to electrodes, but these days I suppose you never knew for sure. The important thing was that there was no sign of either Ron Curtin or the Hammerhead.

The first fellow who'd held up his fingers backed away a few feet and inspected me with a rather forlorn expression, as if he'd seen better specimens.

"Should we give him coffee?"

"No. It'll skew the results. Just wait another few minutes."

"Could somebody please tell me where I am, and what this is all about? And maybe loosen these ropes." My hands were numb.

The second man moved into view. Mid-twenties and full of himself. Black stretch pants and a black synthetic top, with his hair mussed. One of the guys who'd grabbed me, probably. The other fellow in the suit tilted his head in a pose of curiosity, but he no longer looked worried.

"I'm staying for the questioning," he said.

"Of course."

"I really need to pee," I said.

"Give him some water. He probably needs a drink."

"Oh, yeah," I said, "that'll help."

"Get him a jar, or a glass from the canteen. I'll unzip him."

"Are you serious?"

He was. The suit left the room. The cocky young man in black squatted in front of me like a prostitute eager to conclude business and move on to the next customer. He unbuckled my belt and unzipped my trousers as I squirmed in the chair. Then he frowned, seemingly uncertain about what to do next.

"Scared to touch it, or worried I'll get it all over you?"

"You right-handed?"

"What?"

"Are you right-handed?"

"Yes."

He untied my right hand. The suit brought in a McDonald's cup. Medium. The way my bladder felt, maybe they should've supersized. I flexed the wrist of my free hand, which tingled as the feeling returned, then went about my business while the young guy held the cup with surprising poise. If it hadn't been such a relief I probably would've done something stupid and juvenile like spraying him.

The suit wrinkled his nose and took away the cup, which was filled alarmingly close to the brim. Then the other guy pushed up a small table to my right and set down a full glass of water, which I greedily drained.

"Got anything to eat?"

"Later."

"Mind telling me where I am?"

"The U.S. embassy. You'd better be damn glad we got to you first."

"Actually, that's not how I remember it."

"Okay, but we got you."

"The other guys were Russian?"

"Just like old times, huh? And believe me, you wouldn't be peeing into any cups with those guys."

"A samovar, you think?"

"Funny. In your pants, more like it."

"You guys are the best."

But in spite of everything, I *was* relieved. Being abducted and then bound to a chair by my countrymen might still lead just about anywhere, I supposed, but it seemed preferable to the alternative.

"Does my father know I'm here?"

"He has no idea about any of this."

"That's not what I asked."

"You'll be released into his custody. Provided you cooperate."

I exhaled slowly. By now my head was completely clear, and I felt better after the water. Maybe I would be all right.

The suit returned, this time with a man in a white lab coat carrying a silver hard-shell briefcase, which he placed on the table and snapped open. The guy in black removed the rest of my bindings and backed away toward the door. Then, without a word, the man in the lab coat unrolled a black band, wrapped it tightly around my right bicep, and secured it with Velcro, as if he was about to take my blood pressure. He secured two thinner bands around my chest and began connecting sensors to the fingers on my right hand.

They were hooking me up to a polygraph. I was about to be fluttered.

I suppose it could have been an aftereffect of the knockout drug, but for a moment I experienced a sensation close to dizziness. It was as if the room were in motion and I was whirling on a long comet tail of history, preparing to land at the very point where all of this had started half a century ago, when Dad had been in an identical position. They'd hooked him up to an older version of the same machine and placed him before an inquisitor, all in the name of security. A moment that changed our lives, and now I would relive it. But I doubted my captors felt that way. To them this was more like battlefield cleanup, carting the last litters of the wounded from a very old and dormant field of action.

Rather than freaking out, I began to relax, fortified by the moment of solidarity with Dad. I realized then that I was ready for any question.

"All set," the technician said.

I flexed my hand and drummed my fingers on the table.

"Don't do that," he said.

The young fellow in black introduced himself.

"I'm Peter West." Then, gesturing toward the suit, "This is Arnold Harrison."

"Am I really supposed to believe those names?"

"Believe what you want, as long as you answer the questions completely and truthfully. Are you ready to do that?"

"Fire away."

West started me off with a series of easy questions to establish a baseline response. Name, age, home address, and so on, although about halfway through they threw in a wild card.

"Have you ever had sexual relations with Austrian national Litzi Strauss?"

"Yes."

West checked with the technician, who nodded.

"Within the past week?"

I decided to test the machine.

"No."

Another look. The techie shook his head. West frowned and tried again.

"Have you had sexual relations with Austrian national Litzi Strauss at any time during the past seven days?"

"Yes."

A nod. A short time later they got down to business.

"Tonight at the bookstore, did the Russians take possession of the Lothar Heinemann book?"

"There was no Lothar Heinemann book."

West didn't even bother to check with the techie.

"We monitored your phone conversation. We know there was a book, whether Lothar's name was on it or not. Did the Russians take possession of it?"

"Not to my knowledge. I told them I'd put it in a burn box. That got their attention long enough for me to get away."

West raised an eyebrow and nodded.

"Not bad. Where was it really?"

"In the desk. A locked drawer. If you haven't found it by now, then I guess they have it."

West looked over at the white coat. Then he frowned.

"You're lying."

"So you really haven't found it?"

"Answer the question."

"I got rid of it."

"Where?"

"Down the coal chute. A flap behind the file cabinet."

West seemed surprised when my answer passed muster.

"How did you know to put it there?"

"Earlier instructions. I'm a good listener."

West looked at Harrison, who shrugged. The CIA must already have checked the cellar but come up empty. Maybe the Russians had it. Then I remembered the scrape of footsteps I thought I'd heard below. Lothar must have arranged for someone to be there to retrieve it. Many of those old cellars, I knew, had connecting doors that had been installed during the Second World War so that people could escape through their neighbors' houses in case their own homes collapsed in an air raid. Ziegler himself might have been down there, the old rat. I smiled.

"Why are you smiling?"

"It was a good book. I enjoyed reading it."

"Why didn't you take notes?"

"Lothar asked me not to."

West shook his head, seemingly unable to comprehend the idea that I'd actually done as I was told.

"Tell us about the contents."

The questions continued in this vein for the next hour or so. I kept my answers as vague as possible, which wasn't all that difficult considering that I truly couldn't remember the material down to the finer details in the way that West wanted. I knew the names of the bookstores, of course, because they were ones I'd visited myself, and I easily remembered all the code names. But the dates and times, the sequences of the various couriers, and the finer points on who learned what, and when, and from whom, had already faded, so much so that after a while West finally threw in the towel.

"Shit, this is worthless."

"You think Lothar still has the book, don't you," I said. "Him or one of his people."

West shrugged.

"As long as it's not the other guys."

"Why do you even want it, after all this time? To expose it or bury it?"

"You're not cleared for that answer. Let's just say that maybe it's not so bad that you don't remember too much. But obviously you formed some sort of conclusion after reading it, or you wouldn't have said what you did to Lothar on the phone."

"About Lemaster being guilty? That was Lothar's conclusion. I didn't say it was mine."

"But your handler still wants to know, doesn't he?"

"Yes. I take it you know his name."

"Giles Cabot has made himself pretty obvious lately. Especially by Agency standards."

"Pretty neat trick for a guy in a wheelchair."

"You were up there for the Nethercutt funeral, weren't you? That's probably when you came to his attention."

"Probably."

"How did he first make contact? Was it that weekend?"

"No. Later."

I led them through the process, from that first anonymous message in Georgetown, typed on my own stationery, right up to the messages he'd sent me in Prague. I said nothing of what I'd learned about my father's past, or Litzi's, which meant I said very little about the events in Budapest. Neither of them seemed troubled by my apparent omissions. In fact, West seemed downright charmed and intrigued by my account.

"Christ," he said. "It's like something you'd read in a novel."

"I think that was the point."

"Well, we'd like you to finish it for us," Harrison said. "Write one last chapter, then close the cover for good. If you're up for it."

Now they had me. Almost.

"Why not use one of your own people?"

Harrison cast a nervous glance at the technician.

"Let's talk generally for a moment, shall we?"

He pulled up a chair and motioned to the technician to clear away his tools. The man in the white coat stripped me of the various monitors and sensors, then packed up his briefcase and left. No one said good-bye as he shut the door.

"You ask a very good question," Harrison said. "Let's just say that the work that needs to be done is likely to occur on territory outside our authorized area of operations. Places where a private citizen is certainly free to do as he chooses, even a particularly nosy and intrusive one, but not an employee of the Central Intelligence Agency."

"So you want me to go to Block Island, to where Cabot lives?"

"We want you to bring this matter to a conclusion. If it involves activities on U.S. soil, then we're not permitted to have a role in it. So you would be free to determine the latitude of the work within your own discretion as a private, law-abiding citizen."

I almost laughed. Lawyers, I thought. Spies were powerless once you let lawyers into the equation. Maybe this explained why legal thrillers had overtaken espionage novels on best-seller lists in the wake of the Cold War.

"Okay, then. What is it that you *don't* want me to do?"

"Find Cabot's stash, then dispose of it."

"His stash?"

West picked up the thread.

"All the Angleton people had one after they retired. So did the Dark Lord himself, as it turned out. Things that were never supposed to leave the building, but somehow did anyway, most of it having to do with all the stuff that no one knew they were up to."

"Like the running of Headlight, Taillight, and Blinker."

"Precisely," Harrison said.

"And even poor old Mary Meyer's diary?"

"Actually, that turned up in one of Angleton's safes at Langley. Apparently it was just a curiosity for him."

"Strange man. I had a run-in with him once, when I was a kid."

"We know," Harrison said. "That was in his safe, too, in an old daybook."

I was amazed, even charmed in an eerie sort of way.

"But what we didn't find were things like his appointment logs, all those accounts of every lunch and every Agency visit he ever got from goddamn Kim Philby."

"I can see why he'd have stashed those."

"You and every two-bit historian who ever came up with a cheap conspiracy theory," West said.

"Maybe he sent them to Area 51. Have you checked Roswell?"

West laughed. Harrison wasn't amused.

"We think Nethercutt had a stash as well, and that after he died his old rival Cabot came over from next door and found it. That's probably what set off this whole thing."

It made sense. It also explained some of the contacts and documents Cabot had come up with. New information would have made him feel empowered enough to reopen his old investigation.

"So it stands to reason," West said, "that Cabot must also have a stash. He's probably had one all along, but now it will have Nethercutt's stuff, too, plus whatever you've sent him."

"How am I supposed to find it?"

"Bait," Harrison said. "One last item that you'll send his way, juicy enough that he'll want to put it away immediately for safekeeping."

"Which is another reason you wanted Lothar's book."

"We'll come up with something else. Any ideas?"

I shook my head.

"How were you communicating?" Harrison asked.

"It was pretty much a one-way street. He'd send messages, and I'd do as he asked. Litzi was reporting my movements for a while, but after that I have no idea how he was keeping tabs. The only other channel from my end was a dead drop, next to the Franz Josef statue in the Burggarten."

Harrison shot a questioning glance at West.

"Worth a try," West said. "He's probably still got somebody checking it. Whatever we come up with, you can put it there the day you fly back. On your way to the airport, even. By the time it's delivered you'll be in place."

"On Block Island?"

"I never said that. Never even mentioned it."

"So where's this bait, then?"

"We'll come up with something. Then we'll shoot it over to your father's place before you leave. In the meantime, book a flight to Boston and a rental car. If you have any trouble getting a spot on the ferry, let us know and we'll see to the arrangements."

"You're trusting me to handle the tradecraft once I'm there?"

"Once you're on U.S. soil, we're not trusting you to do anything. I hope that's understood."

"Perfectly."

"But you've read all the books. Obviously you have some idea of how these things work. If he was expecting you, that would be one thing. But he won't be."

"What do I do with this stuff if I find it?"

West handed me a slip of paper.

"Here's an address. By certified mail, if you please."

It was a post office box in Herndon, Virginia, in care of someone named Elliott Wallace. Fake name, no doubt. An all-purpose conduit for all sorts of Agency detritus.

"You're trusting this to the U.S. Postal Service?" I asked. "Whatever happened to dead drops?"

Harrison took over.

"This is an address that automatically receives special handling. Besides, setting up a dead drop in certain locales would imply operational activity."

"So this is to keep the lawyers happy."

"It's for your own protection."

"Maybe I should just destroy the material."

"It's U.S. government property. Anything that needs to be destroyed, we'll manage."

"With Breece Preston's approval?"

Harrison looked over at West, who cleared his throat.

"Just use the address, Mr. Cage."

"One final piece of business," Harrison said. He handed me a pen and an official-looking sheet of paper. "Date and signature at the bottom, with your full name printed underneath."

It was a document the Agency called a nondisclosure agreement. I'd seen Marty Ealing persuade people to sign them on behalf of some of our shadier clients. Basically it was a pledge not to disseminate or publish any information I obtained as a result of any employment for the Central Intelligence Agency.

"I thought I wasn't working for you?"

"Not in any official capacity, no."

"Then I'm not really employed, so this doesn't apply to me."

West looked uncomfortable. Harrison attempted to head me off at the pass.

"We've made these things stick before on far more tenuous associations. But if you don't wish to sign it, fine. We'll cease all association with you here and now, including any sort of security guarantees for your remaining time in Vienna."

Nice people, aren't they?

"What about on Block Island? Who guarantees my security there?"

Harrison sighed, exasperated. I refused to pick up the pen.

"How 'bout if we go off the record a minute, Bill?" It was West, easing into the role of good cop.

"I thought we already were."

"Well, yes. But I mean way off the record."

"Okay."

"Ron Curtin is in custody. He was sitting in the back of that Russian van."

"So they *were* working together, him and the Hammerhead."

"Yes. After competing for a while they eventually joined forces. Let's just say they both stood to be embarrassed by dredging up too much of the past. Frankly, they're probably just as happy to let us take custody. That way they don't have to fight over it now. Anybody but Giles Cabot or *Vanity Fair,* as far as they're concerned. But if it makes you feel better, we'll gladly make sure that both Curtin and the Russian remain in custody until you're done. Deal?"

"What about afterward?"

"Then they'll be worried about us. You'll be off the hook."

So I signed it. And in doing so presumably signed away any hopes for publishing a story. Just as well, perhaps, especially if a magazine piece would have meant exposing my father's involvement, or Litzi's. After all their painstaking effort to maintain their privacy, why blow their cover in an act of journalistic vanity, even if it meant I still had to work for Marty Ealing. Maybe I'd grown up. Just because the CIA's motto said that the truth would set you free didn't mean everyone had to know it.

"Tell me," I asked, "was any of this meeting taped or recorded?"

"Do you seriously think we'd want this conversation appearing in any kind of official record?" Harrison said.

"Then why be so careful every time I mention what I might be doing on—"

"No need to say it."

"See what I mean?"

He shrugged. "We're careful because, well, you just never know, do you?"

"That would make a nice Agency motto if you ever get tired of the old one."

Harrison opened the door. "I'm told that your father has been contacted and is waiting downstairs. We'll maintain a security presence on your behalf for as long as you remain in Vienna, right up until the time you board a plane back to the States. Go anywhere else and you're on your own."

I then asked the question that had already started to nag at me.

"What will you do with this information? Use it, destroy it, or just bury it?"

He smiled.

"Good luck, Mr. Cage."

38

Dad was less than thrilled with my treatment at the hands of our government. The polygraph angered him even more than the abduction, the injection, or the way they lashed me to a chair. But I think he was secretly envious that they'd assigned me to close the case.

"They'll probably give it a name," he said. "You'll end up in their archives, with your own operation."

"Doubtful. It's unofficial. Less than unofficial, if you get right down to it."

"Doesn't matter. Those people can't take a dump without assigning a code name. They can't help themselves."

We were seated with Litzi around his dinner table. It was noon. After getting in the night before at nearly one a.m., the long hours had finally caught up with me, and I'd slept until eleven, troubled throughout by bizarre dreams. We were now working our way through a pot of coffee, chocolate croissants, and the last of the cold cuts.

"I never would've believed Giles Cabot was capable of engineering all this," Dad said. "Ten years ago maybe. I'd always heard he was a vindictive son of a bitch. But the way he looked at the funeral I wouldn't have given him another month. I don't know whether to tell you to be careful for your own sake or for his."

"I do seem to remember a pretty capable fellow pushing his wheelchair."

"Kyle Anderson. Someone said he was a former Agency knuckledragger. Dirty deeds galore in Latin America. He's been Cabot's personal assistant for years. Probably the one who typed those messages on your Royal. Probably also the guy sending those K-Fresh emails to your fake Russian in Prague. The best part now is, you get to find out for yourself."

Litzi, having experienced firsthand how such assignments could go wrong even with the best of intentions, was more circumspect.

"Do the bare minimum, then get out," she said. "Even that will probably be too much."

"At the very least maybe I'll get my books back."

"Of all the things he did, that was the strangest," Dad said. "What was the point?"

"Lothar said Cabot always believed there was something about the books themselves that made them valuable to the courier system. Not that he ever found out what it was. Maybe Cabot thought that as a courier I might have ended up with one of the books. So he stole them to check for himself."

"Typical Agency overkill."

"Even after how he's used me, I'm not looking forward to breaking an old man's heart. I hope there's a way to do this gently."

"There never is," Litzi said. "You'd be better off spending the weekend with your son."

Someone from the Agency was supposed to drop off a parcel in the afternoon, containing whatever bait they'd rigged for Cabot. I was then supposed to place it at the dead drop the next morning, on my way to catch a 9:40 flight to Boston. It connected through Paris and was scheduled to arrive at 2:05 p.m. I had a car reservation on the 6 p.m. ferry from Point Judith, which would put me on Block Island by seven. Then I was on my own.

In the afternoon Litzi and I went shopping for supplies. I noticed Agency men fore and aft. They were constantly chatting into cell phones, and they didn't seem to mind if anyone saw them. Maybe that was the point.

I'd decided that the best approach to snooping around Cabot's farm would be to pose as a bird-watcher, so I bought a hat, a rucksack, outdoor clothes, and a pricey pair of binoculars. I would pick up a guidebook and map on the island. Bicycling was a popular way for getting around there, so I planned to rent a mountain bike suitable for trails and open fields.

The Agency had given me a diagram showing the lay of the land around Cabot's ten-acre property, plus a photo of his gray clapboard farmhouse, which sat on a grassy rise with an eastward view of the Atlantic. On the diagram someone had not so subtly marked an X on a small nature preserve that abutted his land. Presumably it offered the best vantage point.

Litzi and I ate an early dinner, but kept our wine consumption to a minimum. We said good-bye afterward, parting with plans for her to visit Georgetown later that fall. A real vacation this time, with no more secrets between us. I was already wondering what David would make of her.

When I got back to the apartment, Dad was in one of his most familiar poses, seated in the easy chair across from his great wall of books. He was flipping through the old courier copy of Oppenheim's *The Great Impersonation* that I'd brought back from Szondi in Budapest.

"You should turn in early," he said, which was what he'd always told me the night before a big race.

"I will. Although the jet lag's never half as bad on the way back."

He nodded toward a sealed, unmarked envelope on an end table.

"They dropped that by around four."

Neither of us was curious enough to open it, probably because we knew it was fake. If Cabot also figured that out, my assignment would become that much tougher.

"I'd forgotten how silly Oppenheim's dialogue comes across these days," Dad said. "It's like Gilbert and Sullivan without the music." He shut the book. "So you said Lothar's a pretty good writer?"

"Especially for a first-timer."

"Who would you compare him to?"

"Hard to say, since his book's in German. Adam Hall, maybe?"

Dad was impressed.

"I always liked Hall's Quiller novels. One of the few nonspooks who got the details right. He's buried in Washington, you know?"

"Adam Hall? I thought he was a Brit?"

"He was. Elleston Trevor was his legal name, although he was born as Trevor Dudley-Smith. He's in a little Catholic cemetery, probably only a mile or two from your house."

"How the hell did you know that?"

"I know all sorts of useless trivia about these damn things, and for the past twenty years it's been going to waste. It's time I put it to use again, so I've come up with a new project—finding the new whereabouts of Lothar's lost book. Might as well revisit a few of my old haunts, don't you think?"

"Think Lothar will pick up your trail?"

"Oh, I know he will. I'm betting he'll be flattered."

"He'll be rooting for you. I think he liked the idea of finally having a reader."

Dad reopened the Oppenheim.

"It has to be better than this old stuff and nonsense." He shook his head as he gazed at the cover. "And say what you want about that bastard Szondi, at least he knows how to treat a rare book."

"What do you mean?"

"Well, look how he's marked the price. This little sticker on the protective jacket. I've never understood why so many booksellers routinely take the best items in their store and scribble the amount in pencil on the flyleaf. It's a small thing, but why deface their very own holdings? I've never understood it, and . . . Well, I'll be damned."

"What?"

"He wrote the price inside, too. Damn fool."

"Let me see that."

Dad handed over the book. I again considered Cabot's theory that the books themselves were somehow important, apart from any code. On the inside of the plastic protective cover there was another small sticker, aligned perfectly with the one on the outside. They were back-to-back.

"Do you have a razor handy?"

"Medicine cabinet. You're not going to slice up the Oppenheim, are you? Even bad prose doesn't deserve that."

"I want to peel back this sticker, the one on the inside."

The look on his face told me he'd figured out what I was up to. He headed briskly down the hall and returned with a bare blade.

"Careful, it's double-edged."

He stood over me as I peeled up a tiny flap of the red circle. The middle of it, I realized now, had no adhesive. Only the edges were sticky. And there, just beneath the center, was a tiny disc of film, which for nearly forty years had remained there, well hidden from prying eyes.

"Good Lord," Dad said. "Microfilm."

"You have anything we can look at it with?"

He fetched a large magnifying glass from a desk drawer.

"Still can't read the print," he said. "But I'm betting that's a CIA letterhead, up there at the top."

We looked at each other, his expression a blend of marvel and dismay.

"Looks like Cabot was right about at least one thing," I said. "Lemaster was passing secrets."

"Which makes me wonder if he might be right about *every*thing. I feel like a bigger fool than ever, doing all those favors for Ed. Shouldn't you give this to the Agency?"

I considered the idea for about half a second.

"Hell, no. They had their chance with me. Besides, now I've got the perfect offering for Cabot. Who needs an artificial lure when you've got live bait? I'll put the microdot back on the dust jacket and slip the book into the dead drop, with a note telling him how it works."

"He'll be thrilled."

"I know *I* am. I'm beginning to think this might even work."

39

A horn blast from the dawn ferry, reliable as an alarm clock, awakened me to my first morning on Block Island. I'd just enjoyed my soundest night of sleep in days. The ocean air probably had something to do with it. So did my new sense of security.

At the ferry terminal in Point Judith the night before, I'd telephoned David to let him know I was safely on American soil, and to expect me back soon in Georgetown. Having earlier heard my account of the strange Nethercutt funeral, he perked up right away when I mentioned Block Island.

"One last mission?" he said jokingly. "Sounds risky."

"Oh, you know what they say," I answered, playing along. "'Caution is the enemy of discovery.'"

"Hey, I just read that in *A Spy for All Seasons*!"

Which, come to think of it, was probably where I'd first seen it as well, too many years ago to count.

"Glad you found a copy. Maybe in a few days I'll have more of them for you."

"Reading you loud and clear, Dad."

"Yes, well . . ." Had I missed something in that exchange? "Aren't you just about due for fall break?"

"Coming up in two days."

"Going anywhere?"

"Still deciding."

"Well, drop me a text when you know, now that my cell phone's back in action. And I should probably give you the name of my hotel."

We traded small talk a few minutes more before it was time for him to head to dinner.

"Good luck, then, Dad."

"Thanks. Same to you with your schoolwork."

"Schoolwork. That's a good one, Dad."

"Uh, right. I'll call when I'm back."

Goodness. He was certainly getting wrapped up in those spy novels, if my one little reference got him that fired up.

But what intrigued me more, I suddenly realized, was the way the Lemaster quote—"Caution is the enemy of discovery"—made the perfect counterpoint to the advice Jim Angleton had given me when I was seven years old: "Caution is the eldest child of wisdom."

Might Angleton also have uttered the same advice to Lemaster at one time, only to have his operative turn those words upside down in a later novel? I recalled Valerie Humphries's tale of Angleton marking up his copy of *The Double Game* as if it were the Rosetta Stone, the key to everything. It made me wonder what must have caused Lemaster's words to pop into my head just now, and why David had reacted to them so sharply. The mind works in strange ways, I suppose, especially when you're still a bit foggy from a transatlantic flight.

After hanging up, I'd conferred with a weathered old shipping clerk at the ferry terminal, who assured me that none of the trucks for FedEx, DHL, or the other delivery services ever went ashore before nine a.m.

That meant today was probably the earliest Cabot could receive the book with the microdot, and even that would be pushing it. His farmhouse was less than two miles from my hotel, which gave me a few hours to eat breakfast, rent a bike, and get into position.

Block Island is only about ten square miles, and even on a bicycle you can reach any part of it in less than half an hour. The drawback to such coziness, especially now that most of the tourists were gone, was that I'd stand out. This was evident when I went down for breakfast at 7:10. I was alone in the hotel dining room.

I scanned my map and drank coffee. The view out the window was of circling seagulls and slate clouds. The air held a premonition of winter, a briny rawness that made you long to curl up by a fire with something hot to drink. Litzi would like it here. Thinking of her made the room seem more desolate than ever.

"Here's a refill for you."

The waitress had materialized at my elbow. She spotted the picture of Cabot's house right away.

"That's a nice old place. You house hunting?"

I pushed a napkin over the photo, which only made me look more suspicious.

"Early stages. Just browsing for now."

"That's what they all say."

She slid the check beneath the saltshaker and glided away.

Small places like this didn't keep secrets well. If my snooping was too obvious I'd soon draw unwanted attention.

It felt good to stretch my legs on the bike, cranking it uphill in low gear as I pedaled out of town. The air was cold enough to numb my fingers, but sweat soon dampened my back beneath the rucksack. I'd packed a lunch and a big bottle of water along with the binoculars. Hardly anyone was on the road, which again made me feel conspicuous, and as I passed the few scattered houses near the turnoff to Cabot's, I imagined his neighbors looking up from their breakfast tables to wonder who the stranger was.

His property was right across a gravel road from Wils Nethercutt's. Their facing boundaries formed a rough V, reaching its vertex at the paved road to the south. The northbound dirt road bisected the V. The farther up it you went, the farther away you got from each of the diverging property lines. I was looking on the right for the nature preserve. The map showed that it was a quarter mile up the hill.

Halfway there I passed a footpath that crossed the dirt road from either side, with gates at the threshold of Cabot's and Nethercutt's properties. It was overgrown, barely used. Knowing their history as rivals, I wondered how many years it had been since anyone had walked from one place to the other.

A small wooden sign marked the entrance to the nature preserve. Sandy trails disappeared into the underbrush. I locked the bike at a rack and pulled the binoculars and bird book from the pack. An older couple emerged on foot from one of the trails, half out of breath from their morning stroll. The man took a look at my gear and frowned.

"Little late to be bird-watching this far north, isn't it?"

"Oh, you never know. You always get some stragglers on the flyway."

Whatever that meant. He looked skeptical.

"Well, good luck with it."

Great. If I looked out of place to them, how would I look to Cabot and his assistant if they spotted me up on the hillside, poking around in the brush? Too late to worry about that now.

I trooped through the browning underbrush, stirring sparrows from cover. It smelled good up here, the clean scent of late autumn. Nearing the top of a slight rise I spotted Cabot's shingled rooftop, and as I crested the hill the whole place came into view—the weathered front porch with its wooden railing, green shutters, and glass-paned aluminum storm door. The porch faced south, and I was facing east, with the Atlantic visible beyond the house, down the slope of the island. Maybe two acres of brown grass surrounded the house, enclosed by more underbrush. On the far side was a pretty stand of birches, already stripped of their leaves. An oyster shell driveway led up to a clapboard garage, where a black Jeep Cherokee with rusted rear panels was parked outside. Unless there was something else parked inside, this was the only vehicle, and I presumed it was Kyle Anderson's.

I found a viewing spot that offered reasonable cover and sat in the crunchy brown grass, scattering a few grasshoppers. I pulled out the binoculars to scan the house. Every curtain was closed. They were the lacy kind, like you saw in Europe. No smoke from the chimney, but who's to say he'd even have a fire going at this time of day, or at all? A heating-cooling unit to the left of the house hummed into action, throbbing like a refrigerator in an empty kitchen.

It didn't look at all like the nerve center for the kind of odyssey I'd just been on. Then again, the most effective spies in my favorite books were always ordinary-looking men—Folly with his lumpy suits and split-level home in the Virginia 'burbs, Smiley the Chelsea homebody, wiping smudged glasses with his necktie. In their world, and in Cabot's, James Bond and Johnny Fedora were aliens from Planet Hollywood.

Such thoughts kept me occupied for maybe an hour before I began to grow restless. I got out the bird book, flipping the pages. The only ones I'd seen since arriving were gulls and sparrows. I was admiring the long red bill of the American Oystercatcher when I was startled by the slam of a storm door.

I looked up and saw the big fellow I remembered from the funeral, Kyle Anderson, stepping off the porch and walking up the drive. I followed with the binoculars, and when he disappeared into the underbrush, I stood, ready for pursuit. I was on the verge of leaving when he reappeared with a folded newspaper in hand. There must have been a delivery box at the end of the drive.

He went back inside. A few seconds later I heard faint strains of music. A symphony by Mahler, another Austrian-Bohemian like Litzi.

I gazed east toward the sea. In only a few hours it would be nightfall on her side of the Atlantic. Nothing else stirred. I hunched lower into the grass. This was tougher work than I'd expected.

Just after eleven a.m. I took out my lunch, eating the sandwich but saving the apple and the chips. By two-thirty they were also gone, and shortly after four o'clock I swallowed the last of the water. Only four other people had wandered past me on the trails, and fortunately none had seemed overly curious about the middle-aged man with binoculars.

I stifled a yawn and stood to take a leak, scattering more grasshoppers. I had just zipped up when I heard tires popping against the shells on the driveway. I moved back into position and there it was, a white FedEx van with blue and orange trim, rolling to a stop behind the Jeep. Cabot's handyman in Vienna had worked fast. I raised the binoculars and settled back onto the matted grass.

The deliveryman left the engine idling as he carried a clipboard and a small box across the porch. Anderson answered his knock and signed for the package with the door ajar. The afternoon sunlight caught the gleam of something or someone behind him, and as the deliveryman retreated I saw the spokes of a wheelchair. Adjusting the focus, I made out the outline of a seated figure, mostly in shadow. The only distinguishable feature from this distance was a shock of white hair, which I saw just as Anderson was shutting the door. Cabot had the bait. The only question now was if and when he'd bite.

Nothing more happened until dusk. Lights came on in the kitchen and living room, and I thought I heard a television. Anderson emerged shortly afterward, still alone, and not carrying anything. He wore a light jacket but there were no bulges in the pockets. It was six o'clock.

When he got into the Jeep, I headed back toward the bicycle, eager to catch him before he drove out of sight. I made it down to the junction of the paved road just in time to see his taillights receding in the opposite direction, toward an intersection where he turned right, toward town. I would never catch him, but the town was small enough that it would probably be easy to find the Jeep.

Half a mile down the turnoff I saw the Jeep parked in the lot of a natural foods store, well short of town, one of those boutique groceries where everything sells at a premium. Only two other cars were there, so I kept my hat on and my face down and went inside. Anderson was seated toward the back, at a small metalwork table by a coffee counter where a milk frother was hissing.

"Order's up, Kyle," a girl called out.

He thanked her and grabbed his mug, then sat back down to browse through the store's copy of the *New York Times* while he sipped foamed milk from the top of his cup. Anderson hadn't struck me as a latte guy, but I guess you never know. I picked up an apple and a bottle of fruit juice, then eased toward the meat counter, pretending to look at the Delmonicos marked at $17.95 a pound.

"Help you, sir?"

"Just looking."

After a few minutes more I began to feel conspicuous, so I paid for my items, then sat on the small front porch, gazing off into the gathering darkness. I checked my watch. 6:20. Ten minutes later I heard a chair scrape followed by the beeping of the register. I averted my face as Anderson emerged with a six-pack of beer and a grocery bag—probably the makings of tonight's dinner—then hopped into the Jeep. If he'd noticed me on the porch, he hadn't reacted, but I still felt uncomfortable.

By the time he got back to the house the whole interlude would have lasted nearly forty minutes. It had the feel of a daily ritual, and I filed it away as a possible window for action. God knows he must get stir-crazy, cooped up all day with Cabot, especially with winter coming.

By the time I got back into position it was nearly too dark to see where I was going on the path. The whine of a stove fan filtered up from the house, and before long I smelled meat frying and heard the first notes of an old Van Morrison album.

I gave it another two hours. By then it was so chilly I could barely keep my teeth from chattering. At nine a light went on upstairs, and the ones downstairs switched off. Bedtime for Cabot. I packed up, groped my way to the bicycle, and pedaled to the hotel, oddly drained by the long and mostly uneventful day. I walked into town for a late dinner, but hardly had an appetite until the waitress brought a steaming bowl of chowder and a tall glass of beer, which got the juices flowing enough for a cheeseburger and fries.

"Here for the fishing?" she asked.

"Bird-watching," I said, sticking stubbornly to cover.

I was in bed by ten-thirty. If Cabot bit, he would do it soon, so I set the alarm for ninety minutes before the dawn ferry, then fell asleep to the muffled sound of voices from the TV in the next room.

The sun was a sliver of orange peel peeking above the gray rim of the Atlantic when Anderson propped open the storm door and pushed Cabot's wheelchair onto the porch. I raised the binoculars, fingers freezing, and saw a frowning old man draped in an Army blanket. Two claw-like hands poked from the opening, clutching the FedEx box in his lap. He had swallowed the bait. Now he was about to run with it. I stood, ready to move.

Anderson pushed the chair down a ramp to the ground. Then Cabot waved him off. His right hand let go of the box and punched at a set of controls, guiding the chair forward under its own power. Anderson followed him around the left side of the house toward an oyster shell path that led across the back lawn and disappeared into the underbrush. I'd brought the bike up the trail with me today to be better prepared for a quick getaway, and I pedaled hard toward the dirt road, quickly reaching the pavement and turning toward Cabot's place. Then I turned up his driveway. If they'd changed course in the meantime and were now coming out in the Jeep, then I'd meet them head-on, busted for sure.

But as the house came into view I saw the Jeep still parked at the garage. I hid the bike in the underbrush and ran toward the house, using it to shield me from the trail in the back. I went the same way they'd gone, to the left, then peered around the corner toward the back. They were still somewhere off in the brush. I sprinted across the back lawn to follow them.

Twenty yards into the brush the path became a plank walkway that curved left through marshland, with high grasses and reeds to either side. I slowed down, not wanting to make a clatter on the boards or come upon them without warning. I heard voices and stopped. Just around the bend I could see that the walkway led to a small dock on a salt pond. They were out on the end of it, and Anderson was lifting Cabot out of the wheelchair into an aluminum skiff with an outboard motor. I kept out of sight, following their progress by sound—a few grunts of effort, sloshing water from the rocking skiff, the pull of a starter rope, then the sputtering roar of the motor. I smelled the oily smoke and heard Anderson rev away from the dock. When I peeped around the corner, the skiff was heading toward the center of the pond, and their wake was coming ashore through the reeds. Anderson was at the stern, steering with the motor. Cabot sat up front, propped on boat cushions, his white hair stiff in the breeze. He stared straight ahead, as rigid as a carved bowsprit.

It was too risky to move farther out the walkway, so I stepped off the planks and immediately sank ankle-deep in the goo. The muck nearly pulled my shoes off as I moved awkwardly forward, pushing through the high grasses until I was a few feet from the water's edge. I still had cover but could see across the pond.

Anderson angled the boat left as a loon dived out of sight. He throttled back and cut a small circle as they reached a faded orange buoy, like the ones lobstermen use. Cabot's initials were marked crudely on the side. Anderson cut the engine and nimbly latched on to the line of the buoy with a boathook, which he used to pull them closer. When the bow bumped the buoy, Cabot himself grabbed the line and gave a few feeble tugs before Anderson stepped forward in the rocking craft and began hauling up the line, hand over hand. By now I had the binoculars out and could see everything in detail.

He pulled up at least ten feet of streaming rope before the rusting cage of an old crab pot emerged in a cascade of water. The trap dripped as he swung it into the skiff. A gray canister was inside it, roughly the size of a cooler and dripping with algae. They both looked around the pond a few seconds to see if anyone was watching. I held my breath and kept still. The wet ooze had filled my shoes, and my toes were numb.

They turned their attention back to the trap. Cabot muttered something, and I saw Anderson working at a combination lock. A metallic snap was audible across the water. He opened the side of the trap, pulled out the canister, and slowly unscrewed the top. It was watertight, and inside it was a yellow dry bag, the kind kayakers use. It, too, was marked with Cabot's initials. Inside the dry bag were four sealable plastic bags, each big enough to cook a turkey in, and each was filled with banded stacks of documents and folders. It was Cabot's stash, his Holy Grail of stolen and privately collected intelligence. Mine, too. My breath came in short bursts. Between the cold and the excitement it was all I could do to hold the binoculars still.

Cabot opened the FedEx box and withdrew the Oppenheim book that I'd left at the Vienna dead drop only two mornings ago. All of my work, and all of his, was encapsulated in this makeshift treasure chest, which Anderson was now resealing to put back inside the trap. He clicked the lock, took one last look around, and heaved the bulky crab trap back over the side. It sank in a hiss of bubbles.

That's when I realized I'd better get the hell out of there. But it was too late now to try to beat them back up the path. Anderson had already pulled the starting cord, and even if I made it through the muck in time I'd make a terrible racket, and leave muddy tracks on the planks.

So I crouched lower in the reeds, soaking myself and the binoculars as the skiff swung around toward the dock. I shivered nervously as I listened to them go through the whole routine in reverse, with Anderson lifting Cabot back into the wheelchair. All the while I hoped Anderson wouldn't notice the path I'd cut through the reeds. Fortunately some clouds had come up, and it was still gloomy enough that visibility was poor once you left the open space of the pond.

I heard the whine of the wheelchair motor. Neither man spoke as they headed back toward the house. After they passed I remained still for another ten minutes, waiting for the storm door to slam shut. My fear was that Anderson would go into town in the Jeep and see my bike stashed in the brush at the head of the driveway. But after the door closed there was only silence, except for the lonely call of a loon. I sloshed back to dry land and worked my way around the perimeter of the underbrush, an arduous but necessary route to keep anyone in the house from spotting me. It took me nearly an hour to reach the bicycle, and I didn't breathe easily until I rolled onto the main road and was on my way into town.

Back at the hotel, the desk clerk gaped at me as I trooped across the lobby holding muddy shoes in my right hand. My pants were soaked from the thighs down. The binoculars were dripping, and I smelled like a marsh. I smiled and nodded as if it were all in a morning's work of vigilant bird-watching, and he nodded back, seemingly horrified.

Eric Ambler, I thought. I had become like a prototypical leading man in an Ambler novel, one of those Everyman types who blunders into something bigger than himself, then keeps tripping over his own two feet while the professionals circle for the kill. If it wasn't so foolhardy it might even be funny. Give me enough time and maybe I'd be like Jim Wormold, the vacuum cleaner salesman in Graham Greene's *Our Man in Havana*, who faked intelligence reports to earn extra cash only to have all his dark postings start coming true, leaving him caught in the middle. High comedy, except at the moment I didn't feel like laughing. But at least I knew that Curtin and the Hammerhead were out of the picture, safely detained back in Vienna. That alone made me feel better.

In my room I peeled off the wet clothes and hopped into the shower, and by the time I emerged—clean, pink, and reenergized—I had worked out my plan of action for the afternoon and on into the next day. There were holes in it—almost any ambitious plan has holes when there is only one person to carry it out—but its simplest and most appealing attribute was this: By nightfall tomorrow, for better or for worse, the game would be over.

40

At midday I rented a kayak, bought wire cutters at a hardware store, and studied the map. The pond behind Cabot's house was accessible from a dirt road on the far side, although I'd have to fight my way through another marshy stand of underbrush.

Toward dusk, I lashed the kayak to the top of my rental car and drove it to the spot I'd pegged as the most convenient drop-off. I shoved the boat and paddle far enough into the brush to hide them from passersby. Then I drove to the nature preserve, where I parked on the shoulder of the dirt road and walked to the lookout spot. I hoped my hunch about Anderson's habits was correct.

Shortly after six p.m. he emerged from the house, right on schedule. He headed for the Jeep while I headed for the car. I gave him enough time to make the turnoff, then I drove to where the kayak was stashed and parked on the shoulder.

The remnants of an old path offered easier and drier access than I'd expected, and the boat was light enough to drag through the grass and sand. The hard part was climbing into the snug cockpit and casting off without turning the thing over. It tipped alarmingly as I shoved off with the paddle. But it finally eased into the pond, and I quickly reached the buoy. I grabbed the line to stop my progress, then held on for dear life as the boat rocked and wobbled beneath me.

I waited for the waters to calm and took my bearings. The loon from this morning was still on patrol, keeping his distance. A night heron prowling near Cabot's dock eyed me suspiciously. The only sounds were of bugs and the wind.

Taking a deep breath, I began hauling up the slimy line, a chore that told me just how strong Anderson must be. Every foot was hard-earned, and each great tug threatened to capsize the boat. But my excitement mounted as the line coiled on the deck, and I gasped with joy when the rusting trap finally broke the surface with its treasure inside.

The trickiest part was balancing the trap on the deck while getting the wire cutters out of my pocket. A mosquito buzzed my ear, Cabot's last line of defense, and I began clipping open the rusted mesh. It snipped easily, and I peeled back a panel large enough to reach in and take hold of the canister. It was bigger than I'd expected, and cumbersome to hold while I shoved the trap back off the deck. Bubbles rose as I watched it disappear into the murk.

I opened the canister and removed the yellow dry bag marked with Cabot's initials. I put the open canister back in the pond, where it immediately filled with water and sank. The lid floated, so I took it with me and paddled back to shore. Getting out was easier than launching, and within ten minutes I'd tossed the dry bag into the trunk of the car and lashed the kayak to the roof. Only one car passed while I was tying down the boat, and it didn't even slow down. On my way back into town I saw Anderson's Jeep, still parked at the natural foods grocery. Enjoy your latte, Kyle. I was giddy with excitement.

I dropped off the boat at the rental place just before closing, then returned to the hotel. As I passed through the lobby, the desk clerk looked at me with even greater curiosity than he'd shown in the morning. I was again wet, with leaves and brambles stuck to my trousers. The yellow dry bag dangled from my hand like the catch of the day at the fisherman's dock. I held it so that he didn't see Cabot's initials, but otherwise I was feeling downright cocky, so I smiled and waved.

"Beautiful day, wasn't it?"

"Yes, sir."

Sometimes it was brazen or nothing in this business.

I spread the items across the bed. The size of the archive was astonishing. Cabot's trove could be roughly divided into four categories, one for each of the plastic bags. The largest was the contents of a fat folder marked "Nethercutt." Most of its holdings were stamped with an *H* for Project Honetol, the name Angleton gave to his ruinous mole hunt when he began it in 1964.

Nethercutt, being one of Angleton's most zealous disciples, had spirited away quite a haul, and I'm sure that if I'd known as much as a historian about all the contacts and ops, then I would have been able to make sense of everything. As it was, the only Nethercutt materials I could put into context pertained to either Lemaster ("Headlight"), his Soviet source Nijinsky, or Headlight's communications network.

Among the most relevant items was a summary of an interrogation with Yuri Nosenko, the defector whom Angleton and his own Soviet pet, Anatoly Golitsyn, had never believed, and who had therefore been locked away in a bunker. Nosenko named four KGB "traveler" agents with roaming rights to all of Central and Western Europe. One was code-named Dewey, the longtime recipient of all those goodies from Lemaster.

The Nethercutt file also included material on the Soviet agent Leo, or Trefimov, the one Litzi and I knew as Vladimir just before he was murdered. There was a summary of the criminal associations he developed after the collapse of the Soviet Union, which mentioned his relocation to Vienna in the late 1990s. This was the material Cabot must have used to track him down and set up our meeting.

There were also several 1972 Nethercutt memos to Angleton, which outlined Nethercutt's involvement in quashing the publication of Lothar Heinemann's novel. Not one of them mentioned the book's title, or Lothar's pen name, which helped explain why Cabot hadn't found it.

The second batch was a collection of Cabot's own Agency files. The findings of Valerie Humphries's research were there with regard to the points of intersection for Lemaster and Dewey. There were also records of Cabot's recent correspondence with Vladimir and with Milan Bobić, my old consular adversary from Belgrade.

At the very back of the Cabot folder was a long list of antiquarian book dealers across Europe. Many had tiny checkmarks by their name. Der Flügel was prominent among them, but obviously when Cabot called he hadn't known which title to ask for, and I suspected that Lothar had alerted Ziegler to deflect any queries that came in by phone. I'd lucked out.

The third, and smallest, portion of the cache was made up of my own contributions—the negatives of Vladimir's KGB documents, my one written report, and the copy of Oppenheim's *The Great Impersonation*. By the look of it, Cabot had placed the microdot right back on the dust jacket, as if to better preserve it for use in an official proceeding.

The fourth bag was in some ways the most interesting, even though the materials had little or nothing to do with Edwin Lemaster. It was a huge stack of pages from Angleton's office diary and appointment logs from September 1949 to May 1951, the period when the British mole Kim Philby had been a frequent lunch companion and a regular visitor to his office. Incredible material, in other words, for any CIA historian.

As I flipped through the pages, scanning Angleton's odd marginalia and notes of his discussions with Philby, all sorts of key operational details jumped out, meaning that he had leaked them directly to the infamous mole, often doing so after a very wet lunch in which he regularly consumed boatloads of martinis. Anything Ed Lemaster would've leaked might well have been tiny by comparison. In fact, if Lemaster had truly been a Soviet operative, his main role could have been to help fuel Angleton's mistrust of people like Nosenko.

I realized then what the CIA desired most from my unofficial mission to Block Island. It was the Angleton stuff—the logbooks, the diaries, and all of the Honetol material that Nethercutt had squirreled away. The more personal game that I'd gotten so caught up in involving Cabot, Lemaster, Preston, Dad, and Litzi was the merest of sidelights, a means to an end.

The idea that a popular author might once have betrayed them was probably worth keeping under wraps, especially if Preston and his new Russian business partner were involved, since Preston still made millions from the government. But in the bigger picture of the Agency's legacy, the Angleton stuff carried more weight.

It was nearly midnight by the time I finished going through it all, and I was exhausted. I packed everything back into the folders and slipped the dry bag into my luggage for safekeeping. Then I slept soundly, ready to finish the job once and for all.

41

In the morning I headed to the post office, carrying the documents in a couple of plastic laundry bags from my hotel room. I bought a pair of large flat-rate boxes and stuffed everything inside. I consulted the slip of paper with the CIA address in Herndon, Virginia, considered it one last time as a possible destination, then decided against it.

Where should I send the boxes, then? Not to my town house. And not to David, I thought, remembering how I'd been used without my knowledge in so many spy games. My ex-wife, April, probably would have helped if I'd asked nicely, but it was unfair to expect her to take on that kind of responsibility. Enough innocent people had already been harmed in this venture.

Then I remembered that this was the time of year when Marty Ealing went on his annual two-week romp to Las Vegas. Ostensibly it was to touch base with a few clients, but everyone in the office knew it was mostly an excuse for Marty to fool around on his wife. I mailed the box to myself in care of Marty at the office address for Ealing Wharton. I knew I could count on his secretary, Anne, in a way that I could never count on him. Then, once I'd had time to make my own copies, and only then, I'd forward all the originals to that P.O. box in Herndon.

"Will these go out today?" I asked the clerk. He looked at the wall clock.

"Noon ferry. Soon enough?"

"Perfect."

Just before noon, with plenty of time to kill, I went to a short-order place by the dock to watch the cars load onto the ferry. I ordered a beer and a basket of fried clams just as the postal truck rolled aboard. The clams arrived as the horn sounded. I watched the crew cast off the lines, then toasted myself with the beer as the ferry eased away in a blast of diesel fumes and churning seawater. I bit into a clam. Crunchy-hot on the outside, cool and juicy in the middle, the taste of the sea. Life was sweet. I ordered a second beer and went back to the hotel to pack. Then I snoozed for an hour.

But by the time five o'clock rolled around I was anxious. One more job to do, and it was the riskiest. I got back on the bike, which by now had twigs in the spokes and dried mud on the frame, and pedaled to the nature preserve to take up my usual post. At six p.m. I watched Anderson leave for his coffee break. Then I pedaled toward the house, reaching the paved road just as the Jeep's taillights disappeared toward town. I rolled up the driveway, stowed the bike out of sight, and knocked loudly at the front door. I checked my watch. I figured I had thirty-five minutes to finish my business and get the hell out of there.

Before long I heard the electric whine of Cabot's wheelchair, then the bump of the tires against the door. A curtain stirred on the window atop the door. The old man's eyes flashed in surprise. He backed up the chair and shouted, the voice raspy but stronger than I expected.

"Come in."

When I opened up, he was grinning crookedly, as if he'd been expecting me all along.

"My assistant is away at the moment, but I suppose you already knew that." He frowned at my rucksack, and waved me back toward the porch. "Leave that outside, if you don't mind."

"I do mind. I've brought you something special. One last contribution to the cause before I officially resign from your employment."

He grinned again, but more uneasily this time. I followed him down a hallway toward the back of the house while he spoke over his shoulder.

"The microdot was much appreciated. You practically beat it back across the water. I'm just sorry you never found Lothar's book."

"Oh, but I did. An excellent read, too."

He looked back at me as we reached the end of the hall, and gazed with new appreciation at the rucksack.

"Patience," I said. "First you have to answer a few questions."

"Of course." Now that he thought he was about to get what he wanted, he had decided to be accommodating. We entered a study that was wall-to-wall books. At a glance I recognized many familiar titles, all from the genre that my father, Ed Lemaster, and I had once read and collected so passionately. Cabot watched me taking it in.

"More complete than even your father's library," he said. "Probably as good a place as any for us to wrap things up, don't you think?"

I took a seat in what must have once been his favorite place to read, a big wing chair with crinkled brown leather and a floor lamp to its right. He pivoted the wheelchair to face me.

"You said you had questions?"

"Why me? And why Litzi and my father? Was I really a better choice than some ex–field man, or was pulling our strings half the thrill?"

"You make it sound unsavory."

"Did you have some sort of score to settle with my dad?"

"Certainly not! Your dad's a wonderful fellow. A little stuffy and overly deliberative, but that's the way of diplomats. I meant no harm. The experience was good for you, was it not? You finally got to discover why the wheels of fate rolled over you so mercilessly back in Belgrade. And you learned a valuable lesson in human nature—that no one is trustworthy, no one is what he appears to be. Could I have simply hired some old hand to work in your stead? Perhaps. But I don't command the resources I once did, especially considering the hefty transfer that was necessary to ensure Trefimov's cooperation, the fellow you called Vladimir. Although I'm pleased to note that all the money earmarked for that purpose has been safely returned."

"After you had him killed, you mean."

"Not at all. I only made his whereabouts available to a known creditor, who, acting in the way that such people always act, carried out the deed quite on his own."

"After leaving behind my copy of *Petrovka 38*."

"That was a favor they did for me. To keep you interested. I knew Litzi could take care of any complications."

"What about poor old Bruzek in Prague?"

"Not my doing. You'll have to ask the clumsy Russians, or that thug Curtin, what went wrong there. Although, for the prices Bruzek charged, I would have happily pushed those shelves myself."

"Nice."

"You met him. You saw what he was like. In fact, you'd already met him, when you were a boy. One of many reasons you were the perfect fit—the old girlfriend with the intelligence connection, the whole flap in Belgrade, *both* of them. But most important, of course, was your susceptibility to the power of all those books." With great effort he raised his arms to encompass the walls. "I was sure you'd be attracted by the possibility of being able to walk across those pages one last time, not just as a reader but as a *participant*, a companion, even, to all those characters you grew up with."

"How could you be sure?"

"Because at one time I would have been just as susceptible. I have only been in this wheelchair since retirement, yet with the Agency I was forever deskbound. I could only read the reports from those far-flung places, just as I could only read those novels.

"I also knew something else about you. Any careful reader of those books always suspects that at heart they're not really fiction. It's what made me first suspect Ed Lemaster. From the moment I finished *The Double Game*, I saw so much of Don Tolleson in him that I began to worry. Me and Angleton both. Dick Helms wouldn't even read it, and you'd be shocked at how much Dick loathed le Carré. 'Too cynical,' he said. 'We'd never use *our* people that way.' Poor naïve Dick. And Ed got away with it, too. Until now. Thanks to us, the truth will finally come out. You'll be the one to publish, of course. I'm happy to let you take the glory."

"I'm afraid I have to tell you that I've signed a nondisclosure agreement."

"With whom? You can't possibly mean—?"

"The Agency had a little chat with me in Vienna just before I flew back to the States."

Cabot's expression went stony. Already winded from his speech, he now sagged with disappointment. I almost felt sorry for him. I checked my watch. Twenty more minutes at the most.

"But don't let that stop *you*," I said. "And don't worry, I didn't come empty-handed."

Cabot rallied, leaning forward in the wheelchair as I reached into the rucksack. I pulled out the yellow dry bag with the GC initials, then turned it upside down and shook it loudly to show him there was nothing inside.

"What have you done?" The gleam faded from his eyes. His breath began to rattle in his chest. "Where have you put everything?"

"Don't worry. It's all in a safer place now."

"You don't know the meaning of safe! I've seen what you're like, blundering halfway across Europe."

It felt like a fitting exit line, so I stood, knowing there was nothing he could do to stop me. I felt a stab of shame, taking advantage of him this way. The letdown of the hollow victory, exactly as Lemaster always described it. But he deserved it, if only on behalf of Litzi and Dad.

Yet I could also see now that he was a dying man. Even a twisted dream is still a dream, and a traitor is still a traitor. He continued his breathless rant as I picked up the rucksack to go.

"The only good you did was by default! You never even delivered the one item I wanted most!"

Then, oddly, disconcertingly, his face lit in triumph, which puzzled me until I turned and saw Kyle Anderson in the doorway. The big man had arrived without a sound, at least fifteen minutes ahead of schedule. His left hand was on his hip. In his right hand was a menacing-looking sidearm, pointed at my chest.

"What's the rush?" Anderson said. "We get so few visitors that we always like them to stay awhile."

He frisked me quickly with one hand, then gestured toward the chair. I obliged him by sitting back down.

"Hands on your head before I blow it off."

He moved up behind me and put the barrel behind my ear lobe, chilly to the touch. Then he pressed it uncomfortably against the base of my skull.

"The funniest thing happened down at the market," he said. "I bumped into old Ben and Abigail, and they told me they'd seen a bird-watcher up at the preserve just the other day. Damn strange for this time of year, they thought. So did I. So I hurried on back, just in case. Lucky for all of us, huh?"

He spoke to Cabot.

"If you want I can shoot him now, then take his body out in the skiff. There are enough weights in the shed to have him submerged and forgotten by morning. There will be some serious cleanup, but nothing I can't handle."

The hopeful, rational side of me expected Cabot to immediately veto the idea. Instead he sat there drawing shallow breaths, pondering every possibility.

"It's not that easy," he finally said. "If the Agency arranged for his visit, then he's part of something larger. I won't live long enough to pay any consequences, but you will."

"Let me worry about that."

Cabot shook his head.

"The whole point of this was to end up on the right side of history, to crack the case of the Great Mole Hunt, our very own Philby. I won't get there by rubbing out the son of a diplomat."

"This can't be a real op," Anderson said. "For one thing, there's no backup."

"You checked?"

"No. But we'd know by now. He'd be miked and somebody would have dropped me. But he's clean. No mike, no weapons, no GPS beacons. Clean as a virgin and just as stupid. And if he's the one they sent, then you know it's off the books, meaning they won't even bother to come 'round for the cleanup."

There was a long and disconcerting silence as Cabot reconsidered.

"But we no longer have the material," Cabot said. "The location might die with him, and it's too late for that kind of setback. And you're wrong. There *will* be follow-up. Someone upstairs will want to know what happened."

"You said it yourself, this guy's not good enough. If he's stashed our things, we'll find them. But no one will find him. I can finish it outside if you want, take him somewhere even safer than the pond."

There was a sudden glimmer in Cabot's eyes, and you could tell he was giving the idea one last hearing. Then the light dimmed, and he sighed deeply, another long rattle more forlorn than the others.

"It's over, Kyle. Go into town. Have a beer."

Anderson kept the barrel pressed against my head for another few seconds, then withdrew it and backed away. I exhaled, but didn't move. Behind me, Anderson sighed wearily.

"I'll wait out on the porch in case you—"

"*No*, Kyle. Take the Jeep into town, that's an order. I'll be the one to finish it, and I'll do it on my own terms."

"Yes, sir."

"I want to hear the engine start, and I want you to call from the phone at the Mohegan Cafe. Stay put until I phone you back. Understood?"

"Yes, sir," he said. His glumness was infuriating. He would have enjoyed killing me, and he left the room with the disappointed air of a hunter who'd failed to bag his limit.

He'd parked the Jeep farther up the drive than normal to keep me from hearing his arrival, but we heard the departure just fine—the roar of the engine, then the cracking of the shells beneath the tires as he reversed at full throttle. We saw the swing of his headlight beams through the lacy European curtains, then he was gone.

"Roll me over by the window," Cabot said.

I did.

The sky was brilliant, a starry night.

"Fresh air, that's what I need right now."

Cabot didn't have the strength to push up the sash, so I did it for him. He pulled his blanket tighter as the night air rushed in, but he seemed to relish the autumn scent of burning leaves, a hint of brine. The moon shone through a scudding cloud.

"Move closer," he said. "Look off to the right."

I did as he asked, and for a shaky moment I wondered if he'd given some coded order to Anderson to lie in wait across the lawn with a sniper rifle. But the only sound from outside was the sigh of the wind in the brush.

"Do you see that small rooftop maybe two hundred yards off, to the right?"

"Yes." It was lit by a neighbor's floodlight.

"That's Nethercutt's outbuilding. It's where we found his papers. After Wils died, I went over to comfort Dorothy. Then I told her I needed to go through his old belongings for the Agency."

"She believed you?"

"She never knew how bad things really were between us, or what all the fighting was about. She gave me the keys. It was alarmed seven ways to Sunday, but she told me the code for the keypad. Even then it took quite a while to find it."

"The floorboards?"

He frowned.

"Wils was better than that. It was in his refrigerator, behind a false wall. Cold storage."

The pun made him wheeze with laughter, which returned the disturbing rattle to his breathing. It tired him enough that he had to pause before continuing.

The phone rang, and he sighed with impatience.

"You'll have to fetch it. On the end table. The cord will reach."

I handed him the phone. The volume was turned up high, and even I could hear the clink of glasses and the general roar of the tavern crowd at the Mohegan. It brought back memories of my dinner there with Dad the night of the funeral, and the way we'd first discussed this strange set of neighbors, Nethercutt and Cabot, as we carved our prime rib.

Cabot hung up. I shut the window and took the phone back to the table.

"By now I suppose you've seen what I found there," Cabot said. "I was quite excited. Finally I had the leads I'd always needed to try and nail the bastard. Trefimov, if I could find him, plus a few other odds and ends. But the existence of Lothar's book, that was the real revelation. Years ago Wils had put out the word that every copy had been destroyed, and I'd believed him. Now I knew there was still one out there. There were other leads, too, of course. But I needed an operative, a traveler. Kyle was eager to go, but none of his talent is between the ears. He never could've passed muster in Europe. Then I saw you and your father at the funeral, and I knew right away. And when that bastard Preston—he was Ed's first handler, you know, the very fellow who let this happen right under his nose—when he got up in my face about letting sleeping dogs lie, well, hell, how could I do anything *but* go back on the hunt?

"I sat up late for six nights running, assembling the pieces. The more I went over it, the more everything came together, just like a plot line in one of Ed's damn books. I had characters, twists, scenarios. It only took a few phone calls to set it up. I sent Kyle down to Georgetown to put some of his old tricks to work. I hired a few cameos here and there . . ."

"Like the girl in Georgetown."

"With a red carnation. Your son is a sharp one. She knew he'd made her."

"What if we hadn't seen her?"

"No matter. It was window dressing. Like the story Litzi told you about the man in the seersucker."

"You reeled me in perfectly, I'll give you that."

"But you really found Lothar's book, didn't you? That must be why they grabbed you."

"Read it cover to cover. He had all the code names. He had pretty much everything."

Cabot's eyes were aglow, partly in envy, partly in fascination. But the glow was tenuous, flickering. I sensed he was down to his last reserves.

"Tell me," he asked, voice fading. "He *was* guilty, wasn't he? Our man

Edwin? He was one of theirs, correct? You can tell me, now that you have everything else."

I could hear the rattle of his breath up close now, and when I'd rolled his chair to the window I'd sensed the frailty in his birdlike lightness. I knew then with the certainty that only arises at moments like this that the real reason he'd spared my life was because he was dying. It softened something in me, or maybe I just decided that there had already been too many casualties. So, even for all his ruthlessness, why not part on a note of gentleness, a note of grace? No more hollow victories.

"Yes," I said. "He was. I'll never be able to write it, of course, but he was."

For that moment, at least, I think I even believed it. It was sobering to think that I had helped uncover a traitor, one whom I had greatly admired for most of my life.

"Surely you can find some way to get around that agreement, can't you?" Cabot said, his voice querulous again. "You could work with a coauthor. Handle his 'research,' that sort of thing. They wouldn't dare sue you and risk having everything else come out."

"Maybe I will," I said, humoring him. "But it could take a while."

"Of course."

He probably knew I was lying, but he played along for both of us.

"So there's your bonus then, in lieu of payment and expenses," he said. "Thanks to me, you'll be a writer again. You'll have your career back."

Not that he really gave a damn about that, the crabbed old bastard. But he deserved a few points for bothering to pretend.

Cabot ran out of steam then. His head sagged to his chest, and a long, tired breath sputtered out of him. If he'd been able, I think he might have died on the spot. Instead, after a brief pause, I saw his chest rise as he finally inhaled. He didn't look up again. He just flapped his right hand in a weak farewell. Without a further word from either of us, I left the house.

I was on full alert the entire bike ride back to the hotel, expecting the Jeep at every turn. But I made it back without incident, and sighed deeply in relief upon entering the well-lit lobby.

I'd made it. I'd succeeded. I was done.

It was time to go home.

42

The desk clerk seemed pleased to see me looking clean and dry for a change, so I smiled and nodded as I crossed the lobby.

"Good evening, sir," he called out cheerfully. "Did your friends ever catch up with you?"

That stopped me.

"Friends?" I tried to sound offhand.

"Two of them. Looking for you earlier."

I eased over toward the desk, lowering my voice.

"They, uh, must have missed me. What did they look like?"

I braced for a description of Kyle Anderson and some equally brawny pal.

"Oh, one was a younger fellow. Checked in yesterday right down the hall from you. Then this morning, after you went out after breakfast, there was an older gentleman. Very nice man, here for some charter fishing."

Two men, and it wasn't even clear they were working together. Yes, it was definitely time to leave Block Island.

"I'll keep an eye out for them."

I looked around nervously, but the lobby was empty. Then I headed down the hall toward my room, more determined than ever to catch the next available ferry. Fortunately the door was locked securely, just as I'd left it. I turned on the light, retrieved my suitcase from the closet, and tossed it onto the bed.

That's when Breece Preston stepped out of the bathroom, holding a gun.

"I was beginning to wonder if old Giles was going to do all the dirty work for me," he said. "I take it he wasn't too pleased with what you'd gone and done, but I suppose cooler heads prevailed."

Preston put his left hand in his trouser pocket and pulled out the little green Certified Mail receipts from the post office, which I'd put in my shaving kit for safekeeping.

"Good job finding all that old crap of his. And thanks for not sending it to Langley, or whatever bogus P.O. box they must have given you." He looked down at the receipts. "Marty Ealing's office. Not one of your better moves, although it will certainly make my job easier once I'm done here."

"What's that mean?"

"Why don't we discuss it over drinks? I've already poured yours." He nodded toward the bedside table, where a hotel glass brimmed with a cocktail on the rocks.

"What is it?"

"Kentucky bourbon, your favorite."

"I prefer it neat."

"Well, this will have to do. Have a seat. I insist."

I sat on the bed, eyeing the bourbon. He walked around to face me, still standing, and now blocking my path to the door.

"Drink up."

"You're not joining me?"

"Maybe in a moment or two."

I picked up the glass and sniffed. It smelled only like bourbon.

"What else is in here?"

He smiled, which told me all I needed to know. I put down the glass.

"I guess you want it to look like a heart attack or something."

"You can never know for sure what a coroner will say in a backwater like this. But if you'd prefer I can always shoot you. Now that I have these"—he held up the mail receipts—"it's six of one, half a dozen of the other."

"How long have you been following me?"

"Didn't pick up your trail until I saw you heading into the post office, or I'd have moved sooner. It's a little tough getting out of the Pakistani tribal areas on short notice. But with Ron out of commission . . ." He shrugged. "Fortunately you started using your cell phone again or I might never have found you. Once I saw you were calling from Point Judith, it wasn't too tough figuring out the rest. What'll it be, then? Your choice, but I haven't got all night."

So this was to be my bad ending, then, no better than what had become of Folly in his final chapter, or poor old Alec Leamas in his, writhing at the base of the Berlin Wall. One went out gracefully, the other in a despairing surge of anger. The only emotions I seemed to have at my disposal were fear, rage, and frustration. I thought of David, of my dad, of Litzi. Even of April, standing in morning sunlight in her kitchen as someone telephoned with the news.

"Well?" He leveled the gun at my chest. There was a big ugly silencer on the end of the barrel. What I really wanted to do was jump to my feet and lunge at the gun, if only to make this as difficult and messy for him as possible. But nothing I'd learned in the survival class had taught me how to cover that much ground without getting blown away first. So I grasped for more time instead.

"What are you so worried about in all this? Humiliation, because Ed went bad on your watch? Or were you the one who turned him?"

"You haven't earned those answers, you sloppy fuck."

He extended his arm and tensed to fire. I grabbed frantically for the glass. Just in time, apparently, because he relaxed and lowered the gun. I responded by lowering the glass, wondering how long I could keep him going back and forth.

"Goddammit!" he said, raising the gun once again.

Then someone knocked at the door.

We flinched. Preston put a finger to his lips and slowly shook his head, then whispered to me, "You don't want to get some poor maid killed, do you?"

"Police!" a man's voice shouted gruffly. "You reported a robbery, sir?"

The smugness drained from Preston's face, and he slowly lowered the gun. In one motion I threw the bourbon at his head, glass and all, and bolted up from the bed, bumping past him as he spluttered and spat at the toxic liquid. Then I opened the door onto a local cop, knees bent, gun pointed.

The cop jumped back, almost as startled as me. It was a miracle he didn't shoot me. I raised my hands, showing they were empty, then sidled past him into the hallway as I blurted, "The other guy has a gun! He's the one who's robbing me."

Preston apparently had no stomach for such an even matchup, or perhaps he was too smart to involve himself in the shooting of a policeman. He dropped his gun to the floor, held up his hands, and began pleading his case.

"Officer, this is a ridiculous misunderstanding."

The policeman look relieved, but didn't lower his guard.

"I'm sure you'll have plenty of time to explain," he said.

Just as I was becoming convinced that this would end well, I heard a door open down the hallway behind me. Of course. The second man. I braced for yet another twist that would turn the situation back in Preston's favor, but when I turned I saw David step from the room.

Impossible.

In fact, it was so disorienting that for a fleeting moment I wondered if I hadn't actually been shot and was dreaming up the entire scene from some last moment of consciousness while I lay flat on my back across the hotel bed.

"Hi, Dad."

Then David smiled, and the thought disappeared. He was real. I was alive. And Breece Preston was in handcuffs, still dripping poisoned bourbon from his eyebrows.

To hear David tell it, everything had worked exactly according to my plan. He'd been there for the past two days, he said, watching my back just like I'd asked him to.

"*Asked* you to? Where'd you get that idea?"

"From your signal, Dad."

"My signal?"

"You know. 'Caution is the enemy of discovery.' It's what Folly says to Snelling in *A Spy for All Seasons*. You knew that's what I was reading, so I figured you were sending a message, especially since you were calling from an unsecure line and couldn't just come out and say it. Then when you asked if I was traveling anywhere for fall break, I put two and two together and came on up."

I shook my head, not sure whether to laugh or get angry. Because I remembered the scene he was talking about, and had to admit there was a certain bizarre logic to the conclusion that he'd drawn from my words.

Folly utters the key phrase just before departing for a risky meeting with a dangerous contact at a safe house in Leipzig. In response, his operative Sam Snelling takes the initiative to act as a backup, and by doing so saves the day.

Had my knowledge of that scene somehow triggered, at some subliminal level, my own wording in my conversation with David? As much as my rational side argued "no," another part of me wondered. Who's to say what sort of miracles the powers of fiction can conjure up, especially when they're shared between father and son at a time of imminent danger?

In any event, with his imagination on overdrive, David had grabbed a flight up to Boston on the first day of his break, and then caught a bus and a cab to the ferry, arriving on Block Island without a car during my third full day on the island. He caught up with me the next morning, but hadn't made contact—exactly the right tradecraft. Within a few hours he'd detected Preston watching me at the post office. From then on he'd made it his business to keep more of an eye on my pursuer than on me.

That's how he ended up seeing Preston break into my room not long before I returned from Cabot's. He then phoned the local police, who, despite a painfully slow response, nonetheless showed up in time to set things right.

"We're going to have some explaining to do to your mother," I said.

David smiled.

"You should've seen the way she rolled her eyes when I told her what I was reading."

I knew exactly what he meant.

The police kept us occupied for nearly two hours as we gave statements and filled out forms. At that point a couple of state policemen arrived by helicopter to take Preston back to the mainland, along with a sample of the spilled bourbon. By then the day's last ferry had departed, so we grabbed a bite to eat at the Mohegan Cafe and called it a night.

With my room now smelling of booze, and temporarily off-limits as a crime scene, I bunked in one of the twin beds in David's room, still not quite believing that he had managed to avoid my detection for the previous day and a half. Obviously he was better at this business than I was.

Even with a few beers in my belly I stayed awake for the better part of the night, jumping at every sound until I finally nodded off well past midnight. I awakened with a start at the cry of a seagull to see that it was nearly dawn.

We dressed, grabbed a quick breakfast, then rolled aboard the early ferry just as the sun was coming up. When we reached Point Judith

I followed the stream of departing vehicles to the first main junction, then deliberately turned in a direction that practically no one ever took.

I pulled over to the shoulder, where David and I sat and watched as the rest of the cars and trucks disappeared in the other direction, streaming toward the tidewater horizon of sawgrass and marshes glowing amber in the morning sunlight.

No one followed us.

43

Giles Cabot died the following month. The burial was private, with no invited guests, although it was easy enough to imagine Anderson and a few neighbors—Ben and Abigail, perhaps—gathered around a sandy grave site against the backdrop of an angry sea. The obituary in the *Post* was effusive in its praise of Cabot's national service, but made only glancing mention of his role in Jim Angleton's Great Mole Hunt, and none at all of his suspicions concerning Edwin Lemaster. As usual, the first draft of history had come up short, and I suspect later installments will fare no better.

The better news in the paper that day appeared on the jump page of a lengthy story about the military drawdown in Afghanistan—a throwaway mention that, as part of the cutbacks, the Pentagon had canceled its contract with Baron Associates. Baron's chief executive, Breece Preston, was not available for comment. But it was speculated that his business was now on the verge of bankruptcy following similar cancellations in Iraq and Colombia, and the recent financial collapse of a partner firm in Moscow.

A few days later, just when I was getting used to the idea that strange, unsigned messages containing excerpts from spy novels were no longer going to be coming my way, a sealed envelope postmarked in Maine dropped through my front door mail slot. It had no return address. Its only contents were twenty pages of typescript from the first chapter of an untitled novel featuring Richard Folly, his first appearance in nearly twenty years. On the back of the last page there was a brief unsigned handwritten note:

"Thought you'd enjoy a sneak preview. Nice work in Europe. If Alexei visits, please give him my regards."

The handwriting confirmed what the authorial style had already told me—this was the work of Edwin Lemaster.

News of Folly's resurrection made me happy. The prospect of a surprise visit by someone named Alexei, presumably a Russian with spook connections, did not. For several days I debated whether to install new locks, get a dog, or even leave town for a while. Having just quit my job at Ealing Wharton, I was free to do as I pleased. I also considered calling my pals in Vienna with the CIA. But something about the friendliness of Lemaster's gesture—was he finally calling a truce, even after my recent foray to all his old haunts?—stayed my hand. So, with Litzi due to visit in only a week, and David professing to actually be looking forward to meeting her, I decided to sit tight.

Yesterday, at about nine in the morning, a hunched old man knocked at my door and told me in a heavy Russian accent that his name was Alexei. He was the most harmless-looking fellow I'd seen since Lothar Heinemann, so I was immediately on my guard. I invited him inside. He bowed rather formally and asked if I could brew him a cup of black tea with sugar and milk. I obliged him and we sat down on the couch.

"My apologies for appearing at your place of residence uninvited," he said, "but I find that the reception is often warmer in these matters if I do not telephone in advance." He lifted the teacup from the saucer as if to display the proof of his good judgment.

"What exactly do you mean by 'these matters'?"

He set down the cup.

"Things from the past. I have come a long way, and I have many questions."

"*You* have questions?"

"About Edwin Lemaster. He was kind to me, just as you are being, but he would not speak with me. He suggested instead that I see you. He stated without reservation that you are the top authority, not only about his life in books, but his life as a spy. And that is my interest. Because once it was *my* job to be the person who knew all about Edwin Lemaster."

"For Soviet intelligence?"

"Yes. I was known then as source Glinka."

"I think I'd better get you another cup of tea, Alexei."

"That would be most kind. But do you have vodka as well?"

"Even better. But first I have a question of my own. This job of yours—you must have been doing it, what, at least thirty years ago?"

"Almost forty."

"Why, then? Why do you still want to know?"

He shrugged.

"My wife asks me this also. She tells me we are fortunate to be living in this country. She believes that if some people knew what my job once was, that we would not be allowed to stay. So I must ask you to be . . ." He searched for the word.

"Discreet?"

"Yes."

"I will be."

"As for why, it is not so easy to explain. An American I know describes it as 'professional curiosity.' I spent two years of my life searching for a single answer, and never found it. That kind of failure stays with you, like an old pain that cannot be relieved. Do you not agree?"

"Oh, I agree completely. What was the question you could never answer?"

"It came in the form of an assignment from someone very high within the intelligence apparatus, a man known as Oleg."

"I've heard of Oleg."

Alexei nodded gravely.

"He was an important man. He wanted me to establish without doubt the fidelity of a double agent of ours known as Pericles. In your intelligence apparatus he was known as Headlight."

So there it was at last, the final bit of evidence, the solid link between Lemaster, or Headlight, and the stray name of Pericles that Valerie Humphries had come across only one time.

"Lemaster, you mean."

"Of course."

"And?"

"I spent months going through his reports, and those of others. I followed in his tracks, and in the tracks of his contacts. He never once detected my presence, I am proud to say. But the months became a year, and one year became two. And even then all that I had was a hunch that I can best describe by telling you my nickname for him, which in those days I did not dare to repeat."

"A nickname?"

"A Russian word which means 'Cube.'"

"Why 'Cube'?"

"Have you studied mathematics?"

"It was never my best subject."

"Surely you know what it is to cube a number?"

"Ah. Multiplying it by itself twice. Like two times two times two."

"Exactly the example I had in mind." He waited for me to figure it out.

"A double that's doubled? That's what you suspected?"

"Yes."

"Is this what you reported to Oleg?"

"Do you think I was suicidal? My assignment was to verify his fidelity. If he was a double of a double, then Oleg would be ruined, and others above me along with him. Meaning that I, being at the bottom, would suffer most."

"But you're sure? You're sure you were right?"

He shook his head, looking woeful.

"I have never been less certain of anything. That is why I have come here. It is the one question I never answered."

"So you thought you'd just ask Ed himself, and he sent you to me."

Alexei nodded hopefully, as if we'd finally reached the moment of truth.

"Mr. Lemaster said you have done much recent work on this question. Groundbreaking work, he called it."

I smiled. Say what you would about Edwin Lemaster, he still had his contacts, and he still had a sense of mischief.

"Why don't I tell you what I know—or what I think I know—and then we'll compare notes?"

"That is very fair. It is generous. Please, begin."

So I told him what I'd learned, and where I thought it fit, and I told him Lothar's conclusions as well. We collated and cross-referenced my findings, checking and double-checking the chronology, the logic and the possible gaps. And when we had reached the end of our chat and nearly the end of the vodka, we both realized something quite curious.

"I still haven't answered your question, have I?"

He nodded solemnly.

"But is that not, in itself, a kind of answer?" he said. "Because if you are a double, and then a cube, and then perhaps even two to the fourth power, would you not at some point transcend all questions of loyalty or betrayal? At some point, does not everything become artifice?"

"Sounds like perfect training for a novelist. No wonder Angleton went crazy. Cabot, too, in a way."

Alexei smiled.

"The same happened with Oleg. A secret hospital in the Urals. The American is the only one I know who remained sane."

"Ed, you mean?"

"No, no. His recruiter. His original handler. The man who first brought him to our attention as a possibly valuable asset."

"Do you mean Thresher?"

"Yes. He, at least, was trustworthy. I have often wondered what became of him."

"I take it you never met him, then, or knew his real name?"

Alexei shook his head.

"It was Oleg's most closely guarded secret. And with the state he is now in, I suspect no one will ever know."

"You may well be right."

Alexei's glass was empty. I moved to refill it, but he waved me away and stood, no more wobbly than when he'd arrived.

"I must catch a train," he said. "But I thank you."

"No, I thank *you*. You've been very helpful."

We shook hands. Then he departed. I watched him shuffle down the sidewalk toward Wisconsin Avenue, and almost as soon as he was out of sight I realized that I didn't know his full name or where he lived. He must have been very good at his job.

Was he a plant, a subterfuge? Some last trick from Lemaster to try to convince me that he had never betrayed his country? Or, better still, to place Breece Preston in an even more unfavorable light?

I have no idea. And frankly, that's fine, because recently I took up a new profession in which ambiguity, uncertainty, and even unresolved questions are strengths, not weaknesses.

I am writing a spy novel.

It is about a popular and respected American writer who was once a popular and respected spy. His life is an interplay between fact and fiction, light and darkness, image and illusion. I am trying to use my imagination to its limit, but I must confess that many particulars will be loosely based on a huge cache of copied documents and confidential reports, a trove that remains easily accessible to me even though, at the moment, it resides at an undisclosed secure location. The only thing further I will say on that subject is that access does not involve the removal of any floorboards. As Giles Cabot would say, I'm better than that.

The originals of these documents are presumably still in the possession of the Central Intelligence Agency, unless of course no one ever checked the post office box in Herndon, Virginia.

Someone at the Agency must have gotten wind of my plans, because recently one of their employees phoned me. I wasn't surprised that they knew, since I'd told Marty Ealing what I was doing the day I gave notice, and he's a terrible gossip.

The caller sounded young and inexperienced, but he wasted no time in sternly reminding me of the nondisclosure agreement, and the possible consequences of violating it.

"It's a novel," I said. "Completely made up. Ed Lemaster's name won't even be mentioned."

"So this isn't for *Vanity Fair*?"

"No. There won't be a single fact involved."

"Okay. But you also should be aware that former employees must also submit novels before publication."

"But I was never an Agency employee, as you know. And the agreement I signed covers only the facts." He wasn't quite sure how to respond. I felt a little sorry for him.

"Well, just be careful, then."

"Oh, I will. Very careful."

He apologized for bothering me. Then he wished me luck.

Sometimes even the idle wishes of a nameless CIA man come true, and this morning a reputable publishing house in New York telephoned to offer me a contract based on my cover letter, an outline, and fifty sample pages.

Tonight, David and I will celebrate with our usual fare at Martin's Tavern. I doubt we will see a woman wearing a red carnation, but you never know. He and I have already made plans to meet my father this December. In Berlin, of course. What better place, now that each of us in his own way has played at being a spy.

I figure my book will take about a year to finish, but I've already roughed out the plot, sketched the characters, and have an ending in mind. I've also decided that the opening words will not appear in the first chapter, or even in the prologue. They will be printed on the epigraph page, right up front, so that no reader can possibly miss them.

They go like this:

This is a work of fiction. Any resemblance to actual persons, living or dead, events, or locales is entirely coincidental.

APPENDIX

Warfield Cage's Library of Espionage First Editions
The following are **222** books, by **48** authors, **18** of whom worked in intelligence (their names are in **boldface**), **6** more of whom worked in foreign ministries or a war/defense office.

Of these, **57** of the books were published prior to 1950.

BY AUTHOR

Allbeury, Ted
—*Snowball*, 1974
—*The Special Collection*, 1975
—*The Lantern Network*, 1978
—*The Alpha List*, 1979
—*The Other Side of Silence*, 1981
—*No Place to Hide*, 1986
—*A Wilderness of Mirrors*, 1988

Ambler, Eric
—*The Dark Frontier*, 1936
—*Uncommon Danger* (U.S.: *Background to Danger*), 1937
—*Epitaph for a Spy*, 1938
—*Cause for Alarm*, 1938
—*The Mask of Dimitrios* (U.S.: *A Coffin for Dimitrios*), 1939
—*Journey into Fear*, 1940
—*Judgment on Deltchev*, 1951
—*The Levanter*, 1972

Bingham, John (Lord Clanmorris)
—*A Fragment of Fear*, 1965
—*The Double Agent*, 1966
—*Brock and the Defector*, 1982

Buchan, John
—*The Thirty-nine Steps*, 1915
—*Greenmantle*, 1916
—*Mr. Standfast*, 1919
—*Huntingtower*, 1922
—*The Three Hostages*, 1924
—*The Courts of the Morning*, 1929

Buckley, William F., Jr. (Blackford Oakes series)
—*Saving the Queen*, 1976
—*Stained Glass*, 1978
—*Who's on First*, 1980
—*The Story of Henri Tod*, 1984
—*See You Later, Alligator*, 1985
—*High Jinx*, 1986
—*Mongoose, R.I.P.*, 1987
Burgess, Anthony (Army intel cipher work during WWII)
—*Tremor of Intent*, 1966
Childers, Erskine
—*The Riddle of the Sands*, 1903
Coles, Manning (Adelaide Frances Oke Manning [**war office**]
and Cyril Henry Coles [**British intelligence**])
(Tommy Hambledon series)
—*Drink to Yesterday*, 1940
—*Pray Silence* (U.S.: *A Toast to Tomorrow*), 1940
—*They Tell No Tales*, 1941
—*Without Lawful Authority*, 1943
—*Green Hazard*, 1945
—*The Fifth Man*, 1946
—*Let the Tiger Die*, 1947
—*A Brother for Hugh* (U.S.: *With Intent to Deceive*), 1947
—*Among Those Absent*, 1948
—*Diamonds to Amsterdam*, 1949
—*Not Negotiable*, 1949
—*Dangerous by Nature*, 1950
—*Now or Never*, 1951
—*Alias Uncle Hugo* (U.K.: *Operation Manhunt*), 1952
—*Night Train to Paris*, 1952
Conrad, Joseph
—*The Secret Agent*, 1907
—*Under Western Eyes*, 1911
Cooper, James Fenimore
—*The Spy*, 1821
Cory, Desmond (Shaun Lloyd McCarthy) (Johnny Fedora series)
—*Secret Ministry*, 1951
—*This Traitor, Death*, 1952
—*Dead Man Falling*, 1953
—*Intrigue*, 1954
—*Height of Day*, 1955
—*High Requiem*, 1955
—*Johnny Goes North*, 1956
—*Johnny Goes East*, 1957

Furst, Alan
—*Night Soldiers*, 1988
Gainham, Sarah
—*The Stone Roses*, 1959
—*Night Falls on the City*, 1967
Garner, William (Michael Jagger series)
—*Overkill*, 1966
—*The Deep, Deep Freeze*, 1968
—*The Us or Them War*, 1969
Grady, James
—*Six Days of the Condor*, 1974
—*Shadow of the Condor*, 1978
Granger, Bill
—*The November Man*, 1978
—*Schism*, 1981
—*The Shattered Eye*, 1982
—*The British Cross*, 1983
Greene, Graham
—*The Confidential Agent*, 1939
—*The Quiet American*, 1955
—*Our Man in Havana*, 1958
—*The Human Factor*, 1978
Hall, Adam (Elleston Trevor)
—*The Berlin Memorandum* (U.S.: *The Quiller Memorandum*), 1965
—*The Ninth Directive*, 1966
—*The Striker Portfolio*, 1968
—*The Warsaw Document*, 1971
—*The Tango Briefing*, 1973
—*The Mandarin Cypher*, 1975
—*The Sinkiang Executive*, 1978
—*The Scorpion Signal*, 1979
—*Northlight* (U.S.: *Quiller*), 1985
—*Quiller KGB*, 1989
Hamilton, Donald (Matt Helm series)
—*Death of a Citizen*, 1960
—*The Wrecking Crew*, 1960
—*The Removers*, 1961
—*The Silencers*, 1962
—*Murderers' Row*, 1962
Hone, Joseph
—*The Private Sector* (Peter Marlow), 1971
—*The Sixth Directorate*, 1975
Hood, William (worked for James Angleton)
—*Spy Wednesday*, 1986
—*Cry Spy*, 1990 (last non-Lemaster purchase in the collection)

Quammen, David
—*The Zolta Configuration,* 1983
—*The Soul of Viktor Tronko,* 1987
Semyonov, Yulian (USSR—originally published in Russian)
—*Petrovka 38,* 1965
—*The Himmler Ploy,* 1968 (aka *Seventeen Moments of Spring*)
Simmel, Johannes Mario (Austrian—originally published in German)
—*It Can't Always Be Caviar,* 1959
—*Dear Fatherland,* 1965
—*And Jimmy Went Up the Rainbow,* 1970
Tyler, W. T. (Samuel J. Hamrick, **U.S. Foreign Service officer**)
—*The Man Who Lost the War,* 1980
—*Rogue's March,* 1982
West, Elliot
—*The Night Is a Time for Listening,* 1966
Wheatley, Dennis **(British War Office)**
—*The Secret War,* 1937
—*The Scarlet Impostor,* 1940
—*Faked Passports,* 1940
—*The Launching of Roger Brook,* 1947
Wilkinson, J. Burke **(State Department, NATO)**
—*Night of the Short Knives,* 1964
—*The Adventures of Geoffrey Mildmay,* 1969

BY DATE

1821 —Cooper, *The Spy*
1892 —Le Queux, *Strange Tales of a Nihilist*
1901 —Kipling, *Kim*
—Le Queux, *Her Majesty's Minister*
1903 —**Childers,** *The Riddle of the Sands*
—Le Queux, *The Seven Secrets*
1905 —Le Queux, *The Czar's Spy*
1907 —Conrad, *The Secret Agent*
1908 —Oppenheim, *The Great Secret*
1911 —Conrad, *Under Western Eyes*
1914 —Le Queux, *The German Spy*
1915 —**Buchan,** *The Thirty-nine Steps*
—Oppenheim, *The Double Traitor*
1916 —**Buchan,** *Greenmantle*
1918 —Le Queux, *Sant of the Secret Service*
1919 —**Buchan,** *Mr. Standfast*
1920 —Le Queux, *The Secret Telephone*
—Oppenheim, *The Great Impersonation*

1922 —**Buchan,** *Huntingtower*
1924 —**Buchan,** *The Three Hostages*
1928 —Le Queux, *The Secret Formula*
     —**Maugham,** *Ashenden*
1929 —**Buchan,** *The Courts of the Morning*
     —**Mackenzie,** *The Three Couriers*
1934 —Oppenheim, *The Spy Paramount*
1936 —Ambler, *The Dark Frontier*
1937 —Ambler, *Uncommon Danger* (U.S.: *Background to Danger*)
     —Wheatley, *The Secret War*
1938 —Ambler, *Epitaph for a Spy*
     —Ambler, *Cause for Alarm*
     —Oppenheim, *The Spymaster*
1939 —Ambler, *The Mask of Dimitrios* (U.S.: *A Coffin for Dimitrios*)
     —**Greene,** *The Confidential Agent*
     —**Household,** *Rogue Male*
1940 —Ambler, *Journey into Fear*
     —**Coles,** *Drink to Yesterday*
     —**Coles,** *Pray Silence* (U.S.: *A Toast to Tomorrow*)
     —Wheatley, *The Scarlet Impostor*
     —Wheatley, *Faked Passports*
1941 —**Coles,** *They Tell No Tales*
     —MacInnes, *Above Suspicion*
1942 —**Hunt,** *East of Farewell*
     —MacInnes, *Assignment in Brittany*
1943 —**Coles,** *Without Lawful Authority*
1944 —MacInnes, *The Unconquerable*
1945 —**Coles,** *Green Hazard*
     —MacInnes, *Horizon*
1946 —**Coles,** *The Fifth Man*
1947 —**Coles,** *Let the Tiger Die*
     —**Coles,** *A Brother for Hugh* (U.S.: *With Intent to Deceive*)
     —**Hunt,** *Stranger in Town*
     —Wheatley, *The Launching of Roger Brook*
1948 —**Coles,** *Among Those Absent*
     —**Hunt,** *Maelstrom*
1949 —**Coles,** *Diamonds to Amsterdam*
     —**Coles,** *Not Negotiable*
     —**Hunt,** *Bimini Run*
1950 —**Coles,** *Dangerous by Nature*
1951 —Ambler, *Judgment on Deltchev*
     —**Coles,** *Now or Never*
     —Cory, *Secret Ministry*
1952 —**Coles,** *Alias Uncle Hugo* (U.K.: *Operation Manhunt*)
     —**Coles,** *Night Train to Paris*

—Cory, *This Traitor, Death*
1953 —Cory, *Dead Man Falling*
    —**Fleming,** *Casino Royale*
1954 —Cory, *Intrigue*
    —**Fleming,** *Live and Let Die*
1955 —Cory, *Height of Day*
    —Cory, *High Requiem*
    —**Fleming,** *Moonraker*
    —**Greene,** *The Quiet American*
1956 —Cory, *Johnny Goes North*
    —**Fleming,** *Diamonds Are Forever*
1957 —Cory, *Johnny Goes East*
    —Durrell, *White Eagles over Serbia*
    —**Fleming,** *From Russia, with Love*
1958 —Cory, *Johnny Goes West*
    —**Fleming,** *Dr. No*
    —**Greene,** *Our Man in Havana*
1959 —Cory, *Johnny Goes South*
    —**Fleming,** *Goldfinger*
    —Gainham, *The Stone Roses*
    —Simmel, *It Can't Always Be Caviar*
1960 —Cory, *The Head*
    —**Fleming,** *For Your Eyes Only*
    —Hamilton, *Death of a Citizen*
    —Hamilton, *The Wrecking Crew*
1961 —**Fleming,** *Thunderball*
    —Hamilton, *The Removers*
    —**Le Carré,** *Call for the Dead*
1962 —Cory, *Undertow*
    —**Fleming,** *The Spy Who Loved Me*
    —Hamilton, *The Silencers*
    —Hamilton, *Murderers' Row*
    —Deighton, *The Ipcress File*
    —**Le Carré,** *A Murder of Quality*
1963 —Cory, *Hammerhead*
    —Deighton, *Horse Under Water*
    —**Fleming,** *On Her Majesty's Secret Service*
    —**Le Carré,** *The Spy Who Came In from the Cold*
    —MacInnes, *The Venetian Affair*
1964 —Deighton, *Funeral in Berlin*
    —**Fleming,** *You Only Live Twice*
    —Wilkinson, *Night of the Short Knives*
1965 —**Bingham,** *A Fragment of Fear*
    —**Fleming,** *The Man with the Golden Gun*
    —Hall, *The Berlin Memorandum* (U.S.: *The Quiller Memorandum*)

—**Hunter,** *The Expendable Spy*
—**Le Carré,** *The Looking Glass War*
—O'Donnell, *Modesty Blaise*
—Semyonov, *Petrovka 38*
—Simmel, *Dear Fatherland*
1966 —**Bingham,** *The Double Agent*
—**Burgess,** *Tremor of Intent*
—Cory, *Feramontov*
—Deighton, *Billion-Dollar Brain*
—**Fleming,** *Octopussy and The Living Daylights*
—Garner, *Overkill*
—Hall, *The Ninth Directive*
—MacInnes, *The Double Image*
—West, *The Night Is a Time for Listening*
1967 —Cory, *Timelock*
—Deighton, *An Expensive Place to Die*
—Diment, *The Dolly Dolly Spy*
—Gainham, *Night Falls on the City*
—**Hunter,** *One of Us Works for Them*
1968 —Diment, *The Great Spy Race*
—Diment, *The Bang Bang Birds*
—Garner, *The Deep, Deep Freeze*
—Hall, *The Striker Portfolio*
—**Le Carré,** *A Small Town in Germany*
—MacInnes, *The Salzburg Connection*
—Semyonov, *The Himmler Ploy* (aka *Seventeen Moments of Spring*)
1969 —Garner, *The Us or Them War*
—**Hunter,** *Spies, Inc.*
—**Lemaster,** *Knee Knockers*
—Wilkinson, *The Adventures of Geoffrey Mildmay*
1970 —Simmel, *And Jimmy Went Up the Rainbow*
1971 —Cory, *Sunburst*
—Diment, *Think Inc.*
—Hall, *The Warsaw Document*
—Hone, *The Private Sector*
—**Lemaster,** *A Lesson in Tradecraft*
—MacInnes, *Message from Málaga*
1972 —Ambler, *The Levanter*
1973 —Hall, *The Tango Briefing*
—**Hunt,** *The Berlin Ending*
—**Lemaster,** *The Double Game*
—Littell, *The Defection of A. J. Lewinter*
—**McCarry,** *The Miernik Dossier*
1974 —**Allbeury,** *Snowball*
—Deighton, *Spy Story*

—Grady, *Six Days of the Condor*
—Le Carré, *Tinker, Tailor, Soldier, Spy*
—McCarry, *The Tears of Autumn*
1975 **—Allbeury,** *The Special Collection*
—Deighton, *Yesterday's Spy*
—Hall, *The Mandarin Cypher*
—Hone, *The Sixth Directorate*
1976 **—Buckley,** *Saving the Queen*
—Deighton, *Twinkle, Twinkle, Little Spy*
—Lemaster, *The Cutout*
—MacInnes, *Agent in Place*
1977 —Latham, *Orchids for Mother*
—Le Carré, *The Honourable Schoolboy*
—McCarry, *The Secret Lovers*
1978 **—Allbeury,** *The Lantern Network*
—Buckley, *Stained Glass*
—Grady, *Shadow of the Condor*
—Granger, *The November Man*
—Greene, *The Human Factor*
—Hall, *The Sinkiang Executive*
1979 **—Allbeury,** *The Alpha List*
—Hall, *The Scorpion Signal*
—Le Carré, *Smiley's People*
—Lemaster, *A Spy for All Seasons*
—Littell, *The Debriefing*
1980 **—Buckley,** *Who's on First*
—Tyler, *The Man Who Lost the War*
1981 **—Allbeury,** *The Other Side of Silence*
—Granger, *Schism*
—Hunt, *The Gaza Intercept*
—Lemaster, *London's Own*
1982 **—Bingham,** *Brock and the Defector*
—Granger, *The Shattered Eye*
—Tyler, *Rogue's March*
1983 —Deighton, *Berlin Game*
—Granger, *The British Cross*
—Le Carré, *The Little Drummer Girl*
—McCarry, *The Last Supper*
—Quammen, *The Zolta Configuration*
1984 **—Buckley,** *The Story of Henri Tod*
—Deighton, *Mexico Set*
—Lemaster, *A Glancing Blow*
—MacInnes, *Ride a Pale Horse*
1985 **—Buckley,** *See You Later, Alligator*
—Deighton, *London Match*

—Hall, *Northlight* (U.S.: *Quiller*)
—**Hunt,** *The Kremlin Conspiracy*
1986 —**Allbeury,** *No Place to Hide*
—**Buckley,** *High Jinx*
—**Hood,** *Spy Wednesday*
—**Le Carré,** *A Perfect Spy*
—**Lemaster,** *Requiem for a Spy*
—Littell, *The Sisters*
1987 —**Buckley,** *Mongoose, R.I.P.*
—Quammen, *The Soul of Viktor Tronko*
1988 —**Allbeury,** *A Wilderness of Mirrors*
—Deighton, *Spy Hook*
—Furst, *Night Soldiers*
1989 —Hall, *Quiller KGB*
—Deighton, *Spy Line*
—**Hood,** *Cry Spy* (last non-Lemaster purchase, just after Berlin Wall came down)
—**Le Carré,** *The Russia House*
—**Lemaster,** *Render unto Caesar*
Post–Cold War
1991 —**Lemaster,** *A Final Folly*
1994 —**Lemaster,** *The Sinking of the* Bellwether
1997 —**Lemaster,** *Strength in Numbers*
2000 —**Lemaster,** *Duty, Honor, Betrayal*
2003 —**Lemaster,** *The Tent of the Sheik*
2007 —**Lemaster,** *Remote Control*

Acknowledgments

When your characters and plot spring not only from your imagination but also from a lifetime of satisfied reading, it is difficult to know where to begin saying thanks. David Cornwell, aka John le Carré, is probably an appropriate starting point, since his Smiley novels were my entrée to the classics of espionage fiction, back when the Cold War was as chilly and gray as a January sky over Berlin. And while I'm not a collector of first editions like, say, Warfield Cage, I am lucky enough to have a true first of *The Spy Who Came In from the Cold*, a copy of which the author was kind enough to sign for me several years ago. The novels of Graham Greene, Len Deighton, and Charles McCarry also marked me at a relatively early age, enough to remind me of the Elvis Costello song lyric that asks, "Who put these fingerprints on my imagination?"

Yet, for all my voracious reading, I had no inkling of how widely and deeply the genre had cast its nets until I began researching this novel. James Fenimore Cooper, that guy we had to read in high school? Yes, even he was a practitioner. I owe the work of many sources for that sort of information. Among those worthy of specific thanks are Stephen J. Gertz, who is not only an expert on rare books but also an authority on the quirky phenomenon of the book scout; and Otto Penzler, who, when it comes to spy fiction, seems to have collected, read, and assessed everything ever written. In Budapest, Professor Istvan Rev, a historian at Central European University, offered valuable insights on the fortunes of the antiquarian book trade during the Cold War and beyond.

Thanks are also due to a few dozen former operatives of the CIA, who spoke with me as part of my research for another project, but whose experiences, insights, and, in some cases, authorial forays, helped light my way. I'm particularly grateful for a pleasant afternoon spent chatting with CIA veteran William Hood, whose novel *Spy Wednesday* earned a cameo in this book's chapters in Vienna, the city of his greatest Cold War triumph.

Finally, although Bill Cage puts little stock in so-called nonfiction, I found many such volumes to be quite helpful, especially Tom Mangold's *Cold Warrior*, Evan Thomas's *The Very Best Men*, and Genrikh Borovik's *The Philby Files*.

A NOTE ON THE TYPE

This book was set in Janson, a typeface long thought to have been made by the Dutchman Anton Janson. However, it has been conclusively demonstrated that these types are actually the work of Nicholas Kis (1650–1702), a Hungarian, who most probably learned his trade from the master Dutch typefounder Dirk Voskens.